I
Dau

# Lost Daughter

## Ali Mercer

Bookouture

Published by Bookouture in 2019

An imprint of StoryFire Ltd.

Carmelite House
50 Victoria Embankment
London EC4Y 0DZ

www.bookouture.com

ISBN: 978-1-78681-967-3
eBook ISBN: 978-1-78681-966-6

*For my dad*

# Prologue

## Rachel

### The day of the loss

She waited for what seemed like forever before they came back. The daylight lost its brightness and the shadows lengthened, and still they weren't home. She carried on sitting at the kitchen table staring at the birthday cake in its box in the corner where she'd left it that morning, several lifetimes ago.

She sent messages, but there was no reply. She couldn't bring herself to call. Neither of them would want to hear from her.

There was plenty of time to think, and remember.

The broken glass... the scream... the blood.

So much blood.

*I don't want her to see...*

*You did this? How could you? I hate you!*

*You could have killed him. You stupid bitch.*

She had been so sure. And she had been so wrong. But even if she had been right, there was no excuse and no justification for what she'd done.

Eventually she heard a car outside. A key turned in the door and she heard Mitch say to Becca: 'Why don't you go upstairs and get changed out of your school uniform?'

He must have decided it would be better if Becca was out of the way when he confronted her.

She couldn't blame him for treating her as a risk.

He came into the kitchen. There were splashes of dark dried blood on his clothes. He stood there and gave her a long, hard stare.

She said, 'Are you OK?'

'Not really.'

'Mitch... I—'

'It's too late, Rachel.'

The car outside started again and was driven away into the distance.

Rachel whispered, 'Did *she* bring you back?'

'She did. She stayed with Becca in the waiting room. She helped me take some pictures, too. I thought I'd better keep a record of what you did. They might be useful evidence. In court. I don't imagine that they would help your case if you were to apply for custody.'

Her face was wet. She looked up at him and he was distorted by tears, as if he was dissolving.

'Oh, no, Mitch, please—'

'Save your breath. This isn't right, Rachel. I don't want you here any more, and neither does Becca.'

The door opened and Becca came in. Mitch said, 'It's all right, Becca. She won't be staying.'

Becca stepped closer to her father, as if being at his side would protect her. Her face was like a closed door.

Rachel said to her, 'Is that what you want? For me to go?'

And Becca said, 'I want to stay with Daddy.' Her voice seemed to come from very far away as she added, 'You should leave.'

Mitch said, 'Are you going to respect our daughter's wishes?'

Rachel took in the two of them, standing there side by side: the big, wounded, protective father, and the just-teenage girl, angry and defensive and loyal – to him. Becca folded her arms and lifted her chin in defiance, as if to challenge Rachel to deny her what she'd asked for. Her dear, familiar face was a hard little mask, but Rachel knew what she was thinking as clearly as if she'd said it: *Please, just go, just go, just go...*

Rachel had to be calm, to stop crying. To think. There was a right thing and a wrong thing to do here. She had to get it right.

But she couldn't think. She could barely breathe. And so she said what she knew her daughter wanted to hear.

'All right. If you want me to go, Becca, I'll go.'

# Chapter One

## Leona

The first odd thing about the temp is that she's waiting out front in the cold, instead of staying in the warm in the main reception for the business park. Perhaps she likes her own company, though she doesn't seem to be enjoying it much today. She looks as if she's worrying about something. Something big.

But as Leona approaches, her expression becomes a careful blank.

'I'm so sorry. I didn't expect you quite so early,' Leona says. 'I'm Leona Grey – I'll be taking care of you while the boss is away.'

'I'm Rachel Steele,' Rachel says.

They shake gloved hands. Rachel returns Leona's smile without conviction, and her eyes flicker away from Leona's gaze. Well, that's OK. It's not *necessarily* evasive. Not everybody is confident in their body language.

Rachel is wearing a mask-like layer of foundation, through which it is still obvious that her nose is red with cold. The make-up doesn't disguise the bags under her eyes, either. It wouldn't be unfair to say she looks like death warmed up – but then, who looks their best first thing on a December morning?

'Welcome to Fun-to-Learn,' Leona says, punching in the key code that gives access to the office. 'I should be here at nine tomorrow, but I'll give you the code so you can come and go.'

She holds the door open for Rachel to go through. Rachel is wearing a plain navy-blue coat and high heels; she's smart but inconspicuous, like a court scene extra in a legal drama. Clothes that don't give a whole lot away. Her CV is probably in the boss's desk drawer, shoved in there with other stray bits of paperwork before he went on holiday; Leona could have a rummage round later, find out a bit more about her. Or she could ask the temp agency to send it over again, though she probably won't get round to it.

Rachel looks as if she's a bit older than Leona, probably in her mid-thirties. Chances are she's one of those former professional women who have spent several years away from office life, being run ragged by small children. This might be her first venture back into the workplace she'd abandoned for marriage, several versions of Microsoft Office and a recession later. Yes, that must be it. A stay-at-home mum who can't afford to stay at home any longer.

Sooner or later she'll put out a framed picture of her family on her desk, a reminder to herself and everyone else that her life doesn't stop here.

'It'll warm up when the heating gets going,' Leona says.

She flicks on the fluorescent lights, illuminating a bank of six white desks topped with slightly dusty computers; the boss's desk has a separate spot in the corner, in a glass-walled cubicle. The surfaces are littered with the detritus of office life; files, a birthday card with flowers on it, a stray mug. A strand of purple tinsel has been taped along the top of the padded divider that splits the bank of desks into two separate sides. It isn't quite long enough to reach.

'You're here,' Leona says, showing Rachel to her place and feeling a little bad for her, because it's the worst desk in the office. Rachel will be in the middle of a row with her back to the door, at a distance from the nearest window, facing a whiteboard listing sales targets (decorated today with an additional sketch of slightly forlorn holly leaves), a clock and a pinboard. The chair is a killer: the one no one else wanted.

'Hang up your coat if you like, though I wouldn't blame you if you wanted to keep it on,' Leona says, indicating the wooden coat stand in the corner. Rachel complies. Leona moves round the office, pulls up the blind next to her desk; wintry sunlight streams in.

As Rachel settles into place opposite her Leona sees that her hands are ringless. No wedding ring. No engagement ring. Nothing.

Perhaps Leona has got her all wrong.

Leona takes off her own coat, a big mock-astrakhan number. She's of the belief that coats should be fun, if possible. She hangs it up; her silver bangles chime, and the sleeves of her patchwork top fall back to reveal her wrists.

She turns just in time to catch Rachel staring at her, and it's the first time their eyes have met.

The look on Rachel's face is knowing, sharp with recognition, not sympathetic so much as battle-hardened. It says, *I see you're someone who knows a little something about pain: the kind you choose for yourself because it's a distraction from the kind you can't forget.*

And she's right. Leona doesn't want to forget. She doesn't deserve to forget. There's no hope for her at all unless she remembers.

And Rachel clearly understands that. But how could Rachel possibly know about that kind of pain?

# Chapter Two

## Becca

The lecture theatre, where they are spending the whole day listening to various awful talks, is exactly the kind of facility that had convinced her parents the fees for St Anne's were worth it. Becca has to admit, the school is pretty impressive, as is the indoor swimming pool, the gleaming, state-of-the-art science and language labs, the large, hushed, well-stocked library, and the girls themselves. In their uniform of winter tartan and crested jerseys, they have an air of health and confidence that whispers what the whole school boasts: *money*.

But Becca has always been conscious of not quite matching up to the template of the ideal St Anne's girl. If that was what her parents had hoped she'd become, their hard-earned cash has been wasted.

Her hair is thin and mousy, just curly enough to fluff up and not straight enough to shine; she'd been fair when she was little, then ended up an unremarkable shade of brown. She has only just graduated from a 32AA to a 32A, and she isn't skinny, which would at least be some kind of excuse. She isn't popular, or sporty, or outstandingly clever; she has never had a whole-class party for her birthday, she doesn't have a pony (and has never ridden one), and she doesn't live in a house with two staircases.

And she doesn't have a mother in the way the others do.

Not that anyone really knows about that, except for Amelia Chadstone, whose inside knowledge makes her even more intimidating to Becca.

Becca has known Amelia for years. Back when they were little, Amelia had been cast as the Virgin Mary in the St Anne's nursery school nativity play; Becca had been a sheep. Now Amelia is the ideal St Anne's girl: hockey demon, top of the class, popular and blessed with a long, blonde, swishy mane of hair that she fiddles with almost constantly, as if to ensure that everybody keeps noticing it.

If Becca was pretty or funny or *interesting* it might be different, but she's not one of those girls, like Amelia, who can command the attention of the class, both in lessons and outside them, and who is already beginning to boast about boys.

As if the whole concept of sex wasn't completely disgusting! And as for love and marriage – why would anybody want all that, if they had even the faintest understanding of what it might lead to?

That morning's speakers have been invited to talk to Becca's class on the theme of 'Keeping Calm and Carrying on – Resilience in the Teenage Years'. It's embarrassing, on a par with sex education and the policeman who had come to warn them about drugs and the kind of men who might offer them lifts. Becca is not at all sure she's in danger from the kind of threats the school keeps inviting people in to warn her about. What she's learned, and the others seem not to have realised, is that the people who are closest to you are the ones to watch.

Before the morning break they'd heard from a nervous lady in a purple dress, who had talked to them about mindfulness. Amelia had been scathing about purple-dress lady during the break, as a bunch of her friends listened and giggled and Becca hovered somewhere just outside the group with her water bottle.

'If grown-ups have time to sit around thinking of nothing, that's all very well for them,' Amelia had said. 'But the rest of us have things to do! Anyway, if anybody thought this was *actually* important, we'd be taking exams in staring into space.'

Becca had felt a bit sorry for the purple-dress lady, who must have been through something awful to need mindfulness so much, but she hadn't said so. She had got used to keeping things to herself.

In a way, it is just as well that she is regarded as dull, because otherwise her classmates might be more curious about her family situation than they are. But as it is, her invisibility is a kind of shield.

Amelia has never acknowledged what she knows. But then, why would she? In the normal way of things, they barely speak. However, Amelia could have told other people, and Becca is pretty sure she hasn't. That means Becca is indebted to her, which only makes her even more impossible to talk to.

She ends up just behind Amelia as they pile back into the lecture theatre after the break, and finds herself sitting next to her at the end of a row. Amelia pays her no attention, though; she's busy talking to Millie Parker-Jones, a curly-headed girl who has the distinction of having briefly dated an older boy. *Snogging but that's it*, as Millie had put it. That's the kind of thing they know about each other. There are few secrets at St Anne's. Apart from Becca's. Which is Amelia's, too.

Miss Finch, their class teacher, shushes them sharply before introducing the second and final speaker, a neat little blonde woman in a white shirt and dark-blue trousers.

'Kind of boring, but at least she isn't trying to be fit like the other one. It's so tragic when older women get their legs out. Or their boobs,' Amelia mutters to Millie.

And Becca thinks of her mother, as she had been in the old days – all sharp lines and edges in her red wool suit and boxy handbag, and the heels that clicked as she walked along – or trim and elegant in an emerald-green cocktail dress, smelling of glamour.

Miss Finch tells them all to be quiet once again, and the woman introduces herself as Sophie Elphick, a specialist in cognitive behavioural therapy who previously worked in the probation service. She says, 'I know that today is all about wellness, but I'm here to talk to you about what happens when things go wrong.'

A projector clicks and a PowerPoint slide is displayed on the blank wall behind the nurse. A single word, in black type, in a circle: HARM.

The mood of the lecture theatre abruptly changes. It's like when they were about to watch an ox's heart being dissected in biology: the girls are all torn between apprehension and bravado, the instinct to recoil and the equally strong instinct to act indifferent, to shrug it all off.

'We are all vulnerable, and we can all come to harm in many different ways,' Sophie says. 'We could be harmed by another person, or by something else – something such as disease or an accident of nature. We may even harm ourselves.'

A phrase appears, next to an arrow pointing to the circle: WHO OR WHAT CAUSED THE HARM?

'Things don't just happen; they happen for a reason. Even accidents have causes. When it's a case of one person doing harm to another, and the outcome has been a crime, we describe this as a motive.'

A single word joins the others, forming the second point of a triangle around the central circle: WHY?

Sophie goes on, 'All kinds of harm cause damage, and until there's some kind of resolution – until the original harm is understood and forgiven – the damage will always live on. It might be hidden. It might be recreated in some form by the person who was damaged in the first place, in an attempt to regain control. Or it might be denied or distorted. It could be lied about. But it won't go away.'

The final phrase, the third point of the triangle, appears: HOW IS IT REMEMBERED?

'Now, we're going to talk about the kinds of harm that are most commonly experienced by your age group,' Sophie says.

The next slide is a list of problems. Bullying, loneliness, self-harm… difficult family relationships.

Becca feels herself beginning to sweat, and suddenly her heart is beating so loudly that she can hear the blood rushing and swooshing round inside her head.

Oh, no, this is the last thing she needs – not right here and now, in front of her classmates, Miss Finch, and Sophie Elphick.

All she wants is for today to be over, to have got through it unscathed, without catastrophe, and to be home safe and alone in her bedroom with nobody bothering her and the door firmly shut. At least Dad knows when to leave her alone.

Sophie Elphick is talking about self-harm. *God, is she ever going to stop?* The last thing Becca wants to dwell on right now is blades and blood.

Amelia flips her long, shiny hair over one shoulder and turns to whisper something to Millie. Her shoulders shake with suppressed giggles.

*Everyone else is perfectly fine.* It's just Becca who can't bear it.

It's then that it happens, and there's absolutely nothing Becca can do about it.

It starts with a sound like the humming of telephone wires, quiet at first, which intensifies until it is singing like a sawed note, louder than an orchestra of violins in unison, drowning out the rush of her blood and the pumping of her heart.

The sound has a colour, only at the edge of her vision at first, then bright white like lightning but static and fuzzy. It accumulates, like a car windscreen in bad weather getting silted up with snow. And then the blizzard is a whiteout, and everything turns black.

# Chapter Three

## Rachel

It is three o'clock and the windows are already darkening when the sound of a phone ringing interrupts the trance-like state into which Rachel has fallen at her desk. So far, most of her time at Fun-to-Learn has been spent copying information from an old website to a new one, but the monotony doesn't bother her; she's not sure she would be up to anything more challenging.

It is so unusual for anyone to call her that she's not at all quick to realise the ringing phone is hers.

And then she recognises it and comes to, and it's as if a long-dormant part of her suddenly awakens. There's only one person this call can be about, only one person who really matters.

She lunges for her handbag and fishes out the phone.

It's him, as she had known it would be.

As she heads out of the office she has a fleeting impression of her colleagues' faces turning towards her in surprise. Then she's passing through the little entrance lobby and out into the privacy of the gathering gloom.

'Mitch, what's going on? Is Becca OK?'

'Yes, no need to panic. She's at home. She's all right, more or less.'

From terror to relief in the space of a heartbeat – that's the power Becca has, has always had. Some things don't change.

'More or less?'

'She fainted. The school called me to come and pick her up.'

Rachel should have been the one to collect her – to hug her, to take her home in the car, to give her sweet tea, to tuck her up in bed. But she wasn't. And here she is, alone and shivering in the dark, and the physical yearning is so intense it's like a wave knocking her off her feet – the need to have Becca in her arms, to hold her and reassure her. To be there.

'But she's never fainted before. Did she hurt herself? Is she OK?'

'More embarrassed than anything, I think. She was in the lecture theatre when it happened, and she seems to have just slumped onto the shoulder of the girl next to her. Which was Amelia, actually. Amelia Chadstone.' As if Rachel was likely to forget who Amelia was. Or what she'd seen. 'Amelia thought she'd fallen asleep, so she nudged her and Becca slid onto the floor, and that's when she came to. Amelia felt pretty bad about it, I think. She was waiting with Becca when I got there.'

'That was nice of her.'

Rachel would much rather never to have to think about any of the Chadstones again, but there it is, there's no getting away from them.

Mitch sucks in his breath and says, 'Look, Becca and Amelia are friends. It's not fair on Becca if you have a problem with that. I thought you'd been working on all of that… stuff?'

'I have. And I get that. It's just… I'm worried about Becca. Can I speak to her?'

'She's fine, Rachel. There's no need to make a fuss. Anyway, she's having a nap right now, actually. I think she might have been overtired.'

'Overtired? Why? Have you been making sure she gets to bed on time?'

'Please don't make out that this is somehow *my* fault, Rachel. It's really not necessary. Or helpful.'

'OK. I'm sorry. But… she did look a little pale last time I saw her. Maybe she needs an iron supplement.'

'I spoke to the school nurse about it. She thinks it could be anxiety. A delayed reaction to stress.'

That gives Rachel pause. What Mitch is saying is that it's *her* fault. And that's what the school nurse meant, and that is no doubt what the Chadstones will agree on when they discuss what happened at dinner tonight. That's what they all think.

And, no doubt, they're right.

'Will you take her to the doctor?'

'I spoke to him earlier. He said she should be fine, but to keep an eye on her and bring her in if there are any ongoing issues.'

'Such as?'

'Dizziness, feeling disoriented, nausea, loss of appetite.'

'So… when did all this happen?'

'Oh, around eleven-ish? Just before lunchtime.'

'This happened this morning, and you're only just telling me *now?*'

'Rachel, don't shout at me. If you do, I'm going to end this call.'

She's holding the phone with her right hand; she moves her left to touch the skin of her right wrist and pinches, hard, and keeps pinching. After a moment she's able to speak quite calmly: 'OK, I'm sorry. It's just that I wish the school had let me know.'

'We've been through this. I'm the primary contact. It's not reasonable to expect them to notify us both.'

She pinches even harder. She's going to have a bruise. 'OK, OK, I'm sorry. Look, when do you think it would be all right for me to call Becca?'

'Maybe after dinner? Seven-ish?'

'Seven-thirty?'

'I thought you were desperate to speak to her. What else can you possibly have to do that's so important?'

Silence. Rachel pinches even harder. She says, 'I have an appointment.'

'Oh. OK then. Just try not to call too late. And, Rachel?'

'Yes?'

'I can't guarantee she'll want to talk to you,' he says, and ends the call.

Rachel is suddenly aware of just how cold and dark it is. She lets go of her wrist, rubs it, and puts the phone away. Somehow she manages to remember the key code and make her way back into the office.

Leona looks up as she comes back in. She says, 'Is everything all right?'

'Yes, everything's fine. I'll stay late to make up the time.'

'Don't worry about that. Look, if there's somewhere else you need to be, don't feel you have to stay. There's nothing you're doing that can't wait till tomorrow.'

Rachel sits down. 'There's nowhere else,' she says.

She's conscious of Leona watching her as she starts work again. The other woman is suspicious, that much is obvious. She smells a rat.

Sooner or later, Leona will see her chance and she'll take it. She'll start asking questions. She'll want to know. And that's when Rachel will start running out of options. Evasion will be off the table. She'll have just two choices left: to tell an outright lie, or to reveal herself for who she is.

# Chapter Four

Digby Street is not neighbourly, which suits Rachel just fine. Most of the houses – boxy 1960s semis, slightly ramshackle and prone to leaks – have the look of homes into which as many residents have been crammed as possible. 'For rent' or 'Recently let' signs protrude from weedy lawns, and at weekends, curtains stay drawn across the windows of converted garages and living rooms used as bedrooms. People come and go without anybody else taking much notice, let alone attempting to talk to them.

Her usual spot has been taken by a familiar Ford Fiesta, carefully parked. It is already six-thirty, the appointed meeting time, and she hasn't eaten since the cheese sandwich she'd brought in for lunch. She will have to get through what lies ahead with a rumbling stomach.

She finds a place to leave her car a little way down the road, in front of one of the few houses on the street that has children living in it; there is an abandoned, rain-sodden pushchair on the front lawn, its wheels facing the sky. Having manoeuvred into the space without disaster, she sprints back to the Ford Fiesta. Oh, God – she can't even remember if she managed to make her bed before leaving for the office that morning.

The driver's window slides down before she gets there.

'So sorry – could you give me a minute?'

It's fine. Of course it's fine. Her heart is thumping, but there's really no need to be afraid – it's not like she hasn't been through this before.

She hurries into the house. This is it, the safe ground she has created out of the rubble of her old life – such as it is. She steps round somebody's bicycle that occupies most of the space in the entrance hall. The carpet, the walls – it's all grimy, uncared for. But what does it matter? Nobody she really cares about is ever going to come here.

Upstairs, someone is showering. There is one bathroom between five of them, and it's in almost constant use. Rachel lets herself into her room. A faint pulse of music, the kind that is meant to convey mindless euphoria, reverberates through the walls.

Actually, it doesn't look too bad – no dirty cups or dishes lurking, and she'd folded away the sofa bed and stashed her bedding in the cupboard. This is intimate enough as it is: for one of them to have to perch on Rachel's bargain-basement sheets would be an additional mortification that she could really do without.

She goes back out to the Ford Fiesta and Sophie emerges with her briefcase, presses her key fob to lock the car, then double-checks it. Rachel doesn't blame her; Digby Street doesn't bring out your trusting side. Neither of them says anything as Sophie follows her up the garden path and into the house.

They don't bump into anyone in the corridor – not that anyone has ever asked who Sophie is, any more than they have ever shown any interest in Rachel herself.

Rachel says, 'Can I get you anything? A glass of water?'

'I'm fine. But do get something for yourself, if you'd like.'

'I'm fine, too,' Rachel says. She can hardly stop for something to eat now.

Sophie sets down her briefcase, takes off her coat and folds it over the back of one of the chairs next to the wobbly table. She's dressed slightly more formally than usual, in a long-sleeved white shirt and dark trousers. Maybe she's had an interview, or been in court. Rachel doesn't ask. It is not her business to ask questions; this relationship is strictly one way.

She stuffs her own coat in the wardrobe, though the bedsit is cold enough for it to be tempting to keep it on. She really must have a clear-out. Once she'd moved into Digby Street Mitch had asked her to take all her clothes with her; most of them are too big for her now, and too bright, too look-at-me.

The music stops and starts again, to a slightly more insistent beat. Sophie's non-judgemental face falters and gives way to a frown. She says, 'Is that going to carry on, do you think?'

'Probably, I'm afraid,' Rachel says.

'Never mind,' Sophie says, non-judgemental face back as if it had never been away. 'Do you mind if I sit?'

'Please do.'

Sophie perches on the chair she'd chosen for her coat; Rachel takes the sofa. Sophie reaches into her briefcase and brings out the familiar clipboard with its sheaf of papers.

'I should remind you that all being well, this is going to be our last meeting for a while,' she says.

'I know,' Rachel tells her.

Rachel had thought this would be a relief, but actually, now it comes to it, it seems like another loss. Sophie has been her only visitor, and now there will be none. Also, the regularity of Sophie's visits has been a way of marking time, like the progression of a school term towards the holidays, though with no expected release at the end of it.

A bruise has come up on her wrist; has Sophie noticed it? Rachel rests her other hand over it. She'd rather not have to explain. She has always tried to be honest with Sophie, up to a point. But she's never told her everything, and there's no point starting now.

Anyway, she can talk about the phone call without drawing attention to the bruise. Sophie will doubtless encourage Rachel to think of ways to handle conversations with Mitch more constructively in future. Rachel will mention how terrible the Chadstones make her feel, and Sophie will remind her of the techniques she has learned to calm herself: *Breathe in as if you're smelling a strawberry… and out like you're blowing out a candle.*

They won't exactly avoid the sequence of events that led to Rachel moving out of the family home, but Sophie is all about solutions, and her approach is to divert Rachel from the past – from all of the past, not only the crisis of three months before.

Sophie doesn't believe in guilt. Or obsession. Or rather, she does, but she thinks they're a negative use of energy. She certainly won't be drawn into a discussion about how, if Becca is vulnerable or under par, it's because of her mother.

Rachel's daughter, the baby she held in her arms, the toddler whose first steps she missed. Home is where the heart is, and home is somewhere else, and so is her child. And with the best will in the world, there is absolutely nothing that Sophie can do about that.

# Chapter Five

The notice is already in place when Rachel comes in on the first Monday of her second week. It isn't immediately obvious, and Rachel doesn't spot it until she's hung up her coat, sat down and switched on her computer. And then there it is, the only thing that has changed about the view from her desk since she left on Friday evening, unavoidably in her line of vision beyond her PC screen.

It's on the pinboard on the far side of the window, next to the Christmas menu for the nearest pub and the timetable for yoga classes at the business park gym: a modest poster, home printed in black ink on a piece of A5 paper, displaying a few words and a telephone number either side of an innocuous picture of a cup of tea and a slice of cake. The key message is in big bold capital letters and leaps out at her like an accusation.

ARE YOU A MOTHER APART?

It might as well be a Wanted poster with her own face on it.

She puts on her glasses and the words underneath the picture come into focus. *Christmas isn't always easy.* Well, that's true enough. *But if you're a mother who doesn't live with her child, you are not alone.*

That does not strike Rachel as being true at all.

Leona emerges from the kitchen with a cup of green tea and ginger, her ritual morning drink: the smell of it always makes the office seem slightly warmer. She's wearing a loose-sleeved cardigan that exposes the tattoo of bluebell flowers on the inside of her right wrist, presumably a leftover from a rebellious phase when she was younger.

'Morning, Rachel. How was your weekend?'

'Fine, thanks. Yours?'

'Oh, not bad, thank you. Too short.'

Is it Rachel's imagination, or did Leona give her a sharp look as she approached, before she settled at her desk?

Almost suspicious. No, not suspicious, challenging. Well, it must have been Leona who put the poster up. Rachel decides not to mention it. After all, it is not a conversation she wants or needs to have.


This is the day Mike Findlay, the managing director of Fun-to-Learn, is back from his golfing trip to Spain. He shows up at about half-past nine, a middle-aged man with an unlikely tan and a suit that is too broad across the shoulders, and bids them all a cursory good morning as he strides slightly breathlessly towards the office in the corner. He looks gloomy but determined, as if it's cost him something to make it to this position of lonely responsibility, and to acquire such a very heavy briefcase to carry on the way. Or maybe he just has a post-holiday hangover.

He doesn't acknowledge Rachel, which is fine by her. The less attention everybody else pays her, the better.

At ten o'clock Leona, who seems to be Mike's unofficial deputy, knocks on the door of his corner office and the two of them go off to the meeting room on the other side of the corridor. The change of mood in the office is as instant as in a classroom left to its own devices. Chatty Susan, the sales administrator who sits to Rachel's left, has been unusually quiet and industrious all morning. Now she stretches and allows herself to yawn.

'I reckon Mike's wife must have given him a hard time for going away. He looks a bit browbeaten,' she says to Angry Annie, the product and distribution manager who sits on the other side of the bank of desks. Annie isn't always angry, but Rachel thinks of her that way because of her habit of making long private phone calls of complaint to big companies, and the pride she takes in securing compensation.

An empty place separates Angry Annie from Leona; Rachel gathers that this buffer zone is usually occupied by the IT guy, who is off sick with shingles. Periodically Angry Annie complains of headaches and speculates that she's coming down with shingles, too.

Angry Annie says, 'Well, you can't let your hubby get away with too much, can you? If mine buggered off to Spain for a week he wouldn't half find a long list of chores waiting for him when he came back.'

Susan gets up, goes over to the noticeboard and inspects the poster. She's wearing a jumper with a reindeer on it today; Annie has Christmas tree earrings and a necklace of little baubles that light up.

Susan says, 'Did you see this, Annie?'

'See what?'

'*Come and join our new support group, based in Kettlebridge,*' Susan says, reading the last line of text before the phone number. '*Enjoy a friendly chat with other women who know what it's like. For details, phone Viv.*'

'Viv? Who's Viv?' Annie wants to know.

'Friend of Leona's, I suppose,' Susan tells her. 'I shouldn't think they're going to get many takers, would you? It's not exactly the kind of thing people would want to shout about.'

The blood rushes to Rachel's face. Luckily no one is looking at her.

'Quite,' Annie agrees. 'You'd have to be pretty bad not to get custody or whatever, wouldn't you? Terry's always said that if we decide we can't hack it any more, I can have the house as long as he doesn't have to have the kids. I think there are times when he quite fancies being one of those Saturday dads, not that I'm about to let him get away with it.'

Rachel moves her right hand across the keyboard and surreptitiously pinches her left wrist.

'Is it a coffee morning or something?' asks salesman Jim, breaking off from scrolling through the football results. Jim, who sits on Rachel's right, is in his twenties and is treated with mildly patronising affection by Annie and Susan. Today, in honour of the festive season, Jim is wearing a pair of antlers that make him look like a slightly clueless faun.

Susan peers at the poster. 'No, it's an evening thing. Seven o'clock tonight.'

'Isn't it a bit sexist?' Jim wants to know.

'Come off it. How could it possibly be sexist?' Annie asks.

'Well, it's mothers only, isn't it? It's just for women.'

'What do you care? You're not a dad yet, are you? Unless there's something you're not telling us,' Annie says.

'Yes, well, Leona doesn't have any kids either,' Jim retorts.

'You're a wally,' Annie says. 'Why else do you think she's got involved with this group? She does have a kid, or she did. She gave her up for adoption.'

'That's pretty unusual these days, isn't it?' Susan observes.

'I guess she must have been quite young. Maybe she wasn't really up to looking after a baby.'

'I wonder if she ever regrets it,' Susan says.

Rachel pinches a little harder. Discomfort is distraction and that is good. This job is meant to distract her. It isn't meant to remind her of just how badly she has failed.

'Well, I still think it's sexist,' Jim says.

'There's nothing to stop the dads having their own group, is there?' Annie says.

'Yeah, and if they did, you'd be muttering about why mums aren't invited,' Jim says.

'No, we wouldn't,' Annie retorts. 'Who'd want to join a group of sad dads? I can't think of anything more miserable. Other than a group of unhappy mums.'

'It's enough to make you grateful for what you have, isn't it?' Susan says, turning her back on the poster. 'Even if our kids run us ragged, and then men aren't much help. How about a cup of tea and a nice mince pie?'

'Why not,' Annie says, and gets to her feet. 'Get into the mood for our Christmas lunch later.'

Jim locks his screen to hide the football results and stands, too. Susan says, 'You coming, Rachel?'

'I'll pass, thanks,' Rachel says.

The others wander off to the kitchen, and for the first time since starting work there, Rachel has the office to herself.

It takes a violent effort of will to keep herself from going over to have a closer look at the poster, but she manages it. It's not as if she's going to go, anyway, and there's no reason why it should hold any significance or interest for her, let alone seem to be drawing her towards it.

At twelve-thirty the others shut down their computers and get their coats on ready to go for their Christmas lunch. The timing is ideal, as far as Rachel is concerned: she's expecting something, and the fewer witnesses the better. But Leona doesn't move.

'Sure you don't want to change your mind?' Annie asks Leona. 'I'm sure they could squeeze you in.'

'Someone has to answer the phones,' Leona says. 'You could take Rachel with you, though.'

'I'll stick with my sandwich, thanks.'

Mike the boss breezes out of his office, rubbing his hands together in anticipation.

'Right then, who's driving?' he says.

Annie sighs. 'Me again, as usual, I expect.'

They file out, and the office is quiet once more. Which is a good thing, all told. But also unnerving. With fewer bodies around, Rachel feels unpleasantly exposed. She hopes Leona will pop out for a walk round the business park at lunchtime, as she often does, but no such luck: when the external doorbell rings at half-past one, Leona is still there.

'I think that might be for me,' Rachel says, and jumps up to answer it.

The delivery man hands over the parcel and she signs for it and goes straight out to put it in the boot of her car, then hurries back.

'Treated yourself?' Leona asks as Rachel sits back down opposite her.

The words slip out almost before Rachel has time to stop them.

'Oh, it's not for me. It's for my... I mean, it's a present for somebody else.'

Leona studies her over the tinsel-draped barrier. She has large, clear, light green eyes, to which she never applies any make-up, and very long, very fine, very straight ash-blonde hair, like a child's.

Leona says, 'I'm not your boss, Rachel.'

'I'm sorry, I'm not sure I follow you...'

'I know I've been explaining to you what you need to do. But Mike's the boss. We're just colleagues. Which means you can talk to me. If you want to. You don't have to feel you can't.'

'I don't. I mean, I don't feel that way.'

'OK. Good.'

There is a small but conspicuous pause.

'You must have seen my poster,' Leona says. 'And I guess the others might have talked about it? So you probably know that I had a baby I gave up for adoption.'

Rachel nods. She can't bring herself to speak.

'I just think that sometimes groups can be helpful. A chance to get together and talk about the things we have in common, and maybe the things we don't. And Christmas can be difficult. We thought we could make it a kind of anti-Christmas party.'

'I have a daughter,' Rachel says. The words sound strange. Not as if she's lying, but as if she isn't telling the whole truth. 'She doesn't live with me. She lives with her dad. That delivery was a new coat for her. For Christmas.'

'I thought it might be something like that,' Leona says.

Already Rachel feels as if she has said too much. She doesn't want to get into explanations. Not here, not anywhere.

'But I'm not really one for groups,' she says. 'Or parties, come to that.'

Leona stares at her sceptically, then retreats back behind the barrier.

Rachel makes a concerted effort to get back to work. But out of the corner of her eye she can still see the poster. And she can't help but think of the person she used to be, back when she was so sure she was loved that no gathering, however full of strangers, held any fear for her.

# Chapter Six

## Rachel

### Sixteen years before the loss

Rachel inspected her reflection in the tinsel-framed mirror mounted on the wall opposite the bathtub. The frost-white glitter she'd put on her eyelids was still in place, though the silver top she was wearing now had a red wine stain on it as a result of someone's overenthusiastic dancing.

Music reverberated through the walls and floorboards, underlaid by a steady buzz of conversation. It was a good party: noisy, busy, full of people drunk on punch and festive goodwill. And yet she felt out of it. Everybody else seemed so carefree and so uninhibited, and so... *young*, even though they were mostly the same age as she was. Perhaps she should just get tipsy, too, and let herself go.

'What do you think of Mitch's girlfriend?' someone said outside the bathroom door.

*Oh no.* Somebody in the queue was talking about her. And she probably wasn't about to say anything flattering.

'She's quite pretty, I suppose.' That was Mary Smart, who was going out with Mitch's old schoolfriend, Hugh Chadstone. 'I hear his parents don't approve, but then they're probably not very happy with him dumping law and going off to Cornwall to study art, either. I guess you can see their point.' There is the click of a cigarette lighter, a leisurely exhalation, and then Mary carries on.

'She's not a student, you know. I guess she decided not to go, or maybe she didn't get in. She's a secretary.'

'Really? Where does she work?'

'I don't know. Somewhere in London. She and Mitch are *long-distance*. Sometimes I think that means things last longer than they would have otherwise, you know?'

'Mitch is so gorgeous, though.'

'Well, if that kind of bohemian look is your thing.'

'So what about you and Hugh?'

'Well, you know – treat 'em mean, keep 'em keen. Men are like animals, you have to let them know who's boss. If you don't they start thinking they're the ones in charge, and then you're really in trouble.'

The other girl laughed, and suddenly Rachel couldn't bear to stand there and listen to them any longer. She opened the bathroom door and stepped out.

Mary and her friend, who were smoking a joint, stared at her in open-mouthed astonishment. Mary had on a red felt elf's hat; her friend had come in white, and was wearing a halo and angel wings.

'Nice party, Mary. Thanks for making me feel welcome.'

And with that she walked off. She was conscious of Mary and her friend watching her, still at a loss for words. The corridor and stairs were crowded, but people made way for her. In the hallway, Hugh accosted her: 'Hey, Rachel, have you seen Mary anywhere?'

Hugh's face was red with drink – Rachel had only ever met him when he was either sozzled or hungover – and his Santa beard was dangling round his neck like a woolly cravat. The rest of his party outfit consisted of a plaid shirt, red cords and desert boots. A fair few of the boys Mitch knew from his school, which had been a private one, dressed in a similar way – it was a kind of unofficial uniform, Rachel had decided. Mitch himself didn't dress like that – he usually wore black, often second-hand, and increasingly threadbare since his parents had stopped giving him an allowance.

'Mary's gone to the bathroom. She'll be back in a minute,' Rachel said.

Hugh's face brightened. 'Oh good. Have you had much of a chance to chat with her or anything? It's just that I'm a bit worried she might be going off me, and I was wondering if she might have said anything? I know how you girls like to talk.'

'No, I think she likes you, she's just trying to play it cool. Just don't tell her I told you. Maybe you should try playing it cool, too?'

'Well, thanks for the heads up,' Hugh said. 'I'll try.'

'Do you know where Mitch is, by any chance?'

'I don't, I'm afraid. I'm sure he's around, anyway.'

Rachel squeezed past Hugh and into the living room. The lights were off, and people were dancing. She couldn't see Mitch at first. Then she spotted him on the far side of the room, deep in conversation with a girl in a glittery catsuit. She couldn't leave him for two minutes without him being seized upon by some opportunistic woman. She picked her way round the dancing in the centre of the room and joined them.

'—so that was when I really knew that it was over,' the glitter-girl said, and then saw Rachel and fell silent.

Mitch's smile of greeting faded and was replaced by concern. 'Rachel, are you all right?'

'Yes, fine,' she said.

'How about we go to the kitchen and see if there are any beers left? Nice to have met you,' he said to the glitter-girl, as an afterthought. 'Hope it works out.'

'Sure,' said the glitter-girl forlornly, looking daggers at Rachel.

The kitchen was quieter, further away from the music. There were a few people there talking – it was the stage of the night when people started having heated debates about nothing in particular, or committing to lengthy comic anecdotes, or crying. Mitch took a couple of the beers they'd brought out of the fridge and passed her one.

'Cheers,' he said. 'You're not upset that I was talking to that girl, are you? I think she just wanted to bend someone's ear about her ex. He's here, apparently.'

'No, no, that's all right. I know you're irresistible to girls with sad stories to tell.'

She smiled at him, and he relaxed. He said, 'So what's up?'

'Oh, nothing.'

'It's *definitely* not nothing.'

'OK.' She swigged a couple of mouthfuls of beer. 'I overheard Mary talking about me.'

'Oh.'

'She said your parents don't *approve* of me.'

Mitch looked horrified. 'I'm really sorry, Rach. I promise you, I never said anything like that to her, and if it came from Hugh then he's obviously got the wrong end of the stick. Which, to be fair, wouldn't be that unusual for him. Anyway, we both know it isn't true. It's *me* they don't approve of.'

'You've always been really evasive about what they think of me—'

'OK then, for what it's worth, my dad says you're a grafter and I could do with learning from your example. And my mother disapproves of everything I do on principle, but if that ever changes I'm sure she'd love you. But look, you don't really care about what my parents think, do you? Because you shouldn't.'

She shrugged. He moved closer to her, put one hand on her hip and gave her that wicked grin that meant he was thinking of what would happen between them later, when they were finally alone. She felt her irritation begin to dissolve: after all, what did it matter what anybody else thought? He was the only one who really counted.

'My parents don't *know* you, Rachel,' he said. 'And they don't *want* to know me, at least not right now. But our lives are about us, not our parents. Right?'

'Right. I know. But Mitch… Did you tell Hugh – or Mary, or whoever – that I'm a secretary? Because I'm not, actually. I *was* an executive assistant, and they've made me office manager. I mean, I know it doesn't sound that different but it's actually a step up from—'

'OK,' Mitch said. 'I might have got a bit confused. But you know I didn't mean anything by it. I would never put you down, Rachel. And if Mary was being mean about you in any way then she was totally out of order.' He gazed at her fondly, reached up to tuck a strand of her hair behind her ear; the last traces of her annoyance disappeared. 'You've got so much more going for you than she has, anyway. She's *exactly* the kind of person who'll get married to someone like Hugh and settle down to have kids in the country, and wake up in twenty years' time and wonder where her life went.'

'What do you think *we'll* be like in twenty years' time?'

'What do *you* think we'll be like?'

'Well… you'll be a famous and successful Turner Prize-winning artist, being exhibited here, there and everywhere.'

'And you'll be running an international business empire.'

She beamed at him. They often talked like this: it was a favourite game, and the way he'd tried to distract her and keep her spirits up in the aftermath of her dad's death. He smiled back, relieved to see her happy again, and leaned in to kiss her – just fleetingly, but it was enough to give her that glorious hazy feeling that all was right with the world, as long as they were together.

He said, 'Do you want to dance?'

'Always,' she said, and he stood back so she could lead the way to the living room.

# Chapter Seven

## Viv

Viv has hosted many different groups at Park Place over the years, from the church flower arrangers to the town square improvement committee. It never usually makes her nervous; she likes it – she likes to keep busy. But she's nervous today, and so she does what she always does when she doesn't quite know how else to occupy herself: she bakes.

Pottering round her clean, orderly kitchen, listening to a nice bit of Mozart, she's almost contented. She's going to make barm brack, an old-fashioned loaf cake that she will serve sliced and buttered. The bowl of mixed dried fruit has been soaked overnight in sugar and tea, and is now dark, wet, tannin-scented and plump as if ripe again. She folds in the white flour and stirs it. Now it looks like the beginnings of a cake. All that is missing is a child to lick the spoon.

She pictures him the way she always does, conjuring him up, and the image is part memory and part a wish, and she's comforted.

While the cake is in the oven she vacuums and dusts the living room – best to have everything shipshape. George, bless him, would have reproached her for fussing round like this. He had been crankier than ever after his retirement, and made her cranky, too, by being underfoot all the time, though she had tried her best not to show it.

It had been a bit of a nightmare, really, those last few years. The sneaking off, the lies, the constant niggling fear of discovery, and the worry about what finding out would do to Louise and Elaine – even though they were out of the house and living their own lives – and more particularly, what it would do to her husband. Because George would have known, then, that she wasn't the wife he thought he'd had all these years: reliable, steady, honest as the day is long. Nope: she is – was – a deceiver, and their enduring and apparently successful marriage had, in fact, been based on a lie.

A necessary lie; a lie that had propped them up, given something to cling to, and shaped them. Because the more George had niggled and complained and condemned and sulked – almost as if he knew, deep down, that she was surreptitiously going against his wishes – the more she chatted and bustled and baked.

It hadn't been fair to George, not really. Still, it's far too late to do anything about it now.

When they were younger, in the early days of the marriage, there had been times when they would lie in bed together and talk about which one of them would go first. George had always been insistent that it would have to be him. 'I'd never be able to live without you,' he had said. It hadn't really been morbid; it had seemed a remote, hypothetical prospect, like the end of the world. Quite romantic, really. A way of affirming how precious the present was: of acknowledging how much their togetherness mattered.

But then she had got pregnant. He had been tender with her then, too. So full of hope. It was before he had learned how much there was to be afraid of.

Sometimes you just had to lie, even though it seemed the worst thing in the world to have done when your thoughts and memories were boiling away inside you and your husband was next to you snoring obliviously, sleeping the deep sleep of the man whose heart might have been broken but whose conscience was untroubled.

God forgive her.

The timer goes off and she returns to the kitchen. Nutmeg, cinnamon, allspice: the scent is instantly consoling. Her back protests as she stoops to take the barm brack out of the oven. She can't have that. She can't afford to get frail. Can't get old. Or at least, can't get old and infirm. Yes, the years are ticking by, but as long as she's in reasonably good health it doesn't matter too much, does it?

George had been at peace when he passed; his time had come, and he had been free to go. But it isn't like that for her. She isn't free, and she can't leave. She has to stay strong and well.

She has so much still to do. She's still needed, and George never knew how much.

Perhaps, in a way, she had lied to protect him from ever having to know.

She sticks a skewer in the barm brack and it comes out clean. She covers the loaf tin with a clean tea-towel and sets it aside to cool so that it'll be easy to turn out, and switches off the oven.

Mustn't get forgetful. That's not an option either.

Best not put it off any longer. When you're frightened of something, you should just try and get it over with. If you can.

She goes to the hall cupboard, opens it, and there it is, to the side of her anorak, her good woollen overcoat and her mac: a blank, slightly battered green baize noticeboard. It still has a faintly ecumenical scent from all those years in the church office – the odours of cold old building, pine floor cleaner and modestly dispensed incense have all soaked in.

It isn't a big thing – it is perhaps two feet high and one foot across, about the height and breadth of a toddler with arms outstretched – and it is light, but still, pain shoots down her spine and into her thighs as she bends to drag it out, and then lifts it.

She grits her teeth and carries it to the living room and props it up against the antique armchair, which George had never let anyone sit in and is so horribly uncomfortable she still discourages visitors from using it.

Now for the photo.

There aren't many to choose from. A slim packet, which now lives in the bottom drawer of the sideboard. For years it had been hidden, like a teenage girl's diary, under their mattress – George could be relied upon never to help change the sheets, so there was no risk of discovery.

She has never shown these photographs to anyone.

She flicks through them and makes her selection. The snap looks a little bit faded, even though it's never been out on display. It shows a little boy in a brown corduroy jacket and red wellies, standing in a muddy lane. A happy boy. A boy who likes puddles, and doesn't mind the rain.

The Blu-Tack is in the drawer where it always is, along with the tape and parcel paper, the scissors and the drawing pins. It won't do to pin or stick this, though. It won't do to damage it.

She had suggested to Leona that it might be best for the ladies to bring copies of their pictures, just in case, and had mentioned this to the one or two who had called in response to Leona's flyers and posters. But she had neglected to organise a duplicate for herself. All it would have taken was a little trip to the photocopier at the newsagent's. But she hadn't done it. She really was getting forgetful.

Or maybe it was just that she had wanted to put this off to the last possible moment, because she was afraid of how it would make her feel.

She places the rest of the photos carefully back in the packet and sticks the one she has chosen on the noticeboard. Not at the top or in the middle – that would be presumptuous. Tonight is not just about her. So she picks a spot towards the bottom, somewhere to the side.

It is only then that she allows herself to sob, and not for long.

A car passes by outside; the house is quiet again, and sweet with the smell of cinnamon. She kneels on the rug and gazes at the picture of her son as if she could will herself back there, to that muddy lane, to a long-ago day that was just beginning to clear, and the pain in her back seems to vanish.

# Chapter Eight

## Rachel

It is snowing as Rachel arrives, just enough to be decorative but not so much as to give people an excuse to stay away. Worse luck. She doesn't really know what she's doing here. Still, she's made it this far. It would be ridiculous to go scurrying back to the bedsit now.

It certainly is pretty where Viv lives; it's like being in a Christmas card. The fine flakes whirl and gust in the glow of old wrought-iron streetlamps, and the red-brick Victorian houses look as if they have just been dusted with icing sugar. On the other side of the road, the trees of the park are ghostly in the gloom.

She finds somewhere to leave the car – it very obviously doesn't belong here, among the executive saloons and family-friendly 4X4s – and makes her way to number 17. All the houses she passes are adorned with lights that glitter discreetly in the darkness, wound round garden topiary or fastened to gabled roofs. Rachel glimpses tinselly trees through the chinks between heavy curtains, and mantelpieces crowded with cards. If Digby Street is a kind of anonymous hell, Park Place is an English domestic heaven.

One house has a nativity display on the windowsill: large plaster figures, faded with age, carefully arranged. The infant Jesus is soundly sleeping in Mary's arms, blissfully oblivious to what is to come.

A blind comes rattling down and hides the scene from view, and Rachel hurries on.

Number 17 is at the end of a gabled Victorian terrace, like a row of gingerbread houses. Unlike its neighbours, it shows no signs of the season. No lights, no garland, no glimpse of baubles or the fairy on top of the tree.

As far as Rachel is concerned, this is as good as a welcome sign. She steps up and rings the bell.

It seems to take an age for someone to come. Rachel's breathing is fast and shallow and sends thin plumes of cloudy white into the icy air. Finally the door opens, and she sees a crisp-featured, apple-cheeked old lady who might have been beautiful once. There's a scent of something warm and spicy coming from inside the house, something enticing.

Rachel says, 'Are you Viv?'

The woman nods and smiles encouragingly. She's wearing pearls and perfectly applied pale pink lipstick, and her silvery hair, which has been tinted blonde, is as impeccably styled as the Queen's. Rachel guesses that she's in her late sixties. She clearly has absolutely no intention of letting herself go.

'I'm Rachel Steele.' Steele is her maiden name; she's always used it at work – it had seemed like a useful way to separate her office self from her home self, the one who had become Mitch's wife and Becca's mother. Sometimes it complicated things having two identities, but it also made her feel as if she had preserved a little bit of her younger self, the girl who had been so determined to make her own way in life and establish her independence. She could do with a bit of that willingness to embrace the new tonight. 'We spoke on the phone about half an hour ago. I work with Leona?'

'Ah, yes. Come on in, you look half frozen. You're very welcome.'

She steps back to let Rachel into the porch and closes the front door behind her. It's like stepping into a warm hug after the cold air outside.

'I didn't actually say anything to Leona about coming tonight,' Rachel says. 'I mean, I saw the poster she put up, but I wasn't sure I was going to make it until I phoned you just now.'

'Ah. Yes. Well, she's here already, and I hope you won't mind, but I took the liberty of mentioning you'd be here. I thought it would be better if it didn't come as a surprise when you arrived. Anyway, I'm delighted you could join us.'

Viv holds her hand out for Rachel to shake, and Rachel clasps it. Viv's touch is light and dry. She's wearing a gold wedding ring and an engagement ring set with one of the biggest sapphires Rachel has ever seen.

'I hope you're feeling hungry,' Viv says. 'We seem to have rather a lot of food, and not many people.'

She leads the way into a sitting room with crimson rugs and long wine-coloured curtains and an open fire blazing. Leona is sitting by the fireplace at one end of a big L-shaped sofa covered in dull gold brocade. She's gazing at the flames, apparently lost in thought, and looks more than ever like an eccentric Renaissance angel on a disappointing day.

'Here she is,' Viv says.

Leona gets up and comes over to offer Rachel a peck on the cheek. 'Good to see you. Well done for coming. I did wonder if you might, but I couldn't be sure, especially as we hadn't really talked about it much. Anyway, I'm sure it's needless to say, but anything that we tell each other here is in the strictest confidence.'

'Of course,' Rachel says.

'Can I get you a drink?' Viv says to Rachel. 'Tea? Coffee? Hot chocolate? Sparkling white wine? It's non-alcoholic, so you don't need to worry about driving. I expect you know Leona doesn't drink.' Rachel hadn't known this, though it doesn't entirely surprise her; Leona is always so controlled, it's hard to imagine her having a couple of glasses and letting her hair down. 'She's very health-conscious,' Viv adds. 'Though she does make an exception for cake!'

'Cake seems like a pretty harmless vice, in the grand scheme of things,' Rachel says. 'I'll just have a glass of water, please.'

Viv takes her coat and goes off, and Rachel perches next to Leona on the sofa and takes in the choice of refreshments on the coffee table in front of them. There is a large bottle of fizz, open, and two old-fashioned wide-rimmed glasses, almost empty. There is also a cake, some kind of fruit loaf with a couple of slices missing, and a large plate of luscious-looking cupcakes, iced in pink with white writing, the same words painstakingly piped onto each one: BAD MOTHER.

'Do tuck in,' Leona says. 'I made the cupcakes. The barm brack is Viv's. It's very good.'

'Maybe later on,' Rachel says. She's too nervous to eat; she'd probably choke. 'I'm really sorry, I didn't think to bring anything. I should have. It was all a bit last minute. I only rang Viv when I got back from work.'

'No, no, don't apologise. At this rate you'll be able to take some home with you. We're a bit down on numbers. Very much down, actually. In fact… I think we might be the only ones who make it tonight.'

'Oh. Well… I suppose it's very close to Christmas. Maybe people are busy with stuff.'

'I don't know. Viv had quite a few phone calls. And not all of them were cranks. But when it comes down to it… maybe women like us have learned to be wary.'

Their eyes meet; Leona gives Rachel a rueful, we're-in-this-together smile, and Rachel does her best to return it.

*Just because you're feeling anxious, doesn't mean the threat you're facing is real*: Sophie Elphick taught her that. This is fine, all fine, sharing a sofa in a strange house with a woman who she met at work and with whom she has something big and painful in common. This is progress, opening up, reaching out.

Leona reaches for one of the iced cupcakes and takes a bite out of it: the word BAD disappears.

'This is what other people think of us,' she says, and finishes it off. 'I thought I'd take the bitterness out of it.' She gestures towards the green baize pinboard leaning against the armchair next to the fireplace and says, 'Anyway, there's plenty of space.'

There are two pictures pinned to the board. At the top there's a photocopy of a snap of a newborn baby swaddled in a yellow cellular blanket, and beneath it is a faded glossy print of a sturdy toddler in dungarees and red wellies. It is not possible for Rachel to guess which child is Leona's, and which is Viv's.

There is something ghostly about the pictures: not sinister, but melancholy. They lend the room a little of the atmosphere of a séance or vigil, as if this gathering is prompted by an unspoken faith that the power of collective longing might call the children back from wherever they have gone, and reunite them with their mothers.

'You see the newborn? That's my girl,' Leona says. 'That's Bluebell. She was adopted when she was a baby. She's nearly seven now. I do have some more recent pictures – her parents send me one every year, and we exchange letters on her birthday. Me and the parents, I mean, not me and Bluebell.'

'Ohh…' Rachel has no idea what to say. The bluebell tattoo on Leona's inner wrist now makes sense.

Viv comes back in and passes Rachel her glass of water. Rachel sips it and swallows, and sets it down with a conspicuously trembling hand.

'We're on to introductions,' Leona says. 'I've just pointed out Bluebell.'

'Pretty name,' Rachel says.

'Yeah, her adoptive parents kept it. I didn't think they would.'

Viv settles into an armchair. 'That's Aidan in the red wellies. He was just three years old then, and he stopped living with me when he was four. He lives in a care home now, has done for years. He's in his forties now. Officially middle-aged.'

There is a silence that deepens until Rachel realises that something is expected of her.

'I haven't brought one,' she says. 'I know you mentioned it on the phone, Viv, but I forgot.'

'Maybe next time,' Viv says. 'No need to bring an original, unless you have a spare of course. We all know how precious photos are, especially if you don't have many of them. Would you like to tell us anything about your child? Or children?'

'I have a daughter. Becca. She's thirteen. I split from her father earlier this year, and we agreed that it would be better for her to live with him.'

Can she really bring herself to add Becca to the pictures on the pinboard? Becca would hate it if she knew. Those other children will have no memories of what their mothers were like before they were parted from them. But Becca does. Becca has been conscious of at least some of what is going on – too much.

And Becca has been asked which of her parents she would prefer to live with, and she has chosen.

'Do you still see her?' Viv asks.

'Yes, once a week, on Saturdays.'

'Viv sees Aidan once a week as well,' Leona comments. Her tone is sympathetic but matter-of-fact, as if they're discussing the routine broken nights of early motherhood, or the trials of potty training. 'I haven't seen Bluebell since she was tiny. I just have the photos. Are you sure you wouldn't like a cake?'

She holds out the plate of cupcakes. Rachel hesitates, then thanks her and takes one. She peels off the paper and discards it and examines the icing. BAD MOTHER. She thinks of the effort that had gone into piping the words, over and over again onto each little cake, and how defiant Leona must have felt as she did it.

What was the name of that Greek myth – the one about the girl who was dragged off to the Underworld and made the mistake of eating something there?

*Persephone.* That was it: Persephone and the pomegranate. The lost daughter who ate fruit in the underworld and swallowed six seeds, which meant that she had to return there for six months of every year, and her mother mourned so hard that she brought down winter on the world of the living. Mitch had told her about it. He'd known about that kind of thing: he'd liked playing Professor Higgins to her Eliza Doolittle. And then he'd used her as a model for a painting inspired by that myth. The only time she'd posed for him.

And now Mitch really does have her daughter. An irony surely not lost on either of them. And she still has the study for the painting, tucked away out of sight somewhere in the bedsit. Maybe she should get it out, put it on display: a reminder of a time before her relationship with Mitch turned bitter. Before Becca, even. When it had just been the two of them.

Anyway, the cake is delicious: a perfectly melting mouthful.

'Before I forget, there's something I have to give back to you,' Leona says to Viv.

She rummages in her handbag, which isn't really a handbag at all but a capacious leather satchel, and takes out a book: an old orange paperback copy of *Kramer vs. Kramer*, with a movie still of Dustin Hoffman holding up a little boy on the cover. She puts it down on the coffee table and says to Viv, 'Thanks for the loan, but this book is the enemy.'

'Oh, really? I thought it was rather interesting. It certainly has a case to make, as does the film – the idea that the mother shouldn't always be the default parent.'

'Exactly. That's what I object to. I'm sure it lingered in the mind of many a judge handing down a final ruling after a custody battle, and it wouldn't have influenced any of them in favour of women.'

She glances at Rachel as she says this. Rachel does her best to look studiously neutral: better that they talk about fictional mothers than that they should start to try to elicit some kind of confession from her.

Leona presses on. 'OK, so here's what I object to. Number one, he learns how to make his kid's favourite breakfast and suddenly he's a hero. Now when would that apply to any woman? A woman's a loser if she *doesn't* know how to do this stuff, not a star if she figures it out.'

'Is that bit in the film?' Viv asks. 'I think it might be, actually.'

'Who cares? It's still annoying. Number two, he's an absolute *bastard* to his wife. In the book more than the film. Like, when she's up the duff and he can't stop himself from shagging her all the time and the doctor has to tell him to leave her alone. What a prick! It doesn't even seem to occur to him to wonder whether she wants it or not. So the book opens with her giving birth and he's just repulsed, he's got absolutely no compassion for her—'

'She does swear at him,' Viv points out.

'Yeah, so what? This is *birth* we're talking about here, not some Jane Austen tea party. I swore at *everybody* when I was doing it—'

'I did, too,' Rachel volunteers.

'So then the poor woman comes down with postnatal depression,' Leona goes on. 'Except nobody calls it that, and he won't let her go back to work, and in the end she's coming out in hives, she has to get away or die. I don't know about any of the rest of you, but *I* can understand that.'

She folds her hands in her lap and looks fiercely round as if challenging them to contradict her.

Viv intervenes. 'I think the father in this book changes,' she says. 'And sometimes people *do* change. And attitudes, and laws. I've seen changes in my own lifetime that I could never have imagined.'

Rachel scans the pictures on the pinboard again, then discreetly looks around the sitting room for other photographs. She's surprised to see a framed family group on the mantelpiece: a younger, golden-haired Viv with a smiling husband and two teenage daughters.

*What kind of double life has Viv been living, and why?*

'In my opinion, Mrs Kramer does the truly loving thing, the really noble and big-hearted thing: she says the dad should have the boy because she can see it's what's best for him at that time,' Viv goes on. 'What could be more generous and self-sacrificing than that? I don't think she's a victim the way you suggest, Leona. I think she's a *hero*.'

'I never said that she was a victim. I said that he was a bastard and it wasn't surprising that she got depressed,' Leona objects. 'Have you ever seen the film, Rachel? I don't suppose you'd be a fan.'

Rachel hesitates. Where had she seen it? On a small TV screen, late at night – one of the various London flats she'd lived in, maybe, or back further still, in her parents' house. Yes, that was it. She'd watched it with her mother.

Something slides down her face; something moist and sticky, like blood. Not blood. Tears.

*Oh God, no – she can't be the one to cry.* She can't sit here sobbing in front of these women and the pictures of the children they're separated from. She can't tell them any more of her story: if she does she has no idea when she'll be able to stop, or what'll be left of her when she does.

She lurches to her feet, banging her knees against the coffee table in her haste to get away, and Viv reaches out as if to stop her but Rachel isn't having any of that.

'I'm so sorry, I made a mistake – I thought I could do this, but I can't,' she says.

Her last clear view of the meeting is of the plate of pink BAD MOTHER cupcakes. She stumbles away and almost instantly finds herself back out in the cold and the dark and the snow. She hurries as quickly as she can towards the safety of her car.

*

She decides to sit for a while before attempting to drive. Everything is very quiet. After maybe five minutes, she feels more or less herself again – merely tired, and ordinarily sad.

What had she hoped for? Nothing. Absolutely nothing. She had only gone along because she was desperate. Then why is she disappointed?

She's exhausted, depleted, broken-hearted: all she can do is keep on working and turning up on Saturdays to see Becca. She's never far from the edge of tears – they're always there somewhere, waiting

for a chance to humiliate her – but for all that, she can't bring herself
to feel anything, or to think about anything: not with regards to
her own situation, and certainly not for anybody else's. She doesn't
want to feel, doesn't want to think.

So what the hell was she doing, coming here?

It's Christmas, that's all it is. Getting through it. Getting used
to the way things are now.

She turns the key in the ignition and Radio 1 comes on. Becca always
used to tease her for listening to it. She doesn't tease her any more.

Rachel puts the car into gear and is about to drive off when
somebody taps on the window.

It's Viv, in a coat that she hasn't stopped to button up. She's
holding a small, shiny package. Something wrapped in foil. A gift
of some kind.

Rachel winds the window down. 'I'm sorry, Viv. It was really nice
to meet you. I guess I'm just not ready to do something like this.'

'I know,' Viv says, and thrusts her offering through the open
window, so Rachel has no option but to take it. It smells faintly
of cinnamon.

'Something for you to eat when you get back,' Viv says. 'It's
barm brack. Have a slice with a bit of butter, and a nice cup of tea.
Call me any time, or pop round. You know where I am now, and
you've got my number. Happy Christmas, and make sure you take
care of yourself. I'm glad you came.'

With that she turns and walks away. She has a particularly
determined stride; it is easy to imagine her with a dog on a lead,
head down against a buffeting wind, bracing herself against the
weather. She's fast, too, and has already disappeared from view by
the time Rachel realises she has neither thanked her nor wished her
a happy Christmas in return.

The foil parcel is heavier than you might expect, soft and slightly
yielding. Rachel puts it on the passenger seat. She feels an unfamiliar
warmth wash over her, like a blessing.

She pulls out off Park Way onto Gull Street, a narrow, low-lying thoroughfare that runs parallel to the river Kett, lined with takeaways and pubs and blocks of flats. There are modest lights strung up above the road, a few bits of tinsel in passing windows, a couple of revellers staggering along in high heels. But otherwise it is quiet. Soon Christmas will be over, and everything will be back to normal.

As she approaches the turn-off for the dual carriageway she hears bells ring out. She breathes in the scent of Viv's baking and is startled to find herself at once intensely grateful and filled with regret.

# Chapter Nine

## Rachel

Eleven years before the loss

'Well, it's certainly pretty,' Rachel said. 'And it's in our price range.'

'In London a place like this wouldn't exist,' Mitch said. 'Not for any money.'

The house they had come to see was just the other side of a small hump-backed bridge and was partially concealed by a tangle of flowers and greenery. Along the front wall, a pink climbing rose had got out of control and run riot. There was no 'For Sale' sign: it had only just come on the market. The windows were shuttered and the house appeared to be sleeping, its creamy stone façade warmed by the June mid-afternoon sun.

Mitch beamed at her and she smiled back. He was obviously in love with the place already, and it was working its magic on her, too. Still, they had to be practical. She leaned against him so she could see, too, as he studied the printout with the details.

'There's an extension at the back that I'd be able to use as my studio. It's commutable – Barrowton's not too far and there's a quick service to London Paddington. It's doable, Rach.'

'Yeah, but it's a long commute. I'd be out of the house first thing and I'd only just make it back for Becca's bedtime. It would mean a lot more time away from home, Mitch.' She reached across to squeeze his hand. 'And a lot more childcare for you.'

'Well, I can handle that, if you're up for it. I kind of like the idea of being a hands-on dad. And I think I could really work here. It'd be good for us. We'd be able to put down roots, make the place our own.'

'We wouldn't know anybody. Apart from the Chadstones,' Rachel said.

Mitch's face fell. 'Oh. That would be all right, wouldn't it? They wouldn't be *that* close. Anyway, I thought you got on with them?'

'It's not that I don't get on with them, it's just that—'

She didn't *mind* them, she just didn't want to have to hang out with them any more than was strictly necessary. Mitch was bound to take this as a criticism; he was stubbornly loyal to Hugh, and by extension to Mary, too.

But then Becca protested that she wanted to get out, and promptly burst into tears.

Rachel got out of the passenger seat, careful of the estate agent's little run-around which Mitch had parked very close to, and went round to release her. The car didn't have air conditioning, and it was hot and stuffy; no wonder Becca was fed up and bawling. Her face was turning the same bright red as her dress. But the minute she was out of the car she stopped crying, and the two of them went hand-in-hand onto the bridge.

Rachel hoisted Becca up so that she could look down into the stream. Becca pointed. 'Fish,' she said.

Rachel turned to see Mitch pointing the camera at them; they'd brought it along so they could take pictures of the property. He put it away in the backpack they used to cart around things for Becca – favourite snacks, toys, a change of clothes, and woe betide if any of it was missing when a crisis struck – and came up to join them. He looked really happy and relaxed, as if they were on holiday, and she suddenly realised she hadn't seen him at ease like that for ages, probably not since before Becca was born.

'You just looked so perfect together, I had to get a picture,' he said. 'But shouldn't you put her socks and shoes on? She could hurt her feet.'

'I'll do it in a minute,' Rachel said. 'I just wanted to give her a chance to calm down.'

The estate agent, a young man in a shiny suit, approached from the other direction, from the garden path that led to the cottage. He was looking sheepish, as if he had a confession to make.

'I'm really sorry, I haven't brought the right key with me,' he said. 'I'm going to have to nip back to the office. Shouldn't take me more than a quarter of an hour. You're very private here, as you can see, but still, it's pretty quick to get into town.'

Normally Rachel would have complained at least a little about the delay, especially as they'd had an hour and forty minutes' drive to get here from London. But the sun was shining, the stream was bright with reflected light and the cottage was lovely. She decided to let it go.

'OK, I guess we'll just take in the view for a while,' she said.

The estate agent got back into his car and sped off, and Mitch came to stand at Rachel's side and put his arm around her.

'You know, I bet Becca would be more relaxed in a place like this. We all would,' Mitch said.

'Look, it's called Rose Cottage,' Rachel said. 'There's a nameplate on the wall. I always wanted to live in a house with a name.'

'Flower,' Becca said, pointing towards the house.

'Yes, they're roses. It's very pretty, isn't it?' Rachel said, and set her down. Becca was getting to be quite a weight, but still wasn't enthusiastic about walking too far; her preferred mode of transport was her father's shoulders.

And a fine pair of shoulders they were, too. There he was, her husband, the father of her child – six-foot-three of knight in shining armour with tousled hair in need of a trim, a trace of Becca's stewed apple on his shirt and bags under his eyes. He was such a good dad – so gentle, so patient. Rachel was struck all over again by how lucky she was, and how lucky Becca was, too. She must be sure never to take him for granted.

Fatherhood, for all its moments of unexpected joy, had worn him out – had worn both of them out: sleep, haircuts, sex, had all gone by the wayside. It had been much harder than she'd anticipated. So much for her plan of setting up her own business while on maternity leave; she was pleasantly surprised to have managed to hold onto her job, given the miasma of tiredness through which she faced working life. But if she could wake up here on Saturday morning… She'd feel as if she was working for more than to pay the bills. She'd be doing it so her daughter could have the kind of home Rachel's own mother would only ever have been able to daydream about.

'Flower!' Becca said again, pulling hard at Rachel's hand.

Well, it wasn't as if there was anybody at home. 'We can have a look in a minute,' Rachel said, 'when you've got your shoes on.'

Becca was perfectly docile as Rachel led her back to the car. Maybe Mitch was right. Maybe the countryside *would* be better for Becca – and for them all.

Mitch stayed on the bridge, gazing down at the water. He was frowning slightly, maybe because the sunshine was so bright, or maybe because he couldn't quite believe that somewhere so perfect could really be within reach.

# Chapter Ten

Rachel allows ten minutes extra in case she gets stuck behind riders or a tractor, and arrives early, but without too long to wait. Perfect timing. And so it should be. She's had plenty of practice. She parks in the gravelled space in front of the little bridge and readies herself to call for Becca.

The cottage on the other side of the stream, beyond the wall and the gate, is like a child's drawing of a house in winter. It has a smoking chimney, big, rectangular windows and a bright red door, and there are patches of day-old snow still clinging to the garden. A magical place. A place she's no longer permitted to enter unless Mitch allows her in; a place she has paid for, and lost.

It's time.

Her heart is already lifting in anticipation, even though she knows not to expect too much. Still, this is it. After what happened, after what she did, this is as good as it gets. As much as she can hope for, or deserves.

They won't have long. Just enough time for Becca to thaw, to forget to be wary and estranged and defensive – if all goes well.

She gets out of the car, walks over the bridge and lets herself through the gate.

There's a Christmas garland on the front door, new since last time. It's heart-shaped and made of holly; the red berries match the paintwork. It doesn't look like the kind of thing Mitch would have chosen – too pretty, too feminine. Becca must have picked it out. Helping to take charge of the Christmas decorations. Being the lady of the house.

She rings the bell. Mitch is always quick to answer, as if to remind her that he's the gatekeeper, that she can't get in or past or round him. He won't invite her in. A Jehovah's Witness or door-to-door energy salesman would get a warmer welcome.

Mitch always found it weirdly difficult to give botherers short shrift. He listened to them; he was friendly and receptive; he was always polite. He gave explanations. *I'm a confirmed agnostic, I'm afraid*, or *I'm happy with my electricity provider, and I don't buy on the door.*

As if he had plenty of time on his hands. Which, frankly, most of the time, he did.

He won't be like that with her.

The door opens and there he is, bearded, grouchy, in his paint-spattered Cornish fisherman's smock. She'd been with him when he bought that. On holiday. A lifetime ago.

'She'll be down in a minute. You might as well wait in the car.'

'OK.'

'You'll have her back at four, right?'

'Of course.'

His hand has healed, but he has a scar and it hasn't begun to fade yet. He sees her looking at it and their eyes meet for a moment before he shuts the door in her face. There is nothing for it but to do as she's told and go back to the car.

But then Becca comes trudging towards her, head down, hands in pockets, hair riffling in the breeze, trying to look nonchalant about everything, as if she's quite grown up enough, thank you, to take all this in her stride. And Rachel's heart rushes out to her; all she wants to do is to envelop Becca in her arms, as she might be able to do if her daughter was a younger child – ten or eleven or even twelve instead of thirteen.

But she knows that would be a mistake. They've had practice for this, in a way: all those weekends when she'd made a big effort to do things with Becca, to make up for not having got home for bedtime during the week, what she'd wanted most was a hug. And Becca had known, and had quickly learned not to give it to her. Not straight away. To make her work for it. Even when she was quite little, she'd been aloof with Rachel on first seeing her after some time apart, as if she either wanted to punish Rachel for having left her or didn't quite trust her not to disappear again. Or both.

And Becca is thirteen now, on the cusp of leaving childhood behind. It is important for her to have her space, to not be crowded by her mother's guilty, needy affection.

Becca gets in next to her and puts on her seatbelt, and Rachel starts the car.

Rachel says, 'You all right?'

'Yeah, not bad,' Becca says offhandedly. 'You?'

'Yeah, not bad.'

Rachel turns the car and drives away.

She has to hold it together, to tread the delicate line that an absent parent has to keep to: calm, patient, under control. Neither overbearing nor chummy, and certainly not demanding. There can be no hint of the kind of ugliness that had taken over when she did what she did to destroy the pattern of their lives together.

She never meant to do Becca harm: and yet she had. Now everything has to go right, as far as it can. And if it doesn't, if she screws up, she could lose the little bit of Becca that she still has: these Saturdays together, and Becca's willingness, in spite of everything, to be with her.

# Chapter Eleven

The multiplex is largely deserted, and Rachel's spirits rise at the prospect of making it to the cinema without bumping into anybody. People are always perfectly nice, or at least, never openly nasty, but the way they look at her makes her uneasy. Whatever they know about her situation, or suspect, it's more than she would like.

She can't think of anything to say to Becca while they're waiting in the queue. Becca has the tense, muted expression that Rachel has seen on her a few times lately, and thinks of as the face of the 'adolescent-in-waiting', halfway between a sulk and a sneer. It makes Rachel nervous of trying to start a conversation; chances are Becca will barely respond. That face means Becca is feeling stressed, and as Sophie Elphick has said to her during one of their counselling sessions, it's hard for someone who is feeling anxious to open up enough to talk. So Rachel decides to bide her time.

How typical, as she stands there in silence with a daughter who looks as if she'd much rather be spending the next few hours somewhere else, that there should be one of those conspicuously happy mums in front of them.

The woman has the kind of blonde hair that speaks of regular cossetting at the hairdresser's, and is wearing slim-cut mustard-yellow corduroy slacks and a tobacco-brown peacoat: the overall effect is cute rather than misguided. She has two children – naturally, she wouldn't have an only child – a small, over-excited girl in a raspberry-pink princess coat and a scampish boy.

There had been a time when Becca had asked when she could have a little sister or brother. Then, somehow, she had known to stop.

The mother-of-two has put her handbag on the floor, open, while she sorts out the tickets. The boy pulls the girl's plaits and the girl shrieks and lurches away and knocks the handbag over, scattering some of its contents. The woman turns round and Rachel sees that her coat is open at the front and she's pregnant – not heavily, but maybe five months or so. Of course. Why stop at two?

Rachel moves to help pick everything up, but the woman thanks her and waves her away. Fair enough: even the seemingly perfect don't want strangers picking over the bits of their life they would rather keep out of sight. Sometimes you just want to be left to pick up your own snotty tissues.

As the woman gathers up the last few bits – a broken-toothed comb and a pair of very small flowered underpants – a shadow falls across the slightly sticky, unpleasantly patterned carpet and a loud voice declares: '*Becca!* Didn't expect to see you here.'

It's Amelia Chadstone. No sign of her parents, thank God, but her older brother, Henry, is loitering nearby.

The other mother ushers her children away. Amelia offers Rachel a polite smile. 'Mrs M, how nice to see you.'

'Nice to see you, too, Amelia,' Rachel says.

Thankfully, it's Rachel's turn to be served, so there's no need for further small talk.

She asks the attendant for two tickets to the film Becca has chosen, having picked it out as the least bad available option. It's a CGI love story with monsters. A little bit of artificial threat, pretty young stars building up to their first kiss – a couple of hours of escape for young girls who may have faced real threat at home.

Behind her Amelia and Becca are discussing the school production of *Oliver!*, which both of them are in. Or rather, Amelia is talking about it, and Becca seems to be agreeing with her.

'I'm sorry, your card has been declined,' the attendant says.

*Oh no. No. Not now. Not here. Not* in front of Amelia Chadstone.

Rachel rummages in her bag. She has no other cards on her – she has been trying not to use them. In her purse there is some loose change and a solitary tenner. Not enough to cover two tickets, and certainly not enough for pizza.

*Shit.*

The attendant tries her card again. Rachel studies the floor as if the solution to her woes might be there; a lone fiver miraculously dropped by another cinema-goer, or a magical mechanism that will swallow her up.

How could she have let this happen?

Behind her the queue is growing. Becca and Amelia fall silent. She's going to have to admit defeat.

'No joy, I'm afraid,' says the attendant.

Rachel takes her card back and turns to Becca.

'We'll just have to have a little bit of a rethink,' she says, and steps out of the queue.

'What's the problem here? Do you need cash? I have cash,' Amelia says to Becca.

'Thank you, but that won't be necessary,' Rachel says.

Henry Chadstone says to Amelia, 'Our film's about to start.'

Inspiration strikes. 'Why don't you go with them?' Rachel says to Becca, holding out her last tenner. 'I'll wait in the car for you.'

Becca hesitates. Rachel is reminded of herself on Park Place, accepting Viv's gift of the foil-wrapped barm brack even though she'd already decided to stay away.

'Have fun,' Rachel says. 'Enjoy the film.'

She thrusts the crumpled tenner into Becca's hand, which opens to receive it. And Becca smiles, and says, 'Thanks, Mum.'

Seeing that smile makes Rachel want to cry. Instead, she stands back as Henry gets the tickets and a couple of tubs of popcorn, and Amelia starts chatting with Becca again. There's no real reason why that should make Rachel uneasy, but it does. One of these days those two are going to discuss her. Maybe they already have.

Everyone has things they don't want other people to see. Or remember. But that is no consolation. She has apologised to Henry and Amelia's parents, and they have responded graciously; things have been smoothed over, at least on the surface. But the thought of what all four of the Chadstones know fills her with deep, abiding shame, and she can't help but feel apprehensive as she says goodbye to her daughter and scurries out to the car park alone.

# Chapter Twelve

Rachel is some way through *Kramer vs. Kramer*, which she had bought after Leona mentioned it, when Becca reappears.

*Please let her have enjoyed the film. Please, please can at least that part of today have gone right?*

'How was it?' Rachel asks, switching the radio off and putting the book aside.

Becca gets into the passenger seat, slams the door, shrugs. 'It was all right. Can we get something to eat? I'm starving.'

Of course she is; it's well past lunchtime. Rachel has been fretting about this ever since they said goodbye at the entrance to the cinema. Given her complete lack of funds, there is only really one option – unless she's prepared to take Becca back to Rose Cottage early. Which she isn't. This is it: this is their time. It's down to her to make the best of it.

She takes a deep breath and starts the car. 'I'll take you back to my place.'

They don't talk much on the way to Barrowton. Rachel tries asking about school and Becca gives her the shortest possible answers, and in the end they both settle for silence.

*

When they get out of the car it's impossible to miss Becca taking in everything that makes Rachel's current address so different to Rose Cottage: the close-packed houses, the weeds, the smell and sound of traffic, and, in the middle distance, the trains rattling past.

Rachel's upstairs neighbour approaches, head bowed over a pushchair. She's a pale, heavy woman Rachel has christened Miss Spank, after what her boyfriend likes to do to her – or so Rachel assumes, judging by the sounds that filter down through the thin fabric of the building at night.

Rachel attempts a smile. Miss Spank ignores her and trundles on.

There is something scuzzy, a caked substance that looks suspiciously like old vomit, on the path that leads to the front door. Inside the dark hallway, the floor is littered with flyers that nobody has bothered to clear away: invitations to sell gold or old clothes, pizza deals, club nights, opportunities to make 'quick cash fast'. Rachel unlocks the door to the bedsit; Becca mooches in, and Rachel follows her.

There isn't much to see. A net-curtained window looks out onto the road; there are four beige walls, a sofa bed, a tiny table, a TV, a table-top cooker, a microwave, a sink. A lorry rumbles along the road outside, and everything in the room trembles.

'It smells kind of funny,' Becca says, sitting down on the sofa bed. She sniffs. 'Like old sausages.'

'Yeah, that'll be the guy in the next room. He doesn't seem to eat anything else.'

Rachel opens her one and only food cupboard. It is almost bare.

'Spaghetti hoops on toast OK?'

'Whatever,' Becca says.

Rachel sets about heating up the spaghetti hoops and puts some bread in the toaster. It's a bit on the stale side, but not actually mouldy yet. How long is it since she has made food for Becca – or for anybody other than herself, come to that?

She spreads what's left of the margarine on the toast and pours the hoops on top, puts the dishes on the table and finds some cutlery to go with them. Becca comes over from the sofa to join her.

'You know what, I always used to really like these when I was little. I haven't had them for ages,' Becca says.

She tucks in. Rachel thinks of the father in *Kramer vs. Kramer*, finally mastering the art of making French toast. She decides Leona was wrong to be so dismissive of that scene. There's nothing quite like the satisfaction of feeding your child, especially if you're out of practice, and even if you suspect she's pretending to enjoy it to make you feel better.

\*

After they have eaten she takes Becca back to Kettlebridge, and they park near the river and walk along the towpath to the weir.

The drizzle is fine but steady, and they have the scenery more or less to themselves, apart from a couple of dog-walkers and one very determined jogger. How often have they walked along here together? Countless times, with Becca at so many different childhood stages: the squalling toddler in a pushchair, the imperious girl demanding a ride on Mitch's shoulders, the slouchy pre-teen.

'We used to come here often when you were little,' she tells Becca. 'Do you remember? It always seemed to cheer you up.'

But Becca looks at her blankly, as if Rachel is talking about someone else.

They walk over the narrow bridge that crosses the weir, and gaze at the still, pooling water on the upper side and the foaming torrents downstream, bisected by the rigid structure of the sluices. The turbulence in the air is like being beside the sea; the place seems to belong to a different kind of time, where there is constant movement and yet nothing ever really changes.

And then Rachel dares linger no longer.

She hurries Becca back to the car. Mitch will be watching the clock, and she has to prove herself. She has to be reliable.

They make their way through the Kettlebridge traffic and pull up by the bridge on Rose Lane with minutes to spare. Rachel rings the bell, the door opens, Becca disappears wordlessly inside and Rachel is left face to face with Mitch.

She has left the umbrella in the car and the rain is falling a little more heavily now, soaking her jacket and her hair and running down the back of her neck. She moves a little nearer to the doorway so that she's sheltered by the storm porch, as close to Mitch as she dares.

'Good day?' he asks. His arms are folded and she can't see the scar on his hand. She can't help herself, she always has to look at it; it's as if she hopes it will look less bad than she remembers. But of course it doesn't.

'Yeah. We just came back from walking by the weir,' she tells him.

Does he remember that as something they used to do together? He shows no sign of it. He says, 'How was the cinema?'

'We bumped into Amelia Chadstone. With her brother.' She clears her throat. 'Becca went in to see the film with them.'

'With them? And you didn't go?'

She can't bring herself to confess about the disaster with the money, which is yet to be resolved. At least she has enough petrol in the car to get back to the bedsit. She shakes her head.

Mitch frowns. 'So what did you do?'

'Sat and read my book in the car.'

Now it is Mitch's turn to shake his head. 'Well, I suppose if Becca's happy...'

'She seems to be quite good friends with Amelia these days,' Rachel says.

Mitch regards her with suspicion. 'Like I said before, Rachel, you need to be able to deal with that.'

'I know. And I can. I promise.'

'What does your counsellor think?'

'About what?'

'About, you know, whether you're better.'

'She doesn't really make that kind of judgement.'

Sophie's last words before saying goodbye had been: *Remember, it's all a work in progress.* But Rachel decides that now is not the time to relay this, or to explain that she has come to the end of the programme and won't be seeing Sophie regularly any more.

Mitch sighs. 'Well, I hope she's helping. See you next week.'

He shuts the door in her face. There is nothing for it but to turn and walk back to the car. It shouldn't feel like defeat, but it does. Worse than defeat. It's like being a ghost, colourless and invisible, and almost, but not entirely, cut off from the ones she loves.

# Chapter Thirteen

## Viv

Somehow she gets there, though someone nearly bangs into her at a crossroads – her fault entirely. He hits his horn, she brakes, and she glimpses his furious face, framed by rain-streaked windscreen, as he pulls out and speeds out of her way.

*Keep that up and you'll be next*, her husband might have said.

She isn't normally such a terrible driver. But coming here, seeing Aidan like this, in hospital, is a trial, and her nerves aren't bearing up terribly well. It's been a horrendous time for him: not only has he been through the agonising pain of a ruptured appendix, but he's also had to cope with an unfamiliar environment, far from the staff at his care home who know him and are used to him. For him, the abrupt, brutal change in his usual routine is as much of a torment as physical pain. And because it's been an ordeal for him, it's been awful for her, too.

It is a great relief to reach the hospital and find a parking space, but only for a moment, because now she has to go and see him. She isn't ready. She's never been ready for Aidan – has spent her whole life trying, and failing, to be as good a mother to him as it was possible for her to be.

She would love to think that poor George had known exactly what she was up to, and had chosen to turn a blind eye; that he had understood she bore him no ill will for wanting a clean break, everything cut and dried, but still, she needed to do what little she could. Any marriage is full of necessary mysteries, and nobody can ever really know all the secrets of somebody else's heart.

But no, this is just a guilty fantasy. Might as well face facts, she had spent forty-odd years lying to her husband, and the only thing that could have made her feel worse would have been to toe the line and do what he wanted in the first place and never see Aidan again.

And she had lied to the girls, too… If only she had been bolder while George was still alive. She could have told him she was still visiting Aidan, and then she could have told her daughters about Aidan, too. Instead they had found out at the worst possible time, when they were deep in mourning for George – who, despite being a rather rigid sort, had been a good dad, kind and loving and steady.

They had lost a father and gained a brother – but one who had been shut away from the world for most of his life. It had been a shock to both of them. Too much to take in… and too late, much, much too late.

They had their own lives, their own problems and responsibilities. Elaine was bringing up her girls on her own and things obviously still weren't brilliant between her and her ex, though she refused point blank to talk about it and always insisted things were fine – she'd always kept Viv at arm's length. And Louise had done so well in her career, qualifying as a pathologist and climbing the ranks, but it was a stressful, all-absorbing job and she didn't have much time or energy for anything else.

Aidan knows, in theory, about her other children, but has never shown the least desire to meet them. He responds to any mention of them the same way he does to anything that he senses she's reluctant to talk about – by becoming intensely preoccupied with something else, so he can block her out until she gives up and changes the subject to one she's more comfortable with.

This is all new, this hospital. Well, relatively new. Still, she can't help but be reminded of the old building where she had taken Aidan as an outpatient, before he was diagnosed and put into care full time. He had hated it. Had behaved dreadfully. As if he knew what was coming, what the doctors were preparing to say: *infant schizophrenia, ineducable, will never live a normal life…*

Over the years, she has often wondered whether it is not the case – as the doctors imply – that he knows too little; maybe the cause of all the trouble is that he knows too much.

They have tried to make the new hospital nice – nicer than the old one, anyway, though no doubt bad news is still broken here on a daily basis. There is an atrium, as high and airy as a cathedral, with escalators leading up to the different floors, and on the ground floor there is a café that is almost like a real café that people go to out of choice, its boundaries marked out by a grove of small artificial trees standing in steel pots on the marble floor.

She passes the shop where you can buy Slush Puppies and toothbrushes and bunches of wilting yellow chrysanthemums, and tightens her grip on the Tupperware box she has brought for Aidan. Chances are he'll be in no state to eat cupcakes, but they'll keep for a couple of days. That's one thing she has always been able to do for him: bake. Back when he was small she'd been reprimanded by the health visitor for it. It's true that he has always been a little podgy, but he has barely eaten since he came down with appendicitis and was admitted to hospital, and the weight has dropped off him; without it, it is more apparent than ever what a handsome man he is.

Damn it, why shouldn't Aidan eat cake? It's one small pleasure that he shares with the outside world.

She takes the escalator to the first floor.

When he is better maybe they will let him off the ward, and she might be able to take him down to the café. It is some years now since he has seen an escalator; she can barely remember the last time. These days, she doesn't take him out much. She's no longer confident of her ability to manage if things go wrong.

He certainly used to like escalators, though. No, *like* isn't the right word; he had been thrilled by them and also slightly terrified.

He lacks the gift of indifference. The nonchalant shrug is not and never has been in his repertoire.

The escalator will be an outing. An adventure. Something to look forward to.

Now that the stress of the drive is over, she notes that her back is protesting again. Hopeless! She can't afford to be frail. Aidan still needs her. Aidan will always need her.

She couldn't bear it when other people moaned about how busy their children were with their own lives, how they hardly ever called or bothered to visit. Honestly! Didn't they understand that that was the point? Didn't they realise how *lucky* they were?

People tended to think they owned their children, or that their children owed them something, and many of them never seemed to learn that this was not the case. They wanted to take the credit, as if they alone were responsible for the life that had taken root when they planted it. They didn't understand that a gardener might dig the soil and feed the rose and water and prune it, but the blooms and thorns grew of their own accord, and the petals unfurled because that was what they were meant to do, not because anybody made them.

But Leona was not like that.

She had first met Leona at the Kettlebridge craft fair, running a stall selling her own wares – second-hand goods that had been mended and painted to make them better than new. A sideline, Leona had told her: 'Not my day job – not yet, anyway.' Viv had been impressed with the young woman's energy and drive, but hadn't guessed that a lost child lay behind it – the need to escape into being busy, and to try and make something of herself. But it had made perfect sense once she knew, because Viv herself was the same: why else had she spent so much of her life on committees, trying to be good?

She had only found out about Leona's baby because she liked the bits and pieces Leona had been selling so much – refashioned jewellery and handbags, mainly, with a few knick-knacks, freshly painted and decorated bits of crockery and china. She had gone to Leona's flat to look at the furniture Leona had been working on, and Leona had told her about Bluebell almost without prompting. It was a test: Viv had known that straight away, from the look on Leona's face as she told her. Leona wanted to see if Viv deserved to know.

There had been so many occasions when Viv could have said something about Aidan, to so many different people: before George passed and even more so after. Why was it Leona who had opened the floodgates? Maybe it was because Viv barely knew her. Maybe it was because of the tattoo of bluebells on Leona's wrist, which had turned out to be a tribute to her daughter. Anyway, Viv had blurted out the truth then and there, and she had wept, and Leona had comforted her.

The meeting, the support group for other women like them – mothers who for one reason or another, did not live with their children – had been Leona's idea. She had been so sure it would work out that Viv had kept her doubts to herself, but she hadn't been surprised when the other potential attendees had melted away. Misery did not seek company, after all.

But then Rachel had come – the woman with mask-like make-up who was temping in the office where Leona worked for her real day job. Whatever it was that had happened to her, it was obviously still raw and recent. After Viv had given her the barm brack and came back into the house, Leona had said, 'If anybody needs this, it's her.'

But maybe it was really Leona and Viv who needed it. To be able to help someone. To make some kind of difference, when there was so much that couldn't be changed.

Viv approaches the entrance to the post-surgical ward and rings the buzzer for admission.

When you're separated from your child – bone of your bone, flesh of your flesh – they are always frozen in your heart at the time and age at which you parted. Viv knows full well that the Aidan she's about to see is a middle-aged man. Still, it feels as if the son who's locked away from her on the other side of the security door is a toddler still: just as helpless, as needy, and reluctant to submit to unpleasant medical procedures, or remain in an unfamiliar place.

There is a reception desk at the head of the ward, but it is never staffed. After a few minutes, during which she manages to restrain herself from pressing the buzzer again, a nurse comes by to let her in.

Viv doesn't recognise her, but she knows Viv straight away. It's the Aidan factor. He makes an impression on people. Often not a positive one.

'Aidan's doing well, though still heavily sedated,' the nurse says. 'I'll take you to him.'

Viv pauses to take her coat off and hang it up, and smears her hands with antibacterial gel from a dispenser – these seem rather token, hopeful gestures towards the prevention of infection, like lighting a candle in church as an offering for the dead, but Viv has always operated on the principle that something is better than nothing and anyway, it is what the signs say to do. Then she hurries to catch up with the nurse, who walks at a brisk pace that Viv struggles to match.

The nurse is an attractive sort of girl, and Viv reflects that under different circumstances Aidan might have fancied her, and then suppresses the thought. Poor lad, doomed to a life of perpetual virginity, though from the perspective of her three-score-plus years on the planet Viv thinks that maybe he's saved himself a lot of bother.

After the drama when Aidan first came round from anaesthesia and got very upset, they've put him in a room on his own. And there he is, lying on his back in bed, asleep, his arms neatly arranged on top of the covers, one hand covered with bandages and plasters securing the drip in place. There is a large window next to his bed and raindrops are still clinging to the other side of the glass, but Aidan's face and the outline of his body are touched with gold from the unexpected sunlight pitching through a break in the clouds.

He is so peaceful, so composed, it could be a deathbed scene.

She asks the nurse, 'When can the drip come out?'

'Not until after he's shown he can eat and drink for himself, I'm afraid.'

'He's not going to eat and drink with that thing in. He might try and rip it out. It'll drive him crazy.'

The nurse sighs. 'They won't want to take it out only to have to put it in again. The consultant will review him on his ward round – shouldn't be too much longer now.'

Viv puts her Tupperware box of cupcakes on the bedside table. She says, 'If I'm not here when he wakes up, could you please try and make sure he's offered one of these? He may not like any of the food you have. He's a very picky eater.'

'OK, I'll see what I can do. I'll leave you to it. Ring the bell if you need anything.'

The nurse goes out, keeping the door open, and Viv sits down to watch over her son.

He has a window with a lovely view – not of the city but of green hills stretching to the horizon. He'll like that, when he's better. You can just see the road that leads to the hospital car park and there's a bus stop and, sometimes, ambulances, so that'll provide him with diversion.

Aidan tends to notice things that nobody else is interested in. The number of lights above the bed. The make of the car passing the bus stop. The three birds wheeling in a distant corner of the sky. And he has always seemed to see right through her... past the carefully groomed, ageing outer shell to her heart.

It is warm in the sunlight, almost like summer. She closes her eyes and the darkness is tinged with orange. For a moment she allows herself to bask. She imagines herself relaxing, having not a care in the world.

*Letting go.*

*But that is what she must not and cannot do.*

As if an alarm has gone off, jolting her back into wakefulness, she's alert again and the sensation of drifting off somewhere else – somewhere bright and hazy, perhaps near the sea – is gone.

Aidan is still sleeping peacefully, but that won't last forever, and God only knows what state he'll be in when he comes to. Most likely this is the calm before the storm, and soon enough all hell will break loose.

*But that is a good thing*, she reminds herself. *Chaos is a sign of life.* An Aidan who is capable of wreaking havoc on a hospital ward is an Aidan who is still in the world of the living, even if acting in a way that is not particularly convenient for anybody else.

However nice medical people are, it's always made plain that when you're on their territory, you operate by their rules. But Aidan won't submit to that. Aidan isn't very good at rules, unless, that is, they're reinforced with cupcakes.

She has tried to explain this to the staff here, but she's not sure the message has quite got through.

Oh well, if they don't watch out, they'll find out soon enough what a six-foot-tall middle-aged man is capable of in the throes of a toddler's rage.

But to look at him now, you could almost imagine that he was just like anybody else.

He had been such a sweet, docile baby. And then, suddenly, almost overnight it seemed, he had become a changeling child: screaming, biting, hitting, spitting, lashing out, and at peace only when blank, absorbed in rubbing a favourite stick between his hands as if trying to light a spark that was never going to catch because there was nothing for it to catch on.

And then it was down to what the men in white coats said, and she and George had listened to them and agreed to do as they said, and have Aidan taken away.

*You have other children*, the men in white coats had told her. *Concentrate on them. You need to move on, for their sakes.*

Did she love the others a little less because of Aidan? It makes her feel awful to think this, but it's possible. After Aidan, she couldn't help but maintain a small protective space around her heart, to insulate it from future shocks.

At least she'd had Aidan with her for a time. Some women gave birth knowing that their children would be taken from them, or would die or were already dead. And some women sank into such depression that they wished their lives were over, and believed that their babies would be better off without them.

But when she'd first held Aidan in her arms it had seemed as if he and she were the still axis at the centre of everything, and the people and places around them – even George – were distant and peripheral. It would never have occurred to her that four years later she would be saying goodbye to him.

When she left him at the first institution he had lived in, he had turned his back to her, absorbed in the spinning top she had brought because she knew it would divert him. To this day, she doesn't know whether he was indifferent to her departure or oblivious, or stoic and resigned beyond his years – beyond anybody's years.

A normal child would, surely, have bawled, wailed, clutched at her, obliging her to peel his hands off her ankles finger by finger before she could leave him there.

It had been agony. Somehow she had got through that day, and the next, and the next. Housework. Cooking. Looking after George and the girls. She knew George knew how she felt – she could see it in his eyes. 'It's for the best,' he had said to her. 'They'll be able to help him there better than we can. We couldn't go on the way we were, Viv. We couldn't have coped with him, not now he's getting so big.' And she had willed herself to believe him. It was, after all, what all the experts had said.

And then, a week later, she had gone back, and there Aidan had been in the visitors' room sitting in a bright patch of sunlight, playing with the spinning top as if she had never left him, as if no time at all had passed.

She had lived for years with the fear that the others would turn out to be like Aidan – which, in a way, had also been a strange kind of longing. Because if they had, she wouldn't have given them up. She knew that much. She could never have done that again. They'd have had to put her away as well.

But no, the others had been chatty, competitive, possessive, demanding – all the things Aidan never was – and, ultimately, they had gone off and left her, which was how it was meant to be.

Everybody goes in the end, if you don't go first.

But Aidan…

Her halting, imperfect, interrupted love for her firstborn has been the most terrifying and compelling experience of her life, and it is impossible to believe that anything so vivid and powerful could ever be cut off.

But there is no point brooding… Much better to keep herself occupied. She rummages in her backpack – so much more practical than a handbag – for her knitting.

Passing the time while waiting to see Aidan: this has been the story of most of her life. By now she should be well used to it.

She's knitting a baby cardigan, premature size, smaller than the things you can buy for newborns in the shops; she does a lot of these for the hospital. As she works on them she often thinks about the mothers whose children will wear them: all that hope and fear, those hours in the special care baby unit next to the incubators. Watching. Waiting. Praying, whether you call it that or not.

She puts the knitting down in her lap and reaches out to touch Aidan's bandaged hand, very lightly, so as not to wake him.

'We'll get you out of here soon enough, my darling,' she whispers.

# Chapter Fourteen

## Rachel

Always, just when you don't need it, when you can't afford for anything to go wrong, something comes along to cause chaos. Today it's snow, which has snarled everything up even though it's not even that heavy, and somebody else's accident, which has brought the traffic to a near-standstill.

Not her fault. It could happen to anybody. But because of her track record, it matters. It will be harder for Becca to forgive.

The crucial moment – curtain up for *Oliver!* – inches closer, and then passes.

Finally, she turns off at Kettlebridge, and everything begins to move. She has never been more relieved to reach Becca's school.

The car park is full and has been for some time, judging by the light dusting of snow that has settled on every surface. Somewhere round here will be the people carrier she had bought when she was pregnant with Becca, which now belongs to Mitch.

They'd both assumed back then that there would be more children.

'It just didn't happen,' was what she had learned to say if anybody was rude enough to ask.

She leaves her car in an unmarked spot next to a flower bed. The compacted snow of the car park is particularly lethal, and she nearly ends up flat on her backside several times as she picks her way towards the entrance.

Just outside the auditorium she hears music. Girls' voices, raised in unison. Rachel hasn't heard the song for years, but recognises it straight away: it's 'Be Back Soon', the most cheerful of all possible goodbyes.

She takes a deep breath, pushes open the swing doors to the lobby and goes through. It's a cavernous, brightly lit space, decorated with commemorative plaques and students' artworks – big, splashy oil paintings in gilt frames like Old Masters. There is no one there apart from a curly-haired, cardigan-clad young woman who is setting out wineglasses on a table covered with a pristine white cloth, ready for the interval.

Becca's class teacher. *Oh, God, but what's her name?* A blank. How can Rachel have forgotten? It's just further evidence that she's unfit to be here: is barely functioning, even now.

Somewhere in that auditorium the Chadstones are sitting together and watching like proud, proper parents. Probably next to Mitch.

Rachel approaches the teacher, leaving a trail of wet footprints on the pristine floor. She smiles her best smile, apologises, asks if she could just slip in and stand at the back.

'I'm so sorry,' the woman says, her eyes big with sympathy of the this-is-hurting-me-too variety. 'But I just can't. It would be so distracting for the girls. It's not long till the interval, if you wouldn't just mind waiting?'

Her name is *still* a blank, something to do with birds maybe, suggestive of pecking and scratching and then flitting away. Ah yes – Miss Finch.

Miss Finch looks down at the glasses of wine she has set out so far as if it occurs to her to offer Rachel one, and then thinks better of it and faces Rachel again with a bright, slightly nervous smile.

'Maybe you might like to have a look round the art works?' she says, bravely but a little falteringly.

*Don't worry, I'm not actually dangerous*, Rachel feels like saying. *Not to you, at any rate.* Instead she withdraws without saying anything.

She leans against the auditorium doors, as close as she can get, and does her best to listen. Then applause breaks out and the doors are pushed open. She stands aside and watches the other parents emerge blinking into the light to circulate in the lobby, greeting and congratulating each other.

After a while Mary Chadstone descends on her, glass of wine in hand and husband and son in tow, calling out: '*Rachel!* Wasn't Becca brilliant – you must be *so proud!*' and somehow that is even worse than being invisible.

Rachel summons up a smile. Maybe she will be able to get away without acknowledging that she has only just arrived.

'Hello, Mary – how are you?'

'Very well, very well,' Mary says.

'Excellent show,' Hugh Chadstone says.

He is the type of handsome that runs to seed early given too many hours spent behind a desk or in restaurants and not enough exercise: big, beefy, a former rugby player. Henry, the son, who is thinner and geekier, hovers next to him. Defensive. Protective. They're going to let Mary handle this, but are both poised to step in if needed.

And then Rachel spots Mitch coming out of the auditorium.

The rest of the room fades into the background. Mitch sees her and freezes. The tension between them is almost palpable, like magnetism, though the force at work is repulsion rather than attraction. Then he heads straight towards her and comes to a standstill just inches away. He is so angry with her he completely ignores the Chadstones.

'What happened to you?' he says.

Of course, he's furious. He'd be furious with anyone who let Becca down. So would she, come to that.

'It's the snow, the A34 had completely seized up—'

'Oh dear, were you held up?' Mary enquires sympathetically. 'How much of the show did you miss?'

'A fair bit,' Rachel mutters, looking down at the floor.

'I had a terrible journey, too,' Hugh says. 'My train crawled all the way from Paddington. Absolutely maddening.'

'But you still made it on time,' Mitch says.

Mary takes Hugh's arm in readiness to steer him away. 'Lovely to see you again, Rachel. Mitch, we'll catch up soon. Do enjoy the second half, won't you?'

They move away, with Henry loping along behind them, and Miss Finch closes in on Rachel and Mitch, scenting a potential domestic. Her expression is artificially encouraging, as if all it takes to dispel conflict is a little robust positivity. 'If you'd like to begin making your way to your seats, it's about to start again.'

Mitch abruptly turns and marches off towards the auditorium, with Rachel hurrying to catch up.

Her heart is pounding as she takes up her place beside him. He doesn't acknowledge her; he is staring fixedly at the empty stage. In one way it is a relief when the lights go down and the show begins. But it is also terrifying.

There's one thing that is even more guaranteed to fill her with dread than facing the hostility of the only man she has ever really loved.

And this is it: waiting for her daughter to be exposed to the risk of failure. There is no way for her to help or come to the rescue, and nothing for it but to watch and pray that Becca has got what it takes to hold her own.


When Becca first walks out onto the stage Rachel's heart sinks. Becca looks so skinny and vulnerable in the torn red dress she's wearing as Nancy, so different from the girls all around her, with their practised smiles and evident expectation of applause. Amelia Chadstone, stomping about with aplomb as Bill Sikes, is plainly some kind of queen of them all, even more self-assured and indomitable than the rest.

Standing awkwardly with her arms folded across her chest, Becca looks as terrified as Rachel feels on her behalf. Why couldn't they have given Becca a tiny part – something in the chorus, the role of a street urchin or a starving child in the orphanage? Then at least her nerves wouldn't have been so obvious.

But then Becca launches into her solo – 'As Long as He Needs Me'. Her voice falters, swells and rises. And then Rachel realises it is going to be all right. More than all right. Becca is singing her heart out, and it's beautiful – so beautiful and powerful it catches Rachel by surprise.

That voice! How is it possible for such a girl to sing like a woman? Becca is only thirteen; she has never been in love. Where, then, does all that yearning and desperation and devotion come from? How does she *know*?

Rachel's vision blurs and tears leak down her cheeks. She tries to sniff discreetly, but it is hopeless; she will have to rummage in her bag and attempt to dredge up a tissue.

A large blue-and-white handkerchief is thrust towards her, and she takes it.

Next to her, Mitch shakes his head in the gloom.

'You *never* have one,' he whispers. 'Keep it.'

She wipes her eyes and blows her nose and tucks the handkerchief away, half wishing he hadn't just given her reason to be grateful. In a way, it's easier when he hates her.

After the show they stand together to wait for Becca, but don't speak. The Chadstones are on the other side of the foyer, next to the wine table; Hugh and Mary are energetically discussing something while Henry looks on. Neither family makes any further move to join forces with the other.

Finally Becca emerges, her face wiped clean of make-up, dressed in jeans and the parka that Rachel gave her for Christmas, the one that had been delivered to Fun-to-Learn the day she opened up to Leona. A mistake, but one that, thankfully, hasn't turned out too badly, as Leona has made no reference to it since, or to Rachel's visit to Viv's house.

Becca is with Amelia, who sees Rachel and bumps Becca's forearm lightly with her fist in a little gesture of solidarity, as if Becca's mother is understood by both of them to be an ordeal Becca has no choice but to face.

Amelia turns aside to be congratulated by her own family. Becca says to Mitch, 'Was it all right?'

'Not bad,' Mitch says, beaming. 'Not bad at all.'

'Well done,' Rachel says. 'You were amazing.'

'Yeah, what you saw of it,' Becca says.

'Come on,' Mitch says to Becca, 'let's get out of here. There's a fair bit of snow about. You might have to jump out and help me clear it away when we get to Rose Lane.'

'Sure,' Becca says.

The two of them head out, with Rachel following.

Mary Chadstone falls silent as they pass, and then starts talking again with emphatic, almost hysterical relief.

# Chapter Fifteen

Outside the air is still and very cold. The car park has emptied out, but there are still engines revving and headlights picking out distended shadows in congealed lumps of snow.

Mitch and Becca stop on the paving in front of the entrance, and Becca pulls up the hood of her parka.

'Night, Mum,' she says.

The sight of her anxious little face, framed by the furry lining of the hood, makes Rachel's heart ache as if someone has reached inside her to squeeze it. Becca isn't flushed with success as you might expect, as Amelia had been. Instead she's pale with the strain of trying to do the right thing by both her parents, and with the painful awkwardness of it all. And she looks that way because Rachel has failed her. Becca is a child whose father is more of a mother to her than her actual mother will ever be.

'Goodnight, love,' Rachel says. 'Break a leg for the rest of the run. You were great.'

Mitch says to Rachel, 'See you Saturday.' And then he turns, his hands deep in his pockets, and trudges off. Becca hurries off to catch up and threads her arm through his so that they're walking along like a couple of pals, two against the world.

Becca doesn't look back. Rachel watches them go and makes her way to her own car.

The frozen snow is granular and crunchy underfoot, and all her windows are laced with frost, long, delicate, tapering branches spread out like vines reaching for something to cling onto. She sets about scraping it off. No rush; there's nothing much to go home for.

By the time she joins the queue waiting for the exit it has already dwindled, and Mitch and Becca have gone.

The traffic has cleared and she makes it back to Digby Street by half-past ten. There's no doubt that a layer of snow improves the place, and helps to disguise its shabbiness. So far only the road has gone slushy; elsewhere, the coating of white has yet to turn dirty.

Rachel negotiates her way into her usual parking spot. She pictures Becca and Mitch at the kitchen table in Rose Cottage with steaming mugs of hot chocolate in front of them, and one of the snacks that Mitch is so good at knocking up. Tuna melt, maybe, or poached eggs on special bread. Nowhere like home when it's cold outside.

But who is she to feel wounded that Mitch has stepped into the role of being Becca's main guide, protector and cheerleader? Under the circumstances, she's lucky that Becca still wants to see her at all. She hasn't exactly been a positive role model as a parent. She has been an example of what *not* to do.

As she lets herself into the hallway that leads to the bedsit she hears a yowl of satisfaction from Miss Spank upstairs, and this is the final straw. She can't face spending the rest of the evening trying to block out the sound of somebody else's masochistic pleasure.

She turns and lets herself out of the house, and walks rapidly away.

*

She isn't planning to get drunk. Anyway, it will be closing time before too long. Still, five minutes later, she finds herself in the pub round the corner, which she has often driven past but has never felt in the least inclined to check out. Until now.

The Dog and Duck has headache-inducing red carpet and fake beams, and the slightly draughty, waiting-room feel of a place in which people are always coming and going. It's surprisingly busy, which is a good thing, because nobody pays her any attention. Anyway, she's not the only one in office clothes; it's so close to the station it must be a draw for commuters, especially ones who have had particularly bad days and need something to take the edge off before doing it all over again.

She orders a gin and tonic and settles on a stool at the end of the bar, next to the double doors that lead to the ladies. Not ideal, because whenever someone comes through a cold draught hits the back of her neck, but this is no time to be fussy. She tries to occupy herself by fiddling with her phone – the 21st-century substitute for smoking when alone – but doesn't really take in anything she looks at. All she can see is Becca's expression. Long-suffering, but not rejecting her.

That awful capacity a child has to forgive a parent, to keep on loving them whatever happens… It's so familiar. She knows it from the inside. She never would have imagined that she'd give Becca cause to look at *her* like that.

Her drink seems to have disappeared remarkably quickly. *Should she have another? Oh, why not?* She shouldn't really spend the money… but she can always just eat cereal for the rest of the week.

It's then that she meets the gaze of some bloke sitting at a table on the other side of the pub.

He smiles. Nice smile, both sheepish and a bit hopeful, as if to say: *I can't quite believe you've caught me looking at you, but since you have… pleased to meet you.*

He isn't bad, actually. Young – or younger than her, anyway – and Clark Kent handsome in glasses and a check shirt, with shoulders that suggest regular gym attendance. And he appears to be on his own.

If she glares at him, he'll back off. But she doesn't. Instead she tries a small smile back.

He lifts his glass and tilts it towards her, then drinks. She can feel herself blushing. *This is probably a really bad idea – what is she thinking?* Like *she's* going to take some random guy back to the bedsit and try to out-yell Miss Spank.

Somebody comes through the double doors behind her and says, 'Fancy meeting you here.'

Rachel turns to see a woman with long, fine blonde hair, loose earth-coloured clothes and a conspicuous tattoo on one wrist.

Leona.

'You're just about the last person I expected to find making eyes at Mark when I came back from the ladies',' she says.

'I wasn't making eyes,' Rachel says, embarrassed.

'Well, you were barking up the wrong tree if you were. He's got a crush on the barman.'

Sure enough, the Clark Kent-a-like is now gazing attentively in the direction of the bar, and looks very much as if he is hoping his devotion will be noticed.

'He'll flirt with anybody,' Leona says, rather crushingly. 'I probably would, too, if I was as gorgeous as he is. It's like having a superpower. Can I get you another?'

'Probably shouldn't. Work tomorrow. Anyway, what are you doing here? I thought you didn't drink.'

'I don't, but that doesn't mean I can't go to the pub. I like pubs. I don't have a problem with drink, or with other people drinking, at least as long as they behave themselves. I just got to a point where I didn't like the way it made me feel. And I'm not your boss, remember? I'm not about to remind you it's a school night. Anyway, you can have a health-giving fruit juice if you want.'

Rachel settles for another gin and tonic. The barman serves Leona rather more quickly than he served Rachel; obviously being a friend of Mark's is an advantage. Leona gets an orange juice for herself and a couple of packets of peanuts, which she puts on the bar between them and splits open for them to share.

'You should eat something,' she says. 'You look like you're about to keel over.'

'I don't feel great,' Rachel admits. She scoops up a handful of nuts and gobbles them down.

'I feel like Ford Prefect in *The Hitchhiker's Guide to the Galaxy*, persuading you to line your stomach before the earth gets blasted out of existence,' Leona tells her.

'Oh. Do we survive?'

'Kind of. We get to hitch a lift on an alien spaceship. So what are you doing here, anyway?'

'I live round the corner. Just thought I'd pop in.'

Leona looks Rachel over as if surveying an exhibit. 'Do you often just pop in?'

'Never, actually. Is it a regular haunt of yours?'

'Are you kidding? We're here because it's out of the way. I didn't particularly want to bump into anybody.' She holds up her wrist, exposing the tattoo, and flexes her hand. 'It's Bluebell's birthday. She's seven today.'

'Oh.'

'Yeah, it's hard to know what to say, isn't it? Usually I get a letter from her adoptive parents and a new photo. And it hasn't arrived. Not that I'm really in a position to complain. I mean, it's good of them to send anything at all.'

'I saw my daughter this evening,' Rachel says. 'I was late for her school show. I missed the whole first half.'

'At least you saw her,' Leona says.

How many hours has Rachel spent sitting in an office with this woman? Suddenly the boundaries of the workplace dissolve completely, and give way to recognition. Rachel is sitting beside her mirror image.

She reaches for her gin and tonic and realises the glass is empty. She feels faintly dizzy, and the bar looks as if it might begin to spin at any minute. She says, 'Same again?'

But Leona gets to her feet. 'I think I should see you home. You really don't look too good.'

'But what about your friend?'

'I think he'll cope, don't you? I'll probably come back to find he's made yet *another* new friend. Shall we make a move?'

'Look, I appreciate the concern, I really do. But I'm fine. I really don't need you to walk me home.'

'Yeah, well, I'm coming whether you like it or not. I want to see you bright and early at work tomorrow, not find out you ended the evening passed out in a ditch.'

'I thought you said you weren't my boss. Anyway, there aren't any ditches round here.'

'Well, passing out anywhere would be less than ideal. You might as well humour me. Otherwise I'm just going to stalk you and follow you home anyway.'

If Rachel is honest with herself, it is an unexpected luxury to have someone making a fuss about her.

'OK,' she says, and Leona smiles in relief, as if Rachel has just done *her* a favour.

On the way out they pause at Mark's table so Leona can put on her astrakhan coat, which is hanging over the back of a chair. Mark looks up at them questioningly but without surprise, as if random occurrences are par for the course where nights out with Leona are concerned.

'I won't be long,' Leona says. 'Just seeing Rachel home. Try not to break any hearts while I'm gone.'

Mark shrugs and grins. 'That's not me, and you know it. I'm the one who's there for people *after* their hearts have been broken.'

'I suppose there's some truth in that,' Leona says. She turns to Rachel. 'Come on, let's get you home.'

Now it comes down to it, Rachel is embarrassed at the thought of Leona seeing where she lives. *It's not me. It's where I ended up; it's not where I belong.*

'I don't really think of it as home. It's just the place where I sleep,' she says.

'Then it's home, whether you like it or not,' Leona tells her.

Outside the streets are quiet, and most of the houses are dark. The only sign of life is the occasional passing car. The temperature has dropped, and their breath makes clouds in the icy air.

'Viv was asking after you the other day,' Leona says.

'Viv?'

'Yes, the lady whose house you came to. For the inaugural meeting of our group.' Leona pulls a face. 'Some group.'

'Oh... I did think it was a lovely idea. It's just not for me, not right now. But you're going to keep on with it, aren't you?'

'You mean, are we going to try again even though we don't have any other members, and the only one we managed to attract fled after the first five minutes? Well, we are, actually. Being gluttons for punishment. We're meeting at my house next week and then we're going to aim to get together once a month.'

'Good,' Rachel says. 'That's good.'

The smell and taste of Viv's barm brack returns unbidden. Cinnamon and fruit. It is no exaggeration to say that it had kept her going through Christmas. A little bit of solid comfort to indulge in once in a while. It had seemed festive, somehow, even though it wasn't a Christmas cake. Just because it had been a gift.

All that baking, that generosity, shouldn't be in vain.

They arrive at the bedsit just in time to hear an unearthly squeal from Miss Spank.

'Wow,' Leona says as Rachel fumbles for her keys. 'Someone's having a good night.'

'Tell me about it. He'll be gone by morning and she'll be miserable.' Rachel manages to get the door open. 'You know, hardly anybody I know has ever been here before. Only my daughter, and that was just the once, and that was because I'd run out of money and needed to give her lunch. And my counsellor used to come here sometimes, but I don't see her any more.'

'I've seen worse,' Leona says. She grimaces as Miss Spank squeals again. 'Better than sobbing, I suppose.'

'Oh, that comes later. I suppose that's true romance for you.'

Leona hesitates, looks Rachel up and down. She says, 'He really hurt you, didn't he?'

'Actually,' Rachel says, 'I was the one who hurt him. Goodnight, Leona. I'll see you tomorrow. Thanks for walking me home.'

She withdraws into the house and shuts the door, and makes her way round the bike in the corridor to the door of her bedsit. As she lets herself in a faint urge to cry comes over her — she had thought she was done with that but Leona's sympathy seems to have brought it back to the surface, like something exposed by a thaw. And Mitch's handkerchief is in her coat pocket, evidence that he, too, is capable of being kind to her, even now.

# Chapter Sixteen

Leona lives in the bottom half of a narrow Georgian house with long sash windows, tucked away behind Kettlebridge town hall on a road that leads down to the church on the riverfront. The neighbouring properties are a whistle-stop tour of different eras in the town's mostly quiet history; Leona's place is squeezed between a 1960s block of flats and a medieval cottage with a low, sunken doorway.

Why has Rachel come here when the expectation is that, sooner or later, she will open up about all the things she doesn't want to talk about? And what will they think of her when she does?

Yet here she is.

There's a brief delay before Leona answers the door. 'Sorry to keep you waiting,' she says. 'Viv's a bit upset.'

'Oh… why?'

'You'll see.'

Leona leads her through a narrow hallway to a sitting room at the back of the ground floor, overlooking a small courtyard garden. There are bright rag rugs on polished wooden floorboards, knick-knacks and art prints, a lamp with a tasselled shade. The pinboard with the pictures of Leona and Viv's children is propped up by the fireplace and Viv is next to it, sitting on a pink sofa covered with a batik throw. She's wearing a neck brace, and it is immediately obvious that she has been crying.

Rachel is so taken aback that for a moment she has no idea how to respond. Viv had seemed so composed last time. Yet here she is with her eyelashes stuck together and beaded with mascara-blackened tears.

Viv dabs at her eyes with a tissue. 'Rachel, dear. How nice to see you again. So glad you could make it. You'll forgive me if I don't get up – I'm not very mobile at the moment. Don't mind me carrying on like an old fool, I'll pull myself together in a minute.'

Rachel perches on a big, round, orange 1960s armchair, while Leona settles at a respectful distance on the sofa.

'Nothing really terrible has happened,' Viv says. 'It's just that I've got myself into rather a muddle with my car, it's a write-off and they've told me I should give up driving. It's not all bad, though. At least Aidan's out of hospital now… that's my son… He had a ruptured appendix, he must have been in agony and the people at the home had no idea till he started getting really quite poorly. He's not very good at expressing himself, you see, which can be very dangerous, believe me. He has what they call *special needs* these days. Learning difficulties. He's always been that way. He's supposed to have a mental age of eight, but that's silly really, there's no comparison. An eight-year-old wouldn't behave the way Aidan behaves when he's upset. A two-year-old might, but a two-year-old wouldn't be as big and strong as Aidan is.'

'What happened to you?' Rachel asks. 'Do you have whiplash?'

'Well, yes, but the car was in a worse state. Anyway, I'm sure I'll learn to do without it, and at least I didn't hurt anybody else. I just need to figure out the bus routes to Aidan's home. It can't be beyond the wit of woman to get to Tring by public transport. Or I'll get a taxi, same as I did to come here tonight.'

'Can't you get somebody to take you?' Leona asks. 'I could ask my liftshare group. Or maybe one of your church friends would drive you there?'

'Oh, no. I wouldn't like to put anybody to any trouble.' Viv hesitates. 'I don't want people seeing Aidan,' she says finally. 'It's not because I'm ashamed of him. It's because I don't want to have to dislike them for the way they react to him.'

'What about your children?' Leona suggests.

'Oh, it's much too far, and they're busy,' Viv says, and it occurs to Rachel that Viv perhaps doesn't want them seeing Aidan either. 'Elaine is a few hours north of here, and Louise is on the south coast and that's hours away, too. Opposite sides of the country, of course. They don't seem to want to stay close to each other any more than they want to stay close to me.' She sighs. 'My fault, most likely. Still, they seem to be happy enough.'

'I don't often wish I had a car,' Leona says. 'But I'm sorry I can't take you.'

Rachel supposes this is her cue to come up with some kind of excuse, or to remain silent until somebody changes the subject. She's under no obligation to offer, and even if she did, Viv would probably refuse. They are near strangers, after all.

The words rise to the surface like a bubble from something breathing underwater.

'I'll take you,' she says.

Then, to make it easier for Viv to accept: 'Tring's not far. It's near Aylesbury, isn't it? Easy. It'd be no trouble.'

Viv pauses, considering, eyes almost closed, as if in prayer. Rachel sees how hard it is for her to accept help, and how used she is to coping with things by herself.

Rachel says, 'Would Sunday be OK? You'd be doing me a favour, actually – give me something to do. Something other than work, that is.' She glances at Leona. 'You see, I live for my time at Fun-to-Learn.'

'Things can't be *that* bad,' Leona mutters.

Viv opens her eyes and smiles.

'That would be very kind of you,' she says to Rachel. 'Let's sort out the details later, shall we? We shouldn't just sit here talking about my problems. How are you two?'

Rachel shrugs and pulls a face, and Leona says, 'I have news.'

'Good news, I hope?' Viv says.

By way of reply, Leona reaches for an A4 envelope lying next to a tray of dips and flatbreads on the coffee table, and extracts a piece of paper and holds it up.

It's a colour copy of a photo of a child: a demure little girl in an immaculate white party dress, her hair in plaits with ribbons at the end, wary and hopeful at the same time.

'This is Bluebell,' Leona says, and her expression is both rueful and fiercely proud.

She gets up and goes over to the pinboard, takes down Bluebell's baby photo and pins up the girl in its place. The change of picture changes the mood of the room; Aidan the toddler is fuzzy and nostalgic, a small figure lost somewhere in the past, but Bluebell is self-conscious and immediately present, looking out at them as if poised to hold her own in conversation, or, equally, to keep her thoughts to herself.

'The adoptive mother got in touch,' Leona says. 'A little bit after Bluebell's birthday, but better late than never. They've moved to the south of France – her husband's working on a big engineering project there. It's strange to think of Bluebell growing up so far away. But anyway, she said Bluebell's been asking about me. A lot. She wanted a photo. Of me. Of course it took me forever to decide which one to send.'

'Does she want to meet?' Viv asks.

'I don't think so. Not yet. It hasn't been mentioned. And I haven't asked,' Leona says. 'It'd be a big step. Even bigger now that they're living abroad. I mean, I suppose it's not *that* far, but it seems different. And Bluebell's still very young. Her adoptive parents will want to be sure that she's ready. But, maybe one day…'

'Are *you* ready?' Viv asks.

Leona shrugs. 'Are any of us ever ready? With things like that, the really big things, I think you can only know after the event. If you're lucky. But, you know… it starts me off daydreaming. What it'd be like to hold her. After all this time. Maybe to become part of her life, in some small way. Not a big part. Maybe like some kind of auntie. To be told when she's getting married even if I don't get an invite to the wedding. Maybe even to get to visit her after she's had a child of her own. To hold her baby.'

And Rachel sees for the first time that to lose a child is to lose the promise of grandchildren, too. Not something she had ever considered. Would a future Becca want her mother to be part of her life if it moved in that direction? Or would she not trust her enough? Would it fall to Rachel to send birthday and Christmas presents in exchange for the occasional photo, and maybe a few awkward, well-intentioned visits – to be the grandparent Becca's child or children didn't really know, without them really knowing why?

Viv is looking at Leona with a strange mix of tenderness and sadness.

'That's lovely, Leona,' she says. 'There's nothing wrong with being hopeful. Hope is what makes it possible for us to keep going. It's much more useful than despair.' She sighs. 'Having grandchildren is a wonderful thing. Not that I see mine as often as I would like. I get to Norfolk maybe twice a year. It's an awful drive. Much too tiring for Elaine to do all on her own. I suppose I'll have to figure out how to do it by train now.'

Presumably Aidan would never have children. This loss strikes Rachel as keenly as if it were her own. Then Viv turns to her and says, 'Did you bring along a picture of Becca?'

Rachel attempts to take a deep breath, and is surprised to find that her throat feels small and tight.

'I did,' she says.

She rummages in her bag for her copy of *Kramer vs. Kramer*; she had slipped the photocopy in there to keep it flat. It's the one Mitch had taken of her with Becca when they first went to see Rose Cottage; she'd taken it with her the night she left. She'd blown it up on the copier at work and cropped it so that she's visible only as a hand holding Becca's. There but not there.

The memory it conjures up is so vivid and sweet, and yet it seems so remote that it could almost be a glimpse of some other woman and her daughter, a snap from some other life.

Becca had gone with her so trustingly then... but she certainly doesn't trust her now. Sophie the counsellor had said that it would take time, that the ability of human relationships to repair themselves was as astonishing as the ability of the human body to heal. But not all wounds got better. And maybe Becca is right to be unsure.

The noticeboard seems suddenly far away, and difficult to reach; she's acutely conscious of every movement. She knows that they're all watching her and waiting, and it doesn't make it any easier that they know how she feels.

There are a couple of spare pins stuck in the baize, and she uses them to mount the picture of Becca in the space under Aidan in his wellies, and next to Bluebell. To Rachel's surprise, Becca doesn't look out of place. It's as if her picture has always been missing.

Her hands are steady. This is surprising, too.

'I haven't got many pictures of Becca,' she says. 'But I love this one. It was taken the day we first came to see our house in Kettlebridge. It was a beautiful summer day, and we were all excited at the prospect of moving somewhere new.' She stops short of saying that Mitch took the picture. Her voice is already shaky.

Viv says, 'What a precious memory. It's a very loving picture. You must be so proud of her. And I'm sure she's proud of you, too.'

'Hardly. I'm a wreck,' Rachel says. 'Most days I feel about a million years old.'

Was it tactless to say that to someone so much older? But Viv doesn't take offence. 'Well, you might *feel* like that, but you certainly don't look it,' she says.

'Yeah, well, it's amazing what a bit of make-up can do.'

'Oh, you don't need all that stuff. You're a very attractive young woman. I know the magazines are all for telling you that you need the latest foundation and so on, but we all know that's just so they can keep on making their money, don't we? Soap and a little pot of Vaseline is as good as any of that nonsense, and a bit of lipstick if you want to be cheerful.'

'Some January sun and a toy boy wouldn't hurt either,' Leona murmurs.

'I'd rather have someone to sort out my garden than a toy boy,' Viv says. 'At my advanced stage in life, one really can't be bothered with all that palaver.'

Rachel turns away from the noticeboard and sits down again. There is a strange but not unpleasant sensation in her chest, as if her heart is opening up and expanding, suffusing her with warmth.

# Chapter Seventeen

The home where Aidan is cared for turns out to be a friendly-looking mock Tudor building set back from the main road and surrounded by gardens. Viv suggests that Rachel wait in the reception area, but once she has made herself known to the staff and logged her registration number, Rachel opts to return to the privacy of her car.

What must it be like for Viv, only being able to see her son with a member of staff somewhere not far off? Rachel has asked whether Viv ever takes Aidan out of the home, and Viv changed the subject, which Rachel took to mean that she doesn't, for reasons that she would prefer not to disclose.

Rachel has come equipped with a flask of coffee and a Sunday paper. As she reads it is quiet around her, although at one point she looks up and sees a small party heading off into the grounds with a selection of gardening tools. At the head of the group is a large man with an unusual, tip-toeing gait; at the back is a stooped, elderly woman who stops every couple of paces to sniff the air and mutter something, and is encouraged to move on by a woman in a red windbreaker over pink overalls that surely must be the home's staff uniform.

Rachel wonders if Aidan likes to go out and work outside. She remembers what Viv had said about wanting someone who could help her out in the garden; if he wasn't here, maybe that could have been Aidan… Surely it would be a comfort for Viv to think of him digging the earth and tending seedlings, or perhaps, if that requires more focus than he is capable of, just feeling the breeze and sunlight on his face. Better than being cooped up inside with the central heating turned up and the TV on loud, making little sense of it, waiting for the next thing to happen.

When a little more than an hour has passed Viv emerges and gets into the car. She looks much better than at their last meeting; the neck collar has gone and she's dressed in bright colours – a teal raincoat, knee-length deep-green leather boots. On the drive over she had been resolutely light-spirited, girlish even, as if on her way to a party.

She says, 'Aidan told me it was time for me to go. He's watching us, so could you give him a little wave, if you don't mind? Look, that's him at the window, top right.'

There is indeed someone standing at the window, waving as vigorously as if his life depends on it. A man, taller than Viv, fair-haired, a little tubby, dressed in a sky-blue T-shirt. Rachel reciprocates.

'He doesn't like it if I stay too long,' Viv explains, waving, too. 'It's not that he doesn't love me, or even that he wants to see me go. It's just that this is the pattern. He doesn't like it if the pattern changes. All relationships are like that, to some extent, don't you think? You find a way of doing things, and you get comfortable. That's why he always wears the same blue T-shirt every time I come to see him. It's his favourite. He's got a stock of them, so we don't have to worry about it getting lost in the wash.'

*If he can't cope with a different T-shirt, how's he going to cope when, one day in the distant future, you can't come to see him any more?*

This must have occurred to Viv, too. Maybe she tries not to think about it. When you're up against the inevitable, what else can you do?

Rachel reaches the turning onto the main road; Viv looks back to catch a final glimpse of the home before they leave it behind. Then she rummages in her handbag for a packet of tissues and discreetly wipes her eyes.

'I've found the only way I can cope with things is not to dwell on them too much,' she says. 'I just try and take everything as it comes. But the car accident, you know… that was a shock. And I have this back pain that comes and goes. Nothing too terrible, but I can't help feeling that it's a warning sign.' She sighs. 'I hate not being able to *do* things.'

'But you can do what you need to do, can't you?' Rachel says. 'And there's nothing wrong with having a little bit of help.'

'Well, I don't really like needing help. And I'm sure you're the same. Though being young and healthy as you are, you've got plenty of time before you need to worry about turning into an old crock like me. Last thing I ever wanted was to become someone who's a burden on others. Do you have any elderly relatives to worry about, Rachel? I know a lot of women of your age do.'

'My father passed away years ago, and my mother died last spring. My father-in-law isn't with us any more either, and my mother-in-law has married again and seems to have found a new lease of life. She and her other half are fit as fleas and spend all their time on cruises. Anyway, I'm absolutely the last person they'd want to accept any help from. Mitch's mother always disapproved of me, and now I imagine she feels completely vindicated. She's always been down on Mitch – that's my husband – as well. He's an artist, and she's never quite forgiven him for not becoming a lawyer. His brother went into the family business, and he's definitely the favourite son.'

'Art must be a hard way to make a living,' Viv observes. 'So, this Mitch… you're still married?'

'For now. Probably not indefinitely. But, you know… We only separated in the autumn. I don't think either of us are in a rush to make it to the final curtain.'

'Well, divorce is a nasty business. My daughter, Elaine, had a dreadful time when she was going through it. Expensive, too. I hope you've seen a decent lawyer. I know a good chap in Kettlebridge, if you'd like his details.'

'Oh… it's very kind of you, Viv, but I think things are settled, for now. I got a redundancy payment last year that paid off a big chunk of the mortgage, and we've agreed that Mitch and Becca will stay in the house until she's twenty-one. That's very important to me, that she shouldn't lose her home. The school's given us a bursary to help with the school fees, and I'm sending Mitch a bit of maintenance – not much, the rent on the dump I live in is extortionate, but hopefully by and by I'll get a better job. Not that I'm saying anything against Fun-to-Learn, but that's just a temporary thing – I'm doing maternity leave cover. Sooner or later I'll have to move on to something else.'

'Forgive me if I'm speaking out of turn, Rachel, but… what about custody? Are you happy with the way things are at the moment?'

Rachel slows down sharply for a crossing, and doesn't speak again till they're past it and on a narrow country road. It's been a beautiful drive; the hills and fields spread to the horizon on either side of them, a landscape simplified by winter bareness.

'I gave Becca up because that's what's best for her,' she says.

'I suppose I, of all people, should understand that,' Viv says softly. 'And yet, you know, I do sometimes wonder about Aidan. Whether I could have kept him. Whether it would have been better if I had. Times have changed, and if he was a child now I think I would be given different advice. But that's my story, not yours. I can see how much you love your daughter, and that you're doing your best for her.'

Tears spring to Rachel's eyes. But she can't start bloody crying while she's driving.

'Please, Viv, don't be nice to me. You'll set me off.'

'Oh, dear. I'm sorry. Sympathy can be lethal, I know. But it doesn't do you any good in the long run to keep things all bottled up. I know that, too. Consider me all ears if you ever want to talk about it.'

'I don't think I can. If you knew you wouldn't see me in the same way.'

'Try me. I've lived in a small town for most of my life. There's not much that shocks me.'

Rachel hesitates. What is it about sitting next to someone in a moving car that invites confidences? They're in a safe little bubble, suspended in time between the visit to Aidan and the return to their separate lives. It could almost be possible for her to confess.

'I suppose you could say it started when my mother died,' she begins, and then stops.

Viv lets the pause linger until it becomes a silence, though not an uncomfortable one: she's waiting to see if Rachel wants to say more, but isn't going to push her. Finally Viv says, 'It's not a small thing, to lose a parent. Comes to us all, if we're lucky enough to live that long: we all end up as orphans sooner or later, making do with our memories. Trying somehow to make sense of it all, because that's what people do, even when there's no sense to be found.'

Rachel breathes in, breathes out again. 'I think that's the bit I'm struggling with. I still don't really understand what happened to me, and what I did. But I just don't trust myself any more.'

'Have you noticed how people tend to think they've got what they deserved? Whether you're pleased with yourself or blame yourself, it's easier to believe you had it coming. When Aidan was little, when it became obvious that he had some problems, I thought it must have been something I'd done. And I wasn't the only one, actually.'

'But in the end… you stopped feeling like that?'

'It took a priest to tell me it wasn't my fault,' Viv says.

There is another little silence. Then Viv goes on: 'Anyway, you obviously had an awful time of it last year, what with one thing and another. This year will be better, you'll see. Good fortune can come as unexpectedly as disaster. Peppermint?'

'Thank you.'

Viv drops a sweet into Rachel's upheld hand and Rachel palms it to her mouth. Peppermints! Her mother had always carried them in her handbag, too. In every other way, though, Viv is nothing like her mother.

The landscape they're driving through is changing, becoming steep and hilly with twists and turns and sharp drops; trees crowd out the view, which occasionally opens up as far as the horizon and reveals the deep valley they're alongside. She fixes her eyes on the road ahead, and does her best to think of nothing else.

# Chapter Eighteen

## Rachel

Six months before the loss

The cardboard urn with the ashes in it was both heavier and lighter than you'd expect the remains of a life to be. It was a similar weight to a small child: easy to carry, but still substantial.

When they collected it at the crematorium, Mitch had asked, 'Can I help with that?' and she had given him the look that means, *I can manage.*

Because she *could* manage. And she had. The job, the commute, the household chores, the parenting… the panicky phone calls when something happened and Mitch wanted Rachel to tell him what to do, like when Becca had come out in a weird rash and Mitch didn't know what it was. (Neither chicken pox nor meningitis but an allergic reaction to laundry detergent, as it turned out.) Or, more usually, when he couldn't find something, like Becca's clean PE shirt or school trip permission slip. Nine times out of ten it was nothing to worry about, but it terrified her when he rang her at work just the same.

And she would carry on managing. She had organised her mother's funeral, and she would go on to sort out clearing and selling her mother's house, the home she had grown up in. And good riddance. There would be some satisfaction in emptying the place of every last trace of what had gone on there, and turning it over to someone new.

They didn't speak at all on the way home. Mitch, who was driving, had obviously decided she was in too dark a mood for him to risk an attempt at conversation. He was taking all this so personally. If she was angry he assumed it was with him, and she seemed to be incapable of explaining to him that she wasn't, not in particular. Not more than usual. She wasn't even angry, not really. It just came out that way.

She sat in the passenger seat, holding her mother's mortal remains on her lap, and then carried the urn with care over the bridge to the cottage and up to their bedroom, where she placed it on the floor by her side of the bed.

Mitch followed her up. He pulled a face when he saw where she had put the urn to rest. An 'ick' face, the sort of face with which he would respond to anything physical that was slightly disgusting.

'Really?' he said. 'You mean you expect me to sleep in the same room as your *mother*?'

'Oh for God's sake, Mitch. No, I wouldn't dream of asking you to do anything you didn't want to.'

She picked up the urn again.

'I'll put it in a corner of the living room then, *if* that's all right with you. Oh, and I'll be sleeping downstairs tonight,' she said, and barged past him on her way out.


Next morning she was up at five, even earlier than usual, tidying away her bedding because the last thing she needed, on top of everything else, was for Becca to see it and start asking questions and worrying that her parents were about to split.

She made coffee, dressed in the skirt and blouse she'd put out the night before, managed something to eat. It was going to be a long day. Frank, who had always been the most sympathetic boss you could ask for, had urged her to take some more time off. But the fact was, they needed her there. Also, if she was really honest, she *wanted* to go back to work. She wanted to be busy, to be rushed off her feet; to be stressed rather than sad. It was the only thing that was going to make her feel like herself again.

Mitch knew that, of course. He knew her better than anyone, always had.

'Just don't pretend this isn't what you want,' he had said to her years ago, just after the end of her maternity leave, early one morning when she was about to dash out of their flat in London to catch the train to work. She had literally left him holding the baby. The crying baby. Becca had been just ten months old, and oh Lord, she could cry like no other child. It was quite unbelievable the volume and pitch that could come out of a person who was otherwise so small and helpless.

Right now, though, Mitch and Becca were both still soundly sleeping.

Nothing much disturbed Mitch's sleep. He had that extraordinary male gift of being able to not worry about things. Maybe it wasn't exclusively masculine, but it seemed that way. He could leave the kitchen in a mess, the ironing undone. He didn't see the dust – somehow he could filter it out, it didn't bother him. He called this *not sweating the small stuff.*

*If you want me to do this, Rachel, if you want me to hold the fort and keep the home fires burning, you have to let me do it* my way.

And he had a point. She had to admit it. She had no right to try and tell him what to do.

Sometimes he accused her of being controlling. He knew how much that hurt her, and he knew why. But maybe it was true.

Her reflection in the bathroom mirror was a bit of a shock – pale, tired, gaunt. She slapped on make-up to compensate: foundation, blusher, but no mascara, in case she felt the need to retreat to the loos at some point and cry. Expensive foundation. She still couldn't quite believe how much she had spent on it. Neither would Mitch if he knew. But she had to try something; she needed to look like her usual self at work.

She hadn't wept yet. She knew Mitch thought that was weird of her: he had cried buckets at his dad's funeral, and even more when his mother got married again and completed the process, which had started long ago when he got involved with Rachel, of washing her hands of him.

*My mother was never bothered about being a grandmother to Becca,* he had said to her. *And yours wasn't really up to it, was she?*

Joanie Steele was beyond being anything to anybody now.

Rachel picked up the urn and carried it through the house to the kitchen, where she set it down to unlock the back door and then took it out to the garden. It was light, but only just; the sun was low in the sky and the air was still very cool. The garden looked unfamiliar, as if it was not quite hers but still belonged to the creatures of the night: the slugs and snails, the hedgehog, the local cats on the prowl, the bat and the moths.

When the hospital rang to tell her the news about her mother the cherry tree had been picture perfect, covered in great pink ice-creamy clumps of blossom. Now it was past its best. Within another couple of days the grass would be carpeted with browning petals. The hops were beginning to grow, though, winding up the side of Mitch's studio, and the rose bushes were covered with buds.

She prised the lid off the urn and set it aside. Then she walked over to the border and began to shake out her mother's ashes.

A thick, steady stream whooshed out, dusting the peonies, coating the feverfew and the St John's wort and the still-leafless branches of the jasmine. It was grey and fine and heavy, and its flow was steady and unstoppable, like a sand-timer: no going back now. It made Rachel think of volcanic dust, of molten rock and dark clouds emerging from volcanoes and the petrified bodies at Pompeii, caught and covered before they could flee.

A breeze blew the dust into her hair and eyes; she could taste it on her tongue. The flow of ash was thinner now, dwindling to a slender ribbon making its way from the vessel in her hands to the earth. She thought of the line of blood that had once connected her to the woman whose remains she had just dispersed, how her mother would have felt her move the same way she in turn had felt Becca move inside her.

She allowed the final trickle to fall, obscuring the high shine of the glossy green leaves of the laurel bush.

Mitch said, 'Rachel... what are you doing?'

He was in his dressing-gown and old slippers and pyjamas; his hair was wild and his face was still puffy from sleep. He was standing on the patio as if hesitating to venture further, like a child who had been woken by his parents arguing and had come out to stand on the stairs, but didn't quite dare to intervene.

Mitch said, 'You scattered her ashes *here*? Don't you think we should have talked about this? I mean, is this even legal?'

A very clear picture of her mother came back to Rachel: down on her knees, frightened, picking up shards of broken glass.

'I had to do something for her,' she said. 'I did little enough to help her while she was still alive. This garden is one of my favourite places in the world. I couldn't think of anywhere better for her to be at peace.'

She picked up the lid and dropped it and the urn into the bin. Mitch followed her into the house. She soaped her hands at the kitchen sink. There was a pain in her midriff that was like a stitch. She wanted to cry – she wanted to howl – but it was too shocking for that. Her mum had been alive and now was ash in the garden: there was no way to make sense of it.

Mitch put his hand on her shoulder: she shrugged it off.

'You *did* try to help her,' Mitch said.

'Not hard enough.'

Mitch sighed. 'I just don't know how Becca's going to feel about this.'

'How I'm going to feel about what?' Becca asked. She was standing in the doorway in her pyjamas, rubbing her eyes.

Rachel rinsed her hands and dried them. 'I just scattered your grandmother's ashes in the garden,' she said.

'Oh,' Becca said. 'Can I see?'

'I don't think you should,' Mitch said. He reached for the keys and locked the back door.

Rachel found she couldn't breathe. Her husband and child were looking at her as if she frightened them.

'I have to get to work,' she said, and went off to collect her things and leave the house.

# Chapter Nineteen

Rachel has taken up running. Not because it's supposed to keep depression at bay – in her experience, you want the little blue and yellow pills for that – but because she has recovered sufficiently for it to be a possibility. There had been a time when it had taken every bit of energy and willpower she had to stay alive, or at least, to keep on going through the motions: getting up, getting dressed, eating, going to sleep. Embarking on a programme of regular exercise would have been beyond her. But suddenly, as the darkness of winter has begun to lift, the urge to push herself a little has come back.

She heads out as soon as she gets back from work, and when she returns to the bedsit she hears her phone ringing inside.

Her key won't turn in the lock; she fumbles with it and flings herself across the room to grab it from the table.

There's only one person it could be, and only one person it could be about.

ICE MITCH. She still has him stored as her 'In Case of Emergency' number.

A grouchy, achingly familiar voice says, 'Are you all right? You sound as if you're about to have a heart attack.'

'I'm fine,' she says, trying to steady her breathing. 'I've been out for a run. Is Becca OK?'

'Yes and no,' Mitch says.

She settles down at the little table.

'What's up?' Her breathing is starting to slow now, though her heart is racing as if she were still running.

'I got a phone call from the school this morning.'

'And?'

'Becca's class teacher is worried about how she's doing. There's been a definite slacking off, she says. Homework not done on time, lack of attention in class, that kind of thing. Plus one really blatant example of copying Amelia Chadstone.'

'Copying? That doesn't sound like Becca. How did they find out about that?'

'It was a piece of maths homework, and they'd made exactly the same mistakes.'

'Maybe Amelia copied off Becca?'

'Come on, Rachel. Amelia's top of the class in pretty much everything, apparently. And Becca has always struggled with her maths.'

'If Amelia's so clever, how come she made mistakes?'

There is a pause. 'Rachel,' Mitch says. 'We've talked about this before. You mustn't let what happened back in the autumn colour your judgement. I know it's awkward for you that the girls are friends. But they are.'

'OK, I'm sorry. Maybe I'm not handling this very well. It's just come as a bit of a shock. I mean, I thought Becca was doing fine. It's a very academic school, and she might not be top of the class but she's always seemed to be coping. And she's really come into her own in the extracurricular stuff. She was brilliant in *Oliver!*'

'Well, yes, but that's all done with now, and her studies are what really count.'

'How can you say that? You're an artist.'

Another pause. 'Barely. Most of the time I copy Old Masters and paint reproductions of people's photos of their pets. And I've never made much money from it, as you know. The last thing I want is for Becca to turn out like me. Anyway, they want us to come in for a meeting. Together. They're going to get in touch with you as well, but I thought I'd give you a heads-up first.'

There is a pause while Rachel absorbs this.

'I don't think it's that serious yet,' Mitch adds. 'It's just that they like to nip problems in the bud if they can. They don't want her going into some kind of downward spiral. I mean, I can see why they might be concerned. I just don't want them to treat this like it's happened because Becca's just being lazy or something. The poor kid's had a lot to cope with. If things have gone off the boil a bit academically, sure, we need to get her back on track, but I don't think they should blame her for it.'

*Because it's my fault.* Rachel pauses, takes a deep breath. She says, 'Have you spoken to Becca about all this?'

'I've tried. I don't think she wants to talk about it. And she's still refusing to engage with the school counselling services. I think we just need to go in and talk to the school and hear what they have to say. Put on a bit of a united front. For Becca's sake. But for this to work, Rachel, I need to know that you can handle it. You can't go in there and pick a fight with me, or make some kind of scene or start throwing wild accusations around.'

Another pause. Rachel moves her left hand, the one that isn't holding the phone, to her right wrist and begins to pinch. She feels as if she's being forced to swallow something. A huge, unpalatable, toxic lump: guilt, grief, regret… and, yes, anger – anger that she can't afford to show. Or even allow herself to feel.

Somehow, she forces it all down.

'OK,' she says.

'Good,' Mitch says. 'I expect they'll suggest a couple of possible times for the meeting. We can sort that out by email. Oh, and Rachel…?'

'Yes?'

'It's good that you've started running. Maybe it'll help. The last thing Becca needs right now is for you to start going backwards.'

He ends the call. Rachel puts the phone down and stares at the red mark on her wrist. She thinks of Leona with her bluebell tattoo, and of Viv's cosy sitting room with all its knick-knacks and photographs, but no picture of her firstborn child on display.

Sometimes a painful reminder is what you want. And sometimes it's more than you can bear.

# Chapter Twenty

Rachel takes no chances about arriving early for the meeting at St Anne's. Even so, Mitch is already waiting outside the headmistress's office when she gets here.

He has washed his hair and trimmed his beard for the occasion, and has even had a go at ironing a shirt. He's left the top two buttons of his shirt undone. His chest hair is beginning to turn silver now; she doesn't remember it that way, always thinks of it as dark.

He looks pale and tired and profoundly uncomfortable, as if he'd rather be almost anywhere else, and he doesn't smile at her as she comes in. The fat, twisty line of the scar on his hand is redder and angrier than usual, as if it's been itching and he's been rubbing or scratching it.

'You made it all right, then,' he remarks as she settles onto the chair one along from the one next to him.

Remembering the awfulness of turning up late to Becca's show is like a stab to the heart. And yet she has so much more to reproach herself for.

'Yes, no traffic problems this time,' she says.

He studies her more closely, as if her appearance might offer a clue as to how far he can rely on her to behave herself in the meeting.

'You look different,' he says eventually. 'Like you've got less make-up on. It suits you.'

She feels herself blush. 'Thanks.'

Her expensive foundation has run out, and in the light of Viv's comments about soap and Vaseline, she has decided not to replace it. After all, whatever Viv did was obviously working for her – Rachel has never seen an older woman with such good skin. And it certainly saves time in the mornings.

Mitch says, 'So how do you think you're doing? I mean, are you up to this?'

She folds her arms and presses them close to her chest; she's doing her best not to do the pinching trick.

'I've been OK. I mean, I think I've been doing pretty well.'

*Why is it so difficult for her to speak to him without sounding as if she's got something to hide?*

'I don't want to intrude,' Mitch says. 'I want you to have the space you need. But I've got to be sure you can cope, Rach. You have to be the mother Becca needs you to be. Especially now. Is there anything I need to know?'

She shakes her head. She doesn't trust herself to say any more.

The door opposite them opens and Becca's class teacher comes out. She looks, as ever, girlishly sweet in a pretty dress and cardigan; her curly hair is pinned back from her face with Kirby grips. But her expression is sombre.

'Mr and Mrs Moran? We're ready for you now.'

*Mr and Mrs Moran*... still. It seems a long time since anyone has called her Mrs Moran. It makes her feel like an imposter, as if she should start issuing an explanation: *At work I'm Rachel Steele – Ms Rachel Steele, I suppose, but Mrs Moran is still technically correct, we're not divorced yet, only separated, my bank account and rental contract are in that name, so I suppose you could say that's who I really am*...

They get to their feet. Miss Finch holds the door open; Mitch holds back to let Rachel through first.

There had been a time when she had teased him for his old-fashioned manners. Now, though, she's grateful to be treated this way by him. At least it is an acknowledgement that she's a woman, even if she's no longer a woman he wants.

She goes through into the headmistress's office and the others follow. Mrs Mellon is sitting, not behind her desk – which is large and executive-looking, and occupies one corner of the office – but on the L-shaped sofa in front of it. Immediately the meeting feels more like a medical consultation than a face-off between someone who is providing a service and two potentially dissatisfied customers.

Rachel's spirits sink. Mitch is right; chances are this is not going to be about Becca as much as it is going to be about her.

There is a file – Becca's file, presumably – on the coffee table in front of her. Next to the file is a box of tissues in a silver holder, which Mrs Mellon must have moved there in anticipation, because last time she and Mitch were here it had been sitting on a corner of the desk.

They had come here then to plead extenuating circumstances, and to ask for flexible terms for payment of the school fees. Rachel had cried, which was better than getting angry. In the end the school had given Becca a bursary that reduced the amount of money they had to find, though there was no guarantee that this would continue to the next academic year. Which is just another reason why Becca cannot afford to fall behind.

Mrs Mellon stands and shakes Rachel and Mitch's hands in turn. She is an imposing figure, more authoritative than kindly, and her touch is firm and swift. She graciously invites everybody to sit, and Miss Finch takes the place next to her. Rachel settles next to Mitch and tries to take deep breaths without anyone noticing.

Mrs Mellon kicks off: 'This is rather a difficult conversation to have and I'm sure we all regret that it's necessary, but I know I'm right in saying that we all only have Becca's best interests at heart.'

'*This'll hurt me more than it hurts you*,' Mitch mutters.

Mrs Mellon looks mildly startled.

'I beg your pardon?'

'I can't remember if my old headmaster ever actually said that,' Mitch explains. 'It would have been pretty hypocritical if he had. He was the kind of sadist who used to do quite well in the educational establishment – in a certain kind of boys' school, at any rate.'

Mrs Mellon raises her eyebrows as if she's not sure whether to be insulted, and Rachel suppresses a wild urge to giggle. She had forgotten that Mitch could be like this, so... *bold*. And protective. This is his way of sticking up for Becca; he's never been one to let other people put her down.

Of course, it could turn out to be counterproductive. And Becca is technically something of a charity case, so alienating the school probably isn't wise...

'They were into caning back then,' Mitch goes on. 'Seems extraordinary now, doesn't it? Still, I guess we all feel like taking it out on somebody sometime. Anyway, I'm digressing, aren't I? I'm sorry, Mrs Mellon, you were saying?'

'You must understand, Mr Moran, this is not a disciplinary matter. This is a pastoral discussion.'

'That's good to hear. Because when I spoke to Miss Finch, it almost sounded as if Becca was in some kind of *trouble* for not doing as well as she used to do. Well, as you know, Becca's had a difficult time lately. I would hate to think that you were punishing her for that. Or that you'd brought us here today so you could threaten to kick her out, rather than working with us to try and help her.'

Mrs Mellon has turned slightly pale. She allows a silence to fall over the room, and when she next speaks her tone is determinedly light and controlled.

'Of course we *all* want what's best for Becca. We were wondering if there might be anything either of you could share that would help us to unpick what's going on.'

Mitch says, 'I think we've already told you everything you need to know. We split up.' He glances at Rachel. 'Becca's mother hasn't been well. We went through all this on the application form for the bursary. How much more detail do you need?'

'We have all seen that when Becca decides to commit herself to what she's doing – when she's truly motivated – there's no stopping her,' Miss Finch says. 'I think we can all agree that she turned in a sterling performance in *Oliver!* It occurred to me that maybe being involved in the show had given her a sense of family that she now is missing again. Or it could have given her self-esteem a temporary boost, which has inevitably worn off.' She looks from Mitch to Rachel. 'We do sometimes see, in a situation like this… that it can be more difficult when there's ongoing hostility between the parents.'

'Obviously, what happened was a shock for Becca, and it's a big change to adjust to. But I think it would be fair to say that we came to an agreement about the terms of our separation fairly quickly and I, for one, would certainly describe the relationship we have now as a cordial one,' Mitch says. 'We've done everything we can to give Becca as much continuity as possible.'

'That was partly why I moved out,' Rachel says, and her voice doesn't sound nearly as steady as she would like. Her vision is misting and she hopes she won't need to reach for the tissues in a minute.

Mitch glances at her nervously. He moves his hand closer to her, pats her gingerly on the knee. The right hand. The scarred one. He hasn't touched her for months. Since the day she left.

'I think what Rachel means to say is that we've had our difficulties, but we've done our best to always put Becca first,' he says.

'That is admirable,' Miss Finch says, with just the kind of face she might wear if one of her pupils claimed the dog ate her homework. 'I'm sure you've done your very best, as you say.' She glances at Mrs Mellon, who gives her an almost imperceptible nod.

'Well, it seems there may be no immediately obvious reason for the current tricky patch,' Miss Finch says.

'We've tried to persuade Becca to go to counselling, but she won't hear of it,' Rachel said.

'We have a comprehensive programme here to support the girls' wellness, as you know, so you can rest assured that we're doing all we can to support Becca and all our other students,' Mrs Mellon told her. 'Let me show you what triggered our concerns.' She opens the ring binder sitting on the coffee table and hands out a pair of identical printouts. 'These are your copies to keep,' she says, and Mitch and Rachel automatically thank her.

The first page is a spreadsheet filled with numbers. The second is a series of graphs, all of which tell the same story: a wavering line, followed by a steep descent.

'These are Becca's marks since the New Year, and as you can see, it is not going the way we would like,' Mrs Mellon says. 'Sometimes this kind of pattern can be resolved swiftly, especially with good, prompt parental reinforcement. If not, however, we at St Anne's can find ourselves in a very difficult position. There are so many wonderful girls we would like to admit, and we have to say no to far too many of them, which is why it is such a cause for regret when one of our girls appears to be struggling to make the most of all her opportunities.'

'I knew it. You're saying that if Becca's marks don't pick up, you're going to expel her,' Mitch says.

'Mr Moran, if Becca falls behind with her studies, we all need to ask ourselves whether this is really the best possible place for her to be.'

Mitch's gaze flickers towards the small framed watercolour of a riverside scene, just about recognisable as the Thames in Kettlebridge, hanging on the wall next to a wooden cross.

'Are you an art lover?' he asks, pointing at the painting. The scar is a crimson slash on his raised hand, impossible to miss.

'I hope I can appreciate beauty, yes.'

'Modern art?'

'I stop with the Impressionists, I'm afraid.'

'I thought you might,' Mitch says.

'You have must have much more knowledge than I do where art appreciation is concerned,' Mrs Mellon says smoothly. 'Thank you both so much for coming in. I think this has been a really good preliminary discussion, and, of course, we'll all continue to keep

Becca's wellbeing at the forefront of our minds. Now, unless there are any questions you'd like to ask...?'

Mitch pulls a face and shakes his head. Rachel remains silent.

'Do liaise with Miss Finch going forward, though you're welcome to make an appointment with me at any time,' Mrs Mellon adds.

She and Miss Finch are quick to rise; Rachel and Mitch stand more reluctantly, as if loath to concede defeat.

'I'll see you out,' Miss Finch says, and accompanies them at a brisk pace to the front of the school building, where she bids them a quick goodbye and they suddenly find themselves outside.

*

It is as if they have been ejected; everything looks slightly unfamiliar, the way it does after a shock. It is the beginning of a beautiful evening. The light is a fading blue; a silver half-moon is high in the sky, its outline hazy with mist. The air smells sweet and promising and the miniature decorative trees set in tubs around the edges of the car park are stippled with the bright green of new growth.

Mitch says, 'I'll talk to Becca again about the counselling thing.'

'OK. It'll probably be better coming from you. She seemed to really resent it when I suggested it.'

'I don't hold out much hope of success. And, you know what, maybe we should just try and listen to her, too. She might not be ready to open up about how she feels. You know how private she is. Our trying to force her could actually be having the opposite effect. She knows what this meeting was about – that in itself might be the shock she needs. And I'll keep an eye on things, make sure she's spending enough time on her homework and so on. Rachel...'

'Yes?'

He gazes at her and there is something in his face she hasn't seen for a long time. Affection. Pained affection, but affection neverthe-less. A kind of guilty tenderness.

He reaches out almost as if unthinkingly to brush a strand of her hair back from her face, then drops his scarred hand as abruptly as if it's betrayed him.

'I know how hard you're trying,' he says. 'Just don't overdo it, all right? For all our sakes. Don't feel you have to start raking over the past. It won't help. What's done is done.'

'Mitch...'

'Yes?'

'It's just a thought, but since she was in *Oliver!*, Becca does seem to have got a lot closer to Amelia Chadstone, and I just wondered...'

He glares at her, the almost-closeness of a moment before completely forgotten. 'What?'

'Well... what if Amelia isn't a particularly good influence? Maybe she's a bit of a distraction.'

Mitch rolls his eyes in exasperation. 'Come on, Rachel. I know you feel bad about this, and so do I, but Amelia's a model student. You can't blame her. If Becca's having problems it's our fault and nobody else's.'

He turns abruptly away and heads for their old family car. It's pretty dirty. Mitch never could be bothered to wash it; that chore that had fallen to Rachel, who had hardly ever done it either.

*It's our fault.* Not *it's your fault.* It was generous of him, in a way, to share the guilt. Generous, but wrong. Because *she* was the one who had turned Becca's world upside down.

The sun is surprisingly warm on her skin; the sighing breeze riffles the new leaves on the boughs of the decorative saplings. Mitch doesn't look back, doesn't wave. He accelerates away and she's suddenly alone.

# Chapter Twenty-One

Viv and Rachel's Sunday trips quickly begin to adopt a pattern. Rachel arrives at Park Place at half-past twelve, giving Viv time to get back from Sunday service and have something to eat. Then they set off for Tring. Viv is eager; they talk, and Rachel finds herself telling Viv things – little things, mainly, inconsequential things, about her week at work or what she had watched on TV the previous night. Sometimes she talks about whatever she had done with Becca the day before, or what she is thinking of doing next – bowling, perhaps, or a trip to a beauty spot, or the cinema again.

She never goes into details about the events that had preceded her separation from Mitch, and Viv doesn't ask.

Aidan is always the same, too, always dressed in the same T-shirt; each time, he waves Rachel goodbye from his window.

Then, on the way home, Viv is silent, and Rachel lets her be.

But after the meeting at St Anne's, Rachel is unusually quiet. She can't quite bring herself to talk about it.

On the way to Tring, Viv offers her a peppermint; she takes one, and keeps on driving in silence. After a while Viv says, 'Rachel, what's wrong?'

'Nothing's wrong.'

Viv doesn't say anything; she just waits until Rachel says, 'I suppose there is something, actually. I got called in for a meeting at Becca's school, with Mitch. Her marks are down, and they told us that it might be because of the situation between us.'

'Oh. Oh dear. I imagine that's left you feeling rather dreadful. And very worried, naturally. I suppose you've had a chat with Becca about it?'

'No, I haven't had the chance. I mean, she knows about the meeting, and I've been trying to get her to see a counsellor for months. But she always just shuts down when I bring it up, and I don't think Mitch is having any luck either. When he tried to talk to her about all this after the meeting, Becca just headed the whole thing off at the pass by telling him there wasn't a problem and she was going to pull her socks up.'

'And are you happy with the way the school has handled it? I only ask because from what I hear St Anne's can be pretty ruthless. They chucked out the granddaughter of one lady I know because the poor girl wasn't quite up to it academically.'

'That's exactly what they were implying they'd do to Becca! Frankly, I'm confused about the whole thing. I'm furious with them, but I'm even more furious with myself. I don't think Becca would be having these problems if it wasn't for me. I just want her to be all right.'

'Well, you know, children go through ups and downs. All children, and I include Aidan in that. When he was little sometimes it seemed as if he'd never progress. And then, all of a sudden, he would. Just at his own pace. Anyway, whatever is going on with Becca will most likely work itself out. But you mustn't beat yourself up. How will you be ready for her when she needs you if you've worn yourself out worrying that you've failed her? You mustn't doubt yourself. You've got so much to give – I can see that, Leona can see that, even your husband can probably see it, unless he's a complete idiot. One day Becca will see it, too.'

'She just doesn't really talk to me. And I don't blame her.' Rachel hesitates, takes a deep breath. 'When Mitch and I broke up I wasn't in a very good way. I ended up taking medication for a little while, and having some counselling. Things are a bit better now. More stable. But for a while I wasn't really myself, and that was so hard on Becca – to see me change like that.'

'Oh, Rachel. I'm so sorry. And you lost your mother not so very long ago, didn't you? Sometimes I think these things can be cumulative. So, you're not taking any medication now? I only ask because I was prescribed Valium for a while in the eighties, after Aidan went off to live in a home, and it was hell to stop.'

'No. I was worried about that. But I stopped when I started working at Fun-to-Learn, and it was all right, actually. I didn't go back under. They don't know about it, though. The temp agency gave me a health questionnaire to fill in that asked if I'd ever had depression, and I just left that bit blank. Maybe it wouldn't have been a problem, but I was desperate to get work and I thought it might make it harder. I haven't actually told Leona that, so maybe keep it to yourself? It might put her in an awkward position if she knew.'

'Rachel, your secret is safe with me. I'm sure you could tell Leona, though. She wouldn't say anything – she'd be on your side. And I hope your employer would be more sympathetic than you think. After all, it's something that very many people experience, at one time or another. This isn't why you think Becca ought to be with her father, is it? Because if every mother who has been through an episode of depression gave up custody, there'd be a heck of lot of women in your situation, and suddenly the playgroup I help with at church would be packed with dads.'

'It wasn't just that,' Rachel says. 'I mean, I was depressed, but it was more than that.'

She slows down for a turning; they're nearly there. She's aware of Viv waiting for her to say more.

'I had to leave, Viv,' she says. 'Becca didn't know everything that had gone on, but she'd seen something she should never have seen. She was scared of me. This is the only way I can regain her trust. From a distance, bit by bit.'

Viv sighs. 'I've said this before, Rachel, and I'll say it again; when you're ready, if you ever really want to talk about what happened, you can tell me. *I* trust you. And regardless of the person you might have been last summer, or what you might have done, or thought about doing, the person you are now has received the ultimate stamp of approval – to my mind, anyway. And on that note… I don't know how you'll feel about this, and you don't have to if you don't want to, but I think Aidan would like to meet you.'

'Really? Is that what he said?'

'Well, not exactly. I deduced it. He wanted to see your car. That's his way of showing curiosity about you. If you don't mind, and if the staff don't mind, if you just stay put in the car park as usual, I'll bring him out to have a look?'

'OK,' Rachel agrees. 'I'd be delighted. I'm honoured.' And it is true; she's profoundly flattered.

'I think of Aidan as a kind of divining-rod,' Viv says. 'He can bring out people's kindness, and also their cruelty. All he has brought out from you is goodness. I suspect, Rachel, whatever you may have done or not done, that you're not the terrible person you sometimes seem to think you are.'

Rachel is conscious of the older woman studying her; then they turn onto the approach to Aidan's care home. Viv turns to face it and lets out a little sigh that could be either apprehension or relief, and says, 'Nearly there.'


After Rachel has been alone in the car for a little while, a small expeditionary party emerges from the front of the building: Viv and Aidan, who is slightly taller than her, and a carer in pink overalls just behind them.

Aidan is holding Viv's hand. Somehow this looks right, even though he should be much too old for it. He is wearing the usual blue T-shirt with an unzipped hoodie and grey jogging bottoms and Velcro-fastened trainers, and there is something about the way he walks that suggests an uncertainty about the relationship between his body, the ground beneath and the space around him, as if it might all be dramatically reconfigured at any moment. He appears baffled but determined. Viv looks pleased and nervous and – this is unexpected but shouldn't be – *proud*. Rachel wonders how long it is since she's introduced her son to anybody.

Rachel gets out of the car and says hello. Aidan scowls at her fleetingly and says a loud hello back as he launches himself forward as if to run away, though it turns out he is only setting out to walk around the car, observing it closely and occasionally pausing to tap or sniff it.

'Is it OK?' Viv asks.

'Sure,' Rachel says. 'It's not very well cared for, I'm afraid. He's probably going to come to all sorts of dreadful conclusions about me.'

'It doesn't look that bad to me. You should see mine,' says the carer, whose name badge reveals that she's called Coral.

Aidan says, 'This is ten years old. The engine is quite powerful, so you could go fast if you needed to.' He peers inside. 'You don't clean it. Do you have a vacuum cleaner?'

'I share one with some other people,' Rachel says. 'It doesn't work very well.'

'Coral says it's good to share, but I don't like sharing,' Aidan observes. 'Other people don't look after things the way I do. I like broken things, for example. Other people often just throw them away. But I don't think being broken makes something bad. Just because you can't use it in the way you want to, doesn't mean you should put it in the bin. You can do something different with it.'

He comes up very close to Rachel, puts his hand on the sleeve of her jacket and looks up into her face. He says, 'You drive my mum. Nobody drove her before.'

'This is Rachel,' Viv says. 'You can say hello to her.'

'I know, and I said hello already,' Aidan tells her.

He pushes his face closer to Rachel and for a crazy half moment she thinks he is about to kiss her, but instead he sniffs her hair. Then he withdraws and studies her again. His interest is more forensic than friendly: she feels as if she's being scanned, as if details to which she's oblivious are being logged for future reference.

'You're going to come every week,' he says.

'Well, maybe not every week,' Viv says. 'Rachel's very kindly helping me out for now, but she does have a life and a child of her own. And a job, too.'

Aidan ignores her. He says, 'You should come inside with us. It's not very interesting, but you can carry on reading your book if you like. You could have a cup of tea. Also, Mum brought cupcakes. I'll let you have one.'

'Oh no, I'm fine here,' Rachel says, although actually the prospect of tea and cake is appealing.

'You sure?' Coral asks. 'You could have the visitors' lounge to yourselves.'

And again Rachel has that feeling of being sucked in deeper than she had planned. But then she thinks, *What the hell?*

'OK,' she says with a shrug.

Viv reaches out glancingly to touch Rachel's arm, and says, 'Thank you.'

Rachel retrieves her handbag and locks the car. Viv takes Aidan by the hand again, and Coral and Rachel follow them as they lead the way back into the home.

The lounge turns out to be quiet and pleasant: it is more comfortable than the institutional waiting room, and has a well-worn, weary vibe that Rachel supposes must come of long use by many visitors who have given up being angry or sad that their lives have brought them to such a place, and are simply grateful to have somewhere to sit.

She perches on the overstuffed sofa; Aidan comes over and holds out the Tupperware box of Viv's cakes, his face as serious as if he were offering her a life-changing bribe, or a proposal of marriage. She takes one and he retreats.

'You can play on the computer if you like, Aidan,' Viv says. 'Aidan doesn't really like to make conversation,' she adds for Rachel's benefit.

'I don't understand why people talk when they don't have anything to say,' Aidan explains.

Viv and Aidan go off to Aidan's room to retrieve his iPad, leaving Rachel alone. She finishes her cupcake, sweeps the crumbs off the sofa into her hand and finds a bin for them, and tries to relax.

She takes in the faded pastel watercolour of a tree-lined river hanging on the wall, the poster advertising a charity helpline, the small tub of plastic toys. She thinks about Viv coming here by herself all these years. Not giving up.

And then, as suddenly as if somebody outside had flicked a switch, sunlight pitches in through the window opposite her and bathes the whole room in gold, and she sees it for what it is: a place where two worlds meet, and nothing but love keeps them together.

# Chapter Twenty-Two

## Rachel

### Six months before the loss

As Rachel passed through the revolving door to the office she checked her watch: five to nine, respectably punctual for someone fresh back from compassionate leave.

She wished the receptionist a more than usually friendly good morning. As she showed her pass to the security guard she noticed a smear of something grey, like dust, on the lapel of her blouse. She brushed it off without thinking. And then she remembered what it was.

They had been in this office building for a year, since her boss sold his business to a much larger company. Her desk was on the tenth floor, beside a window from which it was just possible, if you stood in the right place and craned your neck, to make out the fairy tale form of Tower Bridge.

As she logged into her PC there was a discreet sound of throat-clearing just behind her. It was Elizabeth Mannering, who Rachel didn't usually have much to do with – she was too senior, and ran a different part of the business. She was also a bit intimidating, an impeccably groomed blonde who apparently had a high-flying lawyer husband, plus a live-in nanny to take care of her two small sons.

'Rachel.' Elizabeth smiled at her sympathetically. 'I hope everything went all right?'

'Oh, yes, very well, thank you. I mean, as well as these things can.'

'That's good to hear. And your little girl – how did she cope with it all?'

Rachel glanced at the framed photograph on her desk: it was of Mitch with Becca by Kettlebridge lock, taken a couple of years ago. Becca had still been in primary school then, and happy to smile unselfconsciously for the camera.

'Not so little any more,' she said. 'She'll be thirteen in September. Anyway, she seemed to cope with it all right.'

Becca would only ever remember her grandmother as a strange old lady who didn't like leaving the house and smelt of gin. It was painful to acknowledge it, but there hadn't been much of a relationship there to mourn. It could have been different… if Rachel's mum had been able to live a different kind of life.

If Rachel had been a better daughter, maybe she would have been able to save her.

A meeting reminder flashed up on her PC screen: *Catch up with Frank.* She must have accepted the request when she'd logged in remotely at some point over the last week, though she had absolutely no memory of it. She locked the screen and got to her feet.

'I'd better go,' she said. 'Frank wants to see me.'

A strange expression came over Elizabeth's face – sombre and ever so slightly smug, the face of someone who knew something Rachel didn't.

'Of course. Well, it's good to have you back.'

Rachel hurried off to see Frank, and tried to quell her anxiety at the question it was impossible not to ask: *Why was Elizabeth being so nice to her?*


Frank's office was bigger and less cluttered than the one he'd had in the old building where they'd been based before the buyout, but it still had some of the familiar paraphernalia. The various industry awards for successful public relations campaigns were lined up on a shelf next to the darts board, and in the corner there was a sign saying 'TIME' and the bell that he always threatened to ring if meetings went on for too long, though Rachel couldn't remember a single occasion when he had.

She rapped at the door and he looked up. He was one of those English gentleman types whose only conspicuous concession to ageing was going grey, which had turned him from a boyish charmer to a silver fox; he was always bright-eyed and fresh-faced, even first thing in the morning, though he did have a weakness for very strong espresso. She could smell coffee, and it looked as if he'd just had a breakfast pastry at his desk.

'Ah, Rachel. Yes, come on in, and shut the door behind you.'

*Was that a bad sign?* Any meeting that had to take place behind a closed door was potentially ominous.

He got up from his desk to greet her. He was only slightly taller than she was with her heels on, and not quite as broad as Mitch; he had the build of a still-lithe tennis player, whereas Mitch was more of a former rugby player.

But anyway, Mitch would hate it if he thought she was comparing them. There had been a time when he had teased her about fancying her boss, though it seemed like ages since he had teased her about anything.

And she didn't fancy Frank, obviously. She admired him, naturally; he'd set up his own business, he'd made a success of it, and he'd achieved an undisclosed, though presumably large, sum of money when he'd sold it to the conglomerate they now both worked for. Still, she had never countenanced the idea of being attracted to him. The only man she had ever had eyes for was Mitch, and anyway, Frank was too old for her, and he was her boss. That said, Frank was possibly the only man other than her husband who she had allowed herself to trust.

Frank gestured towards the meeting table in the corner; it was small and round and café-sized, with room for no more than four people to sit round it.

'Please, take a seat.'

She did, and he settled opposite her.

'How are you?' he said.

'I'm OK, thank you. Ready to crack on with things.'

'I don't doubt it,' he said. 'I suppose what I'm trying to ask is, are you fit?'

She shifted in her chair. 'You're not thinking of making us do some ghastly team-building physical challenge, are you? Because I can tell you right now, I'm not doing anything that involves putting on a wetsuit. Not for any charity under the sun.'

'I didn't mean it literally,' he said. 'I meant, are you sure you're fit to be here, back at work?'

'Frank, if I felt I needed more time I'd have taken it, as you've suggested.'

He contemplated her for a minute. 'Good,' he said. 'And as for the wetsuit, any decisions about future team-building exercises will be out of my hands.'

She gaped at him.

'You're not leaving.'

'I am. I'm taking early retirement. The only crucial task that's left for me to do is to talk to you about what *you* want. They're not planning to replace me, so in terms of organisation, if you stayed in your current role you'd be reporting directly to Elizabeth, with all the same responsibilities that you have at present. However, there is another position that I'd be very happy to recommend you for. Daniel Royce, who runs the regional network, is looking for someone to set up and run a new branch, specialising in exactly the same area that you've always worked on with me – supporting clients in the public sector. Does that sound like the kind of thing you might be interested in?'

'A new regional office? Where?'

He was trying to present it neutrally, but still, he winced as he said it: 'Cambridge.'

*Too far. Much too far.* 'I don't think I could, Frank. It would be an awful commute. Impossible.'

Frank sighed. 'I thought you might say that. But would you think it over, at least? In lots of ways it's a great opportunity. You'd have plenty of autonomy, and it should mean a significant pay rise – around a third more than you're getting now. Plus they'd be willing to pay relocation costs. I know it would be a lot of upheaval, but Cambridge isn't a bad place to live. And I really think you could make a go of it. You deserve this, Rachel. I'm just sorry to spring it on you at such a difficult time, and I do appreciate that it might not fit in with your personal life. But Daniel's impressed by what he's heard about you, and if you want it the job's pretty much yours. I just need to let him know sooner rather than later.'

'I see,' she said. 'To be honest, you've caught me completely by surprise.' She realised she was waving her hands helplessly in front of her, and put them firmly down on the table. 'It's been an intense couple of weeks, and I thought returning to work would make it feel like I was getting back to normal. But now it's all changing. I just… I can't quite believe you're going.'

'Neither can I,' he said gently. 'But the time comes when you have to move on. I realise it's been a very tough time for you, Rachel. But you shouldn't miss out on something because of a loss in your private life. You were a huge part of the success of my business, and I don't have any hesitation about putting you forward for a promotion.'

She was appalled to realise that she was not all that far off tears.

'Thank you,' she said.

'Think it over,' Frank told her. 'Talk about it with Mitch.' He glanced at the photograph on his desk, a graduation day snap with his ex-wife on one side, his older daughter in a mortar board in the middle and the younger daughter outsmiling everybody else. 'I know how much your family matters to you. Mine always complained that I worked too much.'

'Mitch won't like it,' Rachel said.

He looked at her directly. He had seen her day in, day out, for years. He would notice the heavier than usual make-up, the signs of fatigue.

'You have to make the decision that's right for you, and that means what works for your family,' he said. 'There'll be other opportunities, and life isn't just about scaling hierarchies. You have a valuable contribution to make, whatever you choose to do.'

His hand darted forward and plucked something from behind her ear. He held it out to show her: it was a bit of cherry blossom.

'What have you been doing, rolling round in the garden?' he asked, getting up to drop the blossom in the waste-paper basket.

'Something a bit like that,' she said. 'Anyway, what are you going to do with yourself now? You must have plans. I've never known you not have plans.'

'Oh, I do, believe me. The only problem is going to be fitting everything in.'

'I'm going to miss you,' she said.

'I'm sure we'll keep in touch. If you have time, that is. Let me know what you decide.'

He went back to his desk, and she realised the meeting was over and got to her feet.

'Rachel?'

He was holding something out to her in a paper bag.

'Hang in there,' he said, and handed it over.

She didn't need to look inside to know that it would be her favourite Danish pastry, with cinnamon and icing on top. Whenever they'd had a particularly tough deadline to meet or a disappointment or a success, Frank brought in breakfast for the team. This time it was just for her.

'Thank you,' she said, touched her fingers to her forehead in salute, and withdrew.

*

When she got home that evening Mitch was in the kitchen, taking a beer out of the fridge. Probably his second. He always cooked with a beer to hand. He and Becca had already eaten; the dirty dishes were still on the table, with stray peas and ketchup clinging to them. Mitch had given up on waiting for Rachel to get home for dinner years ago, after one spoiled meal and hungry Becca tantrum too many.

'Where's Becca?'

'Showering.' Mitch took the cap off his beer bottle and dropped it by the dirty dishes. 'Then we're going to have a Wii tournament. Care to join us?'

'I have some work to catch up on, actually.'

'Ah, you're just afraid we'll thrash you. Beer?'

'Not for me. Like I said, I've got some work to do.'

'Suit yourself.'

She took the least dirty pan off the hob – he must have used it for the peas – and took it over to the sink. There was ancient, ingrained limescale round the taps, and the trim between the worksurface and the splashback was alternately stained and, where she had attempted to scrub it clean, scratched.

They'd always intended to redo this kitchen. They still hadn't got round to it.

'Rachel,' Mitch said. 'What's up?'

She put the saucepan back on the hob, put the kettle on to boil water for pasta and turned to face him. He was leaning against the fridge, nursing his beer.

'Nothing's up,' she said. 'Frank's taking early retirement, and I've been offered a promotion. It would mean more money. Quite a bit more money. But it's based in Cambridge.'

Mitch couldn't disguise his shock. His face was a mask of astonishment: mouth downturned and tight like a child faced with a disagreeable dinner, eyebrows raised.

He said, 'Are you interested?'

'It's got to be worth thinking about. It might mean you could give up doing the commissions and imitations. Go back to doing your own work.'

He composed himself, ran a hand through his hair, folded his arms across his body and raised the beer to his lips again, then held the bottle close to his chest.

'I don't mind the stuff I'm doing,' he said. 'OK, it's not going to do anything for my reputation, but the art world has pretty much forgotten I exist anyway.'

'But, Mitch, you have so much talent. You should be making the most of it. Remember what that art critic said about you, after you did the *Persephone* painting? *One of the most promising* enfants terribles *on the block?*'

'Yeah, but I'm not an *enfant* any more, not by any stretch, and I think I'm well past the point at which I ceased to be promising,' Mitch said. 'Anyway, this isn't about me, it's about you. I don't think you want to do this. I think you know this new job would be too much for you. And you're looking for me to say no to give you an easy way out.'

She found the nearly empty packet of dried pasta in a chaotic cupboard, tipped it into the saucepan, covered it with water from the just-boiled kettle and lit the gas. Her fingers came away greasy from contact with the dial.

'It's not just about me,' she said. 'It's about all of us. Since we're mainly dependent on my income.'

'Ooh, the breadwinner card,' he said. 'Well, I honestly don't know why you're asking me then. Why don't you just go ahead and do what you want?'

She closed her eyes and counted to ten, unclenched her fists, opened her eyes and forced herself to look at him.

'Because I care what you think,' she said.

'Do you?'

She nodded, and he visibly relaxed, found a space on the work surface behind him for his beer, and held out his arms to her.

'Come here,' he said, and she did, and he embraced her and drew her close.

'I've been worried about you, you know,' he said. 'You've had so much on your plate lately. And you haven't been sleeping. You know, you should go to the doctor about that. But I bet you haven't made an appointment yet. Have you?'

She shook her head.

'Look, if you really want to do it we'll make it work – but we need to find out what Becca thinks. It's just come as a bit of a shock, that's all. Sleep on it, see what you think in the morning, OK? I just feel like you're on some kind of edge right now. And I really don't want to find myself picking up the pieces.'

'You know I can't do any of it without you,' she said.

'*Eww.*' Becca had appeared at the kitchen door, her hair wet from the shower, already in her pyjamas and dressing-gown. 'Do you have to?'

Mitch released Rachel, and Becca grudgingly permitted her mother a brief embrace.

Rachel asked, 'How was your day, sweetheart?'

'Good. I'm all ready, Dad – how about it?'

'Prepare to meet thy doom,' Mitch said. Becca whooped and charged off and he grinned at Rachel and followed her, still clutching his beer.

Rachel found a jar of pesto at the back of the fridge. Mouldy. Sometimes her diet these days was not much better than when she first left home. And even if she did accept the chance of promotion, that was probably something that wouldn't change.

The next morning she went into Frank's office and told him that she was grateful for his support and encouragement, but had decided she would prefer to remain in her current role.

And almost instantly, as he began to tell her he understood her decision, she regretted it.

# Chapter Twenty-Three

## Becca

The last time Becca had been in Amelia Chadstone's bedroom had been just after the thing that happened on her thirteenth birthday – that's how she and her father have come to refer to it, *the thing that happened*, the least painful, most evasive description possible.

Thankfully, Amelia hasn't referred to it at all; the only thing they've talked about is the disco. At least they've both got their outfits sorted. Amelia's discarded clothes are scattered all around, an incongruous contrast to her pink-and-white bedroom; she's going through a phase of liking black and grey and things with rips or zips or both, while her room has pale candy-striped wallpaper and a big, exquisitely detailed dolls' house in one corner. Maybe the décor is Mrs Chadstone's choice? Or maybe it suits Amelia for her parents to keep on thinking that at heart, she's still a little girl.

Becca offers to help Amelia put her stuff away, but Amelia says not to bother, that's what mums are for. She has been sitting in front of her lit-up dressing-table mirror for the last half-hour, doing her hair and make-up; Becca is sitting cross-legged on the bed. The air reeks of perfume.

'That'll do,' Amelia says, and pouts at her reflection. 'Now it's *your* turn.'

She gets up, picks up her schoolbag, takes the exercise books out of it and puts them on her desk. Then she kneels on the rug at Becca's feet, upends the bag and shakes it. A slew of small objects spill out: nail varnishes, a tube of highlighter, a Curly Wurly bar.

'You don't really wear make-up, do you?' Amelia says. She looks immaculate; her skin is impossibly flawless, her eyebrows perfect arches.

'I'm not very good at putting it on,' Becca admits.

Amelia picks out a lip gloss and sits down next to Becca on the bed. 'Here. Let me.'

She opens her mouth wide to show what she needs Becca to do, and Becca copies her, then Amelia puts the lip gloss on her, then pulls back to inspect her handiwork.

'Not bad. You've got quite a nice mouth, actually,' she says, and puts the cap back on.

Becca says, 'Did you seriously nick all of that stuff just while we were in Kettlebridge today?'

Amelia rolls her eyes.

'Aren't you scared you'll get into trouble?'

'Of course. That's what makes it fun. I could teach you, if you like.'

'No, thanks. It's just way too predictable to turn into a juvenile delinquent if you already come from a broken home.'

'You're only a delinquent if you get caught,' Amelia says, and stoops on the rug to gather everything up. 'Here, do you want this? I've already got loads.'

She holds out the lip gloss to Becca, who shakes her head. She's reluctant to become a receiver for stolen goods – even from Amelia Chadstone.

Amelia shrugs. 'Suit yourself.'

She drops her haul into her desk drawer, then rounds on Becca with a suspicious expression.

'You're not going to go all judgey on me, are you?'

'I don't think so. I'm not particularly judgey. I mean… I try to keep an open mind.'

Which is true. She has to. Dad had said, *Your mother messed up and she knows it, but she's trying to do better. Try not to be too harsh on her.* And she had tried. She was still trying.

'It's just that the mark-up on all that stuff is ridiculous,' Amelia says. 'You'd have to be an idiot to pay full price for it all. You're not going to tell on me, are you?'

'Like who am I going to tell?'

'I don't know. Not your mum, I guess. But you're kind of pally with your dad, aren't you?'

'Up to a point. I don't tell him everything. I don't tell anybody everything.'

'Little Miss Mysterious. Well, don't you want to see what you look like?'

'Like a slut, I expect,' Becca says.

'You *don't* look like a slut, and as your make-up artist I have to say I'm very offended by that remark. You just look like a slightly fitter version of your usual self.'

Becca gets up and examines her reflection in Amelia's full-length bedroom mirror.

'Well,' she says. 'You don't think it's too much?'

She *does* look different. It's partly the lip gloss; also, she's wearing the new red top Amelia had talked her into buying when they went round the shops after school. It's a bit tighter and shorter than anything Becca usually wears, and shows a good two inches of skin above the waistband of her jeans.

Actually, she doesn't look too bad, actually. She looks older – much older than thirteen; maybe fifteen at least.

'You look hot,' Amelia says firmly.

'Everyone will think I'm desperate to get off with someone.'

'Yeah, well, why shouldn't you? Not that there's going to be much choice tonight. The St George's boys are all totally boring.'

She retrieves her phone from the desk, puts an arm around Becca's shoulders and draws her in, and raises her hand in a self-reflecting salute. There they are in miniature, framed by the perimeter of the screen; the blonde in black and the brunette in red, ready for a good time. They look as if they've deliberately coordinated their outfits.

Amelia is wearing skinny jeans too, and a similar top, though hers is a black T-shirt with a picture of a skull surrounded by red roses, and '*Rock forever*' written round it in gothic script.

Amelia pulls away and taps at the screen of her phone.

'There we are – sneak preview for the squad,' she says. 'I hope you're ready to make an entrance. They are not going to *believe it* when they see you.' She slips her phone into the back pocket of her jeans and looks Rachel up and down. 'You know, you have *lots* of potential.'

'Oh, yeah? As what?'

Amelia shrugs again. 'Whatever you want.' She takes the Curly Wurly bar out of the drawer, unwraps it and offers a piece to Becca, who hesitates, then takes it.

'Won't it mess up my lip gloss?'

'Plenty more where that came from.'

They eat in companionable silence. Amelia scrunches up the sweet wrapper and puts it in her pocket.

'I'll have to throw it out when we get to school,' she says. 'If Mum sees that in my bin she'll kick off. She doesn't like me spending my pocket money on sweets. Little does she know, eh? You know, the main reason is that I never really wanted to be friends with you is because Mum was always so keen on the idea. I suppose it's because my parents knew your parents like a million years ago, and it makes her feel young again or something. Or maybe it's because your parents split up and that makes her feel better about still being married to my dad.' She catches sight of Becca's face and grimaces. 'Sorry. I don't mean to be a bitch. It's not exactly like their relationship is some grand romance, anyway. I think she's really married to this house, not him. If he wasn't away so much, I have no idea if they'd still even be together.'

Becca sighs. 'Yeah, well.'

'Do you hate talking about it?'

'I don't know. Mostly no one asks. Thanks for not telling anybody at school about what happened.'

'Some things are best kept quiet, right? I thought you probably wouldn't like it if it got out.'

'No. Definitely not.'

'Anyway, don't be surprised if my mum starts asking you a load of nosy questions. She's always asking about you. It drives me crazy. Like how are you getting on, have things settled down, all of that. She's more interested in you than she is in me.'

'What do you tell her?'

'Nothing really. That's the point with mums, isn't it? You can't pay them too much attention. It spoils them. You know, I think the other reason she wanted me to be friends with you was that she thought you'd be a good influence. It's because you seem so nice and quiet. Well, that's what people think, anyway.'

'Little do *they* know.'

'Exactly.' Amelia gives her an approving smile.

Becca thinks of the awkward talk she'd had with Dad after he got called into school for that meeting with Mum, the questions he'd felt obliged to ask: was she still feeling upset about the thing that had happened in the autumn? Was seeing Mum bothering her? Would she be willing to think again about giving counselling a go?

She could have answered him honestly. She could have said it was absolutely nothing to do with either of her parents, and that actually, since she'd starting hanging out with Amelia, her studies had become much less appealing. But she hadn't. She had said, 'You two are always on about counselling. I told you already I don't want to go. It's not like it's going to put things back the way they were, is it?' And then she had stomped off to her room. She had left him feeling guilty because that was easier by far than disillusioning him.

Though actually, he probably just blames her mother. And you could argue that she deserves it.

Amelia goes over to her chest of drawers and retrieves a pack of ten cigarettes and a lighter, which she slips into her bra.

'You're not seriously going to smoke at the school disco,' Becca says.

'I might if it's really boring. Don't worry, I'm not going to corrupt you. Unless you really want me to.'

'But won't your mum notice if you come home smelling of smoke?'

'No, because she smokes herself. Three a day, in the evenings, though she doesn't know I know. Come on, we'd better go down. She'll be waiting, and she'll probably want to take photos. She has to have something to put on Facebook so it looks as if she has a life. Don't worry, she won't take any of you, not unless she's asked both your parents' permission, and as far as I know she hasn't actually spoken to your mother since… since the thing, has she?'

'I don't think so, not really. Dad said it was pretty bad when they both came to see *Oliver!* I mean, nothing happened, but they avoided each other, basically. Anyway, I guess they'll have to try and be nice when Mum picks me up tomorrow,' Becca says.

'Awks,' Amelia comments.

'Awks,' Becca agrees. 'So is my lip gloss all right?'

'Sure is,' Amelia says, and they go downstairs together.

*

Amelia turns out to be right about the photos, which take forever because Amelia keeps pulling faces her mother really doesn't want her to pull, or at least, doesn't want to put on Facebook. Eventually a suitable one is taken and uploaded ('You look so nice when you smile,' Mrs Chadstone says, 'I don't know why you couldn't just do that the first time,') and they're on their way.

The school hall is already crowded, and a few girls have ventured onto the dance floor. It's dark, so Becca's outfit doesn't attract quite as much attention as Amelia had anticipated. It is just like when she was in *Oliver!* She had thought that would change things – that she would at least become *the girl who sings*, rather than *the quiet girl nobody really notices* – but the only difference that had made was that she had got to know Amelia better.

And now, once again, Becca has ended up on the outside of a loose cohort of her classmates, playing the onlooker, while Amelia is somewhere in the middle, in the thick of it.

Well, what did she expect?

The disco reminds her a bit of the dances in the Jane Austen adaptations her mum used to sometimes want to watch together on a Sunday – except at least in those days they had dance cards and steps you could learn, and this is just a pool of girls from St Anne's and a pool of boys from St George's, milling about and attempting to merge. Still, on the plus side, it's too noisy to talk, which means there's no point in attempting to make conversation and therefore no risk of being rebuffed. And it's dark, which means it's less obvious that she's on her own.

Meanwhile, Amelia seems to have forgotten her completely. Some boy or other has made an entirely predictable beeline for her; he is tall, and not all that good-looking, but radiates a kind of masculine cockiness that Becca has already decided to find irritating. Amelia is gazing up at him and toying with her hair as if he's Michelangelo's *David* and a superhero rolled into one; nauseatingly, she even lets him hold her hand. Everybody notices, of course, and at one point they slip out together, only to return some time later looking smug.

Slowly, tortuously, the disco proceeds towards the inevitable conclusion: the slow dance. It should be cheesy, the kind of thing that she and Amelia would laugh about later. But actually it's torment, because Amelia is part of it and all Becca can do is watch.

It's not that she really wants to dance like that with anybody. So close! It's creepy and embarrassing. But it would have been nice to be asked, if only so she could say no.

Amelia's just showing off, anyway. She can't possibly be loving it as much as she's making out. Not with that annoying boy.

The song finishes and the lights come up; some of the newly minted couples spring apart as if released by a mechanism, others appear to be glued together. Amelia and her new friend stay locked in a tight embrace, her face buried in his shoulder. It is not possible to tell if her eyes are closed, but Becca is willing to bet that they're not – or not entirely. Amelia wouldn't be Amelia if she didn't take the chance to peek at the effect she's having.

She turns her back on them and goes off to get her coat. The hall reeks of sweat and perfume: she needs fresh air. And anyway, she'd rather wait for Mrs Chadstone by herself than have to watch Amelia being happy any longer.

\*

She makes her way to the exit nearest the car park, which is already busy, illuminated by headlights and filled with the quiet growl of waiting cars. Overhead there is a thin slice of moon, and patches of scattered stars are revealed and then obscured again as clouds move across them. The cool night is a sharp contrast to the stuffy heat of the hall, and Becca puts up the hood of her parka and wishes that both Mrs Chadstone and Amelia would show up as soon as possible, and preferably at the same time.

If Amelia appears first she'll have to pretend she didn't mind being abandoned, and if it's Mrs Chadstone she'll probably have to go back in the hall and drag Amelia away from her new boyfriend. She doesn't really fancy either option.

She stands at a slight distance from a group of girls who are waiting for their parents to arrive and discussing everybody else.

Millie Parker-Jones says, 'Did you see Amelia with Ollie Pickering?'

Amanda Cheam asks, 'Do you know him?'

'A bit,' Millie tells her. 'His brother used to play cricket with my brother.'

Verity Hoddle chips in: 'Did you see them go out together?'

'We *all* saw that,' Amanda says.

'Are they going out now, then?' Verity says. 'They must have kissed at least.'

'More than that, from what I heard,' Amanda says. She drops her voice. 'She *touched* it.'

Verity cries out, 'Ugh, no!' and Millie explodes into disbelieving giggles.

Becca flips her hood down. 'Amelia wouldn't do that,' she says. All three girls turn and stare at her.

'What do you know, anyway?' Verity says. 'You're not even friends. She just feels sorry for you.'

At that point a long adult shadow falls between them. It's Mrs Chadstone, looming over them all.

'Becca – why don't you come and wait in the car? I presume Amelia is on her way?'

The other three girls look sheepish. 'Um,' Becca says, 'I think so.'

She can't help but feel as if she has just won some kind of victory as she follows Mrs Chadstone to her Range Rover, leaving the girls behind her to change the subject and find fault with someone else.

*

'Why don't you sit in the front with me?' Mrs Chadstone says as she unlocks the car. Becca does, though she wonders if Amelia will mind that her rightful place has been usurped. Still, it serves her right for being late.

Mrs Chadstone is wearing a green quilted jacket and knee-high boots; she looks as if she's just come from riding horses, but very clean, freshly perfumed, obedient ones who she has been able to manage without getting so much as a hair out of place. But then, she always looks like that, and Amelia says her mum doesn't ride any more and Amelia doesn't either. It's just a look. A convincing one, though.

'I've never been in one of these before,' Becca says.

'I beg your pardon?'

'A Range Rover.'

'Oh. Yes. Do you like it?'

'Um... yeah.'

There is a pause. *Awks*, as Amelia might say. Which might be the kind of thing Mrs Chadstone would say, too. Amelia probably wouldn't want to hear this, but Becca wonders if mother and daughter might be more alike than they think.

'Thank you for the lift,' Becca says. 'And for having me to stay.'

'You're very welcome. I'm glad you felt able to accept the invitation. I think it was rather brave of you, after... after what happened.'

*OK. Here we go.* Becca is grateful to Amelia for having forewarned her. And at the same time she's annoyed with her for not being here to come to the rescue.

'Oh... it's fine.'

'Good. Because I want you to feel welcome. I know it can't have been easy for you. Since... you know. How is your mother doing these days?'

'She's OK. She's got a new job. I don't know what she's doing, exactly, but it's somewhere nearby. She met some new people. So I think that's helping.'

'Oh! New people? What kind of new people?'

Is she fishing to find out if Mum has a new boyfriend? Becca is tempted to say, *none of your business*, because it isn't, really, but you can't say that to a grown-up. As it happens, Mum has talked quite a bit about her two new friends: one who she works with and who makes jewellery and stuff as a hobby, and one who's really old and bakes a lot of cakes. Mum has even started driving the older one, Viv, for like an hour each way every Sunday to see her son, who's got something wrong with him and lives in an institution. It doesn't sound like much fun to Becca, but she can tell it makes her mum happy. It seems better than a new boyfriend, in a way: less likely to get dramatic. And it's a change: in the old days, when her mum worked in London, she never had much time for hanging out with friends.

But Becca doesn't feel like explaining this to Mrs Chadstone. She doesn't know why not, exactly – it just seems like it would be the wrong thing to do.

'I don't really know much about them,' she says.

'Well, do you know how she met them? Is it like a self-help group or something? I know people with the kind of problems your mum had often find those quite useful.'

'Actually, I think she got to know one of them through work.'

'Oh, I see. That must be nice for her. I assume they're all women, these friends? Or is it like a mixed group?'

'Like I said, I don't know,' Becca says. She vaguely remembers Mum saying something about Leona's friend Mark who's gay, but that doesn't seem like the kind of thing Mrs Chadstone needs to know either. 'I guess I wasn't really paying attention.'

Mrs Chadstone sighs. 'Well, that's great news. Your dad must be relieved that she's doing so much better. And tell me, how's he getting on?'

'He's fine, you know, same as ever.'

'Is he? Well, good for him. You know, your parents and I go back a long way.'

'Yeah, I know.'

'I don't suppose you know what set your mother off, do you?'

'Not really.'

This also feels like something else she probably shouldn't go into. But then again, why not? It's not like she's been sworn to secrecy or anything, and Mrs Chadstone has always been really nice to her, even after the thing that happened on Becca's birthday. Not that they had talked much immediately after that, stuck in that awful, crowded waiting room while people stitched Daddy up on the other side of the double doors.

Mrs Chadstone stays quiet, as if she's waiting to see what Becca will say next. Sitting here in the front seat, with a grown-up really listening to her – as if what she has to say is important, and interesting, and worth being patient for – Becca suddenly feels reckless. Why not just tell the truth? It's not as if Mum will ever know that she's had this conversation, anyway.

'I guess, you know, it started after my grandmother died,' she says. 'We didn't use to see all that much of her, but it was still a big thing. And then Mum had some stuff going on at work. But as for what made her behave like that… I don't know. To be honest, we haven't really talked about it.'

Is it disloyal to tell Mrs Chadstone this? Probably. But at the same time, it's a weird kind of relief.

'I think she's too ashamed to talk about it,' Becca continues. 'Maybe one day she'll try and explain. I don't know. I'm not actually sure that she understands it all herself. I think she's probably just trying to put it behind her.'

'Mm. Well, look, I think the thing to remember is that you *can* get over these things, however enormous they may seem at the time.'

'Could you?'

'I'm sorry?'

'I mean, if what happened to my mum happened to you… if you lost your home, and your job, and your health, and your family, do you think you could get over it?'

'Mm.' Mrs Chadstone raps her fingernails on the steering wheel. 'I suppose I haven't really thought about it like that.'

'She lost all the things that made her her,' Becca persists. She doesn't know where this sudden impulse to defend her mother has come from, but she's on a roll now.

The back door of the Range Rover opens and Amelia gets into the car. 'What did I miss?'

Mrs Chadstone turns to face her and makes a point of checking her watch. 'So nice of you to join us. What kept you?'

'I thought I ought to help tidy up,' Amelia says angelically.

'Oh, really? And I suppose Becca just didn't feel like helping?'

'I didn't, actually,' Becca replies. 'Helping's really not my thing. But Amelia seems to be pretty keen on it.'

Amelia giggles. Mrs Chadstone sighs and starts the car.

*

That night Becca can't sleep.

It's not because of the put-you-up bed that Mrs Chadstone has made up for her in Amelia's bedroom. She's perfectly comfortable, or would be if she could relax enough to drop off.

Next to her, Amelia is sleeping quietly and peacefully. If only Becca could do the same... but she's both tired out and wide awake, and the night seems to go on forever.

It's not because of her failure to interest anybody at the disco despite all Amelia's efforts – though that does make her wonder what on earth is wrong with her. It's not even anything to do with the slightly weird conversation with Mrs Chadstone.

No: what haunts her is the memory of the thing that happened on her thirteenth birthday, right here at the Chadstones' house, and the look on her mum's face afterwards when they were back home and she came down into the kitchen and saw them eating the birthday cake, and said: *I'm going now.*

And then she had left, and it had both been what Becca wanted and not what she wanted at all.

# Chapter Twenty-Four

## Rachel

The Chadstones live on the outskirts of Kettlebridge in a large Georgian house that is easy to miss if you don't know exactly when to turn. It's set back from the road behind a high wall, and partially concealed by the tall old trees in the front garden. Rachel can never remember what it's called, but it's something tasteful and suggestive of space and greenery, like Lawn House or Ivy Place or The Chestnuts.

She thinks of it as the House with Two Staircases. Once upon a time there would have been servants living there, people like her great-grandmother who had been in service and married the coachman. Now there is just plenty of space and whatever discreet help Mary hires in to keep everything immaculate.

Rachel hadn't known anyone who lived in a house like this when she was growing up. Becca seems to take it for granted, and Rachel both finds this disconcerting and is secretly pleased about it. Becca will be able to take wealthy people in her stride; she won't be fazed by them. She won't have to school herself not to be dazzled or intimidated, to see past the glow of money to the person on the other side.

Mary had married Hugh as soon as they'd both graduated; it had been a big, traditional white wedding in a church in Oxfordshire, not far from Kettlebridge, all paid for by the father of the bride. Mary's dad was a stockbroker, the same line of work Hugh had gone into, and even looked like Hugh, just older and fatter; Mitch and

Rachel had both been struck by the physical resemblance. But he had given a long, affectionate speech about his daughter, and Rachel, who hadn't expected to be touched by it, had ended up in tears. Also to her surprise, she had been impressed and moved by Mary and Hugh's obvious devotion. She had come away wanting what they had – not the fancy wedding, but the sureness, the security. And Mitch must have felt the same, because he had proposed not long afterwards.

Mary and Hugh had been the first of Rachel and Mitch's peers to get married, and the first to start a family; when Rachel got pregnant, Mary and Hugh had been the only other couple they knew who already had a child. Henry had been a toddler then, and Amelia had arrived soon after Becca. Mary had never gone back to work, though – she'd briefly been in public relations, same as Rachel, before giving it up for family life.

Rachel sometimes wondered if Mary minded having never really got her career off the ground. Her day-to-day life seemed impossibly leisured, a round of lunches and shopping and sessions at the gym. But perhaps, deep down, she was bored.

It wasn't the kind of thing they ever talked about, though. They had never become close; neither of them had ever quite let down their guards. Of course they had got off on the wrong foot to begin with. Maybe things would have been different – easier – if Rachel hadn't overheard that conversation at that long-ago party. And maybe not. They'd made an effort for Hugh and Mitch's sake, and later on, because the girls were in school together. But it had never come naturally.

And as for Hugh – he had always been perfectly friendly, but whenever Rachel ended up talking to him it was like trying to communicate with someone from a different species. He commuted to London, too, and she still sometimes saw him on the train or in the Barrowton station car park, though there was a mutual, unspoken understanding that while they would greet each other in passing, they were not obliged to make conversation.

What a relief it had been to get to know Viv and Leona... To have friends of her own, who knew her as she was now and accepted her completely. It was astonishing how quickly they had both become embedded in the routine of her life: Leona at work during the week and Viv on Sundays, which otherwise would have been a miserable comedown after the precious Saturdays with Becca. Viv and Leona were her antidote to loneliness. She'd taken to spending her lunchbreak at work with Leona more often than not, going to the weekly yoga class at the business park gym, or strolling round the grounds, talking about current affairs – Leona was more political than she was and had strong opinions on almost everything, from global warming to prison reform. You couldn't talk about TV with Leona because she never watched it, but you could with Viv, who had a secret weakness for soaps and really twisty thrillers... The three of them complement each other. Or so she likes to think.

But then, she has still never explained properly to Viv and Leona what she had done to make Becca reject her. And Mary had been there when it happened.

No wonder Viv and Leona are easy for her to talk to. They still don't really know her. And Mary does.

Last time she had come to the Chadstones' house it had been early autumn, though she had been oblivious to the colours of the leaves. Now it is spring, and there is blossom everywhere and she barely notices that either. She's returning to the scene of the crime, and it fills her with shame.

*

She parks in a corner of the broad gravelled area in front of the house, which is almost filled with the Chadstone family's cars. Hugh must be at home; his Jag is parked next to Mary's Range Rover. He'll probably stay out of the way and leave it Mary to handle her, though he might be listening out, ready to intervene if needed.

The shiny new Mini must be Henry's. No doubt Hugh and Mary will get Amelia a car of her own, too, when she's old enough. It seems highly unlikely that she and Mitch will be able to afford one for Becca – Rachel can barely cover the costs of running a car for herself – but maybe things will have picked up by then, who knows. And anyway, Becca will have the use of Rachel's car, and Mitch's, and somehow or other they'll scrape together money for driving lessons.

Maybe Becca will get a Saturday job, same as Rachel did as a teenager, and pay some of the costs herself. It wouldn't do her any harm… would probably be good for her. The main thing is to encourage her. Not to be like Rachel's dad, who had said there was no point Rachel wasting her earnings because she'd never pass her test.

The crunch of her footsteps as she makes her way to the front door is as loud as a warning signal, as if she were a would-be intruder whose bad intentions have already been foiled.

It's Mary who answers, looking fresh as a daisy. Botox? Or maybe it's just lots of sleep and a happy marriage and a clean conscience.

'Hi, Rachel, good to see you. Come on in,' Mary says, with a consciously gracious smile.

Rachel's instinct is to decline and bolt for the safety of the car. But she can hardly refuse when Mary is being so magnanimous. She puts her right hand to her left wrist, pinches hard, and steps in.

The hallway is sweet with the scent of the huge bouquet of spring flowers standing on a mahogany side table. Hanging on the wall to one side, back in place, is the watercolour of the garden at Rose Cottage that Mitch had done the previous winter. There's no sign of any damage; you'd never know that it had ever come to any grief.

She's glad to see that it is intact. It's one less thing to feel remorseful about.

'The girls are just about up and dressed. They haven't been terribly lively this morning,' Mary says. After a pause that is just short enough not to be rude, but just long enough to let Rachel know she's not expected to accept, she adds: 'Can I offer you anything? Cup of tea? Coffee?'

'Oh, no, we should be heading off.'

Mary's smile has more than a hint of relief in it. Rachel imagines her telling some friend or other about it later: *Poor woman. It's so difficult. I really didn't know what to say to her.*

She makes a conscious effort to remember her manners. 'Thank you so much for having Becca to stay, and for picking her up last night.'

'Absolute pleasure. Becca's welcome here any time, Rachel. I really want you to know that. They seem to have had a fun evening.'

'Oh good,' Rachel says. She had messaged Becca to ask if she'd enjoyed the disco, but hadn't received a response.

'They looked gorgeous,' Mary says. 'See, I took some photos.'

She picks up a smartphone from the side table and shows Rachel a couple of snaps. Amelia is pouting and posing, her arm flung coercively around Becca's shoulders. It's obvious that Becca didn't really want to be photographed, but in other ways she looks quite different to her usual self; she's wearing shiny lip gloss, and a tight red top Rachel doesn't recognise.

'I put a couple of Amelia online, but you don't really do Facebook these days, do you? I'll email them to you,' Mary says.

'Thanks,' Rachel says.

'So how's everything with you?' Mary asks, adopting an encouraging, receptive expression. 'Is there a new romance in your life, by any chance? Becca mentioned that you've made some new friends.'

Why has Becca been talking to Mary about her? And why is Mary so interested, anyway? It's almost as if she *wants* Rachel to be seeing someone else. As if that would be a sign that she really had moved on, and had once more become a fully functioning member of the human race.

*Suck it up*, Rachel tells herself. *Don't make a scene.*

'Yeah, not that kind of friend.'

'Oh well. Maybe in time. Good for you, anyway. It all sounds really *constructive*.' She drops her voice. 'And how's Becca doing? Hugh mentioned that Mitch had told him there had been some issues at school.'

Once again Rachel has to suppress her reflex reaction, which is to object to Becca's problems having become pillow talk for the Chadstones. Of course Hugh and Mitch talk… surely that's a good thing? They've always gone for the occasional drink together. But she has generally assumed that they talk about nothing much, or at least nothing personal, and that this is part of the point: that what they both get out of the friendship is an easy, undemanding companionship that doesn't involve discussing or analysing anything emotional – that is actually a rest from all that.

'I think Becca's doing OK now, actually,' Rachel says. 'I mean, there were some concerns. But it all seems to be going the right way.'

'Oh good. Good. It's always worrying when there are these little blips, isn't it?' Mary reaches out and squeezes Rachel's arm. 'You know, it's great to see you doing so much better.'

Becca comes downstairs, her schoolbag hanging off one shoulder; she's also carrying an overnight bag Rachel doesn't recognise. She averts her face from Rachel's gaze as if she can't bear to look at her. Amelia, groomed and golden as ever, is just behind her, her eyes glued to the screen of her phone as she walks down the stairs.

'God, Ollie just liked *another* of my pictures,' Amelia announces. 'Mum, I think I might have actually got myself a stalker.'

'Don't be silly, dear,' Mary says. 'Stalking's actually a very serious offence. Ollie Pickering is a very nice boy who just happens to have taken a shine to you.'

'Ollie Pickering needs to learn how to play it cool,' Amelia mutters, then, to Becca: 'Come here, you.'

She draws Becca into a flamboyant embrace, then withdraws almost instantly and turns back to her phone.

'See you Monday,' Amelia says without looking up.

'Darling, you're not posting *another* picture, are you?' Mary says.

'Well, you'll be able to see for yourself, won't you? Since you insist on stalking me, too.'

Becca turns away. 'See you,' she says gruffly. 'Thanks for having me, Mrs Chadstone.'

'It's a pleasure, dear,' Mary says.

'Thanks, Mary. I guess I'll see you around,' Rachel says. She holds the front door open for Becca, who barely acknowledges her on the way out, and then makes her escape.

'I can carry your bag,' she says as she catches up with Becca.

'No need,' Becca says, with a sullen glance.

A crunching sound announces the arrival of somebody else: Henry Chadstone, dressed in running clothes and sweating lightly. He veers across the gravel towards them and comes to a halt by the car.

'Hey, Becca,' he says. 'Morning, Mrs Moran.'

Becca manages a small sound of acknowledgment, but otherwise seems to be completely tongue-tied and doesn't respond to Henry's slightly nervous smile.

What must this boy think of Rachel after what he'd seen last time she was here? And Amelia, too – but Amelia had just ignored her, and Henry's impeccable politeness is more of a challenge.

'Morning, Henry,' she says. 'Been far?'

'Did the loop down to Kettlebridge lock,' Henry tells her, and starts stretching out his hamstrings.

'That's a good run,' Rachel says. 'Well, enjoy the rest of the weekend.'

'Yes, you too.'

Rachel unlocks the car and goes to take Becca's overnight bag, but Becca resists and puts it in the boot herself before getting in the passenger seat. Rachel settles beside her as Henry disappears into the house. She says, 'So how was it last night? Did you have a good time?'

'It was all right. It wasn't that great,' Becca says. 'Mum, I'm actually not feeling too good.'

'Oh, I'm sorry – what's up?'

'I didn't sleep very well, and I just got my period,' Becca says. 'I know we're meant to be having a day out and everything, but I think I might need to go home and go to bed.'

*Well, she does look pale. This isn't necessarily just a ruse to get out of spending time together. Or a reaction to being back at the Chadstones' house after what had happened here in the autumn...*

Maybe Rachel should be pleased that Becca doesn't feel obliged to put a brave face on things and soldier on, and is willing to tell her how she's feeling. Becca is private to a fault – once she'd started her periods, she was reluctant to discuss the subject with Rachel ever again, all the more so once Rachel had left the family home. Becca certainly showed no signs of wanting or needing her mother's support; if she did, it had been even more important to her not to admit it.

'Are you sure?' Rachel says. 'You can come back to mine and curl up on the sofa and we can watch TV together, if you like.'

But Becca shakes her head. 'I'm sorry, I just want my own bed,' she says, and there is an edge to her voice that suggests she's not all that far from bursting into tears.

'OK, sure, whatever you want. I'll just let your dad know.'

Rachel takes out her phone, makes the call. She's conscious that Mary must be aware that they're still parked in the forecourt, and is probably wondering why they haven't left yet.

Mitch picks up almost straight away and says, 'What is it?'

'Hi... Becca's not feeling very well. She wants to come home and go to bed. Is that OK?'

There is a pause.

'Sure,' Mitch says. 'Sure, if that's what she wants. Look, can I speak to her?'

Rachel passes over the phone. Becca listens to her father and then says, 'It was fine, Dad. Don't fuss. I'll see you soon, OK? Love you. Bye.'

She ends the call and passes the phone back to Rachel.

'Sorry, Mum,' she says. 'It's just… I don't really feel up to it, that's all.'

'You don't have to feel up to anything to spend time with me,' Rachel says, but Becca doesn't reply.

They drive back to Rose Cottage in silence. It is only when they're finally parked in front of Rose Cottage that Rachel finally blurts out, 'Was it OK for you, being back there?'

'You mean at Amelia's house?' Becca says. 'Sure it was OK. Why wouldn't it be? It's fine, Mum. Don't worry about it. It's almost like nothing ever happened.'

Becca gets out of the car and opens the boot. Rachel hurries to her side and says, 'At least let me carry your stuff.'

Becca shrugs and stands back, and Rachel takes her things to the doorstep of Rose Cottage, where Mitch is standing with his arms folded, waiting to let Becca in.

He has on the blue canvas fisherman's smock that he wears over his clothes when he is painting; there is a dab of fresh cadmium yellow on his sleeve. He smells, faintly but unmistakeably, of linseed oil and turpentine, a once-familiar odour that Rachel had almost forgotten. To come across it again is a shock – not an unpleasant one, but disorientating, as if time has just dissolved and allowed the past to emerge from whatever has been hiding it.

Becca takes her bag from Rachel, murmurs something inaudible and slips inside.

Mitch doesn't quite manage to smile at Rachel, but he doesn't glare at her either. He says, 'You all right?'

'Yeah, you?'

'Not bad. So… how'd it go? The handover, I mean.'

'Oh, fine. In and out. No big deal.' She attempts a smile. He doesn't look convinced. 'I see they've got your painting fixed up and back in place,' she goes on. She can't meet his eyes as she says this. 'It looks really good.'

Silence. She looks up. He is watching her, not angrily, but with reproachful resignation, as if to say: *I know you feel bad. And so you should.*

'I see you're back on the oil paints now,' she says.

'Yeah, it's another reproduction. My dabbling in wishy-washy watercolours is over.'

'You've never done anything wishy-washy.' He shrugs. 'Anyway, I hope Becca feels better soon. Is it OK if I phone later to see how she's getting on?'

'Sure. Did you see that there's a picture of her in the school annual report?'

'Oh, no. I haven't got my copy yet, I don't think.'

'It's a good one. I've got it somewhere – I can show you, if you like?' Then he says the words that Rachel had never expected to hear him say again: 'Why don't you come on in?'

And so Rachel steps over the threshold of her former home and finds herself back in a place that she had only thought to see again in her dreams.

The doormat still says *Welcome*, though she only knows this because she bought it; the rainbow colours of the letters have long since been obscured by dust. The hall carpet is the same as ever, worn and slightly grubby. It is all so familiar that the novel details leap out: inexplicably, there is an empty cereal packet at the foot of the stairs, and amongst the jumble of shoes in the alcove by the front door is a pair of women's boots she has never seen Becca wear. They are black, buckled, with a Cuban heel. A low heel, but still… a heel! Becca has never had a pair of shoes with a heel before. Not that Rachel is in any position to lay down the law.

In her dreams, she drifts through the house as a ghost, or is locked inside while shadowy intruders rattle at the door, and Rose Cottage is never quite as she remembers it, though she doesn't always register the differences at the time. Rooms might have grown or shrunk or changed colour and there are unexpected people there, people who she hasn't seen for years or who are no longer living:

her mother weeping quietly into the washing-up while her father drinks in front of their old TV, school friends she has drifted out of touch with or colleagues from the job she has lost.

It still doesn't seem real. It's as if this is just another dream version of the house, and the Rose Cottage of the here and now is somewhere else, still in a world she has lost access to.

Mitch says, 'Come on through to the kitchen. I'll go find the thing,' and she does as she's told.

The kitchen table. Rectangular, oak, indefatigably sturdy; they had chosen it together soon after moving in. Many birthday teas and Christmas dinners had been set out on it. She and Mitch might even have had sex on it, or at least near it, though she actually can't quite remember.

She sits down and Mitch comes in with the school's glossy, A4 annual report. The scar on his hand is less noticeable today; it's beginning to fade – it's a little closer to the colour of skin, a little further from the colour of blood.

He sets the report out in front of her, open to the right page. The picture is of Becca as Nancy in her torn red dress, singing her heart out.

'There's something else you might want to see, too,' Mitch says, and puts down a proof copy of Becca's most recent school photograph next to the report. Becca looks acutely self-conscious in it, as if she's trying to smile without showing her teeth.

Rachel says, 'Would you order me a copy? Biggest size possible? Let me know how much I owe you for it and I'll transfer the cash.'

'Will do. Just don't expect Becca to appreciate it. She *hates* it,' Mitch says, and almost smiles.

'Well, I like it. Is it OK if I go up and check on her before I leave?' Mitch shrugs. 'Sure.'

And so Rachel goes up the stairs and knocks on Becca's door. From inside, a muffled voice says, 'Yes?'

'It's me. Mum.'

Cautiously, and as gently as she can, she pushes the door open. Inside the room it is dark; Becca has drawn the curtains and is already in bed.

She says, 'Is it OK if I come in?'

'I'm trying to sleep,' Becca grumbles, which Rachel takes as a yes.

She advances into the room and comes to a halt about a foot from the bed, just close enough to reach out and stroke Becca's hair back from her forehead, which she would like to do but doesn't quite dare. She stoops and gazes at Becca in the gloom and says, 'Well, you take care. I hope you feel better soon.'

Becca's thin white hand shoots out from under the covers and grabs hers; it is startlingly cold. She had forgotten that Becca is always cool to the touch. It used to be a family joke.

'I'm sorry about today,' Becca says.

'It doesn't matter,' Rachel tells her. 'All that matters is that you're OK.'

Becca releases her hand and Rachel retreats back towards the hall. She pauses in the doorway to take in the room for what is likely to be the last time, at least for a while.

'I'll see you next week. Sleep well,' Rachel says. She withdraws and shuts the door.

*

Mitch is sitting at the kitchen table downstairs, staring into space. He gets to his feet as Rachel comes in.

'All right?' he says finally, and she sees that it is time for her to go, and that, quite possibly, he is already regretting letting her in, but that at the same time he is worried about Becca, and feels slightly out of his depth.

'She'll be fine,' Rachel says, since some kind of reassurance seems to be called for. 'I'd best let you get on.'

He accompanies her to the front door. But then, in the hallway, he seems to hesitate before showing her out, and she can't help but feel that he is waiting for her to say something, or to ask him something – as if there's a conversation that they ought to be having, but that it's down to her to initiate.

All she can think of is to ask him what he is working on.

'It's a Canaletto this time. I'm actually learning a lot. I can't really recapture it, of course, even doing it brushstroke by brushstroke with the whole thing mapped out in front of me. It's a lesson in humility if nothing else.'

'Like reassembling the code,' Rachel says.

'I suppose it is,' Mitch agrees, and their eyes meet.

What she sees there is fear. He is afraid of her. Even now. No wonder he hasn't wanted to let her in the house.

And then he ushers her out and closes the door behind her.

# Chapter Twenty-Five

Finally, the time has come for Rachel to do something that, not so long ago, would have seemed impossible.

She is expecting visitors.

She's back in the bedsit by 6.30, plumping up the sofa cushions and wiping down the few surfaces; at least there isn't much of the place to clean. She tries to tell herself that there is no reason to be apprehensive: this is Viv, who she drives to see her son every week the day after seeing Becca, and Leona, who she sits opposite at work. They are not going to take against her simply because they have seen inside the place where she lives. But she's still nervous; she's nervous because she wants so much for it to work – for this evening to be the proof that her rehabilitation is complete, that she can enjoy a perfectly ordinary pleasure like having friends round. Or is at least capable of taking her turn to host a support group.

When the doorbell rings – 7.30 on the dot – it's a relief that the waiting is over.

She takes a final look round. It is still light, the soft kind of light that comes from a blue evening sky in early spring, the kind of light that Renaissance artists sought to capture for cherubs on chubby clouds to bathe in. A forgiving kind of light, in which the bedsit doesn't look despicable, but merely neglected; it is the home of someone whose energies are all directed elsewhere.

And then she goes to let them in.

*

As soon as she sees them on the doorstep – both pleased and excited to be out together in the evening, and to have come somewhere new – her anxiety begins to lift.

'Come on in,' she says. 'You'll have to excuse the state of the place. It could all do with a lick of paint.'

'I'm sure it's absolutely fine, but we don't care about the place, dear. We're here to see *you*,' Viv says, and steps forward into the hallway to peck Rachel on the cheek. She's carrying a Tupperware box and a bottle of sparkling elderflower cordial, which she hands over to Rachel. 'Cupcakes from me – the fizz is from Leona. I gather she has something to celebrate, but she wouldn't say a word about it until we were all together.'

'I actually haven't told anybody else at all,' Leona says, coming in behind her. She's carrying the noticeboard. 'You two will be the first to know.'

She sets the noticeboard down by the wall opposite the sofa, and gives Rachel a hug; she smells faintly of patchouli. Then her attention suddenly shifts, and she moves away and makes a beeline for Rachel's chest of drawers, and the small square of painted hardboard propped up on it: the study Mitch had done years ago for his painting of Persephone, the one and only time that he'd used Rachel as a model.

She says, 'I know this painting. Isn't this by Mitchell Moran?'

'It is. He's my husband,' Rachel tells her. 'It's a study for a larger painting, which is probably the one you've seen, though it's in a private collection now.

'But you're Rachel Steele,' Leona says. 'I mean, I know you said your husband was an artist… but I had no idea it was Mitchell Moran you were talking about.'

'Steele's my maiden name,' Rachel says. 'I've always used it for work. I had no idea you would have heard of him – he did that when he was pretty much fresh out of art school, and then a collector bought it and it ended up being part of the Provocation exhibition – do you remember that? It attracted quite a lot of attention because some of the other works in it were thought to be shocking.'

'I skived off school to go to that exhibition!' Leona tells her. 'I'd heard my parents talking about it – there had been a story in the paper. They disapproved, which was why I wanted to go. But actually, I didn't really like it. Apart from this. I still have the postcard of it that I bought.'

Viv moves closer to the painting, too, and retrieves a pair of spectacles from her handbag to help her inspect it.

'It's you, isn't it, Rachel?' she says. 'He's painted you as one of those poor unfortunate women who get locked up in bunkers by deranged men.'

'Is it you?' Leona glances back at Rachel as if to check. She appears puzzled, as if Rachel doesn't quite match up.

'Yes,' Rachel says. 'It's me.'

The painting is so familiar to her that it is a long time since she has really looked at it. It's become a symbol of something else: of Mitch's talent, which she has always admired, and of how crushed he had been by being briefly celebrated for his work, and then ignored. But she's proud of it, too. It's proof that there was a time, long ago, when she and Mitch wanted to try and work together, and bring out the best in each other. And maybe they had.

The painting shows a young woman in a dim basement with a handle-less door, lying on a bed next to a table with a cut pomegranate in a dish on it. A calendar hangs on one wall, a newspaper on the floor has the headline 'Missing', and through the high barred window it is possible to see a lone snowdrop sprouting in a patch of grass in front of a slushy pavement.

Rachel had worn a favourite red jumper and jeans for the sitting; Mitch had wanted her in clothes that she wore often, so she would look as if she was in a situation that she had got used to. But that wasn't quite how it had turned out.

As a portrait, it wasn't a particularly accurate likeness – Mitch had struggled to capture her as well as he wanted to, probably another reason why they'd never repeated the experience. But he had conveyed something about her that she'd barely been aware of at the time: frustration and pent-up energy. The young woman in the painting doesn't look at all resigned to her plight; she looks furious, and as if she's absolutely determined to escape.

'It's amazing to see it like this,' Leona says.

Viv doesn't look quite as impressed as Leona. She asks, 'Is he well known, Rachel? You'll have to forgive my ignorance. I don't know very much about modern art.'

'There was quite a lot of buzz around him when he did that painting,' Rachel says. 'Then the collectors and the people who write about these things moved on. As they do. And he got discouraged, and lost heart. He doesn't do much original work any more. He does commissions for a dealer in Henley – paintings from people's favourite photographs – and he turns out a lot of copies of Old Masters, which brings in a bit of money.'

'It can't have been easy, sharing a house with an artist. I imagine they're rather untidy,' Viv says.

'He is a bit,' Rachel agrees.

She puts the elderflower cordial and the Tupperware down on the worktop by the sink; Viv takes off her jacket and passes it to her, and Rachel hangs it up in the wardrobe. Leona is still studying the painting.

'I've always thought it's about freedom,' Leona says. She sounds affronted, as if the painting is a personal possession that the other two have just insulted. 'I can't believe Mitchell Moran has been living in living in Kettlebridge all this time, and I had absolutely no idea.'

'Well, he is.'

Leona straightens up. 'Do you think you might be able to put me in touch with him?'

'Leona,' Viv interrupts. 'Rachel might not feel entirely comfortable with that.'

'It's not just because of this painting,' Leona says. 'I'd like to talk to him about business. Look, this is jumping the gun a bit – I was going to wait till we had the fizz open – but one of the things I was going to tell you is that I'm leaving my job, so I can concentrate on my own business full time. It's taken me years to get to this point, but I think I've got enough interest to make a go of it. And some kind of collaboration with Mitchell Moran would be amazing.'

Rachel stares at her. 'You mean your second-hand furniture business?'

'Pre-loved. And it's not just furniture. Yes.'

'Is that wise,' Viv asks, 'at a time when so many small businesses are struggling?'

'My running costs are very low. Everything's online. And I have savings. I have thought this through, Viv. Though to be honest, I suppose it's just that the time feels right, for all sorts of reasons. Will you keep it under your hat at work, Rachel? Mike knows, and he wants to tell everybody else, but he hasn't got round to it yet.'

Viv looks concerned, but Leona is defiant, as if she's just asked something perfectly reasonable and can't see why Rachel wouldn't comply. *Does she really think Mitch is about to collaborate with her on a line of revarnished odds and sods from junk shops?* Well, if she does, she's in for a surprise.

'Of course I can put you in touch,' Rachel finds herself saying. 'I can't guarantee he'll respond, though. But I'll mention it to him when I next see him.'

'Thank you.' Leona is flushed, as if she's just fought and won a minor battle. Maybe she's more anxious about going it alone than she's letting on, and is clutching at straws.

'Here, let me take your coat,' Rachel says. With the passing of winter, Leona has stopped wearing the astrakhan number and is instead cocooned in a big belted cardigan, which she now slips out of and hands over. Underneath she's wearing a rose-printed tea-dress; the vintage look suits her, though with the tattoo on her wrist and a heavy pair of biker boots, she doesn't look entirely like a Forces sweetheart.

She does have a good eye. *Who knows, maybe her business will be a success?*

'Please, sit down,' Rachel says, and the other two women settle on the sofa, opposite the noticeboard and the pictures of Becca, Aidan and Bluebell: Aidan with his puddles, Becca barefoot in her red dress, and Bluebell looking back at them.

'I should have come to pick you up,' Rachel says. 'I didn't realise you were going to lug that all the way here.'

'Oh, it was no bother,' Leona says.

'Our taxi driver was very curious about it,' Viv tells her. 'He was too polite to ask, though. I think he might have thought we were going to have a séance. Or maybe he thought we were amateur sleuths, trying to crack a case about missing children. Anyway, Rachel, there was no need, you do enough chauffeuring for me as it is.' Viv turns to Leona. 'She won't take petrol money, either. I keep giving it to her, and she keeps handing it back and telling me to give it to charity if I feel so badly about it. The Red Cross are doing rather well out of our arrangement.'

'I think it suits you both,' Leona observes. 'I'm starting to feel like a third wheel.'

'You could never be that!' Rachel says. 'If it wasn't for you, Viv and I would never have met.'

'Quite right,' Viv says. 'Though even with all Leona's efforts, we still haven't managed to attract any more members.'

'We're the club that no one wants to join,' Leona says.

'Their loss,' Rachel says. 'Shall I open the elderflower cordial? Would you both like a glass?'

'Absolutely,' Viv says. 'And then we can toast your new venture, Leona, and you can tell us your other piece of news.'

'Ah. That,' Leona says, blushing again, but she doesn't immediately volunteer any more information. Maybe all the fussing about

Mitch's painting, and the thoughtless request to be introduced to him, was all just displacement activity. Perhaps this really is big news – too big to be easy to tell.

In which case there's only one thing it can be about.

Rachel finds glasses and opens the cordial and pours it out, and Viv proposes the toast: 'To new beginnings!' and they clink and drink, and it is almost as Rachel had imagined it might be, the three of them united against the world and ready to take it on.

And then Leona tells them.

She has had a letter from Bluebell's adoptive mother, inviting her to come to France to visit. And as soon as she has managed to tell them this, she bursts into tears.


'I'm just not sure I'm up to it,' she says later, when she's calm again and Viv and Rachel have both cried, too, and have embraced her. 'I feel like I'm auditioning for a chance at forgiveness, and I'm doomed to fail. It's not as if anything I do now could begin to make up for what I've done. Bluebell is a child, and children don't make allowances – they expect their parents to be superheroes. She knows I gave her up – why would she want to let me in her life again? What if this is just curiosity, and once this visit is over, she decides she doesn't want to see me again?'

'You don't need courage to do things you find easy,' Viv observes. 'You need it for the things you're scared of. You'll go, and something good will come of it. I know it will.'

'I hope you're right,' Leona says. 'God, I haven't even checked if my passport's still valid. I haven't been abroad for ages. I've been saving every penny for my business. In the end it was the letter about Bluebell that pushed me into taking the plunge, actually. In comparison with meeting her, it just didn't seem like that big a risk.'

'Work's not going to be the same without you, but I'd say Bluebell's done you a favour there. It certainly sounds as if you were ready to leave,' Rachel says. 'Anyway, Bluebell wants to see you. That means you're welcome. When do you think you'll go?'

'Not definite yet. But soon, I think.'

'Well, let me know when and I'll see if I can give you a lift to the airport.'

As Leona thanks her and accepts, Rachel's attention drifts back to Mitch's painting. Who was she kidding, to think she was beginning to free herself of everything that had brought her down? Leona is the one who is escaping, not her; Leona is the one who suddenly has the chance to change her whole life. And she's jealous. It is horrible to be jealous of a friend who is coming within reach of something she has longed for. But she is.

She knows the feeling all too well: that mix of sorrow and anger, of resentment and self-pity. And she also knows where jealousy can lead, and how far it is possible to fall. And how much she still has to lose.

# Chapter Twenty-Six

## Rachel

### Three months before the loss

Later on, she couldn't tell when she had entered the Deep. By the time she came to think of it that way, it felt as if she had been there forever and would never leave.

Although it was hard to pinpoint, it must have been sometime in the weeks that followed her mother's funeral, but it wasn't an on-off moment like a switch or something breaking. It was more a steady sinking, a sense of increasing pressure and distance from light and air, of the surface closing somewhere overhead as she drifted deeper into the chill and the gloom. Sometimes she panicked and started to struggle; sometimes all she could do was keep falling. It didn't make any difference what she did or didn't do. She was still there.

The first imperative was to carry on as normal. Other people didn't seem to be able to tell how far away she was, which was how she wanted it. Mitch knew, of course, but that was different. Frank noticed, asked if she was all right. *Yes, thank you*, she was fine, just a little tired. He looked at her sceptically and made suggestions, which she listened to and filed away under 'one day'. At his leaving drinks she nodded and chatted and smiled and thought how strange it was, the chitchat and pretences, all those people with their desire to save face and belong. She kissed Frank goodbye and wished herself elsewhere, and afterwards she missed him.

By midsummer she was almost used to it. The Deep was where she lived now: it was already difficult to imagine that she would ever feel any other way, or that anything might ever be powerful enough to bring her back up to the surface.

And then it did, out of the blue, on an occasion that should, in the ordinary way of things, have been pleasant and quickly forgettable: a rare night out, drinks in a pub in Kettlebridge for parents of girls in Becca's class to mark the end of the school year.

And when it did, the shock of it was so great, so excessive, that it was impossible to make sense of it, or to trust the evidence of her own senses. And, rightly or wrongly, the cause of the shock was Mary Chadstone.

The Deep was not entirely unlike her previous existence. It was just everyday life with the light sucked out of it. There were blue skies and sunny days, all the usual signs of summer. But for her there was darkness, which permeated everything, flattened it, and made it unreal. The world around her might as well have been the view from the train windows that she rattled past twice a day on the way to and from work; she was cut off from it, and submerged somewhere out of reach.

And yet there she was, going through the motions, keeping up appearances, trying to seem like anyone else.

She went to work, she came back, she tried to eat. Her body had begun to shrink; it was as if she was on a strict diet, exerting colossal discipline. Actually, it was more as if she was melting away. She slept sometimes, but more often than not she lay awake, worrying about this or that. Things to do with work or the house; missed objectives, fire hazards, money. Things left undone. Life was a slippery monster that had got away from her, and worrying was her way of attempting to wrestle it back into her grasp.

It didn't work.

Mitch was a glowering, unsympathetic presence. He hated her being in the Deep. She tried once or twice to talk to him; he recoiled from her, didn't want to know. She had always been the optimistic, upbeat one, the encourager; was this what it had been like to be him, with her throwing his fears and inadequacies back at him? She knew he was afraid: of weakness, of sickness, of being dragged down with her. But also, that felt like kidding herself, soft-soaping the truth. Surely it was understandable if he was repulsed by her, the broken-down, barely-there person she had so suddenly become. She couldn't really blame him for wanting to keep her at a distance. She was at a distance from herself.

At any rate, he had been proved right. There was no way she could have coped with taking on a promotion.

Mitch told her again to go to the doctor. She went to the doctor. It took forever to get through to make an appointment; then something came up at work and she had to cancel it. Eventually, she made it. The doctor was sympathetic and reserved, a precise, professional woman with a bob and a bead necklace that was just the right length to sit under her collar. She asked Rachel a list of questions that must have been asked many times before. A checklist. She handed over leaflets, lists of useful websites, said to come back in a fortnight. Well, what had Rachel expected? Not much. Certainly not a magic wand, a sudden transformation. Nothing happened quickly in the Deep.

It seemed inevitable that any official help would come slowly and reluctantly, if at all. Still, the doctor had listened to her, had acknowledged the possibility that there was something wrong with her, something that it might be possible to treat. A disease.

Perhaps that should have been a comfort, to think that what she was experiencing was a series of tricks her mind was playing on her: to see her life in terms of symptoms, identifiable by a checklist.

But it wasn't, because she was too ashamed.

Through all of this, Becca shone: a bit of life that Rachel, miraculously, had helped to bring to the world, a twelve-year-old girl who was blissfully, innocently preoccupied with her own business. French vocabulary, the new jeans she wanted, when could she have her ears pierced, why couldn't she have a dog? Rachel continued to dole out the usual sorts of answers, cajoling, prevaricating, encouraging, reminding, and, on occasion, making excuses. (Mitch's allergies were the excuse for not getting a dog. Also, Mitch just didn't like dogs. But the onus was still on Rachel to justify the refusal.) The sense of going through the motions persisted. She loved Becca with all her heart, and yet even that was not enough to bring her out of the Deep and plug her back into the living present. She watched her daughter tenderly but as if from somewhere else, as if she were a ghost.

And she saw Becca with Mitch, and she was grateful to him for the ordinary, glorious pleasure he took in spending time with their daughter, talking to her, sharing things with her: exhibitions and art galleries, the new game they had bought for the Wii, old episodes of *Friends*. And she hoped that the kind of attention he gave Becca, his implicit respect for her, his willingness to talk to her and listen to her, his instinctive protectiveness, would make Becca strong. Strong in ways that Rachel herself had never been. All Rachel had was willpower, her desire to show people what she was made of, but that had ebbed away now and left her with nothing.

What she wanted for Becca was for her not to have to feel she had to prove herself: to know that being herself was enough, and was safe. To know beyond a shadow of doubt, even to the point where it was possible to take this for granted, that she was loved. To have a firm foundation; to have love like a home to come back to.

Already, somewhere in the Deep, the question was beginning to form, and was all the more irresistible because it was so painful to her. *Wouldn't Becca be better off without her mother?*


She wasn't even particularly worried about the drinks for parents of Becca's classmates. She'd made the effort to find a babysitter, overruling Becca's protests that she didn't need one and was perfectly capable of looking after herself; maybe Becca was right, but Rachel had begun to see potential dangers everywhere, and she'd only spend the evening worrying if she knew Becca was alone in the house. Mitch had suggested that he could stay home and mind Becca instead, but it was a long time since they'd been out socially as a couple. Surely it would be good for them? Maybe it would even help her to feel a little more normal.

And Mitch agreed to go because she wanted to, but not without grumbling about how boring and pointless it would be, and how the other men would be corporate types who would talk about their careers and investments and personal bests and he'd rather just stay in with the telly. She would remember that, later, and wonder what would have happened if, instead of protesting that they never went out together any more, she had thrown her hands up and said, *Fine, don't come, I'll go on my own.*

Maybe it would have been better.

Or perhaps the moment of reckoning would have just come another time.

There was a signal failure outside Barrowton the evening they were due to go out, and her train home was delayed. When she got back Mitch was terse and preoccupied; having not wanted to go out at all, he was now anxious not to be late. But they were anyway, finally arriving at the Merry Miller pub about an hour after the drinks gathering had got under way.

It was a dull, potentially rainy evening, and the other parents had sensibly not attempted the beer garden, but had settled around a long table inside. They were mostly mothers, with only one other dad besides Mitch – so he needn't have worried about being left out of any man talk. Most of them were a little pink in the face;

obviously a couple of drinks in, and maybe a little more relaxed than was, strictly speaking, good for them.

Mitch went off to the bar to get a round in, and one of the mothers, a woman with very curly hair – double-barrelled surname, something-Jones – moved her designer bag from the chair next to her so Rachel could sit down.

'Have you been at work today?' She had red wine stains on her lips.

*Yes, and what did she have to say for herself? Not much.* She'd had a rotten day, and a humiliating meeting with Elizabeth Mannering, her new manager, who had expressed concern about a few slip-ups she'd made lately and wanted to supervise her more closely. If Rachel had been feeling more buoyant she might have tried to turn what had happened into some kind of mildly entertaining anecdote. But really, what was funny about screwing up at work because your mother had died and you'd lost your nerve?

Curly-haired double-barrelled-Jones had been at work, too, as it turned out.

'Just a couple of days a week at one of the colleges in Oxford,' she said. 'You work full time in London, don't you? Honestly, I can't think how you bear that awful commute. Still, at least you've got Mitch to keep the home fires burning. It must be wonderful being married to a real artist. I saw the painting he did of your garden, the one the Chadstones have – it's absolutely gorgeous.'

She was referring to a small watercolour Mitch had done the previous winter, as a kind of experiment; it wasn't a medium he'd ever made much use of, and when he was younger he'd been dismissive of it, regarding it as the sort of thing that keen amateurs might dabble in. He'd long since lost that youthful arrogance, though. She had been delighted to see him working on something of his own, a piece of work that wasn't a commission or a reproduction, and when they'd had the Chadstones round for dinner and Mary had admired the painting, she had encouraged Mitch to let them buy it. She had thought the sale might boost his confidence, and that he might do more along the same lines. But then he'd gone back to turning out exactly the same kind of work as before, and had been, if anything, even more down on himself than ever.

'It is a lovely painting,' Rachel agreed.

'He's so gifted. I'd love to be able to paint, wouldn't you? Has he ever painted you?'

'He did once. You might be surprised by how boring it is,' Rachel said.

'Boring?'

'Being painted. Lying about doing nothing for hours. I don't know, I think maybe I'm a bit too impatient to make a good muse.'

'Oh, I'm sure you're not. After all, it's all about doing something for someone you love, isn't it?'

In the corner, the mother who sped round Kettlebridge in a silver Mercedes was deep in a giggly conversation with another woman Rachel had never seen before. They had to be talking about sex. They were laughing in that show-offy, conspiratorial, *naughty-us* way that meant they were getting it, and discussing it, and didn't mind who knew it.

But Rachel was not getting it, and they were the last people she would want to confide in.

She got up and said she was going to see if Mitch needed any help bringing their drinks over from the bar, and went to join him.

He was loading glasses onto a tray. He didn't turn and see her, and she was just about to call out his name when Mary Chadstone arrived and swooped down on him as if there was nobody else in the room.

As if greeting a long-lost lover.

He stopped what he was doing and they embraced, courteously but fondly. And then, when they let each other go, he reached forward to tuck a strand of her hair behind her ear.

Rachel immediately felt like a voyeur. As if she had just witnessed something private, something she had no right to watch but was drawn to anyway: something that she couldn't help but recognise as attraction. And when she approached, she felt as if she was interrupting them.

After they had all settled back at the table Mitch and Mary didn't even talk to each other all that much, and the evening rolled on more or less as might have been expected. But Rachel couldn't shake her impression of what she'd seen.

It was ridiculous to be so upset, it was nothing, all he had done was touch her hair… and he had been glad to see her, well, that was no surprise, since he didn't really know any of the others. They were old friends, a little bit of flirtation didn't mean anything.

But it wasn't just flirtation. It was more than that. It was worse than that. It was *tenderness*.

She drove Mitch back home with questions and possible answers chasing themselves round her head. *Are you having an affair? Are you attracted to her? Is something going on?* But it was ludicrous. Crazy. What evidence did she have?

Why should she need evidence? You only needed proof if you couldn't trust somebody to tell you. And if you couldn't trust your husband, weren't you already in trouble?

He didn't ask why she was so quiet. She parked, as usual, just in front of the bridge that led to the house. Becca must have gone to sleep long ago; the only light on was in the sitting room, where the babysitter would be waiting for them.

And then she went for it.

'Mitch,' she said before he could get out of the car. 'Have you been seeing Mary?'

He froze. 'What do you mean?'

'I mean sleeping with her. Or thinking about it. Or both.'

'Of course not. Why do you say that?'

'She's always liked you. Do you remember when they last came round for dinner? She couldn't praise you enough. *Oh Mitch, you're such a great cook, Hugh never cooks, you're so talented, your paintings are so brilliant, we absolutely must buy one—*'

'As I remember it, you were the one who encouraged them to buy that painting.'

'I thought it'd make you feel better to have a sale.'

'Not to them. Not particularly.'

'Well, she didn't exactly turn down the chance, did it? I guess it gave her an excuse to you round to theirs to hang it. Was that when she made her move?'

'Rachel, that's ridiculous. I don't know why you've got this idea into your head. Come on, we've both known Mary for ages. She's married to my oldest friend. Our daughters go to school together. We aren't attracted to each other, and even if we were, we wouldn't do anything about it. Why would we take the risk?'

'But you touched her,' Rachel said, and began to cry. 'You touched her the way you used to touch me.'

And Mitch held her and soothed her and reassured her. He would never do anything to her, he loved her, she was just tired and overwrought, was there anything else that was worrying her? And she allowed herself to be consoled.

# Chapter Twenty-Seven

## Rachel

Whatever secret mixed feelings Rachel might have had at the prospect of change in Leona's life, they don't last the journey to the airport.

She hasn't seen her since Leona's leaving do soon after Easter, and what with one thing and another, they haven't managed to get together with Viv since the evening in Rachel's bedsit. First, they'd postponed meeting up because Viv had been laid low by a cold, and then it had been difficult to rearrange because Leona had been working non-stop on getting her business off the ground. Now, seeing Leona for the first time in a couple of weeks, Rachel is shocked by the change in her.

Leona is almost unrecognisable as the self-possessed bohemian who had greeted Rachel that first day at Fun-to-Learn just over four months earlier, or even as the friend who had confided to Viv and Rachel that she had been invited to meet her daughter, who had cried with them and let them comfort her, and who had been both overwhelmed and full of hope. Now she's pale and petrified; it's almost as if she's travelling towards another loss rather than a miraculous reunion.

As they turn away from the check-in queue she makes a visible effort to rally. She looks at Rachel but without focus, as if she can't really pay attention to her any more.

'You should go,' Leona tells her. 'Get back to work. I don't want to keep you – you've done more than enough for me. Don't hang around here. I'll be fine.'

'OK. If you're sure… Before I go, I have a present for you. For luck,' Rachel says.

She had to do something. She'd felt so bad about not being unambiguously happy for Leona when she heard the news, this is a gift for herself as much as for her friend. It's a small gift, anyway, something that won't take up too much space. She rummages in her handbag and brings it out: a chunk of unpolished rose quartz in a clear plastic bag. She'd bought it on impulse from a stall at Kettlebridge market that she'd browsed one Saturday with Becca.

'It's meant to promote healing,' she says, 'and unconditional love.'

Leona takes it and examines it; her hand closes tight around it.

'Thank you,' she says, and steps forward to give Rachel a hug. Today she smells soft, talcum-powdery, like lavender; she's someone who is always changing her scent.

Leona withdraws first and heads off in the direction of security, pausing only to look back over her shoulder and wave before she's lost in the crowds. She still has the crystal in her fist.

*

Suddenly alone in the airport, Rachel is disinclined to rush back to the car. There will be plenty of work waiting for her back at the office. And yet she can't really believe that any of it is urgent. It seems like a problem from somebody else's life.

In a little over two hours' time Leona will be in the air on the way to her daughter. She may be nervous now, but surely then her fears will fall away, as she puts more and more distance between her present self and the person she had been that morning and last week and last year, and then, eventually, arrives somewhere completely new.

A display of silk scarves in a cabinet catches Rachel's eye and she pauses to examine them. Not that silk scarves are really her thing, but who knows? Maybe they could be. Maybe she could change, too.

'Rachel?'

*Did she imagine it?* She turns and sees a silver-haired man in smart casual clothes – jacket, chinos, open-necked shirt – with a small carry-on suitcase at his side. He is smiling at her with exactly the sort of slightly puzzled fondness that you might expect from a former boss whose protégé had fallen spectacularly from grace as soon as he left.

'Hello, Frank,' she says.

They kiss, as two former colleagues might be expected to do: lightly, without really touching. He stands back and looks her up and down. Not just puzzled. Concerned.

'I'm sorry I didn't reply to your email,' she says. 'It's been a difficult time.'

'I gathered,' Frank says. 'I heard a little bit about what happened. I would have persisted, but I didn't want to hassle you when you were in the thick of going through something. It seemed like nobody had heard from you. It was as if you'd dropped off the face of the earth.'

'It was a bit like that,' she agrees.

'I'm so glad to have bumped into you. It's reassuring to see you, actually. You look well. Whatever's been going on these past few months.'

'You look well, too. Retirement obviously suits you.'

'I'll let you in on a secret; I actually really miss the office. I've been trying to do a little bit of consultancy work. Pro bono, some of it. If anybody actually wants an old dog.'

'You can teach them the old tricks. I'm sure you can persuade them they're new.'

He beams at her. 'That's what I'm hoping.'

He's always had this ability to seem to not be taking himself, or life in general, too seriously, and it's contagious; she can feel her mood lightening. A passer-by jostles them together, and Frank puts his hand quite naturally on her arm, then moves it away.

'I've often thought about you, wondered how you were getting on,' he says. 'But I thought it wouldn't be right to bother you. I knew you knew where I was. Where are you off to today? Somewhere nice, I hope?'

'Just dropped a friend off. I'm about to head back to work, actually. How about you?'

'A couple of days in Geneva. Work-related, actually; I'm involved with an international charity that's based there. One of those consultancy projects I mentioned. But my flight doesn't leave for ages. Look, do you have a few minutes? Maybe we could grab a coffee? It's too good a coincidence not to take advantage of, us both being here, surely?'

Next thing she knows she's following him to a café. He somehow secures a table with a good view of the passing human traffic just as its previous occupiers are leaving, and attracts prompt service from the weary-looking waitress. Then he turns to Rachel and says, 'So, where are you working now?'

And Rachel finds she's happy to answer. With another former colleague, maybe she would have been more defensive, but Frank has the gift of making you feel better about whatever it is you're doing. So she tells him about Fun-to-Learn. And then, unbidden, she tells Frank about her exit from her old job.

'I probably shouldn't say this, but from what I hear these days Elizabeth Mannering isn't all that secure either,' he says. 'If you get in touch with any of the others you'll probably hear all about it. Did you ever think of working for yourself? You know, going freelance. Setting up on your own. I used to be terrified that you'd leave me to do exactly that.'

'That's the kind of thing you can do if you've got a rich husband or low overheads,' Rachel says. 'Maybe I will one day. I just don't feel in the right place to even begin to think about it right now. I'm just happy to have some regular money coming in.'

'Fair enough. And self-employment can be lonely. You might miss the social side of office life.'

'I could probably cope with that,' Rachel says. 'When I started where I am now, all I wanted to do was keep my head down and get paid. I had absolutely no intention of getting to know anybody.'

'Yeah, I bet it didn't turn out like that.'

'No. It definitely didn't. Actually, the friend I just dropped off here is someone I know from work.'

The waitress brings over their order: an espresso for him, a cappuccino for her, and two Danish pastries – hers with icing and cinnamon. Just like the old days.

'Do you remember when I came in for my interview?' she asks him.

'Of course! Of course I do. It was very short, wasn't it? Partly because I was so preoccupied. And also because you were so determined.'

'I was. I'd had a few rejections by that point. You were up against my wounded pride.'

'Your wounded pride was quite formidable,' Frank says.

'Really?'

'Really. You said the office appeared to be in chaos and I clearly needed a Girl Friday. You made quite an impression, you know, right from the minute you appeared, taking the steps up to the office two at a time.'

She remembers that, too: he had been waiting on an upper landing to meet her and she'd said she was looking for Frank Darling, and he had looked her up and down not as if she was a prospective employee and he was the boss, but more as if she was a visitor he was surprised by. And then he had said, *You found him. Let's go and get this over with.*

He clears his throat. 'So how is Becca? And Mitch?'

*Oh God. He doesn't know.*

'Oh… They're fine. Becca turned thirteen, so I have a teenager now. And she had a starring role in the school show. Turns out she can really sing.'

He doesn't say anything. He just looks at her in that familiar, puzzled way, as if he knows something isn't quite right but isn't going to push her to say what it is.

It would be quite easy not to tell him… to change the subject, and finish her coffee and pastry and say how nice it had been to see him and goodbye.

It would be easy, but it would leave her feeling like a coward, and knowing that she had been too ashamed to tell the truth.

'Mitch and I have separated,' she says. 'I wasn't in a very good state. I… had a kind of crisis. So I moved out. Becca and Mitch are still in the house, and I see Becca at the weekends.'

'I see. I'm sorry to hear that.'

And he really does look sorry. And shocked. As if it matters to him to think of her as being happy. As if it genuinely dismays him to learn that things have gone so wrong for her.

'I don't really know what's going to happen next,' she says. 'Things have settled a bit, and we seem to be getting on a bit better. What I want is to keep things as stable as they can be, for Becca's sake. It's so hard for her. Such a difficult age, when so much else is changing. And she adores her father, always has. He played such a big role in bringing her up, they've always had a really close bond.'

She looks down at her hands. Capable hands, not elegant; as her mother had sometimes pointed out, they were like her father's. A tear splotches onto one, another on the other. She keeps her head down. Frank will have seen that she's crying, but she would rather nobody else knew it.

Weeping in public is the ultimate sign of defeat. At one time she would have done her utmost to avoid it. And yet here she is, with tears tripping down her face in a franchise coffee outlet in one of the world's busiest airports, surrounded on all sides by travellers.

She reaches for her handbag and there it is, Mitch's handkerchief, which she has taken to carrying around with her. No particular reason. She just likes it. So why not? She wipes her eyes and looks up at Frank.

'I had depression,' she says. 'It started after my mother died. I was on medication for a while, and I had some counselling. I'm doing better now, but I feel like it wouldn't take much for me to go backwards again.'

She waits for him to recoil, to make his excuses and leave. He doesn't. He says, 'I know how hard it is. I've been through it, too.'

And she's stunned. Of all the things that he could have said to her, this is the one that she could never have predicted.

'This is not to belittle what happened to either of us,' he says. 'But it does happen to a lot of people. There's no shame in it. Or there shouldn't be.'

She says, 'Do you mind if I ask you when it was? Or would you prefer not to talk about it?'

'I don't mind talking about it to you,' he says. 'It was after my marriage broke up. I felt like a failure. Again, not an unusual experience. But that doesn't make it any easier. Anyway, I honestly think work got me through it. At least it was something I could do.' He smiles at her. 'You always used to cheer me up, too, you know. I knew I could rely on you. That's a rare thing, in any walk of life.'

'You know, when I had that interview with you I was desperate,' she says. 'If you hadn't taken me on I think I really would have begun to despair. Do you remember you gave me an advance on my first month's wages? That gave me my freedom. It meant I could leave home. I didn't even tell my parents I was going. One day I was there, and the next I'd moved out. I know it sounds brutal, but it felt like that was the only way I could do it. Things had been pretty difficult for a while. Actually, it got worse as soon as I got my first Saturday job at the department store, when I was still at school. It was as if even that little bit of independence was a threat.'

And then she tells him why she'd had to go. As she's talking she has the strangest sense of familiarity; something about the way he listens, without seeking either to interpret or qualify what she's saying or do anything other than take it in, reminds her of someone else.

It isn't till much later that she realises who it is who has that same calm, receptive, judicious manner, who expresses sympathy but not shock or anger, and who sees her experience not just as an agonising, damaging personal drama, the way Mitch had perceived it – as something isolating and exceptional – but as a kind of trauma that she has in common with many others. It's Frank's wisdom that she recognises, and the person it reminds her of is Viv.

# Chapter Twenty-Eight

## Rachel

### Nineteen years before the loss

The minute Rachel let herself in, she knew. Everything had seemed all right when she left that morning to start her Saturday job at Pinkney's department store. Or at least, it had been as close to all right as it ever was. But now the house was the wrong kind of quiet, and the atmosphere had that weird electricity that lingered after something bad had happened.

Someone was moving around upstairs. Her mum. Her dad was in the living room, in front of the TV, drinking a beer.

She said good evening. He grunted and didn't look at her. He was a big man, thickset, with brawny arms from the removals work he did, and he was powerful in other ways, too; his scowl could instantly darken the mood of a room. Right now, he was in the tense, silent mood that often came before or after an outburst, and meant he had to be left alone. But which was it – had he already blown up, or was he about to? She withdrew and went quietly upstairs, already dreading what she might find.

Her mum was in the master bedroom. Usually it was immaculate: heart-shaped cushions in pale blue satin arranged on the matching coverlet just so, the vanity set laid out on the white dressing table, the full-length mirror reflecting everything. Rachel's dad had let her choose exactly what she wanted, and had paid for it all with only a few indulgent complaints about the cost. He did that, sometimes. He'd

say, 'No more than you deserve,' or 'Only the best for my girl,' and
Rachel's mum would look tearful and grateful and wring her hands
and he'd tease her: 'No need to get all het up about it, Joanie. What
are you going to do when you really have something to cry about?'

She had something to cry about now, but she wasn't sobbing. She
never did, in the aftermath. The instinct to make everything go back
to normal, to not do anything that he might take as provocation,
was much too strong.

Survival instinct: something terrible happened and she put it
back in its box by just carrying on. Despite how frail she sometimes
seemed, her ability to keep going was nothing short of miraculous.

The room was in chaos all around her, as if it had been shaken by
an earthquake. The mattress had been yanked off the bed, exposing
the frilly valance; the satin coverlet was on the floor, littered with
paperbacks that had been swept from the bookcase. The full-length
mirror had survived but the dressing table had been upended, scattering the vanity set, and the china hand that had held her mother's
necklaces had lost them and half its fingers.

Rachel's mum was in the middle of it on her hands and knees next
to a square of newspaper, picking up shards of glass from the little
hand-blown perfume bottle that had never had any perfume in it.

'Oh, Mum. Are you all right?'

Joanie looked up at her and offered her a smile that was meant
to be reassuring, though her eyes were so sad that the effect was
anything but. Her fair, curly hair had been pulled out of shape, and
her mascara had run and smudged into dark patches.

She was a small, birdlike woman – Rachel's dad hated for her
to put on weight – and her reflex response to suffering was to be
cheerful and plaster a brave face on it. In another kind of life, and
another marriage, she would have been the kind of woman who
had lots of friends and knew all their troubles. As it was, she was
someone other people were wary of. She was unnaturally chirpy;
they thought she was nervous and overwrought.

They had no idea. Or if they did have some idea, it was easier by far for all of them to pretend they didn't.

'I'm fine, love,' Joanie said. 'Just got to straighten up a bit. You wouldn't mind putting those books back for me, would you?'

Rachel picked up *Perdita's Prince* and *Royal Road to Fotheringhay*; her mum was fond of historical romances. As she slid them onto the bookshelf she could feel the anger rising inside her. Best suppressed. But she couldn't keep it down.

'Mum, you don't have to put up with this, you know,' she said. 'He has absolutely no right to treat you like this.'

Her mother froze. Too late, Rachel heard what she must have heard already – the creak of her dad's tread on the stairs.

The door swung open and Jack Steele stood there and stared at them both. He was radiating malevolence: they could have been his worst enemies rather than his wife and child.

'You're late,' he said to Rachel. 'Shouldn't you be getting the dinner on?'

Somehow the words were out of Rachel's mouth before she could stop herself. 'Maybe you should get it on yourself.'

He lunged at her and smacked her across the side of her head and she crashed down and curled up with her arm raised to protect herself. Her head was ringing with the shock of it and then her hearing came back and it began to hurt. She touched her ear and looked at her hand and there was no blood, nothing. He'd hit her but he hadn't punched her, it wouldn't show, it wouldn't be obvious, it would pass, if nothing worse happened she'd be able to get away with it—

He stood there looking down at her; he stepped towards her, and she flinched. He said, 'I've told you before. Don't talk back.' Then he went out and slammed the door.

Rachel's mum said, 'Sweetheart. Are you all right?'

'I'm all right,' Rachel said. And she was, or would be. 'Could have been worse.'

She got to her feet. Joanie looked concerned and frightened: not angry. She never got angry. She didn't see Jack's behaviour as something he was responsible for – she thought he couldn't help it.

It was unusual for Jack to go for Rachel, but then it was unusual for her to challenge him. She'd always been a good girl, beyond reproach. She knew he was proud of her – her school reports, her appearance, her behaviour. 'Never given us any trouble,' he would say to people, and they would humour him no matter how often they'd heard it before, because with Jack Steele that was what you did.

She supposed being proud of her was a kind of love. She was supposed to love him, too – if it was possible to love someone you had to try very hard not to hate.

'I forgot to ask about your day at work,' Joanie said, with an attempt at a smile. 'How was it?'

'It was fine.' She lowered her voice again. 'Do you think that's what set him off? Me being out all day?'

But Joanie didn't reply. Instead she asked Rachel if she would mind making a start on dinner and went back to picking up pieces of glass, dropping them onto the newspaper so they could be wrapped up safely and thrown away.

# Chapter Twenty-Nine

## Leona

As the plane takes off the woman sitting next to Leona gives her a quick sidelong glance, almost says something, then thinks better of it and opens her book.

Leona forces herself to let go of the arm-rests. She must look dreadful. She feels it; she has barely slept. Apart from everything else, she hates flying. It's not being in the air or the possibility of crashing, it's being shut in and not able to get out.

Maybe she should have gone by train. It might have been less claustrophobic. But why should she have it easy?

Her neighbour peers at her again. She's older than Leona, also travelling alone, casually dressed in jeans and a check shirt: the kind of clothes you wear if you don't want to draw attention to yourself, if you just want to be left in peace. Probably the last thing she wants or needs is to get dragged into conversation with a panicky fellow traveller.

Leona has on a backless olive linen sundress covered up by a big Navajo-print cardigan. Not an outfit chosen in order to be forgettable. She can't bear to wear anything that makes her look like everybody else. Still, she can sympathise with her neighbour's desire for anonymity. Her own clothes are a kind of disguise, or armour. *I don't care what you think I ought to look like. I look how I choose to look, and it won't give you any clues about who I once was or where I've been.*

Soon she's going to have to face up to the one person whose opinion of her really matters. And this is just the beginning. One day, Bluebell is bound to want to know what really happened. Why Leona gave her up. And Leona will have to tell her. She owes her that much.

*But when Bluebell knows all of it... will she find it possible to forgive?*

The woman next to her says, 'Excuse me, but are you all right?'

'Yes, yes, I'll be fine. I'm just a little nervous. I'm sure it'll pass.'

'Can I ask the cabin crew to get you anything?'

'No, no, thank you, there's nothing that will help. I just have to get through it.'

'Well, if I can help at all, please just ask,' the woman says, and turns back to her book.

*Can you turn back time? All the way back to the summer of the heatwave, the day I turned nineteen, and the moment when Jake pressed up against me and said, 'Why don't you just ring your parents and tell them you're staying over with a friend tonight?'*

The woman turns a page and Leona stares out of the window. The view of the airport has already disappeared; all she can see is clouds. The sweat begins to cool on her face.

*Lord, I am not worthy to receive you, but only say the word, and I shall be healed.*

Funny what comes back to you when you're on the edge. She hasn't been to church for years. It's not church she objects to so much as church people. The idea of the people, judging her. She can't dispute their right to. It's just that people who are good – good in an upfront, bumper-sticker kind of way – are sometimes difficult to be around when you know that you are *not* good, have forfeited any claim to be good, and will never be able to think of yourself as good again.

Viv is a churchy person, though, and she's a comfort, like the perfect missing granny. But Viv is one of a kind. She's accepting. Maybe because she knows what it's like to live with a secret.

Sometimes, when Leona feels ill or has a pain that she can't explain, she likes to think that maybe it is because Bluebell is feeling the same way. As if there's some kind of psychic bond between them even though they can't see or touch or talk to each other, and know so little about each other.

They say that people who have lost limbs can still feel them. Toes that aren't there can still itch, amputated hands can ache in the cold. Absence is in the mind. Presence, too.

Leona reaches for the bag she has stashed under her seat and finds Rachel's gift. The healing crystal. What harm can it do? None. She holds it tight, sits back and closes her eyes. The crystal, cool to the touch at first, begins to warm.

At nineteen, she'd thrown her life away as carelessly as a child tossing a ball in the park, not realising till it's too late that it's gone too far to get back. Now the plane presses on, taking her forward, taking her back, and the past looms large as a planet she's in orbit over.

\*

What she had thought of as freedom had ended up as the opposite. But it had started with pure pleasure, heady and thrilling, a rush that had made her feel like herself again after months and months and months of being someone else – a mother, who was someone who had no fun at all.

She'd forgotten what it was like to be just like anyone else, to be doing the things that everybody else her age was doing. But there she was, standing on the pavement outside a central London pub at the end of a baking-hot August day. And there *he* was, standing with a group of people her friend Emily had got to know since going to university, which is what Leona would have done that year if she hadn't had Bluebell.

He was tanned, as if he worked outside – either that, or he spent a lot of time sunbathing in the park. The short sleeves of his T-shirt exposed lean, lightly muscled arms, and the thought of being any closer to him made Leona blush and tingle in a way that was something else she had forgotten.

Maybe he was a student, but he didn't look like it – he looked
older, more sure of himself. Emily had been a bit vague about what
her new friends actually did, apart from hanging out and going
clubbing, but Leona knew they weren't all at university and some of
them lived in a squat. This one didn't look like he lived in a squat,
though. Much too well-groomed.

He caught Leona looking at him and gave her a big, lazy grin.

Emily came back from the bar with two pints of lager in plastic
glasses and passed one to Leona. Leona's admirer was still smiling at
her and raised his eyebrows as if to say, *How about it?* Emily glanced
over her shoulder and caught sight of him. 'Happy birthday,' she
said to Leona. 'There's your night sorted.'

Leona shrugged. 'Yeah, well, it's not like I can do anything about
it, can I? I have to get back and anyway, as soon as he knows I have
a baby he'll lose interest.'

'Well, you don't have to tell him straight away, do you? Gorgeous
Jake – *what* a birthday present. Oh, look, I think he's coming over.'

Jake approached with a knowing swagger that suggested he was
used to girls being impressed by him.

'Hi, Emily,' he said, and fixed his attention on Leona. She was
suddenly conscious of her bare shoulders, of the way her strappy
top exposed the shape of her body.

'We haven't met before,' he said. 'I'm Jake.'

'I'm Leona, Emily's friend from school.'

'Leona, like a lion?'

'August birthday. Today, in fact. My mum's not that into astrol-
ogy, but I think she had a bit of a hormone rush after I was born.'

'Well, happy birthday,' Jake said, and looked at her as if he was
thinking about what he might like to give her.

'I'm going to leave you two to get to know each other,' Emily
said, and withdrew to rejoin the group of friends behind them.

Jake shook open a packet of cigarettes and offered Leona
one. She had managed to give up when she was pregnant and

hadn't smoked since, but she barely hesitated before taking it. Night fell around them as they talked, or rather, as he talked and she listened. He told her about the band he was in, the famous people he'd met and toured with before they broke through, the carpentry he did to make ends meet. Every now and then he went off to the bar to buy them fresh drinks and told her not to go anywhere. It stayed warm and the light of the streetlamps was soft and forgiving, and the air smelled of beer and cigarette smoke and perfume; it was just possible to make out the beat of the music from the pub jukebox over the background hum of conversation and laughter.

When the barman called time and she said she'd have to be going, he pressed his hand against the wall beside her as if to block her way and leaned in close so that there were only inches between his mouth and hers.

'You can't leave me,' he said.

'I have to get home.'

He looked at her steadily. It was all too easy to imagine him fixing that same gaze on her as he pushed himself inside her.

'I know you have a baby,' he told her. 'Emily told me when I was at the bar. I hear she's called Bluebell. Beautiful name, and I bet she's a beautiful baby.'

He was smiling at her. It hadn't put him off. He didn't care. He even seemed to think it was a *good* thing, something special that she had done. Leona could have cried with relief.

'I named her after the bluebell wood near the cottage my grandma lived in in Wales,' she said. 'There was a spring there that used to come back every winter and vanish in the summer, and the flowers would grow right next to it. My grandma used to take me walking down there to see them. She never used to let me pick them, though. She said you shouldn't bring wildflowers into a house. You have to leave them to grow and go and see them where they are.'

Was she babbling now? She must be drunker than she'd realised, even though she hadn't had all that much. Out of practice. But Jake didn't seem to mind.

'Emily said this is the first time your parents have let you out since you had the baby,' he said. 'You deserve to have some fun, Leona. Don't you think so?'

'I *have* had fun,' she said.

'Not enough. How can you walk away now? Your mum's babysitting for you, right? Go ring her and say you'll be back in the morning. Tell her you've missed the last bus and you'll be staying at Emily's or something.'

And she did.

Her mum was outraged. Probably justifiably, but Leona was past caring. 'This is typical of you, Leona, we give you an inch and you take a mile. You know how bad my back is these days, how much pain I'm in.' Eventually she hung up. Leona walked back from the phone box to where Jake was waiting for her and Jake said, 'You did it,' and pulled her towards him and kissed her in front of everyone.

Then, as the crowds of people on the pavement were beginning to disperse, he broke a pill in two and gave half to her.

'I'm kind of new to this…' she said.

'You really have been missing out, haven't you?' He took his half and swallowed it down with a mouthful of beer, and after she'd swallowed hers he kissed her again.

'Let's make it a birthday to remember,' he said, and raised his bottle of beer to her. 'Here's to tonight, and all the other very happy nights to come.'

She didn't sleep at all that night in the end. They went clubbing, and after the club closed he took her back on the night bus to his place. A couple of hours later she finally, reluctantly extricated herself from his embrace, let herself out and made her way back across London to her parents' house.

Everything seemed lit up with special promise, even though the pill was wearing off and she was beginning to feel the exhaustion that would dog her until she could finally make it to bed. Well, so what? She was used to being tired. But she was also used to feeling as if all that lay ahead of her was demands and difficulties and chores. Suddenly it seemed as if, along with all of that – the nappy-changing, the making of bottles of formula and plans, the childcare she needed to take up her deferred place at university – it might also be possible for her to be loved.

*

The woman sitting next to Leona on the plane says, 'Are you sure you're all right?'

She's crying. She isn't making any noise, but there are tears on her face. She wipes them away with the back of her hand and says, 'I'm just upset, that's all. Nothing to be done about it, I'm afraid.'

'Oh,' the woman says. 'I'm sorry.'

'Not your fault,' Leona says.

The woman looks as if she would like to say more, but goes back to her book. The seatbelt warning signs have come on and they are descending, plummeting towards the ground. Leona clenches her fist tightly around the crystal Rachel had given her, so that its edges dig into her skin.

If Rachel and Viv knew the truth about why she had given Bluebell up for adoption, if they knew what she had done after she started seeing Jake, would they be still be so willing to accept her? Even among people who feel like outcasts, there's a hierarchy. Viv is clearly blameless, a victim of history who had gone along with the prevailing medical advice of the time, and had given up her son because she believed it was for the best. And as for Rachel, whatever it was that had made her feel so unworthy of being her daughter's main carer, it couldn't be as terrible as what Leona had done.

There were some things you never got over. Losing a child was one of them. And so was being involved in somebody else's death.

She closes her eyes again, and the brakes squeal as the wheels of the plane touch down. The force of the friction pins her in her seat, making it impossible to move. They slowly come to a standstill and she's able to lean forward and get her bag from under her seat and drop the healing crystal into it.

All around her people are stirring and stretching, releasing their seatbelts, murmuring instructions or reprimands to their children, getting up to retrieve bags from overhead lockers. Her neighbour uses a postcard to mark her place in her book and closes it.

'I hope everything turns out all right for you,' she says to Leona.

'Thanks. But I don't think I deserve it to.'

'Yes, well, we don't always get what we deserve. Sometimes that's not such a bad thing.'

The woman gets up and shuffles forward in the queue to leave the plane. Leona stays seated a little longer, gazing out of the window.

*You have to leave bluebells to grow*, her grandmother had said to her. *You can go and see them and enjoy them, but you can't take them home with you. They're best off where they are.*

Somewhere out there is her Bluebell, waiting to meet her, maybe looking at the same French sunshine.

# Chapter Thirty

The house where Bluebell is living is in a small town close to the mountainous border with Spain, surrounded by vineyards. Spring here is different to English spring: warm, breezy, scented, with a tension in the air that suggests the possibility of thunder later. Still, at least it is not too hot to walk. Leona wants to walk; to put one foot in front of the other, and think of nothing else.

She makes her way up and down white, hilly roads, past garden walls loaded with old ropes of jasmine and budding clematis and green wisteria. She doesn't get lost. It is almost unbelievably straightforward. It is also completely unreal.

And then she comes to a standstill on the doorstep.

It's a lovely house, as she had known it would be: big, square, white-fronted, with windows shuttered against the sun. Not that it really matters what kind of place Bluebell calls home as long as she's happy and safe, but it is a kind of consolation to know she's growing up somewhere so beautiful.

Leona reaches for the polished brass knocker on the door. It hits the wood with a hollow thud that seems too soft to summon anyone, but then the door opens and a perfectly pleasant-looking Englishwoman in a Breton striped top emerges and peers at her.

It's Amy. Bluebell's mother. Her other mother. The one who took Bluebell in and looked after her when Leona couldn't, who fostered her and then adopted her.

They have spent a fair bit of time talking via Skype, planning this visit, but this is the first time Leona has seen Amy in the flesh. She looks prettier than on the computer screen. Softer. More like someone you might be friends with. The sense of being tested persists, though. Whatever Bluebell might want or not want, Leona is only here because Amy has permitted it. One false move and it'll be over.

If it goes well, she'll be invited back later, and meet Amy's husband too – Bluebell's adoptive father. Maybe Leona will even have dinner with all three of them – and then, who knows? But if it goes badly...

'Leona. You made it,' Amy says. 'How did you get here? You didn't walk, did you?'

'I did. It wasn't all that far.'

'You found it all right, obviously. How was the hotel?'

'Fine,' said Leona, who had barely noticed what it was like, and had spent the night there not sleeping.

'Well then, come on in.'

Leona steps into the entrance hall and Amy pulls the heavy door shut behind her. The two women stand there not quite looking at each other, as if neither of them is sure what to do next. Then Amy holds out her hand and Leona shakes it. Is Amy nervous? She doesn't look it. But then, why would she worry? Possession is nine-tenths of love, and she has Bluebell and Bluebell will always love her.

Amy studies her with both sympathy and detachment. She's read the files; she knows exactly what happened, and how much Leona has to regret. What must she be thinking? *How can you live with it? With what you did? I know why you gave her up. And now she's mine, and I'm glad you let her go.*

Leona wants to answer her. *I made a mistake, a terrible mistake. A ruinous mistake. And after that I had to choose what was best for her, and it wasn't me.*

She has so much to be grateful for. Amy had kept Bluebell's name: she could have changed it, started over with something of her own choosing. And she has invited Leona here. She has been more than generous. More than kind.

But Leona can't speak.

'Bluebell is playing in the garden,' Amy says. 'Do you want to come through and meet her?'

Leona nods, and Amy leads the way through the house.

All the walls are white and so are the shutters, and the floors are covered with terracotta tiles; it is cool, pale and dim. In winter, though, it would be the opposite, bright and snug and warm, a refuge from the icy dark outside. Amy takes Leona past a sitting room with a brick-surrounded fireplace and into a pristine kitchen. On one of the granite worktops is a tray with small plates and narrow glasses in wrought-metal holders, the sort you use for mint tea, and a dish of macaroons.

Amy has obviously assumed that she will be here long enough to drink and eat. But what if Bluebell gets upset, or just wants her to go?

They head out through the dining room, which has French windows open wide to admit the slight breeze from the small courtyard garden. A grapevine stretches across one wall, its dry, twisted old branches covered with new green leaves. In the middle of the lawn is a sundial, and next to it is a small girl, playing.

It's the Bluebell of Leona's most recent photograph, suddenly here and alive and real and in reach. She's a delicate-looking child with slender limbs and long fair hair, tied back in an immaculate French plait, dressed in a crisply pressed chambray smock and sandals. She's kneeling at the sundial and holding her toys so they appear to be standing on its flat face; in one hand she has a small grey plush elephant and in the other a floppy pink-and-white cloth bug, well-worn and obviously much loved.

Leona recognises the bug at once. It's the one she had packed all those years ago, when the police came for her and the social workers took Bluebell away.

Bluebell says quite clearly, 'Now, time to jump,' and makes the bug dive down from the sundial.

'She has a wonderful imagination,' Amy says. 'Go on, go and say hello. She's been looking forward to meeting you.'

Leona crosses the lawn and steps forward into the magic closed circle of the child's solitary game. She's conscious of Amy just behind her, watching silently from the small terrace, holding back for now but poised to intervene the minute she's needed. Like a mother. A real mother.

Bluebell gets slowly to her feet and looks round. She's the first to speak, and although she's plainly attempting to demonstrate her mastery of grown-up social skills her voice betrays her by a hesitancy that turns the word into a question: 'Hello?'

Something enables Leona to move nearer, as if a forcefield is flexing and giving way to admit her. She squats down by the sundial and says, 'I'm Leona. And you're Bluebell. And what are these two called?'

Bluebell kneels again and holds up her toys. 'This is Bug and this is Babar.'

'Are they friends?'

Bluebell shrugs. 'Mostly.'

She's looking at Leona's tattoo, trying not to stare. Leona pulls back her sleeve and flexes her wrist so Bluebell can inspect it. She's trembling; she hopes Bluebell won't notice.

'I'm not sure tattoos are a very good idea,' Bluebell declares.

'I'm not either. But I like this one,' Leona tells her.

'Is it for me?'

'It is.'

Her hand stops trembling. Bluebell looks up into her eyes. And there it is, back again as if all the intervening years had never passed: that moment when Leona had given her up, not knowing how long it would be for or what would happen next, and Bluebell had looked back at her as if seeing more than Leona could imagine, or begin to know.

# Chapter Thirty-One

## Mitch

Mitch is thinking about Rachel when he rings Leona's doorbell, and only remembers to stop scowling when she opens up.

She's youngish, or at least, younger than him, which he knew to expect – when they spoke on the phone she had told him her story about bunking off school to go to the Provocation exhibition, and buying a postcard of his *Persephone* painting. He'd already become a dad by then, living in the country, past his best, his *enfant terrible* years lost to a fug of domesticity. Not that this enthusiastic, rather strange young woman needs to know that. Let her think of him what she will; God knows it's long enough since he met a fan.

He'd also formed an impression of her as attractive, which, as it turns out, was not wrong.

'You must be Leona,' he says. 'I'm Mitch.'

Crushingly, she doesn't look all that excited. Is he a disappointment in the flesh? He'd had vague hopes of flattering small talk, maybe even a little mild flirtation. He should have known better, given that this whole meeting had been Rachel's idea. She wasn't going to set him up with a soothing ego massage from an admirer. No way. The girl is more likely than not to be a total crank.

But still: a pretty crank. Leona looks a bit as if she's just woken up. She's wearing a long, shapeless dress in off-white cotton, and has a pair of those felt slippers on her feet; her arms and feet are bare. She might look prim if the cotton wasn't ever so slightly transparent, and if it wasn't for the messed-up hair and the tattoo and something feline about her, as if she could be about to either scratch or purr.

It's a beautiful May morning, and warm already even though it's not yet near noon; he is suddenly conscious that he is sweating and his jacket strikes him as unbearably stuffy. But if he takes it off, what if he has damp patches under his arms?

He is ridiculous: the past-it one-hit-wonder artist with the lone female fan, who currently appears to be completely underwhelmed by his presence.

She suppresses a yawn. 'To be honest, I'd forgotten you were coming,' she says. 'I've had quite a lot on my plate lately, what with one thing and another.'

'Well, you're in the throes of setting up your own business, aren't you? It's bound to be a busy time.'

'Yes, there has been that to think about. Also, I've just got back from a trip to France.'

'Nice time of year for a holiday.'

'It wasn't really a holiday. There was someone I had to see.'

Her face changes at the thought of whoever it was – a lover, maybe? Suddenly she seems even younger, and vulnerable. The moment passes and she looks him up and down as if assessing his potential to make trouble. He does his best to appear blameless, which he is, mostly. At any rate, he's pretty sure he's not whatever she's afraid of. Leona Grey is safe with him, as long as she wants to be.

Obviously he passes muster, because she steps back to let him in. It is cool inside the flat, which is an immediate relief. Perhaps he won't need to take his jacket off after all. It is silly to care about making a good impression... but he can't help himself. It seems that he has reached that stage of decline; he is that desperate, that defeated, that any halfway pretty girl's opinion has become important to him.

'Nice place,' he says.

'I know, it is, isn't it?'

'You're not from round here, are you?'

She frowns slightly. 'What makes you say that?'

He shrugs. 'I don't know. You just seem like the kind of person who's come here from somewhere else. I am, too.'

She relaxes a little at that, though not completely. 'I grew up in London,' she says. 'But I love it here.'

The obvious reason to move from London to somewhere like Kettlebridge would be having kids. Obviously not in Leona's case, though. And even though he is rarely curious about anyone, and has been accused countless times of being wrapped up in himself – and not only by his wife – he finds himself saying, 'So, what brought you here?'

Leona stares at him almost resentfully, then thinks better of it and answers. 'I got some work experience with a company out here, and then they took me on. That's where I met Rachel. My stepdad fixed it up – he knew the guy who owned the business.'

'Nice stepdad.'

'Yeah. We didn't always see eye to eye, but it was my fault, not his. When he passed away he left me the money I used to buy this flat. Nobody could have been more surprised than me.' She gives her head a little shake as if startled for having disclosed so much. 'Anyway, would you like a coffee? I'll make you one, and then I'll show you the things I'm working on.'

The coffee is good and strong, the way he likes it. She has some kind of herbal tea that smells of ginger. They take their drinks out into the overgrown but pretty courtyard garden, where they talk about art – or rather, he talks and she listens, which makes a change. Becca glazes over when he attempts this kind of conversation, and Rachel had always been preoccupied with other things. Work, mainly. It was a long time since she had been interested in what he might have to say, and who could blame her when he had turned out to be such a failure as an artist?

But Leona is receptive. Surprisingly so. She doesn't seem to think less of him for once having had some limited success before falling by the wayside; she seems genuinely impressed by the work he had once done, even if it was ages ago. It turns out that they have been to some of the same exhibitions over the last few years, and when she mentions something that is coming up at the Ashmolean in Oxford and suggests they could go together, he doesn't say no. After all – why not? It's not as if he has anyone else to go with. Becca has taken to refusing to accompany him to that kind of thing.

Eventually she stands up and says, 'Right, better get this over with. Time to show the great artist my stuff. I hope you won't be too unkind about it.'

'I'm sure your work is delightful,' he says gallantly as he gets to his feet, suddenly ashamed to remember how down he had been on the whole idea of meeting her when Rachel first suggested it.

She shows him into the front room and says, 'This is where I keep the bigger pieces,' and waits patiently while he takes it all in and attempts to muster a suitable response.

It's bonkers. Completely bonkers. It's a beautiful room, with fine proportions, an original fireplace and the cornicing still intact. He can almost hear what an estate agent would have to say about it – *if* it wasn't packed full of odds and sods of furniture, almost as much as it's possible to fit.

There's a birdcage, a schoolkid's desk, a crib, and bric-a-brac, too: lampshades, vases, candlesticks. It's like being in a mad old lady's attic. Or an artistic kleptomaniac's junk shop. He finds he is at a loss for words.

Leona doesn't seem wounded by his lack of response, though. She looks amused. It's almost as if she knows exactly what he is thinking.

She says, 'Feel free to check out anything that catches your eye.'

He squeezes past the crib to the desk, lifts up the hinged lid, peers inside. Someone has drawn a heart with an arrow through it in blue ink, scrawled names on either side. He shuts it again.

'I don't suppose you had a chance to check out my website?' Leona asks.

'I didn't, I'm afraid. But maybe you could show it to me in a minute, if you wanted to. I mean, I'd love to see it.'

'Sure. I mean, only if you have the time.'

'I have time.'

He sucks in his breath. What is he saying? He's been here quite long enough – now is the time to thank her for the coffee, wish her well and leave. There's absolutely no way he can afford to get involved in some kind of friendship with an ex-colleague of Rachel's. Or with anyone. If he wants to preserve his sanity, he needs to steer clear of all complications from now on. So what on earth does he expect to achieve by staying here any longer?

'You know, you're a lot nicer than I thought you'd be,' Leona says.

'Oh, really? Is that because of what Rachel said about me?'

'No, no. She doesn't really talk about you. It's just, you know, I never met an artist before.'

That does it. He had thought it might be pleasurable to have someone admire him, but it turns out to be unbearable.

'I am *not* nice,' he says firmly, 'and I'm not really an artist any more, if I ever was. I'm nothing special, Leona, whatever they might have said about me once. I'm an under-employed househusband, and when Rachel and I get our divorce sorted I'll be an under-employed *ex*-househusband. So I don't really know why you want my opinion or advice about anything.'

Having delivered this outburst, he can't bear to look at her. He stoops to inspect a wooden stool painted with a design of roses – Leona's handiwork, presumably. The roses are clumsily done, but there's nothing wrong with the stool.

He can even imagine it – maybe denuded of the flowers and decorated with something more subtle – in the kitchen at Rose Cottage. It might have come in handy back in the days when Becca used to come and talk to him while he made dinner, before she went all moody and withdrawn. Her marks seemed to have picked up since he and Rachel had been called into the school for that awful meeting, but the moodiness remains, and it's tedious. No, worse than tedious: sad. There's no one to distract him from his loneliness.

'You've got a good eye,' he says.

'Thank you,' Leona says. 'I can visualise what I want, I just don't have the skill to do it myself.'

He straightens up and gives the crib a little push. It is like an artefact out of a fairy tale, suspended from an overarching stand, and rocks as smoothly as a swing, though it has a very slight squeak that wants sorting.

'Bit of oil would probably fix that,' he says.

She shrugs helplessly. 'Where?'

'Just do all the hinges. That's what I would do.'

What was that old lullaby? *If your something something… Daddy's going to buy you a diamond ring?*

He tries to imagine the infant Becca curled up in the cradle, tiny again, eyes shut tight. But Rachel would never have bought this. It would have been too fussy for her. Too unnecessary. She liked plain, sturdy things bought from reputable department stores. Out of the two of them, she had always been the practical one – at least, in the normal way of things, before she'd lost the plot.

*And whose fault was that?* Not his. It really wasn't.

He'd been protecting her, in a way. And he still was.

Her mother's death had tipped her over the edge; another shock could have had an even more catastrophic effect. It wasn't so much that she was gullible, as that she was vulnerable. What good would it do anybody for the whole truth of the situation to come out? What good would it do her, or Becca? None at all, and that was a fact.

The near-miss had been quite explosive enough. That was the thing about Rachel; she was the kind of person who kept soldiering on, and then eventually blew up.

His mother had tried to warn him, and he had ignored her: *Bad blood will out.* The tendency must have always been there, the potential violence, along with the instability. It wasn't surprising, really. You had to make allowances, considering her background.

He looks up and catches Leona watching him. Her expression is neither pitying nor embarrassed. She looks as if she wants to ask him something, or maybe to tell him something.

'Come on upstairs,' she says. 'I'll show you the textiles and the jewellery.'

He can't help but take in the view of her retreating form as he follows her; it's part and parcel of looking where he's going. The dress doesn't give much away, anyway. A vision of her without it comes to mind – Leona as a 21st-century Botticelli *Venus*, perfect and new – before he makes a decisive effort to reject it.

She leads him into a small spare room with an old-fashioned Singer sewing machine on a table in the corner. The jewellery is hanging on a selection of stands next to the sewing machine, and there are neat stacks of tubs of beads and fabrics and embroidery silks next to the table. She shows him the cushion cover she's working on currently, which is dark grey velvet, embroidered with bluebells. It's the best thing of hers he's seen so far.

He says, 'You're fond of bluebells, aren't you? It's a bit of a motif.'

He wants to sound encouraging, or at least as if he's paying attention. But she grimaces as if he's just said something tactless.

On the mantelpiece over the modest fireplace is a line of postcards of various well-known paintings. He spots Chagall holding his wife by the hand as she flies above his head, a creamy Lucian Freud and Dali's melting clocks. Nothing of his.

'*Persephone* is in my bedroom,' Leona tells him, folding the cushion cover and putting it back next to the sewing machine.

Is he that obviously insecure? He hopes not.

'I haven't seen the real thing for years,' he says. 'It's in a private collection in New York.'

'Would you like to see it again?'

'It doesn't matter whether I see it or not. That's part and parcel of what I do, when it works. You have to learn to let go.'

She grimaces again. 'They say that about being a parent, too, don't they? But it's a hard lesson to learn. Even if you know it's what you need to do.'

He stares at her. She meets his gaze steadily, but seems to hesitate. Once again he has the impression that there is something more she wants to say, but can't quite bring herself to come out with.

'Do you have children yourself?' he asks uneasily. He had assumed that she didn't... there were no signs at all of a kid of any age living in the flat. It felt very much like a place where someone lived alone. In which case, why was she looking at him as if she had something to confess?

'I have a daughter,' she says evenly. 'I had her when I was quite young, and gave her up for adoption.'

'I'm so sorry, I had no idea. I hope I haven't been tactless.'

'No, no, you haven't. It's quite all right. Rachel knows, but she obviously didn't say anything. She actually drove me to the airport... I've only just come back. I'm sorry, I'm not making much sense, am I? I went to see her. Bluebell. My daughter. For the first time since she went to live with Amy, who was her foster mother and then adopted her. They live in France now. Just beautiful. The most amazing place. But now I'm here, and she's there. And somehow I have to carry on.'

She presses her hand to her mouth and he realises that she's about to cry. He pats her ineffectually on the shoulder. 'There, there. I'm sure you've done your best for her.'

But Leona shakes her head vigorously. The tears are coming now, leaking down her face; she's disintegrating in front of his eyes. 'I messed everything up. I was so stupid, I let her down so badly, I'll never forgive myself.'

'Surely it can't have been that bad?' He is now hopelessly out of his depth. 'I suppose it was bound to be difficult, if it's the first time you've seen her since... since you said goodbye.'

Leona wipes her cheeks and makes a visible effort to slow her breathing. He waits, and eventually she says, 'I wasn't talking about the visit. That went as well as it possibly could have done. I mean I messed up when she was a baby, when I was the one who was supposed to be looking after her.' She takes a deep breath. 'Actually, there's something I want to tell you about that.'

And then she says that she had spent some time in prison, and when she came out her postcard of the *Persephone* painting was one of the things that helped her start over.

'It helped me because I'd had it before everything went wrong and it allowed me to feel like I might be able to make something out of the life I had left. It gave me hope. I've always wanted you to know that. I get the impression you're not proud of it any more, but I think you should be. Even if you never paint anything original again, you did something that helped change someone's life.'

He says, 'If anything I did was helpful to you then I'm glad, but Leona, when you started over, that was your doing, not mine.'

She's smiling at him, but her mouth is quivering as if she's about to start crying again. He reaches out and takes her hands in his and squeezes them. She looks down at the scar Rachel had given him and rubs it gently and looks up at him as if to ask a question, and he says, 'Long story.'

'I have a lot of those,' she said.

'The thing about long stories is that you don't have to rush them,' he says, and puts his arms around her and holds her. And then she moves closer and leans against him, and she's crying properly and then she's quiet.

He is conscious of them breathing in time, of his heartbeat and of hers. It's a shock to him, the way they suddenly fit together as if they are meant to be. It's like being someone else. Someone younger and bolder, right at the beginning of something new.

Her closeness blots out everything and everyone else apart from the desire to hold her and not to let her go. The rest of the world isn't there. It's only the two of them, in the middle of a room.

He doesn't consciously decide to kiss her, it just happens. A stupid thing to do. It's a hungry kiss. A clumsy one, probably. The really astonishing thing is not that she hesitates but that she kisses him back, and then the clumsiness and stupidity cease to matter.

# Chapter Thirty-Two

## Rachel

'How nice that we can sit outside,' Rachel says, carrying the tray through the open French windows to Viv's garden.

There are roses and cherry and crab apple trees, a smooth green lawn and terracotta pots of hyacinths. It is a sumptuous late May evening and the air is sweet with the scent of sun-warmed flowers. She sets down the tray on the big teak table and Viv thanks her, pours the tea and cuts them both a slice of the offering Rachel has brought, a slightly flat home-baked sponge cake.

'I hope it tastes better than it looks,' Rachel says. 'I'm out of practice. Actually, I've never had a lot of practice. The last cake I made was for Becca's birthday back in September, and that was a disaster.'

*If only nothing else had gone wrong that day.* But still, there had been a time when she wouldn't even have been able to bear to mention it.

Viv says, 'So how is Becca?'

'Oh... not too bad. Things at school seem to have picked up a bit, in terms of her marks at least. She isn't exactly talkative, though. I'm trying to find things for us to do that minimise the need for conversation, because otherwise we just end up sitting there like we're on the world's worst date.'

'It's a difficult age, isn't it?' Viv says, and shifts uncomfortably in her chair. Maybe her back is bothering her. Her aches and pains come and go, but lately the warm weather has helped; this must be some kind of setback. 'Have you spoken to Leona recently?'

Rachel instantly feels bad that she hasn't. She'd called once, after Leona got back from France, and they had spoken briefly, then exchanged a couple of emails. Leona had said Mitch had been round to see her, but hadn't been any more forthcoming than that, and hadn't seemed at all keen to meet; Rachel had felt a bit brushed off, as if Leona suddenly had more important things to do.

Maybe the meeting with Mitch had been awkward. When Rachel had mentioned it to him, he had said only that he didn't think anything more was going to come of it. She should probably have tried to talk Leona out of the whole idea. She hopes Mitch hasn't hurt Leona's feelings; he is harsh on himself, and sometimes he can be overly critical or dismissive of other people's work, too – except for anything Becca does. Becca is the one person who is always exempt, and who he defends fiercely against any perceived slight.

'We haven't really had a proper chat for a while,' she says. 'I guess I've let things slide a bit.'

'Well, I suppose it's bound to be different now you're not seeing each other every day at work, isn't it? You shouldn't beat yourself up about it,' Viv says. 'You've got a lot of other things on your plate. I think I told you the other day that I'd called her to find out how things went with Bluebell. We had a bit of a catch-up, but I felt she didn't really want to talk about it. Anyway, she called me earlier to say she won't be joining us tonight. She doesn't want to come to these meetings any more.'

'Oh.'

Rachel turns towards the pinboard, which is propped up on the chair opposite her. It's been in her bedsit since she hosted the last get-together back in March. Bluebell, with her direct gaze, looks almost more real than the other two children, the toddler splashing in puddles and Becca in her favourite red dress: at any rate, more as if she belongs to the present.

'I was surprised, too,' Viv says. 'But there we are. People come and go, and we don't always know why. Maybe now her relationship with Bluebell has moved on to a different level, she feels she doesn't need us in quite the same way. She sounded... distant. As if she has other things going on in her life that she wants to save her energy for.'

'I suppose it's fair enough to want to look to the future,' Rachel says. 'When I had counselling, the therapist was very keen on that. On not dwelling on the past.'

Viv sighs. 'I understand that, and it's wise advice, but sometimes you have to let the past come back to you. You can't always resist it. It only leads to trouble. Anyway, she says she's well. I'm sure she'll be on for meeting up at some point in the future, when she's a bit less busy. I think there's a lot of frustrated ambition there; she wants to prove herself with her new business.'

Suddenly Rachel feels close to tears. 'Viv... *you're* not suddenly going to go cool on me, are you? I don't think I could bear it. You're the only person I can really talk to.'

'I'm not planning on going anywhere,' Viv says, and reaches out and squeezes Rachel's hand.

Rachel gestures towards the sponge cake. 'Good, because I hope to inflict a whole lot more dodgy baking on you, given half a chance.'

'It's not dodgy. It's delicious,' Viv says stoutly. 'Now, there was something I wanted to ask you. Are you sure you're still all right with taking me to see Aidan? I know it takes up a lot of your time; it must be a bit of a bind. If you wanted to have a little bit of a rethink, I'm sure I could make other arrangements.'

'It's not a bind at all,' Rachel says. 'I want to keep on taking you. In fact, I insist.'

Viv beams at her. 'Thank you,' she says. 'I can't tell you how much I appreciate it. It's lovely to be chauffeur-driven, of course. But the real treat is having your company on the way. Aidan seems to have taken a shine to you, too. I think he'd miss you.'

Rachel glances at the pinboard, at the pictures of the three children. If Leona has made her peace with her loss of Bluebell, if she has found some kind of resolution, that should be something to celebrate, surely. She reproaches herself for being so mean-spirited: she should be happy for her, not disappointed.

She asks, 'Does Leona want the picture of Bluebell back?'

'She didn't mention it. Anyway, it's only a photocopy.' Viv sighs. 'If this is the end of our little group, if you and I are just going to carry on meeting as friends... do you want *your* picture back?'

'Oh, Viv... That seems so final.'

'Well, look, why don't I hang onto it for now? We can just put it aside and see how we feel, and maybe by and by we could have another go at seeing if anybody else would like to join us. If you don't mind, I'll ask you to pop it back in the cupboard for me before you go. My back is still playing up a bit. And while we're on the subject of me asking you for help, I have another request for you.'

Viv clears her throat. She looks suddenly apprehensive. Rachel says, 'Of course. Anything I can do. What is it?'

'Well... I wondered if you might be willing to accompany me and Aidan on a little trip?'

'A trip? What kind of trip?'

'Oh, just to the café down the road from his care home. It's a big adventure for him, though. I used to take him quite often, but then I lost my nerve. It got to the point where I didn't think I could catch him if he decided to run away. But you run a lot, don't you? So you must be pretty fast. Besides, he almost certainly won't do anything inconvenient. It's just that very slim possibility that he might, and if he did I'm not sure I could cope.'

'Sure. Let's give it a go,' Rachel says, though she's not at all sure she will be able to cope either. 'I'll wear my running shoes.'

'Marvellous. Thank you. He will love it – he doesn't get to go out much,' Viv says, brightening, and the effect is magical – it's as if the wear and tear of the years has melted away, as if she's Rachel's age and not her own.

That seals Rachel's fate: regardless of any misgivings she might have, there's no way she can back out. She will just have to manage. And if Viv thinks she can, if Viv trusts her... maybe, in spite of everything, she needs to try to trust herself.

# Chapter Thirty-Three

## Rachel

### The day of the loss

The two discs of sponge that Rachel had baked the night before were pretty sad-looking, even wedged together with plenty of jam. Still, the cake would look better once there were candles on top, and hopefully Becca would appreciate it anyway.

Now for the bit that took a steady hand: the writing. She needed to get it done before Becca came down – not that it was all that likely that Becca would be up before Rachel left the house, even on her birthday. Having been an early riser all through childhood, Becca had recently developed the adolescent ability to sleep away the entire morning.

*HAPPY 13TH BIRTHDAY, BECCA!* They had agreed that Rachel wouldn't wake her to wish her many happy returns; they had also agreed that Becca could open her presents in Rachel's absence, but that they would hang on until she got home for the cake. Rachel had arranged to leave work a couple of hours early, so hopefully it wouldn't be too long for Becca to wait.

In any case, Rachel wanted to have the birthday cake ready to serve. She also wanted it to be a surprise. Usually Becca had shop-bought cakes, but she had dropped one or two plaintive comments lately about how nice it would be to have home-made, and this was Rachel's rather unsuccessful attempt to show that she could do the baking mother thing along with the best of them.

Except it wouldn't be unsuccessful if it made Becca happy.

The prospect of Becca's happiness was a kind of glimmering on the surface, something that reminded her where the light was. But day-to-day life remained dark and opaque in the Deep, as it had been more or less since her mother's funeral.

Then there had been that awful moment in the pub with the other parents in the summer, when she'd seen Mitch with Mary Chadstone and convinced herself they were having an affair. Despite all Mitch's reassurances, and despite her best efforts, she had found herself brooding about that moment, and tormenting herself about whether he really had been telling her the truth. She'd brought the subject up again more than once, and Mitch had completely run out of patience with her; he'd accused her of being paranoid, obsessive... controlling. The last thing she wanted to be.

'You need help,' Mitch had said, and she couldn't disagree.

She'd booked another appointment with the doctor – the surgery was so busy, it had been three weeks before they had a suitable slot – and had managed to get time off work to attend. This time she'd been put on the six-month waiting list for counselling. There was also the possibility of going for group treatment, but the meeting times didn't fit with her working day and commute, and she was nervous about asking Elizabeth Mannering for flexible hours so she could attend. She'd made a few too many mistakes lately; she had to watch her step. She felt as if she was on probation with Elizabeth, and she didn't want to seem unreliable, or admit that she was struggling.

Her spirits rose at the prospect of being able to put a smile on Becca's face. This should be a special and memorable day for all of them – the beginning of Becca's teenage years.

She found a box to put the cake in, tucked it away out of sight, and let herself out of the house to drive to the station.

It would be a relief to be home early; the atmosphere at work had been strange lately. Unsettling, with meetings taking place between high-ups and certain members of staff in odd places at odd times. As if change might be on the way, and not necessarily for the better.

But the whole country seemed to be in the exact same state; businesses were going under, employees were boxing up their belongings, insolvency teams were moving in. It was a nervous time. She told herself it was easy to get things out of proportion, especially when you were already feeling down.

Soon after nine a message from Elizabeth dropped into her inbox. Titled 'Meeting', it was an instruction masquerading as a request, though it was slightly friendlier than usual; it started with *Hello* and ended with a sign-off, both niceties that Elizabeth usually didn't bother with.

All Elizabeth wanted to know was, *Are you free at noon?* Rachel supposed she had better be, though she wasn't keen on pre-lunch meetings – Elizabeth followed such a carefully controlled diet, that was always when she was most uptight. Rachel preferred her in what people called the graveyard slot, the post-lunch slump, much as one might prefer a predator with a full stomach to one without.

She replied promptly: *Yes, of course.* Elizabeth was one of those people who always expected responses to be almost instantaneous.

Another message from Elizabeth pinged back: *Great! I've booked meeting room three.*

That was unnerving, too. Meeting room three was tucked away out of sight; it was exactly the room you'd choose if you were planning an ambush, and didn't want to attract the attention of the rest of the office.

Or it could just be that it was the only meeting room that was available at such short notice.

At any rate, she wouldn't have long to wait to find out.

\*

When she went into meeting room three at noon Frances O'Halloran, the head of HR, was sitting at one end of the table with a sheaf of documents in front of her. Elizabeth was also already in place, and their expressions were serious and focused, as if they had something to do that needed doing, and were ready to get on with it. As if it wouldn't have been appropriate to joke.

She slid into place opposite Elizabeth and next to Frances, and Elizabeth started talking, with Frances occasionally chipping in as back-up.

It didn't make any sense. She couldn't really follow it, though she nodded along to show she understood. She could barely make out the words. There was a buzzing in her head that drowned everything else out, not so much a sound in itself as a weird, high-frequency vibration.

But she did hear *redundancy*. Also *considered*. And *only your role*.

And she could tell from their faces and from the way they were speaking that they'd already made up their minds. She might be able to resist it, to make it awkward for them, but she wouldn't be able to force a change of heart. As far as they were concerned, it was a *fait accompli*.

Numbers were mentioned. The payout she'd be entitled to. A once-in-a-lifetime sum of money. Enough to pay off their outstanding mortgage. The kind of coincidence that could fool you into thinking something was meant to be, and that you should therefore be philosophical about it.

And that was what made it possible for her to carry on sitting there, apparently listening, and behaving, even if she hadn't always quite managed to do so in recent months, like a model employee.

*

They said she could work from home that afternoon if she wanted to. Yes, she did want to. She had her daughter's birthday to get back for. At one o'clock she left the building with her head held high.

People would wonder why she wasn't in the planning meeting, taking notes as usual; well, let them – let Elizabeth say whatever she wanted, maybe even the truth. It was a fine September day, a beautiful day, and Becca was thirteen. Damn it, if she had half a chance to be there early then she was going to be.

She should get the chance to tell Mitch what was going on before Becca got back from school and choir – best not to tell Becca, not yet, she'd only worry, it would spoil the day for her. She picked up too much of the tensions around money as it was.

Anyway, it wasn't too bad. They wouldn't starve. They'd keep a roof over their heads. She'd get another job. Maybe she could go back to Frank, ask him for a reference – he'd be willing to help, wouldn't he? She'd worked for him so much longer than she'd worked for Elizabeth. Nine to five-thirty, all those years…

All those years. All those missed bedtimes, the parent-teacher catch-ups that Mitch had gone to instead of her, the sports days and appointments at the dentist and the trips to buy new shoes… Taking Becca to school, picking her up again. She hadn't been there. She'd been in the car or on the train or at her desk, working.

And now her employer was getting rid of her as if she was something unpleasant stuck to the sole of a shoe.

It *was* bad… It was bad because the whole of the life they'd built, her and Mitch and Becca at Rose Cottage, was dependent on her salary, and she was barely in a fit state to just keep things ticking over, let alone to have to start applying for jobs and selling herself in interviews and getting to grips with somewhere new.

But she could do it. She'd *have* to do it.

It was bad, but it could be worse. She could fix it. It wasn't anywhere close to the worst that could happen… like Becca being hurt or sick or going missing, the sort of things that happened in her nightmares.

The sun was shining, and life was going on all around her: cycle couriers, red buses, black cabs, men and women in suits, a crocodile of children on a school day out, all obediently holding hands with their partners.

When Becca got home she'd change into the new outfit Rachel had picked out as part of her present and they'd gather round the kitchen table to sing 'Happy Birthday'. Rachel would light the candles on the cake, then stand back to take a picture: Becca's face would be bright with the glow of thirteen tiny flames. And then Becca would take a deep breath and blow them all out, and Mitch and Rachel would applaud her and nothing else would matter.

# Chapter Thirty-Four

Rachel resolves not to dwell on all the things that could go wrong on her little expedition with Viv and Aidan. She takes her lead from Viv, who appears as sanguine and serene as if there were nothing to fear.

They progress slowly from the home to the gates: wrought iron, six feet high, firmly shut. Viv presses the buzzer mounted on the adjacent wall, says a few words, waves at the security camera. Aidan, who is busy looking around at everything – the clouds overhead, the composition of the driveway and the lawn, the view of the house from here – snaps to attention as, with a mechanical creak and a groan, the gates begin to open.

*Abracadabra.*

Viv's face is shining. It's that last-day-of-school exhilaration, the thrill of being released from the scrutiny of the powers-that-be. Whatever might lie on the other side of this moment, right here and now it is possible to breathe.

They pass through. Almost instantly, the gates begin to close behind them. The pavement is narrow and Aidan and Viv go ahead, hand-in-hand, with Rachel hurrying along behind. Passers-by don't stop and stare, exactly – after all, that would be rude – but Rachel can't help but be aware that they're being noticed.

They make a conspicuous trio. Viv is as chic as ever in a jacket patterned with tiny wildflowers, wide-legged trousers and high-heeled shoes; Aidan is dressed in the blue T-shirt he wears every time Viv visits – he couldn't be persuaded to put on any additional layers – and walks with an odd, rolling gait, as if he is at sea while everybody around him is on dry land.

Behind them, Rachel feels that she's attracting attention by association: a tall, lanky, dark-haired woman in jeans and an anorak, who looks neither like a carer nor a relative – what is she doing with them? If asked, she would say she is Viv's friend, but given the discrepancy in their ages, people would probably find that strange. How could she explain that she feels more comfortable – *safer* – with Viv than with any other woman she has ever known?

They don't have far to go: past the municipal park, over the road and into the café. Aidan clearly remembers it, which maybe explains the single-mindedness with which he is heading towards their destination. So it catches Rachel completely by surprise when he stops dead and crouches down on the pavement.

She almost walks into him. Under other circumstances, and if she wasn't already on edge, she might be exasperated; as it is, she's alarmed. Then she sees that he is looking at something and stoops so that she can see it, too. Other people make their way around them, more or less puzzled and annoyed by the spectacle of a man who has decided to crouch down on the pavement and the two women who seem to think it's all right to add to the obstruction he is causing.

Viv appears to take Aidan's sudden pit stop in her stride. She smiles encouragingly and says, 'What is it, Aidan?'

He looks up at her. There's some kind of tentative hope there, as if he has long been starved of praise or reward and is responding to the faint prospect of it. His eyes latch on to Viv's. 'Dead bee,' he says.

'Yes,' Viv agrees, nodding. 'Dead bee, on the ground. Is it sad?'

Aidan looks nonplussed, as if this could be a trick question or is, alternatively, just his mother being incredibly dense. He drops his gaze and studies the bee again, as if it's possible that it might start moving. It's a bumble bee, lying flat on its back; it's strange to be able to observe the hairiness of its fat little body, and to see a creature that is so defined by its movement suddenly still.

'It isn't sad,' he explains carefully. 'It's dead.'

'Does it make you feel sad?' Viv asks.

Aidan considers this and mournfully shakes his head. He straightens up and looks up at Viv again, more searchingly this time. He lifts his hands and presses his thumbs together and flaps his fingers in an imitation of flight, and says, 'Where did it go?'

Viv points at the small body on the pavement. 'It's right there, Aidan.'

But Aidan shakes his head, and Rachel thinks she sees his point: the small residue of the bee bears little resemblance to the quick, loud force of nature it would have been in life. It's a legitimate, if unanswerable, question: *Where did all that energy disappear to?*

Viv asks, 'Should we move it?' and that's when Rachel gets her first glimpse of Aidan's temper. Temper isn't the right word: it's a shocking transition – the Aidan standing in front of them is no longer a sweet, overgrown child, troubled by a dead bee, but a menacing thug who scowls at them and thumps his thigh with his fist and bellows out, 'No! No, don't move it.'

'OK, Aidan, we'll leave it,' Viv says reasonably, and Aidan's rage passes as quickly as it came. He says, as if by way of explanation, 'It's dead,' and then sets off again at a pace towards the café, with Rachel and Aidan hurrying to keep up.

There are two young mothers sitting in the front window of the café with a toddler who is working his way through a big cookie studded with Smarties. As Aidan and Viv go in, with Rachel following, one of the mothers gives them a hard stare and pulls a face at her friend as if to say, *Did you see what we've got to contend with now?*

Rachel catches her eye and glares at her, and she turns sulkily away. Viv, who is at the counter and already asking for tea and cakes, is the picture of equanimity; maybe she hadn't noticed their fellow patrons' response to their arrival.

At least the proprietor is smiling at them. He's a big man, neatly dressed; Turkish, perhaps. He makes a point of saying hello to Aidan, who doesn't look too sure what the form is for such occasions but contrives to say hello in return.

'We don't see you so much these days,' the proprietor says to Viv. 'You keeping well?'

'Yes, just getting older, which beats the alternative,' Viv says. She gestures towards Rachel. 'This is my friend Rachel.'

The proprietor doesn't seem to find this strange at all, despite the gap in their ages. He beams at Rachel approvingly. 'Good to see you. I'll bring everything out to you as soon as it's ready.'

'Thank you,' Viv says, and leads Aidan towards a table at a slight but hopefully safe distance from the mothers and toddler by the window.

Aidan rearranges the salt and pepper pots, then picks up the laminated menu and taps it experimentally against the table. One of the two women sitting at the window is watching them – not the one who turned her nose up when they came in, the other one, but she too appears not to find their company to her taste.

Aidan puts the menu down. He stares at the table and mutters, 'No iPad.' He gives Viv a shrewd look, as if about to propose a deal, and adds, 'We eat, we drink, and then we leave.'

'Absolutely,' Viv says.

'We can talk,' Aidan comments with a shrug. He picks up a teaspoon and begins to drum it on the table.

Over by the window, the toddler is seized by joyful inspiration. He grabs a spoon and begins to bash it in approximate time with Aidan's.

His mother takes it off him and says, 'No, Louis.'

Louis points at Aidan. 'But he's doing it.'

'Well, maybe he doesn't know any better. Maybe somebody should be telling him not to do it as well,' the woman says.

'Excuse me,' Rachel says. 'Do you have a problem?'

'Rachel,' Viv says warningly.

Aidan keeps on tapping his spoon. His face is a blank.

The woman gets to her feet. She says, 'He's making a terrible noise. Can't you stop him? I can hardly hear what my friend's saying.'

'I had the impression you didn't have a whole lot to say to each other anyway,' Rachel says.

'If you can't control him, you shouldn't bring him here,' the woman says, and she and her friend gather up their bags and take the toddler out.

The instant they're gone, Aidan lays down his teaspoon.

He looks appraisingly round the café, which appears suddenly idyllic in the afternoon sunlight, and gives Rachel a slow, canny, quite deliberate smile.

# Chapter Thirty-Five

## Rachel

### The day of the loss

Her train was held up – typical. When she finally made it back to Rose Cottage, the people carrier wasn't there.

Mitch must have popped out for something or other. Anyway, there was still plenty of time before Becca would be back.

Rachel let herself into the house. Something about it – a stillness and coolness in the air, the sense of something brewing – reminded her of meeting room three earlier that day, just before Elizabeth began to speak.

Suddenly the little scene she'd witnessed that night at The Merry Miller pub came back to her, as clear as day, as clear as when she had seen it with her own eyes.

Mitch and Mary Chadstone.

But they had talked about it… she had asked him outright. She had wept, and he had held her and soothed her.

She had asked him again, and he had said, 'You need help,' and she had believed him.

Now all her suspicions came screaming back, and it was no longer possible to ignore them.

*If he had lied… if he was someone who was capable of lying like that, so deliberately, so believably… then what else might he have lied about?*

If he was a liar… then how on earth could she continue to believe in him, and in the life they had built together?

\*

She locked up the house, got back into her car, turned it round, and set off to find him.

It was a quick journey, in spite of the traffic. How convenient it must have been... Two houses with no nosy neighbours: Rose Cottage with its lane and its bridge, and the Chadstones' place with its high wall and screen of towering horse chestnut trees. Two houses, two spouses who commuted to London and worked long hours.

So many questions...

*How long?*

*How often?*

*When had it started?*

*Had they been together in her house, her bed?*

*Was it true?*

She had to know. She drove as if washed along on a tide of urgency, but at the same time she was aware of making a special effort to be a careful driver, a model citizen. This was who she was, even today, even now. A considerate person, a person who did the right thing. She was fair, she was reasonable, she gave others the benefit of the doubt.

She had especially given her husband the benefit of the doubt.

She had thought that was the right – the necessary – thing to do. And he'd made a fool of her.

Mitch had told her she was paranoid, and she'd believed him. It seemed as good a word as any for the return of the old feeling, familiar from her childhood, that the people who were meant to care for her couldn't be trusted. It had even been reassuring, in a way, to know that it was all just in her head. That this time round, the threat wasn't real.

Besides, it was difficult to think clearly about anything in the Deep.

She knew what she was going to see before she saw it. And there it was, at the end of Mary's drive, next to Mary's Range Rover: the people carrier. Mitch's car. *Their* car.

It is the car he had used to collect her and Becca from hospital, thirteen years ago that day. The car in which she had held her mother's ashes.

The car he had used to visit the old friend he had fallen in love with, whose house she was now outside.

# Chapter Thirty-Six

The following Sunday Rachel calls in at Viv's house just after lunchtime, as usual.

No answer.

She rings the bell again.

There is music coming from inside, something classical – Brahms maybe? – rising and falling, not in an operatic way but with the gentle, lilting melody of a folk song. Upstairs, the bathroom window is open. Viv must be at home then – she's always so careful about locking the place up.

Rachel lifts up the letterbox and peers through it. Through the fuzzy rims of insulation, she glimpses a narrow slice of Viv's hallway. It all looks the same as it always does.

Perhaps Viv is in the garden and can't hear her. Maybe something has happened, something that has made her lose track of time? Maybe she's on the phone, or in the bathroom, or has just had to pop out for a minute and will come up behind Rachel on the path any second now, all smiles and apologies.

It strikes Rachel that there is a peculiarly still quality to what she can make out of the interior of the house, as if it is frozen in time or memory. As if there is nobody there to stir the air. But that is just her imagination working overtime.

Has Viv fallen, hurt herself? If so, why doesn't she call out?

Maybe she's unconscious.

Rachel calls through the letterbox and goes round to the side to shout over the gate.

Nothing. The house remains resolutely tranquil. Not even an echo.

There is a sudden buzzing right by her ear and she jumps half out of her skin. It's a bumblebee, seemingly much more certain of its direction than Rachel is; it zigzags past her and zips upwards out of sight.

She gets her phone out of her bag, scrolls through her contacts. *In Case of Emergency…*

ICE Mitch.

What is she going to say to him? *Look, I know it seems crazy but I just wondered what you thought I should do, I'm outside my friend Viv's house and the radio's on and the window's open but there's no sign of her…*

It goes straight through to voicemail. That familiar, grumpy voice: *Can't come to the phone right now, so leave a message.*

What did she expect, that he would suddenly swoop into the scene on a white charger and tell her what to do? Surely she should know by now that no man – especially not her estranged husband – is going to save the day.

She ends the call and rings both neighbours' doors. No answer. It's such a lovely Sunday, everybody will be out – probably walking off leisurely pub lunches down by the river.

This time, when she shouts through the letterbox, she's less surprised by the lack of an answer.

She reaches forward and tries the handle of the gate. To her astonishment, it turns. She pushes it open.

*Abracadabra.*

Rachel goes through. Viv isn't in the garden, which is as well-tended and peaceful as it always is, but with no signs of recent activity; no trug part-filled with heads of weeds or gloves that have just been put aside, no cooling mug of tea.

The back door is unlocked, too. Rachel goes in. She calls out one more time: 'Viv?'

No answer.

She has come to know Viv, to drive her to see her son once a week, to love her. It's for her to find whatever there is to find.

The music is louder now: the radio is on in the kitchen. The washing up has been done – there isn't much of it, a bowl, a plate. It has been stacked neatly on the draining board, some time ago, it seems; it is bone dry.

There's nobody in the living room. Rachel makes her way up the stairs. She feels as if she's flying, as if she's weightless; her steps seem to make no sound. At the same time the air seems dense and liquid; it is possible to move but only because she has magically acclimatised. She's as much part of this strange scene as the altered elements.

Viv is in her bedroom, lying on the floor next to the immaculately made bed. She could be sleeping except she's obviously not. If she was napping, she'd be curled up on top of the covers. Instead she's sprawled on the carpet with her limbs at awkward angles. She doesn't look uncomfortable, however. Nor does she look undignified, or peaceful. She looks like a challenge posed to nature: *How can the human body, the human will, come to this?*

Rachel reaches for her phone. She thinks of Aidan waiting, dressed in his blue T-shirt. As she rings she tries to remember her long-ago first aid training: *mouth-to-mouth, the recovery position. There has to be something she can do…*

But she knows it is too late. Viv has already gone.

# Chapter Thirty-Seven

## Rachel

### The day of the loss

She wanted to throw rocks at the windows. But because she was a good citizen, a model citizen, she rang the bell.

No answer.

Of course not.

She hammered away with the door knocker, stooped to yell through the letterbox: 'Mitch! Mitch, get down here. I know you're in there and I'm not going anywhere.'

The house remained silent. It could almost have been empty. Well, sooner or later he'd have to come down, make his case, try to pull the wool over her eyes. They were probably frantically cooking up a story right now, as he cleaned himself up and zipped himself back into his jeans.

All that time she had spent working, feeling guilty about working, carrying the weight of supporting the family on her shoulders…

How long had this been going on?

How could he do this to her?

How could he do it to Hugh, his oldest friend?

And Becca, the apple of his eye?

And today, of all days. On Becca's birthday. How could he have forgotten what today meant – the pain and fear and joy of it, Becca so small and sleepy and swaddled up tight, his first time of holding her? The three of them together, becoming a family.

And here he is, with someone else. With someone who's supposed to be a friend.

The door swung open and Mitch greeted her with astonishment. 'Rachel, is everything OK? What are you doing here?'

'What are *you* doing here?'

And there was the watercolour of the garden at Rose Cottage, hanging on the wall just behind him. A melancholy, frosty scene, almost colourless: a January morning, soon after dawn. The garden didn't look particularly special – it was a small lawn surrounded by mostly leafless borders – but the light was beautiful. It suggested a desire for something more vivid and intense than the ordinariness of home, even if more transient.

She grabbed for the painting, lifted it off the hook – it came away easily – and smashed it down onto the floor. The frame broke into two and the glass shattered with a satisfying crack and scattered in jagged fragments. She wanted to hurt him back – to smash something he'd made just as he had wrecked everything they'd built together. But it was fuel to the fire: the sight of the damage she'd done just made her angrier.

'You miserable, self-pitying bastard!' she yelled at him. 'How can you stand there and act like you don't know what I'm talking about? For years it's driven you crazy that you couldn't have the success you wanted and I was the one paying the bills and keeping a roof over our heads. I suppose this was your way of getting your own back. Did she make you feel good about yourself, Mitch? Did she flatter you?'

Mitch held out one hand as if to keep her at bay. 'Rachel, you seriously have to calm down.'

'Don't patronise me! The least you could do is admit the truth. How long has it been going on, Mitch? How long have you two been getting away with it? It's not just me you've done this to, it's Hugh. Pretty much your only friend. How could you?'

'What is going on?' It's Mary, who had come into the hallway, taken in the scene and decided to stay at a safe distance.

'What's going on is that you've been screwing my husband, and now I know about it.' Rachel gave Mitch a shove. How could he keep looking like that – so shocked and innocent and untouchable, as if she was the one who was breaking the rules, as if she was making some crazy scene that had nothing to do with him? '*You* told me I was going crazy! You must have thought I was so stupid, believing you. You *liar*!'

Mitch looked down at the mess at his feet. The painting was face down, half covered by the backing board and littered with bits of glass.

'You're hysterical,' he says. He is cold and contemptuous: that just enrages her even more. 'You need to get a grip.'

'Oh, fuck you!'

She could quite happily have grabbed one of those big chunks of glass and stabbed him with it, just to wipe that look of lying superiority off his face.

'You know what you've done! Just *admit* it!'

She shoved him again, and he staggered back and somehow missed his footing and thumped down onto the floor.

He screamed. A great shout of pain and fear. Mitch. Her Mitch. To cry out like that…

What had she done?

How often had she watched her mother fall, listened to her shriek and whimper? And here it was, again – the chaos and viciousness of it, shouting and glass and bits of broken wood…

Blood. Suddenly everywhere, a great gush of it, pouring from Mitch's hand.

'Hold it up. Up!' Mary commanded.

Somehow Mary had got in close to Mitch and was kneeling beside him and making him keep his hand up, to slow the flow of blood, and the flesh of his palm was hanging open and there was gore everywhere – wet, sticky, as bright as paint – and Mitch was groaning, and Mary was pulling off the cardigan she was wearing and wrapping it round his hand to staunch the flow.

*I'm so sorry I'm so sorry* – someone was saying it over and over – it was her, and she was the one who had done this – who had made this happen.

'You could have killed him,' Mary spat at her. 'You stupid bitch.'

Through the open front door came the sound of a car being driven onto the gravel and braking to an abrupt stop. There was music coming from it, something with a fast beat. The music went off, too, and someone laughed.

Mary said to Mitch, 'That'll be Henry with the girls. Becca's going to be here in a minute.'

He had gone waxy, as if he was about to faint. Even his lips were pale. The blood was still pulsing out of him, soaking the pale-blue material of Mary's cardigan.

He murmured, 'Oh no, no, I don't want her to see…'

Rachel stepped forward, reached for the phone on the hall table. 'I'll call an ambulance,' she said.

'Leave it,' Mary barked. 'I'll drive him down to Kettlebridge hospital. It'll be quicker.'

'I can take him,' Rachel said.

Mitch said something Rachel couldn't hear. He rallied and tried again.

'Rachel, I don't want you to take me,' he said.

She froze. He was right – how could she be the one to help him, when she was the one who had made this happen? She was no better than any other abusive spouse…

But it had been an accident.

No. No, that wouldn't do. She had broken the glass. She had pushed him. She had made it happen.

She was just the same as the kind of man who picked a fight with his wife because he was jealous and tried to blame her for having provoked him. And then felt guilty anyway, and tried to make up for it.

Then there was the crunch of footsteps, an exchange between questioning voices – Becca and Amelia – and the door was pushed open a little wider and Becca came in.

Becca gaped in horror at the scene at her feet. Her hand went to her mouth; her eyes were very wide.

'Daddy!' She launched herself towards them.

Rachel yelled, 'Mind the glass!'

Becca slowed her pace and picked her way through the fragments, then crouched down next to Mitch and gazed at him imploringly. She said, 'Are you going to be all right?'

Mitch attempted a smile. 'Oh, I should think so. Might have to learn to paint with my left hand. Could be an improvement.'

He was trying to put a brave face on things for Becca, to make a joke of it, even with his hand torn open and blood everywhere....

Rachel's breathing was making a strange rasping sound, not far off sobbing: it was all she could do to get air into her lungs. Becca swivelled round and stared at her. 'Mum, what are you doing just standing there? You have to *do* something!'

Mitch said, 'She did *this*. We were having a fight. She broke the painting and pushed me so that I fell on the glass.'

'*You* did this?' Becca's face is tight with fear and disgust. 'How could you? I *hate* you!'

'Mitch, I think we should get you down to the hospital,' Mary said, and her voice cut through everything else. 'You're going to need stitches. Do you think you can stand?'

Rachel instinctively stepped forward to help but Mitch gave her a look that made her recoil. She staggered back and leaned against the wall to stay upright as Mitch got to his feet.

'Please, Daddy, can I come with you to the hospital?' Becca said.

'Sure, sweetheart, if you want.'

'Of course I want to,' Becca says, with a fierce look at Rachel.

Mary had slipped her arm under Mitch's elbow to support him; he was leaning on her. She said, 'Can you try and keep pressure on the wound?' Mitch moved his good hand onto the bleeding one. 'That's it. Good. Henry, could you get my bag? It's down by the table.'

Rachel saw that Henry and Amelia were standing inside the doorway, staring at the carnage. Henry darted forward and grabbed Mary's bag and held it out to her, and she took it with her free hand.

'Thank you,' Mary said. 'Would you clear up a bit? Wrap the glass in newspaper. Just make sure no one treads in it. We don't want anyone else getting hurt.'

'Sure, Mum,' Henry said.

Mary said to Mitch, 'Do you think you can walk?'

'I think so,' Mitch said.

'The car's just outside.'

'I might bleed all over it.'

'That's all right. That doesn't matter at all.'

They began to move towards the door; Henry and Amelia stepped back. Mary hissed at Rachel, '*You* can get out of my house.'

Somehow Rachel made herself move. She went out behind Mitch and Mary and Becca, and someone closed the door behind her.

Mary unlocked the Range Rover and the three of them turned and looked at Rachel. Mitch had a little bit more colour in his face; it was Becca who was ashen now. Mary was red-faced and wild-eyed, as if she'd just been fighting. But they all had an almost identical expression of disgust and condemnation.

Mitch said, 'Becca, get in.'

Becca scrambled into the back. Mary stuck by Mitch's side as he leaned against the side of the car and faced Rachel. He said in a low voice, 'I don't know what you thought was going on here, but Amelia asked Becca round to celebrate her birthday. Since Becca wasn't having a party or anything. Mary got in balloons and party food for the girls, the kind of thing they used to like when they were little, and she asked me to come round, too, because she thought Becca would like it if I was there. We were going to head home in plenty of time to be here when you got back from work.'

His eyes were cold and there was nothing in the way he looked at her but hate.

'I never thought I'd say this, Rachel, but you really are just like your father.'

'Mitch, we've got to go,' Mary said. She opened the passenger door and bundled Mitch in, then dashed round to get in the driver's side, started the car and pulled away.

The house was completely quiet. Rachel's car was in front of her, parked at an odd angle in front of the entrance. The people carrier was a little way away.

After the trip to the pub with the other parents in the summer, when Mitch had denied that anything was going on with Mary, she had done her best to believe him, and to put the whole thing out of her mind. But then she had reacted to the sight of that car as if there could no longer be any doubt. As if it was proof.

But it wasn't.

Who knew how soon Mitch would be able to drive it again? What if there was damage to tendons, or nerves?

There were spots of blood on the gravel.

Rachel made it a step or two towards the car before her legs gave way under her, and she dropped to the ground and howled like a child.

# Chapter Thirty-Eight

The day of Viv's memorial service is the first time Rachel has been back to her house since she found the body.

She parks next to an estate car she doesn't recognise, which must belong to Viv's daughter, Elaine. Somehow it's obvious that Viv isn't there. It's not that the place looks untended: Elaine had asked Rachel to help find a gardener to keep things tidy, and Viv's roses are flamboyantly beautiful – more spectacular by far than the unkempt display at Rose Cottage. But even though Elaine and her girls have been staying there, the house is somehow lifeless, the windows all closed and blank.

Rachel rings the bell and Elaine comes out. Out of Viv's two daughters, Elaine is the one who has done the lion's share of the work of making the necessary arrangements, while Louise, the pathologist, has taken a backseat. Rachel doesn't know if Elaine volunteered for this, or feels burdened by it, or both. She's done a good job of sorting everything out, though. She has Viv's observant gaze and brisk, friendly efficiency, but not her meticulous grooming: today she's in a pair of dark trousers and a slightly creased shirt, and comfortably chunky shoes. She hasn't bothered with make-up, and her hair – thick and fair, as Viv's must have been when she was younger – is loose and more than a little wild.

'You ready for this, then?' Elaine says.

'As I'll ever be,' Rachel says.

They get into Rachel's car and join the traffic on Gull Street, then make their way at a crawling pace towards the narrow bridge that spans the Thames and leads out of town.

This is their second meeting; on the previous occasion they had gone to Aidan's home together so that Elaine could decide whether or not to agree to Rachel's request to carry on seeing him. It had been rather like an audition. Luckily, Rachel had passed. Aidan had been so overjoyed to see her that he had run up and down the visitors' room in a mild state of frenzy, ululating and flapping his hands as if that was the only way to rid himself of the overpowering electrical charge of excitement. Then he had settled down, and they had walked into the grounds and ventured out to the café, and this time nobody had stared or made comments. Whatever the staff at the home had said to Elaine had obviously been enough to remove any remaining doubts.

The road twists and turns ahead between lines of old oak trees, their heavy masses of green leaves tainted by the bronze of blight as if smitten by premature autumn.

'I'll take the back roads, so we don't get snarled up in traffic,' Rachel says. 'I always used to come this way with your mum. It doesn't take too much longer, and anyway, we've got plenty of time.'

'Thank you for doing this,' Elaine says. She makes a little gesture with her hands that reminds Rachel of the way Aidan sometimes shakes his, in excitement or anticipation or perplexity. 'You're so good with him. I just don't have the patience.'

'It took us a while to get used to each other,' Rachel says.

'I can imagine. Maybe if we'd been able to get to know each other when we were younger... But it's too late for all that now. This time tomorrow we'll be on our way back to Norfolk. It's simply not practical for us to keep on coming back. As you know, I'm on my own, and my ex-husband is not exactly reliable. My priority has to be my girls. That's why I'm so glad you're here, to keep an eye on things. Mum did a good job, finding you.'

The question hangs in the air for a minute and then Elaine makes it explicit: 'So where did you meet exactly? Don't take offence, but you don't strike me as the churchy sort.'

'We met through a mutual friend. Someone I used to work with,' Rachel says.

Leona had taken her time to reply to the email Rachel had sent telling her what had happened, but at least she'd said she was going to come to the service. Her response had left Rachel disappointed and puzzled. Hurt, too, though it seemed silly, as a grown-up, to still be capable of being wounded by a lapsed friendship, like a schoolgirl who'd fallen out with a classmate. It was as if Leona was being wary, deliberately holding back for fear of getting sucked back into something she'd decided to drop.

'I wondered if you were from one of Mum's groups,' Elaine says. 'They used to drive me mad. There was always a bunch of people sitting round in the house, talking about something. She had a way of collecting lame ducks.' She gives Rachel a quick sideways look. 'Don't take that the wrong way.'

'I'm a lame duck. And we did try to start a group,' Rachel says. 'It was for women who have children they're separated from.'

She has already told Elaine that her daughter doesn't live with her; there was no way not to, since they're picking Becca up. Elaine's reaction had been mercifully matter-of-fact, rather Viv-like in fact, almost as if Rachel's situation was not unusual.

'You don't seem especially like a lame duck.'

'Well, I am. And if I don't seem like one that's something to do with her. I owe your mother a lot, you know.' Suddenly Rachel feels like crying, never a good thing when you're driving. 'I lost my own mother last year. It had been a difficult relationship, and we never really resolved things. But when I got to know Viv… I don't know. It was comforting.'

Elaine sighs. 'Then I'm sorry that you've lost her, too.'

'I keep thinking of things it would have been good to tell her,' Rachel says, and then falls silent because Elaine is the one whose mother's memorial service is taking place later that day, and she owes it to Viv to support her.

'She did too much,' Elaine says. 'Always on the go, always taking on more than she could cope with. I used to try and tell her to slow down, and she wouldn't listen. It's like she spent her whole life trying to compensate. I suppose she must have felt she had to make up for giving up Aidan. Anyway, it's not surprising she ended up having a heart attack.'

'She did really love him, you know. It was very touching to see them together.'

'It's good that she let you help her. That was unusual for her. She was always the one doing the helping.'

'She did help me, too,' Rachel says.

They travel onwards in silence, past fields and trees, and by and by are granted a glimpse of the hills they will have to cross to bring Aidan back.

Aidan hadn't come to Viv's cremation. Probably Elaine still has her doubts about him being present at the memorial service. When she and Rachel had discussed it she'd let slip that Louise, her sister, was not at all keen on the idea, though she had left the organising and decision-making to Elaine. It was also clear that Elaine had come to regret excluding Aidan from the earlier ceremony, and wanted to make up for it. So the prodigal son had been invited: not that Aidan is capable of being prodigal. But he has certainly been exiled from family gatherings until now.

They can't be entirely sure how Aidan is going to cope with this. Rachel thinks he understands that Viv has gone; she had tried to explain, had said that it was something that happened to people when they got old, like cars that stopped working or the bee that they had found on the pavement outside the café that time. Aidan had nodded vigorously and had said 'yes' a lot, and had tuned out any further attempts at discussion by humming increasingly loudly. It was impossible to know how he felt about it. He couldn't say, and clearly didn't want to be asked.

Maybe attending the memorial service would help in some way; it would at least mark Viv's passing, not just for Aidan but for Rachel, too. And even if he disrupts the whole ceremony and they end up with a disaster on their hands, that would be some kind of redress for having spent most of his life shut away out of sight.

Aidan is wearing the favourite blue T-shirt he always used to wear when Viv and Rachel visited; Elaine isn't especially happy with this, but lets it pass.

Rachel sees the T-shirt as a sign that Aidan is ready, and that he understands what is about to happen: that this is his chance to say goodbye. Still, it takes a while to get him into the car.

As she tries to coax him in Elaine looks on from the back seat, arms folded. She doesn't intervene but her impatience is clearly building, and Rachel feels her own anxiety levels rising.

Will Aidan give in before Elaine blows up, or will he refuse to cooperate altogether? He walks round the vehicle, sniffing it, examining it. Rachel tentatively opens the passenger door, which he has just slammed shut, but he responds with alarm and asks her to shut it again.

After what seems like a long time, but is probably only five minutes, he says, 'I can't do it.'

'You can,' she says.

He meets her eyes. He tends to avoid this kind of contact, which creates an impression of shiftiness or, from a more sympathetic perspective, profound shyness. This is a rare, disconcertingly intimate moment. It is as if the light from his eyes is touching Rachel's; she's reminded of a nature film in which two snails meet, and tentatively, flinchingly brush against each other with the stalks of their feelers.

She turns away first. She moves towards the passenger door, more slowly this time, and opens it as wide as it will go.

He stands and stares at the interior of the car. Finally, when it seems as if he will never capitulate, he abruptly scrambles in.

Rachel leans across him to buckle his seatbelt. He looks as if he is concentrating furiously, but not on anything that can be seen.

'Let's get the hell out of here,' Elaine mutters, and Rachel gets in next to Aidan and obediently accelerates away.

As the care home disappears behind them the sensation of escape is so strong that it is almost as if they have lost contact with the ground, as if they're flying, and not to a church in Kettlebridge but to somewhere completely unknown. It is as close to free as Rachel has felt for a long time, and she wonders if Aidan feels the same.

They make it to Rose Cottage a little early, and pull up outside the little bridge.

Having been calm as long as they were moving, Aidan seems to surface as if from a state not far removed from sleep, and stirs restively. Elaine says, 'I think we'd better make this quick.'

For months Rachel has been obsessive about turning up precisely on time, as if to prove to Mitch that she can: that she's reliable, that she can be trusted. She tells herself that these are exceptional circumstances: she's about to accompany a man with learning difficulties to his mother's memorial service. He can hardly object to her calling round ten minutes before she's due to pick Becca up.

Still, she feels both nervous and bold as she rings at the bell. As if Viv is propelling her to break the rules.

To her surprise, it's Becca who answers, dressed in a long black skirt and top and ready to go. Becca has been pretty good about coming to the service, which coincides with their regular Saturday visit time; it won't mean much to her personally, since she had never met Viv, but when Rachel had explained about it she hadn't raised any objections. Instead she responded with the same wary indifference that she extends to almost everything nowadays. If adolescence is the process of hatching into a butterfly, Becca is well and truly in her chrysalis.

Becca gets into the back of the car, and Rachel introduces her to the others. Becca seems alert and receptive in a way she isn't usually, as if having other people with them – whoever they are, and whatever is about to come next – is actually a relief.

'Nice to meet you,' Becca says politely to Elaine. 'I'm sorry about your mum.'

'Thank you,' Elaine says.

'Your mum, too, of course, Aidan,' Becca adds, reddening.

Aidan swivels round and inspects Becca, then reverts to staring out of the windscreen. Rachel tries to catch Becca's eye – she wants to signal some kind of reassurance, *Don't worry, it's difficult, you meant well* – but Becca avoids her.

It's hard to tell which of Viv's children looks more apprehensive. With a sense of heading from the frying pan to the fire, Rachel turns and heads off down the lane.

*

She parks directly outside the church and goes round to let Aidan out. The previous evening she had figured out how to put on the safety locks so he couldn't open the door, but it seems that it wouldn't even occur to him to try. She knows he sometimes goes out in the care home's minibus; maybe it is a rule to remain seated until told otherwise.

'Out you come,' she says, leaning across to unbuckle him.

He emerges to sniff the air and scans the façade of the church as if committing it to memory. The service isn't due to begin for another half an hour, but already a few people are gathered outside, taking a moment to greet each other in the sunshine before going in to take their seats. Some of them look familiar, though it takes Rachel a moment to place them; one of them works in the bookshop in town, and another is a hairdresser she's gone to once or twice.

She takes Aidan by the hand, as Viv used to do, and he doesn't resist. He is a good hand holder; his touch is warm and firm, and, to her surprise, immediately comforting. She hadn't expected the reassurance to be mutual.

They pass through the arched wooden doors into the startlingly cavernous vaulted interior of the church. Here the air is cool and still and the light is soft, as at daybreak or sundown; it gleams from the stained glass and is absorbed by dark wood and old stone.

A woman Rachel hasn't met before is standing just inside, clasping a handful of leaflets on which the order of service has been printed. She's tall and fair and slightly rigid, as if standing to attention, and greets them with an anxious smile.

'Excellent, excellent, you made it in good time,' she says to Elaine. 'The girls have been fine. They're over there, at the front, in the pews reserved for family.'

'You must be Louise,' Rachel says. 'I'm Rachel, and this is Becca, my daughter. I was a friend of your mother's.'

She holds out her hand for Louise to shake. Louise takes it, clenches it tightly for a minute, then drops it and turns to Aidan.

'You must be Aidan.'

Louise's smile is now so stiff it hurts to look at it. She holds out her hand; Aidan looks at her aghast and turns away.

'Can we sit down now?' he asks Rachel plaintively.

'Yes, yes, you go on,' Louise says, thrusting an order of service into Rachel's hands.

Rachel needs no further encouragement. As she ushers Aidan and Becca into the church she hears Louise asking Elaine, 'Couldn't you at least have got him to wear something a little more suitable?' and can only hope that Aidan has neither heard nor understood.

*

Once they have settled in a pew Aidan seems quite happy again, and falls to studying the circle of bronze pendant lights suspended across the nave in front of them.

Elaine is on his other side, with her teenage daughters – shy girls who look a bit overwhelmed by the occasion – next to her; beyond them is the space reserved for Louise. Elaine's ex-husband hasn't come; he's away on holiday with his new partner, and the tone of Elaine's voice and the look on her face as she'd explained this had conveyed exactly how she felt about the pair of them.

Becca is squashed into the corner next to Rachel. Behind them, the church gradually fills up, and hums with restrained conversation. It is going to be quite a turnout.

Rachel inspects the order of service. The picture on the front makes her heart sink: it's a black and white photocopy of a posed studio portrait of Viv as a young married woman, with her husband and their daughters. It is immediately obvious that Louise takes after her father. There is no sign of Aidan.

Aidan notices Rachel looking at the order of service and she quickly opens it to hide the picture; he promptly swivels to look at Elaine's, which she's holding on her lap. But he shows no sign of being bothered. It's as if he either doesn't understand that a decision has been made to exclude him, or wouldn't expect anything else.

The organ launches into some jaunty introductory music – Elaine must have decided to go for something upbeat – and Aidan begins to rock exaggeratedly in time. Louise slips into her place on the far side of the pew. Rachel turns and catches sight of Leona several rows behind, wearing a little pillbox hat with a froth of net. Rachel gives her a tiny wave, and Leona smiles uncertainly back. Maybe they will have the chance to catch up later on.

Then she spots Mary Chadstone on the other side of the church, sitting with a group of women she doesn't recognise. So Mary must have known Viv, somehow or other. Through church, perhaps, or good works in the community; they were both the kind of woman who ends up on committees. No sign of Hugh or the children: they must have opted out.

Rachel quickly turns away. Mary is the last person she feels like facing today; the sight of her is all it takes to conjure up the old, bad feelings of a year ago. Of course Mary will be perfectly civil to her, as usual, which is more than Rachel has any right to expect after accusing Mitch of having an affair with her and attacking him on her doorstep.

How could she have got it so wrong? If only she'd given Mitch time – if she hadn't flown into a rage, ended up out of control, just as he'd said – he could have given her a perfectly reasonable explanation for being there.

Better than reasonable. A *good* reason. A loving reason. He had been there to help Becca celebrate her birthday, at a time when Rachel, under normal circumstances, would not have been able to join them.

She hadn't been well; she'd not been in her right mind. She'd been lost in the Deep. Still, it was terrifying how quickly and completely she'd convinced herself that her fears were justified. And then she'd wrecked everything. It took so long to make a family… and it had taken her next to no time to destroy it.

The vicar comes out into the space between them and the altar, and the tempo of the music changes and becomes more urgent. It is time for the first hymn.

The congregation rises, and belatedly Aidan does, too. Everyone around them begins to sing: *Dear Lord and Father of mankind…*

The tune is vaguely familiar; Rachel attempts to sing it, and Aidan sways gently from side to side. The music has the same effect on her that it often has, of drawing out emotions she has been trying not to give into. Her eyes well up, and she stops singing and discreetly blows her nose. Then she realises Aidan is no longer surveying the lights and arches of the church, but has fallen to studying her instead.

He seems to be curious rather than concerned; he doesn't ask, *What's wrong?* but his eyes say it for him, and the slight apprehension she sees there is her warning to pull herself together. She doesn't want to upset him. She tries to smile at him reassuringly and wills the tears away.

When the hymn is over and they're seated again he says, 'You want to go home,' just loudly enough for her to be sure that everyone sitting near them has heard.

It could be a question rather than a statement; he doesn't really know how to ask questions. On the other hand, he could be right.

But where would she actually want to go back to? She finds herself thinking, not of the bedsit nor even of Rose Cottage, but of Viv's living room with the French windows open to the garden, and the sun coming through. The house Aidan had spent his first years in, then had never been back to.

'We'll both go home in a little while,' she whispers, but Aidan doesn't seem to hear her, and is absorbed in gazing at the lights again.

*

In turn, both Louise and Elaine speak about their mother, and as with all eulogies, their addresses are as revealing about them as about their subject.

Louise's tribute is formal and lengthy; she recalls Viv's churchgoing, her faith and her long and happy marriage, refers to unspecified difficulties that she had overcome in life, and tells a light-hearted anecdote about her baking prowess, which prompts a polite, delicate titter of laughter. It is impossible to tell how much of this Aidan manages to follow, or whether he realises who Louise is talking about; hopefully, he has no idea that he is the difficulty Louise has referred to.

Louise's voice is rather hard to listen to – it is a touch flat, even slightly whining – and Rachel finds her attention drifting. When she has finished Aidan stretches and yawns audibly as if to say, *Thank goodness that's over*, and it is such a precise reflection of Rachel's own thoughts that she has to suppress the urge to giggle.

Elaine opens with a description of Viv that scrupulously avoids the subject of Aidan and dovetails with Louise's account. Viv is presented as a mother who was always busy, whether in the kitchen, the garden, or with various causes, and yet who always kept her house spotless and her hair immaculately curled.

Just when it seems that Elaine is about to wind up, she changes tack.

'It's wonderful to see so many people here – a reminder of how much our mother meant to so many. I'm glad and grateful that her son, my brother Aidan, is with us, and if she could look down and see us I'm sure she would be happy, too.'

Elaine looks directly at Aidan, who sighs and wriggles as if unsure what all the fuss is about. The congregation stirs as if rustled by a strong breeze. Elaine starts back towards their pew and the organ strikes up, and they stand for the next hymn.

The music takes over, its heavy cadences making an irrelevance of old secrets and unanswered questions and washing away everything but the consciousness that Viv has gone, and all of them, in the here and now, have come to remember her.

After a final address from the vicar, it is over. Amid the general shuffling forward, people gravitate towards Elaine and Louise to offer condolences. Aidan, in his blue T-shirt, with his rolling, ship-board gait, is not approached by anybody. But at least there is recognition in the glances that slide over him and away.

# Chapter Thirty-Nine

The service may be over, but they're not yet out of the woods. Aidan takes one look at the crowd gathering in the annexe for refreshments and dashes back along the path towards the church.

When Rachel catches up with him he has stopped in his tracks and is bouncing up and down on the balls of his feet with his fist jammed in his mouth, groaning unrestrainedly. His expression is one of abstract horror.

Thankfully, Becca has had the nous to follow them. Rachel dispatches her to fetch Elaine. It hadn't occurred to her that Becca's presence might actually be helpful, but right now she's thankful to have her at hand.

Aidan allows Rachel to steer him towards a bench, where he sits gently rocking and gnawing at his fingers, attracting pitying and alarmed looks from those who are still on their way from the church to the annexe.

Elaine and Becca appear, and Rachel stands to greet them. She says, 'Would it be OK if we took Aidan for a little walk? I think it would help him calm down. He doesn't want to go into the annexe.'

Elaine agrees, though she looks slightly unsure about the arrangement, in the way that one might when leaving a small child with a new babysitter. But she doesn't wrestle with it for long before beating a swift retreat.

The three of them walk through the graveyard and go down to the river together. They find a place to sit and to Rachel's relief, Aidan seems quite happy to contemplate the sky, the far bank and the water.

Boats chug past, joggers and dog walkers make their way along the towpath on the opposite bank, and ducks circle before realising the three humans on the bench have no bread and giving up on them. To their left, the river narrows to flow under the bridge that is one of the main routes in and out of the town; it's just about possible to see the cars passing over it. Here, though, the traffic is almost inaudible. The sun shines in bright streaks on the slowly moving water and the steady pace of the river holds sway. It seems to seep into them, calming and soothing them all.

After a while they walk to the nearby vantage point where the river Kett, a tributary of the Thames, has been split into two streams to reduce the risk of flooding. The triangular patch of grass at the fork in the river is deserted now, but a scattering of cigarette butts and an empty, dented bottle of cider are evidence of recent occupation.

'Looks like some of your contemporaries have been making merry,' Rachel says to Becca, nudging the bottle with her toe.

'Could have been elderly layabouts,' Becca objects.

'Sweet cider? Come on.'

Rachel takes the bottle away with them, and finds a bin for it on the way back to the church. As it drops in among the rubbish she thinks of messages sent out at sea, and how sometimes there's no way of knowing whether what you wanted to say has got through. *Did Viv think of Aidan as her heart gave way, and if she did, was it with fear or hope?*

This time, Aidan consents to go into the annexe.

It has emptied out but retains the heat of a crowd, and has the wrung-out atmosphere of a children's party venue at going-home time. It is still too busy and confusing for Aidan's liking. He clamps his hands over his ears and begins to hum. Rachel steers him into a corner and sends Becca off to fetch Elaine, who is on the far side of the room, talking to the Kettlebridge librarian.

There is no sign of Leona – she must have gone already. But Mary Chadstone is still there. *Oh God, she's bearing down on them.* Aidan starts humming even louder.

'Rachel! I didn't expect to see you here. Wonderful to see so many people. Such a special occasion. A fitting tribute, I think.'

Mary extends her hand to Aidan; he resolutely ignores her and she drops it with a forgiving smile.

'Good to see you, too, Mary,' Rachel says.

Aidan is humming louder than ever; a few people turn round to look for the source of the unexpected noise, then turn away. Mary surreptitiously looks him up and down, takes in the blue T-shirt and the jogging bottoms and the Velcro-fastened shoes.

'So do you volunteer…?' Mary enquires, with a sweep of the hand in Aidan's direction.

'Aidan is my friend,' Rachel says firmly. The words surprise her, but once they're out she knows they're true. 'We met because Viv had to give up driving and I started giving her a lift to visit him.'

Mary nods understandingly. 'It must have been *so* hard for her. Did you know her well?'

Aidan flings his hands down from his ears. He stares at Mary angrily and emits a strange piercing sound, as aggressively pitched as a fire alarm. Mary winces but maintains a resolute smile.

'I didn't know her for all that long,' Rachel says. 'But I'm really glad I got the chance to spend some time with her.'

'I'm sure. Well, I'd best let you get on. I see you have your hands full. Well done you for helping out. I see Becca's here, too – I'm sure Amelia would say hello.'

She withdraws and Aidan falls silent. His posture has suddenly become rigid, and his face is scrunched up in discomfort.

Elaine and Becca come over. Elaine looks Aidan up and down and says to Rachel, 'So how are we doing?'

Aidan's eyes fly open. So blue, so like Viv's, but blank with uncomprehending terror.

Then there is the unmistakable sound of someone emitting a long, intense fart.

Aidan relaxes and beams with relief. The smell is noticeable. One or two people glance at them in dismay, but Aidan doesn't notice.

'I need to go to the home,' he says.

'Good plan,' Becca agrees.

Elaine hurries off to say goodbye to her daughters, who are to be left with Louise while they take Aidan back to the home. Returning, she glances reprovingly at Aidan, who remains oblivious.

*

On the way back, like a tired child, Aidan promptly falls asleep. The car is filled with the soft sound of his relaxed breathing.

He doesn't stir until they arrive; although he seems dazed and baffled he offers no resistance as Rachel coaxes him out of the car, and goes readily enough with them to the visitors' room.

'It's time for us to say goodbye, Aidan,' Rachel tells him. 'But I'll be back to see you tomorrow. Like normal.'

Aidan peers down at his T-shirt as if he doesn't really understand why it's still on him.

'I'm not going to wear this one any more,' he announces. 'It's finished.'

He doesn't let Rachel hug him goodbye – as soon as she steps towards him he jams his fist in his mouth and groans, and she thinks better of it. Elaine doesn't even try. But as they go out Becca gives him a little wave and a smile and says, 'Goodbye, Aidan, it was nice to meet you,' and even though Aidan doesn't respond Rachel is grateful to her.

Then they're on their way back to Kettlebridge, with Elaine next to Rachel and Becca alone in the back. When Aidan was with them it was almost possible to imagine they were an oddly constituted family of four; this arrangement – the two adults, the lone child – is much more familiar.

Out of the blue, Elaine says, 'You know, I can't help wondering if he could maybe have coped with life in the outside world.'

Is she looking for absolution – reassurance that there's no way such a thing could ever have been possible? Rachel doesn't answer. She doesn't know how to.

Elaine seems to feel the need to explain. 'I was just thinking about it because I know that around the time Mum gave him up, some parents in the same kind of situation opted to keep their children with them. But I'm not sure Dad would have stood for it. Anyway, he's obviously thoroughly institutionalised now. He's so settled, there's no way I would want to uproot him, and Louise feels the same way. Did Mum ever talk about all that with you?'

'Maybe she felt the same as you do,' Rachel says. 'She did once tell me she'd wondered if things could have been different. But I think she felt he was happy and well cared for, and that was what mattered most.'

Perhaps Rachel should have tried harder, encouraged Viv to open up about the decision she'd made. Yet it would have seemed tactless to do so. Worse than tactless – an intrusion. Viv had been so gentle with her, so respectful of the things she didn't want to talk about, that it had seemed necessary to take the same approach herself.

Back at Park Place Elaine says, 'I forgot to say – I think I found the thing you mentioned. If you wait here a moment, I'll bring it out to you.'

She disappears into the house. Becca says, 'What's she talking about?'

'Oh… it's nothing very important,' Rachel says. Then, because this is not true: 'All right, this will sound weird. It's a pinboard with some photos on it, one of which is of you.'

'Of me?'

'Viv and I used to meet sometimes with this other friend of ours, called Leona, and talk about our children. We aimed to get together about once a month.'

'With photos on a pinboard? Why?'

'We missed you. I missed you, and I know Viv missed Aidan and Leona missed her daughter. It was a way of having you there.'

'But you see me every week.'

'I know. But I still miss you in between times.'

Becca contemplates this for a moment; she looks slightly resentful, as if Rachel has just blamed her for something that she's in no way responsible for. Then she says, 'I didn't know Leona had a daughter.'

'No reason why you should. It's probably not the kind of thing I would have told you. She had her when she was quite young, and gave her up for adoption.'

Had she mentioned Leona to Becca? She must have done. It was odd that Becca had remembered – she didn't usually take all that much interest in parts of Rachel's life that didn't directly involve her.

'She was round the other day,' Becca says. 'I think she's working on some kind of business thing with Dad.'

'Is she? He didn't tell me. I haven't been in touch with her for ages.'

'Yeah, they looked at stuff on the computer and then we went to the weir.'

'You went there? That's quite a long walk.'

'Yeah. It was my idea, actually. They asked where I thought would be a good place to go, and it's always nice there in the summer. We all had ice cream at the lock house.'

OK, so there was nothing wrong with Mitch and Becca and Leona going to the weir. It was a nice place. A favourite place. They were lucky to have it close by.

But there was everything wrong with it. It was just plain weird. What was Leona doing ignoring her and hanging out with her husband and kid? Because Mitch *was* still her husband. And Leona was her friend… or had been, until not so very long ago, anyway.

Elaine comes out of the house carrying the pinboard with the photos, and Rachel gets out of the car to take it from her.

'Are you sure you want it?' Elaine says.

'I'm sure,' Rachel tells her, and puts it in the boot.

'Thanks for your help today,' Elaine says. 'We'll be in touch.'

She startles Rachel by pulling her into a quick, clumsy embrace, then abruptly withdraws, as if she's as taken aback as Rachel is by this sudden display of emotion.

'I'm sure it made a difference for Aidan having someone familiar there,' she says. 'I suppose that's what we all need when we're in a strange situation – someone to rely on. I can see that he trusts you.'

'I suppose he does,' Rachel says.

But it is frightening to be trusted, especially by someone as vulnerable as Aidan. A huge responsibility. An honour, and one she can only pray she can live up to.

Maybe Mitch hasn't told her about his meetings with Leona because he's worried that she'll think something's going on? She can see why he might be worried, given the way she'd behaved on Becca's thirteenth birthday.

Aidan might trust her, but Mitch doesn't and neither does she. She doesn't trust herself to see clearly or stay calm, or to keep her head above water. She may have managed to emerge from the Deep, but she will always be afraid of sinking back down again, and losing sight of the light.

# Chapter Forty

It's all still uncomfortably familiar: the same old questions about sex and appetite and arguments and suicidal thoughts and sleep, and Sophie Elphick's carefully neutral expression as she notes down Rachel's replies, each one a number, a score between 0 and 10. The feeling that comes over Rachel as she answers is familiar, too: the same old sense of shame, the awareness of having a weakness, an Achilles' heel. She will always need to be on the lookout for the warning signs: unhealthy thoughts, anger, anxiety, and other signs of strain. She will have to watch herself, and not give in.

But at the same time, it's completely different. This is a one-off follow-up session, designed to assess whether she's continued to benefit from the counselling programme since it ended. It's a reminder – both of how bad things had been and of how much has changed, and how time has moved on and carried her along with it.

It's not just that it is high summer, although that does mean that she feels less closed in with Sophie Elphick than when the blinds were down and it was dark outside; Sophie in a short-sleeved T-shirt looks a little bit more like a casual visitor, less like a professional than before. The bedsit is also quieter than usual, and it is undeniably a relief not to be interrupted by moans of sadomasochistic pleasure from Miss Spank, who had suddenly moved out the week before. Thankfully, none of her other neighbours have chosen this particular time to put on their very loud music, or to stand in the front garden, just outside her window, arguing on their mobiles and smoking. It could almost just be her and Sophie there, as if she lived in her own private house.

But the real difference is nothing to do with her surroundings.

Several of Sophie's standard mood-assessment questions are about a nominal special person in her life, and what her relationship with that person is currently like. Sophie has never wanted to know who she's thinking of, but it's always been Becca. Back in the autumn, she had seen little hope for them; she had been terrified that Becca would eventually reject her completely. But now it is obvious to her – and it must be to Sophie, too, even without the reams of data from all these questionnaires in front of her – that she's more hopeful. Either that, or her situation has become less bleak. Which of the two had come first? She can't be sure, but she suspects that at least some of the improvement is down to Viv. And Leona too, even if she has decided to abandon her and inveigle Mitch into some business venture or other instead.

And Becca. She still often feels as if she's treading on eggshells when they're together: she knows that if she pushes for intimacy, if she tries too hard to encourage Becca to speak openly about her feelings, she'll make her clam up. To some extent that's just who Becca is, at this stage of her life. Surely it's important to respect her right to privacy... But also, to be there for her, to be ready should she ever *want* to talk.

But it's difficult. Becca seems to be doing better academically, but she's cagey about the social side of school. Rachel assumes she's still pally with Amelia Chadstone, but if she mentions Amelia, Becca is quick to close the conversation down or change the subject. Becca is wary of talking about Mitch, too, which has the effect of making much of her home life a no-go area. Maybe it would seem like a betrayal, or maybe it's just easier for her to keep her parents as separate as possible.

But for all that, Becca seems more relaxed during their Saturdays together than she was back in the autumn. More trusting. Rachel tells herself that it's being together that counts, not what they can and can't talk about. Rebuilding, however gradually. Keeping it going.

At one time she thought she'd lost Becca completely. But Becca's still there, and even if she's not particularly demonstrative or affectionate, she doesn't seem to hate her.

When they come to the end of the questionnaire Rachel tells Sophie, 'I get the feeling that my numbers were a little higher than back in the autumn.'

'They were, actually,' Sophie says, scrolling through a couple of pages on the iPad on which she has noted Rachel's scores. 'You had a lot of twos and threes back then. Now you're in the low to normal range.'

'Low to normal. It's not exactly what you'd want as an epitaph, is it? Still, I suppose it'll do.'

Sophie raises her eyebrows fractionally, then drops them. Rachel can almost hear her making a mental note: *Appeared in good humour. Joked.*

'So,' Sophie says, 'is there anything in particular you're concerned about at the moment?'

'Not really concerned, as such. I suppose you could say I have things on my mind. I had a friend, a dear friend who I lost recently; her memorial service was on Saturday. She was an older lady – died of a heart attack. I think about her and her son, how he's coping, how it will affect him, whether he is missing her and can't say. He has learning difficulties. I got to know him because I used to take her to see him once a week, and I'm going to carry on visiting now she can't any more.'

'I see. And your involvement with him – that's something you want to continue then?'

'Oh, yes. It makes me feel close to her, somehow. He reminds me of her. Even though he has no filters – he doesn't hide anything. But there's a kindness about him.' She thinks of the warm touch of Aidan's hand when she led him into the church. 'A sort of solidity. He's very steadfast. When he's decided you're all right, that's that, you're in.'

'That sounds like a beneficial development.'

'It is. The thing I've realised about Viv – that was my friend – is that we sort of adopted each other. I never would have expected to have a friendship like that with someone so much older. But she gave me something I'd been missing ever since my mother died. Before that, even, if I'm honest. Even while Mum was still alive, we were never really close. We weren't able to be.'

There is a pause. Rachel wonders if she's about to start crying. She says, 'I'm sorry. I know these sessions aren't meant to be about dwelling on the past.'

'Well, strictly speaking, it's not a therapy session,' Sophie says. 'It's an evaluation. So if there is something you want to say… Do go on.'

'It seems disloyal. Mum would have hated to be talked about like this,' Rachel says. 'I mean, she would have been *furious*. She was desperate for everyone to think we had a perfectly normal, happy home. After my dad died it was even more important for her to believe that. She clung to it… although she seemed to need to drink a lot to carry on believing it. You'd have thought she barely knew how to live without him. And perhaps she didn't.'

Labels, a diagnosis: that would have made it easier, would have turned their home life into a case study, a kind of story that could be analysed and explained. The end product of various factors, which had generated other factors, spilling out toxic influences like radioactive decay. But for that to happen, it had to be talked about. Words had to be found for it. And her mother hadn't wanted it to be spoken of. What lived on in Rachel's memory was the atmosphere in the house, as physical and present as an unpleasant smell or the sound of traffic in the background: suppressed aggression, the fear that it might cease to be suppressed, and the outbursts that you could never quite see coming, or prevent.

'My dad was what you might call controlling,' she says at last. 'He didn't want my mother working outside the home; he didn't like for her to have friends, or to go out, and if she left the house she had to be back by a certain time. Sometimes if she broke the rules he'd be all right about it. And sometimes she'd do some tiny little thing he didn't like, and he'd explode. He'd shout, break things, push her around, pull her hair. Sometimes he'd put his hands round her neck like he was going to strangle her. He was so strong – when he was like that, when he'd lost it, all you wanted was for it to stop. But however out of control he seemed, he never used to hit her so it would show.

'I learned to keep quiet, keep my head down. When I heard things happening sometimes I'd go in the room... I'd beg him to stop. I think I hoped that me being there might make a difference. Maybe it did, I don't know... if she felt a little bit less alone with it. Then I'd help her clear up afterwards. I know it sounds terrible, we both knew it was terrible, but it was just part of our lives. It's extraordinary what you can learn to live with as if it's normal.

'Then I got a Saturday job, and that changed things. He didn't like it. On my first day he lost it with Mum, and when I came home I was more challenging with him than usual and he hit me, which he never did, normally – he reserved it for Mum. I was more careful after that. But finally I finished school and got a full-time job, and I moved out. I had a plan; I had it all worked out. That was when I was going to rescue her. I knew that if I could persuade her to enjoy herself and relax a little, she would see that life could be different for her, and that would be the beginning of persuading her to leave.

'So I talked her into meeting me. I was going to take the day off, and we were going to get together at a time when we knew he'd be at work.'

The old green pinboard is still where she had left it when she brought it back from Viv's, propped up against the wall opposite the sofa. Aidan, Becca and Bluebell: three reminders. Childhood passed, children changed. Would she have told Viv about all this eventually? Could she have told Leona? She might have, if they'd had enough time. The problem with time was, you never knew when it was about to run out.

'It never happened,' she says. 'A few weeks after I left home he was diagnosed with a particularly aggressive kind of cancer – one of the types you get from asbestos; he'd been an electrician when he was younger, and he'd worked in a lot of buildings that had it. Six months later he was dead. Even though I hated him, it was a massive shock – that he could go from being so strong to so weak so quickly. I think there were two things that kept me sane: Mitch and work. I hadn't been seeing Mitch for that long then, but he was just… I never would have thought I could love a man that much. And I knew there was a whole other world out there for me, that things could be different to the way they had been. I wanted Mum to see that, too, but it was too late.

'She would never hear a word against my dad after he died. She wouldn't let me help her, either. Not with money, and not with the claim for compensation. She started to drink, and let things go – I think she just didn't see the point any more. After she passed away I found out she'd remortgaged the house and racked up loads of debt. I got it sorted, but in the end there was nothing left. Anyway, when I did what I did to Mitch – when I flew into a rage with him over my stupid jealousy – he told me I was just like my father, and that haunted me, afterwards. My father's the last person I would ever want to be like.'

'Do you think you *are* like him?"

'No. At the time I thought maybe Mitch was right. I don't any more. What I did was wrong and I'm sorry I did it – I shouldn't have lashed out the way I did. But what happened to Mitch when he hurt his hand was an accident. It's different to the way my dad bullied my mum all those years.'

Sophie nods. 'We all need to control our aggression, and find ways of channelling it that don't harm other people. That doesn't mean anger is a bad thing in itself. Anger can actually be a constructive emotion, a spur to action: it's what you do with it that counts. But guilt can hold us back. Sometimes it's possible to become attached to guilt, to use it as a way to keep on beating yourself up because that's what you think you ought to do. If you're really sorry for what you've done and have tried to make amends, it may be time to let the guilt go.' She draws a deep breath. 'Do you think there are any points of similarity between your relationship with Mitch and your parents' relationship… any parallels, or echoes?'

Rachel stares at Sophie. This is new territory. 'No, I don't think so. I mean, I always worked. That was really important to me. Mum wasn't allowed to. And Mitch is an artist. He's about as different to my dad as it's possible to be.'

Sophie doesn't say anything: she just waits – that significant counselling pause that means you're being left to work something out for yourself.

'I loved him,' Rachel says eventually. 'As time went on, I knew he wasn't happy. But I always felt that it wasn't really me he was dissatisfied with: it was himself. Maybe somebody else would have brought out something different in him.'

Sophie says, 'Were *you* happy?'

Rachel shrugs. 'I felt I just had to keep going.'

'It's very important to look after yourself, as well as other people,' Sophie reminds her. 'Now, do you remember the techniques we talked about that you can use to calm yourself if you feel your emotions are becoming overwhelming? Maybe we should revisit those.'

This is more comfortable territory for Sophie; breathing exercises, in through the nose and out through your mouth, smell the strawberry and blow out the candle, think of a time and place when you were happy or someone you were happy with. Then the hour is over, and Sophie wishes Rachel well, reminds her of the various websites and group meetings she can turn to for support, and gets up to leave.

On the way out she spots the framed school portrait of Becca, smiling awkwardly against a mottled blue background, which is on the top of the chest of drawers next to the picture of her as a much younger child, in her red sundress, and the study for the *Persephone* painting.

'I hope you don't me asking,' Sophie says, 'but is that your daughter?'

'Yeah, that's Becca.'

'I've met her. It was just before Christmas last year. I was invited to St Anne's to give the girls a talk, and she fainted. I felt terrible afterwards. I hope she was all right?'

'Oh yeah, yeah, she was fine. Bit shaken up.'

'She's been OK since?'

'Yeah, she has.'

'That's good to hear,' Sophie says. 'You know, it's a real achievement to have a positive relationship with your daughter after your own childhood was so difficult. I know it's been a challenging time for you, but it sounds as if Becca's thriving.'

'If Becca's doing all right that's probably more to do with Mitch than me,' Rachel says. 'He's the primary carer.'

'He may well be, but you're still her mother. Whatever you're doing, you've just got to keep it up.'

'I still think I sometimes get things a bit out of proportion,' Rachel says. 'There's this friend of mine, a friend I don't really see any more. Suddenly she seems to be seeing a lot of Mitch. I don't like it. I don't get it. I'm even starting to wonder if something might be going on. But I'm actually scared to try and find out, in case I blow up again—'

'Just remember the breathing exercises,' Sophie says firmly. She holds out her hand for Rachel to shake. 'Good luck.' And with that she takes her leave.

# Chapter Forty-One

Aidan has been quiet and subdued ever since the memorial service. He refuses outright to leave the visitors' room and go to the little café; it is as if he has used up all his tolerance for venturing further afield, and wishes only to ensconce himself in familiar surroundings.

It is a reassertion of the norm, and Rachel supposes this is the adjustment she, too, must make; to pick up where she left off, and carry on with this strange life she has made for herself. She certainly isn't up to jollying him out of it; his mood matches her own. Anyway, it's only been a couple of weeks since the service, and it is not yet two months since Viv's death. Surely in time he will feel ready to leave the home again, if only for a little while.

All that Sunday she has a faint headache, which could be residual stress or might equally be foreboding. She's not wholly surprised when, that evening, her phone rings, and it is Mitch.

'Rachel,' he says. 'How are you?'

He sounds hesitant, almost embarrassed. It's the way people speak when they want something, when they're trying to curry favour and anticipate being refused. It's the way she speaks to Mitch; it's not the way he usually speaks to her.

'I'm OK, thanks. Been better.'

*What do you want, Mitch?* She can't ask outright – she doesn't want to offend him. But he must have a reason for calling, so why doesn't he just come out with it?

She asks, 'Is everything OK? Is Becca OK?'

'I wanted to extend an invitation, actually. I was wondering if you'd like to come over sometime, just for a chat, to talk things over.'

'What *things*?'

'Well – you know. Just the way things are now. And Becca's a big part of that, obviously.'

Is it mean-spirited of her to suspect an ulterior motive? It's fair to say that they have been getting on a little better, overall. But you couldn't exactly call it a cordial relationship, not yet. He usually seems keen to keep her at a distance: so what's changed?

They haven't yet formally started divorce proceedings. That ordeal is yet to come… So far, he hasn't seemed to be in any rush, and she has been inclined to leave things as they are for as long as possible. They've agreed the terms of their separation, and have minimised the disruption for Becca: isn't that enough? But perhaps it isn't. Not any more.

'Should I be talking to a lawyer, Mitch?'

'We probably will have to, one of these days. But I'd just like to approach it all in a different way. I think we need to, for Becca's sake.'

'Is this about the summer holidays?'

She has tentatively suggested that, if Becca was willing, she could take her away for a few days sometime in August, perhaps to Cornwall or Devon. Mitch has yet to come back to her with a definite response. If it happens, it will be the first time she and Becca have spent more than a Saturday together since she moved out of Rose Cottage. The Easter break and school holidays had passed by in much the same way as when she was still working full-time in London, with Mitch looking after Becca at home.

He hesitates. 'It might have a bearing on that. Just come, OK?'

'If this is what you think is best for Becca… then OK.'

'I don't know what time would suit you? Is there any time one evening next week when you'd be free?'

He sounds so wary, so defensive. What on earth can he have to say that he's so nervous about?

'How about next Saturday? Before or after I get Becca?'

'No… no, that won't do. It would be better if Becca was somewhere else. How about during the day? Can you get some time off?'

She's grateful to him for not suggesting that Becca could go home with Amelia Chadstone. Perhaps he has accepted that she still doesn't feel entirely comfortable discussing that friendship, that it reminds her of things she would rather forget. She agrees that she will ask, and they say goodbye.

Well… maybe it really is possible: perhaps they can be more amicable? Why not be hopeful? Sophie had said she was doing better, after all.

That night she dreams that she's Leona, standing in a field of bluebells; and her daughter has been returned to her and is in her arms, but is a baby again, as if she had never been given away.

# Chapter Forty-Two

The door to Rose Cottage is opened not by Mitch, but by a completely different man.

That's the first shock.

But actually, it *is* Mitch – Mitch clean-shaven, with his hair trimmed, and that jagged scar on his hand, pink now rather than red, almost faded enough for someone not to notice straight away unless they know where to look.

Without his long hair and beard, he looks much more like anybody else – like someone who might be spotted mulling over lawnmowers in a DIY store, or pushing a trolley in the supermarket: the kind of domesticated man Mitch once would have been desperate not to become. He seems softer, and more approachable. More settled, somehow.

'Come on in,' he says.

His tone is friendly enough but he looks uncomfortable, as if he is resigned to this particular meeting but would like to get it over with as soon as possible. He is wearing a shirt she hasn't seen before, and – this is the most uncharacteristic thing of all – he has taken the trouble to iron it.

Or has Becca pressed it for him? No way. Surely that would never happen.

She follows him into the kitchen. Is it her imagination, or does the house smell different? Has Mitch been experimenting with new recipes – something with coriander in it, perhaps? Or maybe he has bought a new kind of polish, or a different brand of bleach. He must have had a bit of a clean-up recently: everything looks unusually spotless.

Mitch invites her to sit, offers her a drink; she accepts a glass of water, and he fetches himself one, too.

*When did you fall in love with me?* she had asked him once. And he had said, *The first time I saw you.*

When a couple finally, definitively falls *out* of love – beyond anger, beyond reprisals – is that also a point that can be remembered later? Is that where they are?

'I have something I need to tell you,' he says.

Has he rehearsed this? She suspects he has.

'Go on,' she says.

He grimaces. 'It's not an easy thing to say.'

'Let's build up to it, then. Let's talk about other things. How's work?'

Maybe he is trying to tell her is that he has got a new job – that would explain the haircut, the ironing, the shaved-off beard. And she can see why he might be anxious about it – the basis of his custody of Becca is that he is the one who is around at home. That, and the fact that he is the one Becca wanted to stay with.

And there was the time Rachel had put him in the hospital. It might have been an accident, but she'd still hurt him and Mitch would be able to use it against her in court if he chose.

Mitch says, 'It's all going pretty well, actually. There's been a fair bit of demand for these.'

He gets up and releases a tea-towel from the rubber sucker stuck to the side of the kitchen cupboard – when had he put that up? When had he become the kind of person who thought to put something like that up? He brings the tea-towel to the table and spreads it out in front of her with a flourish that seems entirely over the top: as if it's precious, as if the gesture of showing it to her is important.

It is certainly a perfectly attractive tea-towel, printed with a fetching design of miniature strawberries.

'Very nice,' Rachel says.

'There's a huge market for upmarket homeware, if you get it right.'

He whisks the tea-towel away and hangs it up again before returning to his seat.

'Half the battle is knowing what the market is,' he continues. 'Then you just have to figure out how to reach it.'

Is this really the man who had always been so scornful of anything to do with business, and who had dismissed the public relations industry as a waste of time?

'So what *is* your market?' Rachel asks.

Mitch grins at her like a schoolchild who is delighted to know the answer. 'Our market is the kind of woman who buys expensive shoes and hides them from her husband.'

*Our* market?

'Especially the ones who are stuck at home with small kids and only the internet for company,' Mitch goes on. 'This kind of thing is a relatively guilt-free purchase for them. Anyway, I don't suppose *you* ever did that.'

'Did what?'

'Hid your new shoes from your husband,' Mitch says. He folds his arms and twinkles at her. But the last thing Mitch has ever been is *twinkly*. Just when did he get so happy?

'Of course I didn't,' she says. 'Mostly if I bought new stuff it was to wear to work, anyway, and I paid for it with my own money.'

Mitch looks slightly wounded. 'All right, all right, I was only joking. I'm perfectly well aware that you always earned more than me. You never let me forget it.'

'That's not fair. I bent over backwards not to make a big thing about it. Do you think I wanted to spend hours and hours commuting and working and being away from home, and barely seeing Becca? I did it because I had to. Somebody had to pay the bills, and you either weren't willing or weren't capable of changing things so that could be you.'

'Rachel, keep your voice down,' Mitch says. 'There's no need to shout at me.'

'I'm not shouting!'

But she is. She's furious with him for telling her she has no right to be furious. Why can't he at least admit that she'd had to be the way she was – work-obsessed, constantly distracted and stressed-out – because of the way he was?

'This is ridiculous,' Mitch says. 'I *had* hoped we'd be able to have a civilised conversation. Clearly I was wrong.'

And now Rachel finds herself yelling at him across the table: 'It's you! You're the one who's driving me crazy! I was absolutely fine until I came here and you started talking about... about *tea-towels*!'

They are both on their feet now. He looks disgusted with her, as if she has let herself down and him, too. He says, 'You know, Rachel, at times like this I wonder what I ever saw in you.'

The door opens behind him and someone comes in.

'Is everything all right in here?'

It's Leona, as incongruous here as a shadow without sunlight.

Mitch moves towards Leona's side. Suddenly he is all sympathy: 'Did we disturb you?'

Leona rubs her eyes. Her skin is slightly flushed, as if she has just been sleeping, and she glances at Rachel as if taking in a visitor she has not been looking forward to seeing, but knew to expect. She says, 'I heard shouting, thought I'd better come down. What's going on?'

Why is Leona being so distant – as if they'd never really been friends? And why would she have been napping at Rose Cottage? It's Rachel who feels as if she's dreaming.

Leona, here... In Rose Cottage... And *pregnant*.

She's wearing a strappy raspberry-pink sundress that emphasises rather than conceals her slightly swollen belly. She can't be far along. If she was wearing different clothes, it might not even be noticeable. But as it is... it's undeniable.

It is as if Rachel is barely hanging on to a cliff-face and about to drop. And nobody is rushing to her rescue.

'Everything's fine, everything's under control,' Mitch says sooth-ingly. He puts his arm round Leona and pulls her in towards his side so they're facing Rachel as an interlinked pair, two against one. 'You should probably go back upstairs.'

Leona allows him to hold her close just long enough for it not to seem like a brush-off when she extricates herself and sits down. Mitch moves so that he is standing behind her with one hand resting on her shoulder, as if he is thinking of offering her a massage.

Leona regards Rachel with steely defensiveness, then turns to Mitch. 'You haven't told her yet, have you?'

'Well… I was building up to it when she started shouting,' Mitch tells her.

Rachel says, 'Go on then. What is it?'

Mitch looks from Rachel to Leona, who appears to be lost in thought. He shrugs and raises his hands as if in supplication or denial, the gesture of men down the ages who want only the quiet life that entanglement with women denies them.

'I was trying to tell you,' he says.

Leona looks up and says to him, 'I wish you'd let me do this.' Then she says to Rachel, 'You might want to sit down. This could come as a bit of a shock.'

'Oh, no.' Rachel remains standing, looks from Leona to Mitch. 'You mean you brought me here to tell me… No.' She stares at Leona. 'You mean to tell me that's *my husband's baby* you're having?'

Mitch clears his throat. 'We are separated, remember, Rachel.'

'But you told me you didn't *want* another baby!' Rachel yells at him. 'You said you couldn't face doing it all over again, all the nappies and the broken nights, and we couldn't afford for me to give up work and we couldn't afford the childcare. You told me you thought it would finish us off.'

Mitch makes a small, helpless gesture. 'I know. And that was what I thought. I wasn't in a good place at the time. I didn't think I was ready. I didn't think I'd ever be ready. But this… It just *happened*.'

'You *idiot*. Something like this doesn't just *happen*. The two of you decided to do it, and you did it because you wanted to. I suppose it didn't occur to you to use contraception.'

Leona rests her tattooed hand on her stomach. 'You have every right to be angry, Rachel. I just hope that when you've had time to think about it you might see it differently. This is a baby, not a catastrophe. A little girl or boy. Not that we know yet, either way. I don't want to find out. But I think it might be a girl.'

'Yeah, well, you'll have to forgive me if I don't rush to congratulate you. When did this happen, anyway? I suppose it must have been after you got back from France, right? That's when you suddenly went silent.'

Leona glances at Mitch. She looks frustrated by the way this is going: maybe she and Mitch had fantasised that it would all be sweet and lovely, that Rachel would welcome her and the new baby as if it was no problem at all.

'Yes,' she says. 'That was when it was.'

Rachel turns to Mitch. 'You took advantage of her. She'd just come back from meeting her daughter for the first time since she gave her up for adoption. She must have been all over the place. She was vulnerable. Did you know about all that? Because if she told you and you still went ahead and decided that it would be a really good time to sleep with her, I don't like what that says about you, Mitch. I don't like that at all.'

Mitch folds his arms. 'She did tell me about the adoption. Of course she did. She told me more about all that than you know. But that's the past and this is the future, Rachel. You're just going to have to accept that we're in love and having a baby, and that's all there is to it.'

'That's *all*…?'

Rachel stares down at Leona. It all makes sense now. It's so *obvious*. And yet she never would have imagined that Leona would do this to her. Not in a million years.

'I talked about you to Viv, you know,' she tells her. 'We tried to work out what on earth was going on with you. We thought it was to do with Bluebell, that you didn't want to see us because meeting her had changed things and you wanted to move on with your life. We even hoped that one day you'd change your mind.' She shakes her head. 'Here you are in front of me, telling me what you've done, and I still can't quite believe it.'

Her legs are about to give way under her. She subsides back into her chair, rests her head in her hands and closes her eyes. She can't look at them any more. They have done this to her and they're *happy* about it. Worse still, it is plain that they want – maybe even expect – her blessing.

And as for Becca...

What about Becca?

Oh, Lord.

Of all the further upheavals Becca *doesn't* need... to have her beloved father suddenly absorbed in a new relationship and a new baby, to experience all the pangs of sibling rivalry a decade and a half too late...

Somehow Rachel remembers to breathe. *In... out... Breathe in the strawberry, blow out the candle...*

She straightens up and opens her eyes. Leona is gazing at her expectantly, as if hoping to be forgiven on the spot, while Mitch is watching her as if he anticipates having to leap into action and defend Leona at any moment.

*Just look at him, the pressed shirt, the cropped hair...* He is trying. He is making an effort. He is nearly forty and he thinks he's starting over. New woman, new baby. Ready to do it all again, and get it right this time. To not have to look back and reproach himself for his failures. To be the new man, the new dad – practically middle-aged, but with spunk that still works. Who's still got what it takes to get a younger woman into trouble, thank you very much.

And Leona… this is a second chance for her, too. They both have too much to prove to let how Rachel feels about it come between them. Or Becca either.

This baby is merely an almost imperceptible bulge in Leona's dress but is simultaneously an unstoppable force that has breezed in to rearrange everything.

This baby has made Rachel and Becca redundant, an irrelevance. It – whether it is a he or a she – will take Becca's place in Mitch's heart, and make it possible for Leona to take Rachel's. How can it not be so?

'It's all so soon,' Rachel says. 'If I had known you were seeing each other, that would have been one thing. But this… It's too much.'

Mitch moves away from Leona and sits down. He slumps as if defeated and stares at his clasped hands as if he dares not raise his eyes. The scar is a red streak, a wordless reminder of why he'd asked her to leave.

'I'm sorry, Rachel,' he says.

'It's been a shock to us as well,' Leona interjects.

'I suppose you'll be moving in here,' Rachel says, not even attempting to sound indifferent.

'Well, where I am is fine for now,' Leona says. 'It's still early days. But yes – I'm hoping to spend a bit of time here.' She glances at Mitch, and the two of them smile at each other.

This hurts – it hurts like a lance dipping into Rachel's side – but there is nothing to be done about it, apart from ignoring the pain for now.

But why should Becca have to suffer, too?

She turns back to Mitch.

'Are you going to be able to support this baby?'

'*I* will be able to support it,' Leona says. 'If money is what you're worried about, you shouldn't be. It won't have any impact on your financial arrangements with Mitch. That's to do with *your* child. It's nothing to do with mine.'

How can she be so cold, so objective – as if they'd never been friends, as if she hadn't cried in front of Rachel and let Rachel comfort her, as if Rachel hadn't tried to help her? But she's thinking of the baby now. Rachel is out of the picture.

If that's the way things are to be… then Rachel will have to put *her* child first, too.

'What about Becca?' Rachel says, looking from Mitch to Leona and back again. 'She told me you'd been here, Leona. She said you'd been out for a walk to the weir.'

It is galling in the extreme to think of Leona meeting Becca, right here in Rose Cottage, sizing Becca up, assessing how she would adapt to the arrival of the new addition… And Becca being oblivious. Because Becca wouldn't have guessed, would she? She might perhaps have suspected a flirtation. But not a *baby*…

'About Becca. We were hoping you might help us with that,' Mitch says.

'*Help* you?'

But she already knows what they're going to ask for.

They need to have Becca on board. They want to welcome their child into a world in which its teenage half-sibling, shut away in an upstairs bedroom, doesn't resent and despise it. And even if Becca doesn't play ball, they will welcome the child anyway, and into this house.

Becca will no longer be an only child. Her existence has been reshuffled like a pack of cards, and so has Rachel's.

'You see, I'm hoping to spend quite a bit of time here over the summer,' Leona says. 'We don't want Becca to suspect something, and then feel that secrets are being kept from her – she's such an observant girl, she might have clocked that something is going on already.' (*How dare she? How dare she express any opinion of any kind about Rachel's daughter?*) 'That's why we thought it would be best to sit her down and tell her what's going on sooner rather than later, and certainly as close to the beginning of the summer holidays as possible. In the normal way of things, we might not have needed to think about it quite so early. After all, I'm not twelve weeks gone yet.' She gives Mitch a coy little smile. 'The idea is to let you and Becca know, but not to go public more generally just yet. I'd be grateful if you wouldn't mind keeping it to yourself, at least for the time being. It'll give us a chance to get used to the idea before we have to deal with what anyone else thinks about it.'

'I'm not in a rush to broadcast the happy news, funnily enough,' Rachel says.

Her chest has gone tight again. *Breathe in strawberry, out like blowing a candle.* She surveys the pair of them – her husband, and the friend and former colleague she obviously didn't know quite as well as she thought.

*This is it.* This is all the power she has: to make life easy for them, or, conversely, to set out to be as awkward and uncooperative as possible.

*Of all the women in a woman's life, is there anyone who is more terrifying than the woman who loves your husband after you?*

Maybe only the mother-to-be of his next child…

Leona's baby. Mitch's baby. The screaming, messy, sex-life-wrecking reality that is heading their way.

But also… the sweet milky smell of newborn skin, the knitted bonnets, the tiny babygros… And the pride, too, the watching from a small but slowly increasing distance as the child sits up, takes steps, stays on the other side of the school gates on the first day of term…

It's like looking through a telescope, but it's not Leona and Mitch's future that it brings into view, it's Mitch and Rachel's past.

'We thought it might be best if we all told Becca together,' Leona says.

Leona is fiddling with something – a charm on a necklace, hanging by her chest. Oh God, it's the rose quartz – the present Rachel had given her at the airport when she flew out to see Bluebell.

She sees that Rachel has noticed it and her hand drops, and for the first time she looks ashamed.

Rachel says, 'You mean like those chats good parents have in the movies? The one where they tell the little girl that Mummy and Daddy still love her very much, they just don't love each other any more?'

'Rachel,' Mitch says warningly.

'You could always just hide Leona upstairs and get her to come down and rescue you if the shouting gets too loud?' Rachel suggests.

'No need to be like that,' Mitch says stiffly. 'We're all in this together. We're the adults in this situation, supposedly. Becca is only a child, and she's vulnerable. It's not so long since she was having problems at school. We have to focus on what she needs, and try to put how we feel about it aside. After all, she's had a lot to deal with over the last year.'

*Strawberry, candle. Strawberry, candle.*

'Were you always such a hypocrite?' Rachel asks. 'Maybe I just never noticed it before. Strikes me that you weren't exactly thinking about Becca when you got Leona pregnant.'

She gets to her feet and looks down at them both, sitting at the kitchen table – the one she and Mitch had chosen together, the scene of so many Christmas dinners and birthday cakes.

How much does she know about Leona, really? She had assumed that they were allies, whatever happened; that what they had in common would always be more powerful than all the ways in which they were different, and all the things they had never talked about. And yet Mitch had hinted that she didn't know everything about Leona. And Leona had never told her exactly why she gave Bluebell up.

Rachel turns to Mitch again. 'You said that Leona told you something that I didn't know. What exactly were you getting at?'

'Nothing that need concern you,' Mitch says stiffly.

'If she's going to be spending a lot of time in my house, with my daughter, it *does* concern me.'

'It is *not* your house,' Mitch objects.

'Yes, well, we'll see about that, shall we? Things will be different when Becca's grown up and finished school. Maybe even before that.' She stares at Leona, who is suddenly deathly pale. 'What did you do, Leona? What was it that meant you had to give Bluebell up?'

'That's enough, Rachel,' Mitch says, getting to his feet. 'All that is in the past, and it's nothing to do with you.'

'I know you really don't want to tell me,' Rachel says. 'And you know what? That makes me really want to know.'

'Do you have to be so hostile?' Mitch says. 'Look, we need to think about Becca. Agree a date to sit down with her. Get things sorted.'

'You did this; you tell her. I'm damned if I'm going to,' Rachel says. 'And in the meantime, until I know *exactly* what Leona did, I don't want you leaving her alone with Becca. Ever. I'm going to find out what happened. I have a right to know. And when I do, who knows, maybe it'll make me feel differently about who my daughter should be living with.'

And she turns and walks out.

She waits for a moment at the front door. She can hear a low murmur of voices from the kitchen. It sounds as if Leona is crying, and Mitch is comforting her.

For a moment Rachel is tempted to go back in – to apologise, to agree to do whatever they want. In her heart of hearts, she doesn't believe that Leona would ever have done anything deliberate to hurt Bluebell, or that she poses any kind of threat to Becca now; she had only wanted to hurt her back. Yes, Leona is having a baby, Mitch's baby... but it isn't as if she has crept into Rachel's home and stolen her place. Leona is nothing to do with the end of Rachel's relationship with Mitch. That was already dead; Leona's just the proof of it.

The sound of crying stops. Rachel hears Mitch say, quietly but with absolute sincerity, 'Please don't worry. I love you, and I love this baby.'

There is silence – a soft, caressing silence. He must be kissing her.

Rachel shuts the door – perhaps a little louder than was strictly necessary – and goes out to the car.

No need to rush. Mitch is hardly about to come out and challenge her. She's as free to be here as she will ever be.

She sits there for a while, composing herself, trying to think of nothing, watching the play of light and shadow, the trees. Time seems to unfold and unspool. She sees the house covered in snow, in spring, and bright with summer again. A young child in wellington boots making her way down to the stream. Not Becca. Another girl, or maybe a boy.

When she closes her eyes, it is Viv she thinks of; not in any specific way, but as a warm, comforting presence, encouraging and benign.

*Help me*, she thinks, but there is no answer, or at least, none that can be formulated in words.

# Chapter Forty-Three

## Rachel

### Nineteen years before the loss

The bus was crowded, but her favourite spot, the double seat at the front of the top deck, was still free. She opened her book and started reading, and didn't look up when someone sat next to her. A man. A man who was just a little bit too close, as if he wanted her to notice him. She squeezed along so that he wasn't pressing against her and kept her eyes on her book.

He said, 'Is that good, then?'

He was youngish but older than she was, and smelt strongly of aftershave and weakly of beer. He was wearing a suit and had carefully gelled hair. She avoided meeting his eyes: she didn't want to encourage him.

'Seems all right so far,' she said.

'Only all right? I wouldn't bother then, if I was you. Been at work today?'

'Uh-huh.' Under her coat she was wearing the green and white striped uniform dress of Pinkney's department store, a dead giveaway.

'Me, too,' he said. 'It's been a tough one. But, you know, it's Saturday night, right?'

She made the smallest possible sound of agreement. Maybe he just wasn't going to take the hint. The bus moved off and she looked over her shoulder for a free spot she could move to. But there was nothing apart from the empty seat just behind her, next to a boy with untidy, overlong hair who had headphones on and was staring gloomily out of the fogged-up windows at the Christmas lights.

If only she was sitting there, everything would be fine. He looked like someone who would run a mile rather than pester a stranger into conversation. Unlike the man sitting next to her, who seemed to expect her to be flattered by the attention.

The man in the suit said, 'What's your name, anyway?'

'Look, I'm really not in the mood. I just want to read my book.'

'You don't have to be in the mood for anything. I just thought it would be nice to have a bit of a chat. I'm not a monster, you know. I'm actually a pretty nice guy, if you'd only give me a chance.'

'I'm sorry, but I don't *want* to give you a chance.'

'You really have got a rod up your backside, haven't you? You seriously need to relax. That might be something I could help you with, you know.'

'Just listen to her, would you? She doesn't want to talk to you. Leave her alone,' someone growled.

It was the boy sitting behind them, who'd taken off his headphones and was glaring at her neighbour as if he'd like to bore holes in his skull. He looked as if he didn't much care if he got into a fight, and as if nothing would give him greater pleasure than to be forced to punch the source of his annoyance on the nose.

Rachel's neighbour hesitated, but pride wouldn't let him give up immediately. He said, 'It's rude to listen in to other people's conversations, you know. So how about you mind your own business?'

'That was not a conversation, it was you being a pain in the arse. So why don't you just get lost and give us all some peace?'

The two of them glared at each other. Rachel's neighbour was older, but the boy had the advantage of being slightly taller and broader in the shoulders, and of looking convincingly menacing. Rachel held her breath. This could only go one of two ways; either one of them would back down, or someone was liable to get hurt.

'I was only being friendly,' her neighbour muttered. He got to his feet, stumbled towards the stairwell and disappeared.

A ripple of approval ran round the top deck. A woman sitting on the other side of the aisle stood up to ring the bell and then reached across to pat Rachel on the shoulder. 'You ask me, that one's a keeper,' she said, and went off.

Rachel felt herself blushing. She turned to have a proper look at the boy behind her. He was pale, with a saturnine face and slanting green eyes. He was studying her, too, coolly and assessingly, as if mentally measuring her face for a purpose that he wasn't about to explain.

'I suppose I should thank you,' she said. 'But, you know, I also feel obliged to point out that I can look after myself.'

'I'm sure you can,' he said. 'He was annoying me as well. I don't like bullies, and anyway, I wanted to read, too.'

Rachel leaned forward and saw the book in his lap, a large volume open at a full-colour reproduction of Klimt's painting *The Kiss*.

'I love that painting,' she said.

It wasn't that long since she'd bought a poster of it for her room; she'd been entranced by the romance of it, the man and woman embracing in a shower of gold. Her dad had not been pleased. *Don't stick things on the walls like that. You'll make holes in the paintwork. Anyway, it looks like sick.* She had ended up taking the poster down, and redecorating.

'Everyone loves that painting,' the boy said, and smiled at her. He had a dimple in one cheek. Suddenly he looked mischievous, and surprisingly sweet. 'What are you reading?'

'You might think it's silly. It's the kind of book you have to hide from people you know. Or I do, anyway.'

She held it up so he could see the cover, which was bright yellow with a light bulb on the front and the title written in a circle round it: *Ten Ways to the Life You Want*.

He said, 'So what *is* the life you want?'

She put the book back down on her lap and closed it. 'I want to get a place of my own. That's the main thing, so I'll need to find a job that'll pay me enough to do that. Hopefully in a nice office somewhere. I work in the café at Pinkney's, and I'm like the world's worst waitress. I'm always getting distracted and dropping things.'

She was conscious of trying to make an impression on him. Exaggerating. *Flirting*. Not something she usually did. At school she was one of the quiet ones. Out of school, she stayed home, usually in her bedroom. As far as possible, she kept herself to herself.

'My dad runs a building business, and I did some roofing for him last summer,' the boy said. 'I was useless at it. No head for heights. Everyone else laughed at me.'

'So you're not going to follow in your dad's footsteps?'

'I'm not sure he'd want me, to be honest. Luckily he's got my brother to bring on board. Those two have big plans. They want to have some kind of property empire. My mum thinks I should be a lawyer. She seems to have this idea that I could become their consigliere. Only problem with that is, I have no head for figures and zero interest in proving whether other people are right or wrong.'

'There's not much hope for either of us, then.'

'Oh, I'm sure there's hope,' he said. 'There's always hope, isn't there? It's just a question of finding the right way. I should probably read that book of yours.'

He smiled at her again. That smile was just the best thing. It made her feel like a cat basking in sunshine. She couldn't believe this was happening, right here on the top deck of the 113 bus. To her. She was suddenly conscious of her heart, beating just a little louder and faster than usual.

And then she remembered that she ought to be getting off the bus. Where were they? Outside, the bingo hall went by. She'd nearly missed her stop, and it wouldn't do to be late back.

'I'm sorry, I have to go,' she said, jumping up and lunging for the bell.

As she hurried away she caught sight of the expression on his face – startled and bereft – and it stayed with her as she made her way from the bus stop to her house.

She'd left her book behind; it must have slid off her lap onto the floor when she stood up, and she'd been in such a rush that she hadn't noticed it.

Well, maybe it would be some use to him.

Her dad's van was parked outside the house. As she turned her key in the door she steeled herself for whatever the evening ahead might hold – maybe nothing, it might all be fine, he might even be in a good mood. You never knew.

She set aside the memory of that small, perfect encounter on the bus as if it was a treasure, something to take out and pore over later, in secret, when the day's chores were done.

The following Saturday when Rachel came out of Pinkney's after work someone was waiting for her.

When he saw her he beamed at her and it was just as good as she'd remembered. It was him, the boy who didn't like bullies and liked reading about art, the boy she kept thinking about. He was loitering hopefully with a bunch of roses in one hand and her book in the other.

'I thought you might like this back,' he said, and handed over the book. 'Also, I got these for you. I hope they're all right. I wasn't sure what to choose.'

She thanked him and took the roses and admired them. They were dark red, with velvety petals. Nobody had ever bought her flowers before. Would it be safe to take them home? Her dad would probably have something to say about it.

Still… she had them for now.

'So did you read the book?' she asked him. 'Did you find out the ten ways to the life you want?'

'I did read some of it, actually.'

'You'll have seen the bits I underlined, then.'

'Yes, those were the bits I read.'

She shifted the roses into the crook of her arm so she could put the book back in her bag. 'I'm embarrassed now,' she said. 'Were they corny?'

'No. Not corny, and not embarrassing,' he said firmly. 'Look, I was wondering if you might... you know... like to go out with me sometime?'

He was nervous. He looked as if he'd readied himself for disappointment, as if he was half expecting to hear that she already had a boyfriend or just didn't want to take things any further. He seemed like someone who might be capable of taking no for an answer.

Her heart was doing somersaults. She found she was smiling.

'I don't even know your name.'

'Oh yeah. That would've been a good place to start, wouldn't it? I'm Mitch. Mitchell Moran.'

'Well. That's memorable.'

'Yeah, well, Mitchell is my mother's maiden name. I guess she must have wanted to hang onto it.'

'I'm Rachel Steele.'

He grins at her. 'I like it. Strong name. Though I would have still liked you if you were called Puddlefeather or Milkflop or something.'

'You would?'

'Of course I would,' he said.

She drew a deep breath. This was making her dizzy. She couldn't smell the roses, but she could smell him – a clean, lemony, masculine smell that made her want to come closer, to find out what it would be like to touch him.

'I *would* like to go out with you...' she said.

He looked relieved, but only partly. 'OK, great, but I'm sensing that there's a *but* coming.'

'*But* right now I have to get back home. Are you catching the bus? If you are, maybe we could go together.'

He beamed at her. 'Yes. Good. Let's do that.'

They set off towards the bus stop, making their way through the crowds of shoppers. Without even thinking about it she reached out and took his hand. It felt all right. It felt better than all right; it felt like something she'd been waiting all her life to do, and would be doing many times again.

Something was happening to her, something important. Her world was tilting on its axis. *Was she scared? Maybe.* But the thought faded as quickly as it had come. It was as if he was a promise that she was wrapped up in already.

Just before the bus stop was a newsagent's that had already closed for the day. It was slightly set back from the other shops, and she drew him into the sheltered space in front of it.

'Might as well get out of the wind while we're waiting,' she said.

He let go of her hand and reached up to tuck a strand of her hair behind her ear. The gesture was so tender it took her breath away. And then somehow they were kissing. Everything tiptoed away: the shops, the buses, the passers-by, Pinkney's, the home that was waiting for her. Her eyes were closed and she was conscious only of the two of them and the unseen glow of the Christmas lights, stars and candles and snowflakes strung overhead as if to illuminate their meeting.

She was melting and it was heaven. This was it. This was what love was like: being treasured. Like embracing in a shower of gold.

# Chapter Forty-Four

## Becca

They are going to sing an a cappella version of 'Love Me Tender', and from somewhere, genuine white, rhinestone-studded, flared Elvis costumes have been acquired; they're meant to wear their hair in quiffs and gyrate gently, playing it for laughs.

It is pretty much the very last thing Becca feels like doing, but that is not in the spirit of the competition. It is important to be game, to give it your best shot, to try your hardest for your house. The costume helps. A costume always helps, especially one as outrageous, as different from anything she would normally wear as this.

She takes her place on the stage next to Amelia. They sing and shimmy together as if they're the best of friends, and are rewarded by a storm of applause. And it feels good – too good, like something that's probably bad for you, like being drunk might be, or other things that Amelia does that Becca has decided not to. Suddenly everything makes sense: *this* is what life is about – this giddy feeling, which is completely out of her control but in a good way, the best possible way. It is a triumph, so much so that when the scores are announced later it comes as a slight anti-climax to learn that their house has won the cup.

After the bell rings to mark the end of the day they all pour out into the sunlight. Some head for the coach that will drop them off at outlying villages; a few have parents waiting in the car park; others fall into twosomes and threesomes and foursomes to walk to homes in Kettlebridge. Becca aims to bob along in mid-field, trying, as usual, to be inconspicuous. She notices the other girls putting up umbrellas before she feels the first drops of rain.

She doesn't have one. Or rather, she does, somewhere, but she never has it when she needs it. Mum used to occasionally nag her about that kind of thing. Dad never does.

Someone just behind her says, 'Need one of these?'

It's Amelia, whose umbrella is already up – she likes to avoid getting her hair wet, and complains of frizz, though it always looks immaculate. She comes closer and holds her umbrella over Becca.

'You were good today,' she says. 'Everyone said our Elvis routine was the best.'

'You were good, too.'

The street brightens for a moment as the sun emerges from the clouds; then, just as suddenly, it is gloomy again, the wind gusts and it begins to rain properly. The pavement is spattered with spots of damp one minute, dark and sleek the next.

'Why have you been avoiding me?' Amelia asks suddenly.

'I haven't,' Becca protests.

Amelia rolls her eyes. 'Liar.'

'We're talking now, aren't we? How are things going with Ollie?'

'Really good, actually. Is it because of Ollie that you don't want to hang out any more?'

'It's not because of Ollie.'

'A-ha! Then you admit it is because of *something*.' Amelia aspires to become a lawyer in later life, and occasionally makes a point of pouncing on other people's declarations. 'So what is it?'

By now, the tide of end-of-day schoolgirls has mostly dispersed. The rain is falling steadily and the road is almost just a road again, with a few anonymous passing cars splashing through puddles and next to no pedestrians. No one will overhear, and anyway, Becca can't think of anything to say but the truth.

'I just don't think we're into the same things,' she says. 'You know, the shoplifting and smoking and all of that.'

Amelia takes this in, is almost affronted, then decides to be amused.

'Oh, that stuff? That's nothing,' she said. 'You know I was off school the other day? Well, I wasn't sick. Ollie and me both skived off and went to London. *So* much better than this boring dump of a place. Who wants to hang out in Kettlebridge? Come with us next time, if you like. I promise you, you'd love it. It makes you feel like you're really alive. Being here just makes you feel like you're asleep.'

'Yeah, I don't think so, thanks all the same.'

'Well, I think you need to get over yourself and lighten up. If you knew what I know, you wouldn't care so much about doing what people tell you to.'

'If I knew what? What are you talking about?'

Amelia's face is bright with the thrill of a secret she's about to disclose.

'It's pretty disgusting. I'm not sure I should tell you. You might not be able to take it.'

'I think you're going to tell me,' Becca says. 'I think you want to.'

'Only because I think you ought to know. But you're going to be shocked.'

'Try me.'

'OK. Well, you asked for it. I found out my mum's passcode the other day, and had a look at her phone. And guess who's been texting her? Your dad.'

'So?'

'So *ugh*. He was like, *Call me, we need to talk. I miss you. Kiss kiss.*'

'So he wants to talk to her. Big deal.'

'He *misses* her, Becca. You don't *miss* someone just because you vaguely know them and have kids in the same class at school. He's been *doing* her, and she's too dumb to even get a shitty second phone for him to talk to her on and hide it, like you're supposed to do when you're having an *affair*.'

'Oh, come on. Your mum and my dad are not having an affair.'

'Well, if they're not now they were. It's gross, isn't it? Sorry to break it to you, Becca.' Amelia doesn't look sorry – actually, she looks like she's just scored a triumph. It had always annoyed her when Becca was defensive about her parents; she was harsh about her own, especially her mother, and clearly would have felt vindicated if Becca had joined in.

'I just think you've got it wrong.'

'It's evidence, Becca. You can't write it off just like that. It's the *facts*. Of course they don't want anybody to know. Least of all us. If they're carrying on like that, what right do they have to tell us what to do? I don't know about you, but I'm going to do exactly what I want from now on and I'm not even going to feel bad about it. They're just a bunch of hypocrites.'

'You *want* to believe that. Even if he did say *Missing you*, it doesn't necessarily mean that they were having some great big secret affair.'

'Um, it kind of does, actually. Why else would he have said it? Think about it, Becca. Just open your mind for a minute. All that drama last year, on your birthday? When your mum turned up and started smashing things and hit your dad? She *knew*. She was on to them. She just didn't have any evidence. And then your dad somehow managed to persuade her she was just a crazy lady. Which she pretty obviously was as well, but I guess if your husband is cheating on you and lying to you about it you maybe *would* go a little bit crazy.'

'Why are you so keen to believe it? It's your mum you're talking about!'

Amelia tosses back her long blonde hair. 'You know what your problem is, Becca? You need to grow up. You can't just carry on living in some sweet little dream world where everybody's nice. People are not nice. They're horrible. You might as well accept that and have as good a time as possible.'

A car pulls up next to them; it's Henry Chadstone in his Mini.

'About time,' Amelia says. 'I've got to go. Call me if you want. I'm not doing anything tonight.'

'Does your mother know you know?'

'Yes.' She eyes the downpour. 'She's being very nice to me. I think she doesn't want me to tell Dad.' She holds the handle of the umbrella up for Becca to take. 'Here, have this. You can give it back to me tomorrow.'

Becca takes the umbrella. 'Thanks.'

'Look, I know it's a shock,' Amelia says. 'Even *I* was shocked, and I already think my mum's a total bitch. But it's better for you to know, isn't it?'

'I'm not sure *what* I know.'

'You know enough, don't you? You don't want all the gory details. Are you all right? You look kind of weird. Like you're about to faint again.'

Henry hits his car horn. Becca says, 'You'd better go.'

'Just try not to take life so seriously, OK? You'll never get out of it alive.'

Becca attempts a smile. 'OK. I'll try and remember that.'

'I don't know what you'd do without me,' Amelia says. 'You'd be soaked, for starters.'

She grins and turns away and hurries through the drenching rain to the Mini, and waves vigorously as Henry speeds away.

As soon as she has gone Becca closes the umbrella and puts it down.

Sometimes, when she was little, her dad had let her go out into the garden and run around in the rain. Not the kind of thing her mum had approved of. It had felt wild and magical and free, a chance to do the exact opposite of what you were supposed to do.

And now she will never be able to see him in the same way again.

Maybe this is what being grown up is? Perhaps Amelia is right, and there's no point in trying to be good.

Her hair is dripping, her face is coated with water, her jumper and skirt are dark and sodden. It is astonishing how quickly it is possible to be wet through.

# Chapter Forty-Five

She is sitting at the bottom of the stairs taking her shoes off when her father calls out, 'Becca, could you come in here a minute?'

He sounds a bit odd. No, worse than that – desperate, as if he has been taken hostage but can't let on. She wants nothing more than to retreat up to her bedroom and get into dry clothes, but instead she responds to the summons and goes through to the kitchen.

Oh, crap – Leona is here, *yet again*. Leona, the strange tea-towel lady with the bangles and charms. Becca is not madly keen on Leona coming to the house all the time, but has her and the business venture – upcycled furniture, jazzed-up old tat, whatever – pegged as one of Dad's phases, like tai chi or growing his own vegetables, which means it won't last.

The two of them are sitting at the kitchen table, almost as if they've been waiting for her.

'You're soaked,' Dad says.

She can hardly bring herself to look at him. He is the dad who let her romp in the garden and the dad who has maybe been doing something bad with Mrs Chadstone, and now she's in the room with him it's impossible to reconcile the two.

'Yeah, forgot my umbrella,' she says.

'We should look into umbrellas,' Leona says, gazing into the middle distance as if she can see a bright future there. 'Umbrellas and pac-a-macs. Also, what about wellies? Some people will pay an absurd amount where their children are concerned.'

'I should probably go get changed…' Becca says, moving back towards the door.

'No, wait,' her father says, and it's an order. He never usually talks to her like that.

*What the hell?* Becca has the exact same feeling in her stomach that she gets when a lift suddenly plummets downwards.

'Sit down.'

Becca sits. She has left a trail of damp footprints behind her, and her hair is still dripping a little. Neither of them seems to notice, or care.

But her mother would have cared. Her mother would have insisted on her going up and putting on home clothes and drying her hair, and would have probably made her a hot chocolate, too.

She used to do things like that... When she could, when she was here.

'We have some news,' Dad says. 'Good news. You and Leona here are going to be getting to know each other a bit more. I know Leona wants to spend some time with you over the summer holidays, go shopping and whatever.' He gives Leona a sickening special smile, like he adores her or something. She doesn't look at all sure about what he's saying, but smiles back at him anyway. 'We should all make the most of it,' Dad carries on, 'and try and have a relaxing summer before... uh... the new arrival.'

Becca squints at him as if this might help things to come into focus. It doesn't. *What's he talking about?*

Now Leona is smiling at *her*. Disconcerting, especially as the smile is a sympathetic one. Part of Becca wants nothing more than to jump up and run away. Another part of her wants to thump the table and accuse her father of what she heard this afternoon right in front of this slightly dippy, tattooed, weirdly dressed woman, and see what the pair of them make of that.

'I hope we can be friends,' Leona says.

'Yeah, well, thanks very much, but I don't actually really need any more friends.'

Dad and Leona exchange looks. Dad leans over and takes Leona's hand and keeps holding it.

'You shouldn't speak to Leona like that,' he says manfully, and all of a sudden it's as if Becca's an outsider, someone who needs to be shut out in the dark. 'Leona and I are in love, and Leona is having our baby. You're going to have a little half-sister or brother. Sister, we think, though Leona doesn't want to know for sure.'

He squeezes Leona's hand more tightly, pulls her towards him. *Oh, God, it's disgusting* – she's beaming and he looks proud. Then they turn to Becca with a painful kind of hope, as if they seriously believe she might be happy for them.

She's dumbstruck. This is really happening and there's no way out.

'But you barely know each other. You only just met,' she says. As if that has anything to do with it. All it takes to make a baby is sex, and people seem to do that with pretty much anybody, as soon as they get the chance.

'I know it must be a shock,' Leona says. 'But when you've had time to adjust, I think we could all be really happy together.'

'You're going to move in here? With the baby?'

'Well, yes, of course with the baby,' Leona says with an indulgent smile. She glances lovingly at Mitch – Becca wishes she could shout at them to stop doing that – and rests her hands on her tummy as if it's the best thing ever.

She's weirdly fat there. Now Becca has noticed it she can't see how she had missed it before.

Oh God, the thing that's in there is going to come out, and then Becca will probably be expected to cuddle it and coo over it, too.

'Does Mum know about this?'

Another exchange of glances. 'Yes, we told her,' Mitch says.

'*Right*. I'm guessing that went down well.'

Leona shrugs. 'It's a big change. But you'll all get used to it. You're going to have to. Because this baby isn't going anywhere.'

She caresses her tummy with an almost fanatical look of pride and devotion, which just makes Becca even angrier than before.

'I know this is… complicated,' Leona continues. 'But Becca, this is a *good* thing. Don't fight it. It's a new life. One day, I promise you, you'll love this child in a way you can't now imagine. In the meantime, we're all just going to have to do our best to be kind and considerate of each other.'

'Considerate? That is just total *bullshit*,' Becca says.

She has never sworn at anyone before. It feels pretty good and very bad at the same time. Her dad's face is almost unrecognisable, set and unsmiling. She realises how lovingly he usually looks at her, how fond and indulgent he is.

'It's understandable that you might feel hostile. Becca, I want you to know I really have no intention of trying to replace your mother,' Leona says.

'Just as well, because you couldn't,' Becca says. She isn't shouting: she's pleased to hear that her voice sounds perfectly controlled. 'She may have her faults, but she would *never* do what you've done to her. You were supposed to be her *friend*. And she would never make me sit around soaking wet and listen to her telling me how she was going to turn my life upside down and expect me to *like* it. At least when she messed up she had the grace to feel bad about it!'

'That is completely different,' her father says. 'You owe Leona an apology.'

'You owe *me* an apology,' she tells him. 'Me *and* Mum.'

She pushes back her chair and stands, looks down at her father, pointedly ignores Leona.

'I know about you and Mrs Chadstone,' she tells him. 'You *bastard*.'

'I don't know what your mother's been telling you,' he says, much too smoothly, 'but when she thought I was having an affair with Mary she was delusional. If she's been bringing all that up again and trying to poison you against me, then you need to tell me exactly what she's been saying, for her sake. It could be a sign that she's getting worse again.'

'She hasn't said anything. It was Amelia who told me. She saw a message on her mum's phone. A recent message. You told her you missed her. *We need to talk. Call me, I miss you. Kiss kiss.'* Inspiration strikes – no, not inspiration, the truth. It's like being struck by lightning. She just *knows*, sure as she's standing there. 'You must have wanted to tell her about Leona. About the baby. Have you spoken to her yet? Does she know? I guess she probably wasn't too happy. You weren't still seeing her, were you?'

'Mitch?' Leona says quietly. 'What—'

Her dad's expression is awful to see – cunning and resentful and self-pitying at the same time. He looks cornered, but like he isn't going to go down without a fight.

'Amelia shouldn't be looking at her mother's messages,' he says. 'It's very easy for snoops to get the wrong end of the stick.' He glances at Leona: clearly right now what she thinks matters more to him than Becca. 'I never said I missed her. Amelia's exaggerating, or she's remembered it wrong. But I did ask if we could talk. Mary's been a good friend, and I've known her a long time. I wanted to tell her our news, and pick her brains about how to talk to you about it, Becca. After all, she has a teenage daughter, too. And she knows Rachel, she knows about the situation, and she's been very discreet.'

He reaches out, squeezes Leona's hand. 'I'm sorry. I screwed up,' he says. 'I know I should have run it past you.'

Becca says, 'So? What did she tell you then?'

Both of them stare at her. Leona looks a bit weepy, but Becca can't help that. Her dad looks sheepish and reluctantly impressed. He must realise that he hasn't managed to convince her. He is regarding her with something not far removed from awe, and the truth is a kind of power in her hands, ready to be used.

'I don't believe you, Dad,' Becca says. 'So you might as well stop lying. She probably wasn't best pleased that you'd moved on, was she? But maybe she didn't really care, as long as nobody found out about you and her. So how long did it go on for? Was it just the summer, or did it start before that?'

Mitch lets go of Leona's hand, stares down at the table. 'All right. I suppose I may have allowed myself to get a little too close to her after your mother started having problems. I mean, she'd turned into a completely different person. I didn't know what to do. It all started after your grandmother's funeral, after she scattered the ashes in the garden.' Suddenly he looks completely pathetic. 'You must remember that. She was behaving like a crazy person.'

'*She was behaving like a crazy person because her mother had just died!*'

Becca is shouting now; she's angrier than she has ever been. The injustice of it makes it impossible to be anything else.

'Don't,' Mitch says. 'Please don't.'

Suddenly he bursts into tears. Leona spares Becca a reproachful glance and moves in to comfort him, folding her arms round him like a mother with an overgrown child.

'There, there,' she murmurs. 'It's all over now. There, there.'

The storm is over; Becca's moment of power has passed. She retreats from the room. Nobody follows her. She can still hear her father crying, and Leona murmuring to him.

Her dad has basically just admitted to cheating on her mum – even worse, cheating with Mrs Chadstone, which is so gross and ridiculous Becca can hardly bear to think about it – and Leona seems to think that's just fine. Well, she obviously just isn't a very nice person, given the way she's treated Mum. If she thinks it's OK for Dad to carry on like that, maybe she's done loads of things that are even worse.

It's like Macbeth and Lady Macbeth: both of them are guilty as hell, or would feel that way if either of them had a conscience, but instead they're going to try and convince each other that it's all OK and everything is all right and the other one is still lovely.

Well, they're both horrible, and they aren't going to fool Becca.

But this is her dad. Her dad, who is more fun than anybody else's dad, and more *there*, too. Her dad, who'd taught her how to draw, who'd got her at the end of the day from school all those years and made her tea and let her have extra cake and watched all the Disney films with her and got her maths homework wrong and read her bedtime story and tucked her up for the night...

She slams her bedroom door shut, throws herself down on the bed and punches the pillow.

'I hate you,' she mutters. 'I hate you. I hate you. I hate you.'

But it doesn't make her feel better. Maybe nothing will.

She can hate them all she likes. None of them cares. If she disappeared they'd probably barely notice. Or they'd be pleased to have her out of the way.

She remembers that talk in the lecture theatre the time she fainted. The circle with HARM written in it. Cuts and broken glass and blood. People hurt themselves, sometimes. She has never understood why before, but now she does: it must be because other people hurt you so much worse.

# Chapter Forty-Six

## Rachel

When her phone buzzes and ICE Mitch comes up on the screen it barely seems like an intrusion. She hasn't stopped thinking about him and Leona and the baby and Becca since she left the house.

*In like a strawberry, out like a candle...*

She answers the call. 'Hello?'

He says, 'Rachel. Is Becca with you?' His voice is rough and weirdly distant, as if he is calling from underground.

'Of course not. She's with you. Isn't she?'

'She hasn't been in touch with you?'

'No, I haven't heard from her. Why would I? She's with you.'

Mitch sighs. 'OK.'

*In like a strawberry.* It doesn't work. All the air seems to have been sucked out of her lungs.

Something is wrong. Very wrong.

'Mitch,' Rachel says. 'What's going on? Where is she?'

Mitch clears his throat. 'Right now, I'm not sure.'

Several heartbeats elapse. Time seems to expand, then contract. Rachel says, 'What happened?'

Mitch sighs. 'It's kind of complicated to explain. I don't want to go into all the details. But anyway, Leona and I told her the news and she didn't take it very well. She started yelling and carrying on, and then she stomped off to her room. A bit later on, at some point, she slipped out of the house without telling me, and I don't know where she's gone.'

'What do you mean, she slipped out without telling you? You mean she went out and you didn't even notice?'

'We were in the kitchen, talking. You know how insulated it is from the rest of the house. I just didn't hear her. I didn't realise until I went up to her bedroom and found it was empty.' There is a small, reproachful pause. 'Leona's very upset about it. If you'd helped us like I said, this might never have happened.'

Rachel has shifted the phone into her left hand, and is pinching the skin of her wrist with her right. She makes a conscious effort to stop.

She asks, 'When do you think she went out?'

'Oh… I suppose it could have been, realistically speaking, pretty much any time between say about half-past four and maybe ten to six?'

'You ignored her for all that time? Wow. Leona must have been upset. Did she take her phone?'

'I think so. But she's not answering it. She got changed, too, and hung up all her school uniform. She'd come home soaking wet, for some reason, even though she had a perfectly good umbrella with her.'

'She never has an umbrella.'

'Well, today she had one and didn't bloody use it.'

'Just out of interest, Mitch… what's this umbrella like?'

'I can't see what that's got to do with anything.'

'Just humour me, Mitch. Describe it to me.'

'Well… it's kind of checked? I don't recognise it, actually.'

She can hear someone talking to Mitch in the background. Must be Leona. Then Mitch says, 'It's designer, apparently.'

'Could be Amelia's.'

'Could be anybody's.'

'True. But one of us ought to ring the Chadstones, and it would probably be better if it was you. She might have gone over there. Or if Amelia was talking to Becca just before she came home, maybe she'll have some idea where she's gone. After all, Amelia is Becca's closest friend… As far as I know, anyway. Unless you can think of anybody else?'

Mitch pauses. 'No,' he admits. 'Not really.'

'Then it has to be worth a try, surely?' Mitch doesn't respond. 'So… what happened when you told her about the baby? What did she actually say?'

'Well, not much. She just kind of went into an adolescent huff. You know what they're like. It's not always easy to live with, believe me. Thirteen-year-old girl hormones can be pretty vicious.'

There is a crackle on the other end of the line. Leona says, 'Hello, Rachel. I'm on the phone in the bedroom. I think we need to talk. Mitch, you can listen if you want, or you can leave this to me. I'm afraid I'm going to tell her what Becca told us.'

'Leona, no. Please don't do this,' Mitch said.

'It's necessary, Mitch. She ought to know. Rachel, I'm afraid that Becca isn't just upset about the baby. There's something else. Mitch and Mary had an affair, and Becca found out about it. Mary's daughter told her. She'd seen some messages on Mary's phone – nothing intimate, the relationship is over, but enough to make her suspicious. I'm so sorry, Rachel. It seems to have started last summer. They broke it off after you went over there on Becca's birthday and everything came to a head. Mitch was only getting in touch with Mary because he wanted to tell her about me.'

And there it is. The truth.

The shock of it bowls her over. It's huge, it's too much. It's like the rush of being hit or falling, but she is frozen in place. Leona has stopped talking but Rachel can't speak. There is silence and nothing moves.

She had thought it would be a relief to know for sure. It isn't. It's hell. It's the end, the final killer blow to the love she and Mitch had shared. And it wasn't Leona who had killed it, or even Mary: it was Mitch.

It's an effort to remember to breathe. *Strawberry. Candle.*

She's conscious of the phone, the bedsit, the grey light of a rainy-day evening, Mitch and Leona together at a distance in Rose Cottage, and Becca where? Nowhere that they know. Vanished. And in that instant she knows that Becca was never really lost to her before. That even when Becca rejected her and chose Mitch, even when she slept under a separate roof every night, that was never loss in the way this is.

And something Viv had said comes back to her...

*Hope is what makes it possible for us to keep going. It's much more useful than despair.*

She catches sight of the old green pinboard. The three photos: Aidan, Becca, Bluebell. And she's suddenly glad that Leona's new baby won't belong there.

Will having another child remind her of the one she had given away – will Bluebell continue to haunt her like a ghost-child compounded of what-might-have-beens and if-onlys? But with a newborn, there was so much to do – all the waking-up and baths and puttings-to-bed, the doctor's appointments, and then the playdates and trips to the shoe shop. The farewells at the nursery and at the school gates and before sleepovers, the dropping off at a first shared house or hall of residence, the leaving home, the exchange of promises and endearments at the ends of visits and of phone calls.

The routine pangs of parting that come with a lifetime's slow separation.

The being there.

Anyway, Bluebell is back in Leona's life for real now – she would see her again, they would get to know each other. Bluebell might even meet the new baby. Her half-sibling. Who would also be Becca's half-sibling. Three children: one lost and found, one new, and one missing.

*Breathe.* Suddenly it is possible for her to move again, and the world slams back into place.

'You know what, Mitch? You're a pretty good father. I've always thought that... up until now, anyway. But you were a lousy husband,' she says. 'It would have been nice if you'd had the decency to confess at the time. It might have saved me some heartache. Not to mention thinking that I'd lost my mind. And I don't think much of your taste. With all respect, Leona. But anyway, I can't worry about all that now. I have far more important things to deal with. Like tracking down my daughter, who you two seem to have managed to lose without even realising it. Mitch, you should call the police.'

'Oh, is that really necessary? I mean, I can't imagine they'll actually do anything about it. She's hardly going to be a top priority.'

'Just let them know, OK? At least then they can look out for her. And they might have some advice for us. It can't hurt. It's worth trying anything until we've got her back safe and sound.'

'Mitch, I think she's right,' Leona intervenes.

'Well, all right, but they'll just think I'm wasting their time,' Mitch grumbles. Then, rather resentfully: 'You seem very keen to hand out tasks, Rachel – what are *you* going to do?'

What *is* she going to do? She has to do *something*.

'I'm going to find Amelia Chadstone. Call me the second you hear anything,' Rachel says.

Mitch begins to protest – 'Are you really sure that's a good idea? Maybe I should handle it—' But she cuts him off by ending the call.

# Chapter Forty-Seven

Rachel pulls up right outside the house in a slew of gravel and slams the car door shut with a vigour that echoes across the quiet lawn.

She checks her phone. Missed calls from Mitch and Mary. Nothing from Becca.

Mary's voicemail is in her committee voice, smooth and reasonable and blameless.

*'Rachel, I got your message. Mitch rang me, too. I'm afraid I'm not at all sure that any of us is going to be able to help. I've already spoken to Amelia and she has no idea where Becca might be. I wonder if there might be more fruitful avenues for you to pursue. I'm so sorry that this has happened, and I very much hope Becca will be home soon safe and sound. Do call me back if you'd like. If there's anything else useful that we might be able to do, I'm sure we'd be pleased to assist.'*

Hypocrite. She doesn't want to help, not really; she just wants Rachel to go away. Understandably. Who would want their ex-lover's still-wife making a scene on the doorstep, especially if said wife is also distraught because her husband is having a baby with someone else and her daughter has run away? Nobody. But this isn't about her and Mary. This is about Becca, and the possibility that she might have said something to Amelia that would cast some light on where she's gone.

She listens to her message from Mitch.

*'Rachel? Rachel, please call me. I've spoken to Mary, and she said you'd rung her and she's going to talk to Amelia and call you back. I'm really hoping you haven't just gone over there. That would be a really bad idea, and we've got enough on our hands as it is. Please ring me when you get this. I'm going to call the police.' ... 'Just a sec, Leona, let me finish. Rachel, I'll let you know if the police are going to come round, and if they are you can come back here if you want, so we can talk to them together.'*

End of message. Rachel puts the phone back in her bag and gets out of the car. She rings the doorbell once, twice.

It is so unlike Becca to just take off that almost anything seems possible. Terrible things: falling into bad or dangerous company, harming herself, putting herself in harm's way. It is such a brutal, indifferent world, so full of people who at best are willing to turn a blind eye and ask no questions and stay well out of anything that's not their business, or who at worst might see a lonely and confused young teen as an opportunity...

Some children run away and never come back.

Mary opens the door a chink. She doesn't take the chain off. 'Rachel. I wasn't expecting you to see you here. Did you get my message?'

'I did, thank you, Mary. I'd just like to speak to Amelia for myself, if that's all right. Then I'll be on my way.'

'It's not really the best time,' Mary says. 'We're just about to have supper.'

'It won't take long, and I'd really appreciate it. Given the circumstances, maybe Amelia would understand the urgency?'

'I know you're upset, and looking for someone to blame,' Mary says. 'But this is nothing to do with any of us.'

'I beg to differ, actually, Mary.'

'Go home, Rachel. Leave my family alone.'

'If you'd left mine alone we might not be in this situation.'

Mary blushes an ugly brick red. 'If you've come to fling accusations around, I don't think that's going to be terrifically helpful.'

'It's not an accusation, Mary. It's the truth, and you know it, and actually, somewhere deep down, I know you feel guilty about it.'

Then Amelia pipes up inside: 'Mum, I really don't mind talking to her. Why don't we just get it over with?'

Mary hesitates and the fight goes out of her. It's like watching a parent attempting to remonstrate with a toddler in a supermarket, then sheepishly caving in and buying whatever the child is demanding anyway. She must know that Amelia knows about the affair, and told Becca; quite possibly her husband and most of her acquaintances will also know before very much longer, unless Amelia can be persuaded to keep quiet.

'Let's all try to keep calm heads, shall we?' Mary says, rallying. 'You'd better come in, then, Rachel, but it would be best if you'd keep it short, if you don't mind.'

She takes off the chain so Rachel can step inside, and moves back towards the stairwell as Amelia comes forward. She has changed out of her school uniform into a hoodie and jeans – exactly the same kind of thing that Becca would wear. Just seeing that off-duty young-teen uniform gives Rachel a pang, and she wonders what Becca had been wearing when she left the house, and if they would need to find out. Mitch probably wouldn't have a clue, but if Rachel could look through Becca's wardrobe she might be able to work out what was missing.

'I'm so sorry about all this, Mrs Moran. I didn't mean to make trouble. I'll tell you as much as I can,' Amelia says, commandingly but gently, as if talking to a startled animal. 'I'm afraid I don't think I'll be much help, though.'

Rachel is conscious of Mitch's painting of Rose Cottage hanging on the wall next to her, and of Mary lurking in the background, impotently angry. She focuses on Amelia, who is smiling with innocent sympathy – too innocent? – and regarding Rachel warily, as if she presents some kind of unanticipated challenge.

Rachel says, 'When did you last talk to Becca?'

'At the end of the school day,' Amelia says. 'That's when I told her. About, you know. The thing.' She glances over her shoulder at her mother, who shrinks back against the wall.

'I'm sorry to speak so frankly, Amelia, and I wouldn't do this unless it was important, but I need to be sure: you mean you told her you thought there was something going on between your mother and Becca's father?'

Amelia looks down at her feet. She's wearing a pair of unexpectedly childish slippers, fluffy rabbit faces with pom-poms for noses. 'Yeah,' she says. 'I felt she ought to know. I never thought she'd just disappear like this.'

'I don't think that was the only reason why she was upset,' Rachel says. 'There have been other things going on, too.'

Amelia looks up. 'I called her,' she says. 'She hasn't got back to me.'

Rachel detects a faint note of finality, a desire to wash her hands of the whole business – as if the whole thing had been an experiment with unexpectedly arduous consequences. She says, 'Can you think of anyone else she might be with?'

'I really can't. I'm sorry, Mrs Moran,' Amelia says. 'She doesn't have all that many friends, to be honest. I'm sorry, I know that sounds like I'm being mean, but it really is just what she's like. My guess is she's gone somewhere by herself.'

'How has she seemed to you lately?'

'What do you mean?'

'Well, has she been happy? Unhappy? Worried?'

'A bit withdrawn, maybe, though no more than usual. She's always been quiet. You know what she's like – she tends to be on the edge of things. But we don't hang out that much, so I couldn't really say.'

'Rachel,' Mary says warningly, 'I can't see how terrorising my daughter is going to help you find yours.'

'I'm not terrorising her.'

'Well, she's obviously not very comfortable with being interrogated like this.'

'OK, OK. Just one more question, if I may?'

Time to change tack. Rachel decides to offer a confidence in the hope of eliciting one in return.

'I'm really worried about Becca, to be honest,' she says to Amelia. 'She's just found out her dad's got a new partner and they're having a baby, and I think it might have come as a shock. I just thought, if there was anything you could remember her saying... even if you weren't sure... it might give me something to go on.'

Amelia says, 'Look, I've told you everything I can. I really don't think I can help you. It's not *my* fault if she decided to run away.'

She covers her face with her hands. Her shoulders tremble; she emits a soft wet sound not a million miles removed from crying. Rachel's pretty sure she's faking, but Mary steps forward to put an arm around her; Amelia shrugs her off.

Mary briefly looks wounded, then glares at Rachel.

'That is enough,' Mary says. 'You go off up to your room, Amelia. You've done all that could possibly be reasonably expected of you. I'll handle this.'

Amelia scuttles off, and Mary squares up to Rachel.

'You need to leave now,' she says.

'You don't even care that Becca's gone missing, do you? You know what? You've always looked down on me. Well, I don't think much of you either. The only thing you've got going for you is money.'

'Well, your husband seemed to think differently. And I seem to remember our money was good enough for you when you were trying to flog that painting,' Mary says, gesturing towards the study of the garden of Rose Cottage.

'You don't deserve to have that on your wall.'

'Then take it. You'd be doing us a favour. I'm sick of looking at the thing. It doesn't exactly have pleasant associations. What with you having come around here and thrown it around and made that dreadful scene in front of the children.'

'Ah. That dreadful scene. So dreadful that Mitch decided seeing you was more trouble than it was worth and broke it off. Not that it's taken him all that long to get serious with someone else.'

That seems to strike home. She takes low satisfaction in seeing Mary's face crumple, like a toddler whose treat has been taken away.

'It wasn't like that,' Mary says.

'I don't care. But you're right, I shouldn't have taken it out on the painting. It's not the painting's fault that the two of you did what you did. Anyway, thank you for the offer. I'd be delighted to relieve you of it.'

She puts her hands on either side of the frame. It is very slightly dusty. Up close, the painting is reduced to its constituents: lines and dots and splashes, milky white, pale grey and blue. It's less vigorous than the oil paintings Mitch had made when he was younger, more shadowy and unsure. She decides she likes it for that. It's the work of someone who has lost his way, but hasn't quite given up hope of finding something new. It's honest, even if its maker had not been.

She lifts, encounters resistance, persists, and the painting comes free.

'I don't know what Hugh is going to say about this when he finds out,' Mary says.

'I can guess what he's going to say about you and Mitch. Unless he already knows.'

And that's the first time Mary looks ashamed. She just about manages to maintain her expression of affronted dignity, but it is rigid with effort. She opens her mouth to speak and closes it again.

'Oh. Right. He *does* already know,' Rachel says. 'It's like that, is it? And he forgave you, just like that. Even though Mitch is meant to be his friend. Presumably he gets the same deal, does he? Freedom to have a bit on the side. Classy, Mary. Very classy.'

'Keep your voice down,' Mary hisses. 'There are children in the house.'

'It's a bit late to start worrying about that, isn't it? I think your daughter has a pretty shrewd idea of what's been going on.'

Mary hesitates. Rachel says, 'OK, I get it. She doesn't know the half of it.'

'You don't have to make it sound so sordid,' Mary hisses. 'Yes, Hugh and I have had some problems, and he has seen other people and I found that difficult to deal with, and I confided in Mitch about it and he was very sympathetic. But I didn't mean for anything to happen.'

'Oh, great. So Hugh cheated on you and you decided to use Mitch to get back at him. And then you all let me think that I was crazy when I suspected something. You're all cowards. And you're all liars.'

Once again, Mary can't find anything to say. Her pride appears to have deserted her, and she's visibly deflated.

'I have to go,' Rachel says. 'If you hear anything from Becca, or if Amelia thinks of anything, just get in touch, OK?'

She turns away and goes to put the painting in the boot of the car. The front door shuts softly, almost apologetically, behind her.

No one has called her, and once again Becca doesn't answer her phone. She leaves another message. '*Please, just get in touch. Nobody's angry with you. We just need to know you're safe. If you don't want to talk to me, call your dad... or anybody... just call.*'

Where next?

She could go to Rose Cottage and sit there with Mitch and Leona waiting for someone in uniform to turn up.

Or she could keep looking.

She starts the car and is about to drive away when the front door opens and Henry comes out. He heads straight for Rachel and taps on the car window, and she presses the button to wind it down.

'Mrs Moran?'

'Yes, Henry, what is it?'

'About Becca, did you hear from her yet?'

'No. Nothing.'

'I don't know how helpful this is going to be, but Amelia just told me she and Becca had been talking about going to London.'

'*London?*'

'It wasn't like a plan or anything. Amelia was just going on about how good it was and how Becca should go.'

'Oh, great. When did this come up?'

'Er, today. When they were talking after school. I saw them together. I came to pick Amelia up. Anyway, I thought you should know.'

'OK. Thank you. That's useful. I mean, it might turn out to be. Though it would have been nice if Amelia had thought to tell me herself. Does your mother know you're out here talking to me?'

'No. I think she's running a bath.' Rachel could imagine what Mary had in mind: soaking away the guilt with a large glass of white wine to one side and candles round the rim, crying a little into the bubble bath.

Henry says, 'What are you going to do now?'

'I'm going to head into town and have a look round. Just in case she hasn't gone far.' She might just walk into Costa Coffee or Starbucks and see Becca sitting there, or spot her in the shopping arcade, or the park. There aren't that many places for angry teens to hang out in Kettlebridge.

'Maybe I could come, too?' Henry says. 'I could help. We could split up, cover more places faster.'

She hesitates. He looks down at her earnestly. There's something endearingly geeky about him – she can picture him as a doctor or a lawyer one day, bowed by responsibilities, trying to do the right thing.

'OK,' she says. 'You'd better go and tell your mother. I don't expect she'll like it. But you'll need to be quick.'

Henry beams at her. 'OK. I will be.' And he hurries back into the house.

Rachel hadn't really expected anything to come of her trip to the Chadstones' house – she had just been going through the motions, not knowing what to do. And yet here, against the odds, is an offer of help.

*You see, Becca? People do care about you. They really do.*
If only she could hear her. If only she knew.

# Chapter Forty-Eight

## Leona

After Rachel ends the call Leona goes downstairs and into the living room, where Mitch is sitting as if it is beyond him to move. The phone is still in his hand. He looks like a statue of despair after bad news. He fixes his gaze on her as she comes closer, and there is no hint of affection in it.

'Why did you do that?' he asks. 'You had no right. Were you trying to punish me? Or did you want to hurt Rachel?'

'That's an outrageous thing to say. *You're* the one who hurt Rachel.'

'Yes, and that was before I even met you. What has it got to do with you?'

Leona puts her hands on her belly. 'Because it says something about the man who's the father of my child.'

'So now you think I'm a complete bastard.'

'I don't think that. But you could have told me. I told you everything. Why didn't you tell me?'

He glowers at her. 'Because I knew it would cause trouble. And it has. Now you've gone and lobbed a hand grenade into a situation that's already a crisis. What got into you, Leona? If Rachel goes over there and creates a disturbance she'll probably end up being arrested. Or is that what you want?'

Leona stares at him. 'That is a terrible thing to say.'

Mitch rubs his forehead with his hand. 'You shouldn't have meddled with my family.'

'I thought I was part of your family now. Obviously I was wrong.'

He shakes his head. 'I can't do this now, Leona. I have to call the police.'

'Rachel deserved to know the truth,' Leona says. 'For some reason best known to yourself, you seem to have preferred to leave her thinking she was crazy than for her to be disappointed in you. Who knows, maybe that's your twisted way of still having feelings for her.'

'If that's what you think of me, then why are you still here?'

'I don't know,' Leona says. 'Do what you need to do, Mitch. I'm going.'

'I guess it makes sense that you'd want to abandon ship before the police get here and start asking awkward questions.'

'You'd say anything to hurt me right now, wouldn't you? I'm beginning to wonder how your marriage lasted as long as it did,' Leona says, and goes out and closes the door.


She sits on the stairs in the hallway and calls a cab. Yes, they could be with her straight away. No problem. She gives her home address and asks them to be as quick as they can.

Mitch is on the phone; she can't make out the words, but it sounds as if he is giving answers to a checklist of questions. He must be talking to the police. The tension in his voice is obvious, but also, he sounds relieved. It must be reassuring to feel that he is doing the right thing, and that someone's going to be able to tell him what to do next. It wouldn't be like that for her if she was the one making the call, but then Mitch has never been on the wrong side of the law.

She makes a conscious effort not to think about the things he'd said. He'll regret them later, but struggle to apologise – that stiff-necked pride. Such a weakness. But it's the flipside of his talent: the stubbornness and willpower that drive him to paint can also make him infuriating to be with. Or so she tells herself.

'Your father can really be a disappointment sometimes. We'll just have to hope we can get him into shape,' she murmurs under her breath, and rests one hand consolingly on her tummy, where her baby – her new baby! – is quietly growing, too small as yet for her to be able to feel it move.

When she'd come back from France, from seeing Bluebell, she had felt completely at a loss. Yes, she had seen her daughter: yes, it had gone well – as well as she could have hoped – and it had been agreed that they would meet again. It had been a resolution, of sorts. Bluebell was well; she was happy; there was a place for Leona in her life. But it would not be, and could not be, the place that Leona hungered for.

As soon as Mitch had turned up on her doorstep that day back in May, looking hot and hesitant and disgruntled, she'd known she wanted him. More than that. Had to have him. And she had.

And he'd given her what she needed. A little miracle.

It hadn't been about wrong or right, about good or bad. It certainly hadn't been about logic or caution. It had been about need, and hunger. And here they are, and this time she is going to make it work.

She has stumbled into this family, and now she may be the only one who can help them.

When her taxi arrives she tells the driver she has changed her mind, and gives him an alternative destination. He doesn't object; it isn't all that far away from where she lives. She settles back and watches the lane slip by as she's driven away.

*

On the morning that she had given Bluebell up she had known who it was at the doorbell. She had known, and yet as she went to answer it she had allowed herself to hope that it might not be.

It could have been the lady from across the road, popping over because she'd forgotten something when she babysat Bluebell the night before. It might have been someone who had the wrong address, or was lost. It could have been something perfectly ordinary and everyday, the kind of thing that might have happened yesterday or the day before.

But then she opened the door and saw the policeman standing there, and the car parked in front of the house.

She said, 'Is it about Emily? Is she OK?'

Maybe she shouldn't have asked. Maybe it was incriminating. But she had to know. It was too important not to know.

Because if Emily was OK, the police wouldn't be here.

The policeman was short, not much taller than Leona, with freckles that made him look younger than he probably was. He cleared his throat. 'Emily Davis passed away in the early hours of the morning.'

Leona put her hand to her mouth and bit it. A strange sound came out of her. The policeman carried on talking, as matter-of-fact as if he was someone who'd just come round to read the meter.

They needed her to come with them to the station, he said. To help with their enquiries.

A familiar sound reached her from the basement: Bluebell had started crying.

'I can't,' Leona said. 'I have a baby.'

'We're aware of that,' the policeman said. 'There are some people here who'll look after her while you talk to us. You don't need to worry about her, she'll be in good hands.'

And that was when she saw the other car parked behind the police car, and the people in it. Two women, not in uniforms. There was something about the way they were looking up at her, and at the house, that frightened her more than anything. As if she were a problem in need of careful handling, calling for the kind of judicious detachment and caution you would expect of a pair of professionals.

*

They let her go back into the house to get Bluebell ready and pack a bag for her. Downstairs in the basement Jake was still asleep, or pretending to be. In the room next door Bluebell was sitting up and gripping the bars of her cot. She quieted as soon as Leona lifted her out, and gave Leona her sweetest smile. Two teeth now, and a headful of hair, blonde and curly; she attracted admiring looks wherever she went.

'Hey you,' Leona said. 'I've got you.'

She was suddenly very calm. Unnaturally calm. Maybe it was shock, or maybe it was because she was in the middle of the worst that could happen and there was no longer anything to be afraid of. Or maybe it was because she had to be that way. For Bluebell. Bluebell always became distressed as soon as Leona did, and whimpered the minute she and Jake started arguing.

But it was hard to understand anything, other than that she was in trouble and the social workers had some kind of emergency court order that meant they could take Bluebell into care for now, while Leona was talking to the police. And however nice and gentle they were being with her – they were trying not to frighten her, probably, so she wouldn't panic and try to resist them or run away – underneath all of it was this: they could take Bluebell, whether Leona agreed or not.

And Emily was dead. Emily was her friend, and she had died after taking a pill that Leona had given her. That was the only other thing Leona knew for sure: Emily was dead, and it was her fault.

She put Bluebell back in the cot while she got some things together, and Bluebell sat and watched her and sucked on her comforter. Nappies, the rusks Bluebell liked, a mixture of outfits, a few favourite toys: the blue plastic keys that beeped when you pressed the button, the padded bug that Bluebell slept with. It wasn't that much. It fit in the bag, no problem. Then she dressed Bluebell in the outfit she'd got her for Christmas, the top embroidered with tiny flowers and the little dungarees that matched, and the soft leather shoes that had been a gift from her mum.

Mum would have taken Bluebell, even after everything that had happened. But the backache that she'd complained of for so long had turned out to be kidney cancer, which had gone past being operable, and she was in a hospice. Leona's stepfather was probably there with her right now. No point hoping for any help from him: he hated babies, and he hated Leona even more.

Jake finally stirred himself, and sat up in bed, lighting a cigarette. It was Jake who had come to find her in the club the night before, to tell her Emily had collapsed and the bouncers were dealing with it. It had taken a while to find out that Emily had been rushed away in an ambulance, with her boyfriend at her side.

How had Leona ever found Jake attractive? At this moment he looked like a spoilt, shifty schoolboy, someone obviously not to be trusted. She had been so happy to move in with him, to escape from her parents' house. She had thought it was love. Love and freedom. Lately though, it had been increasingly obvious that he found her a bit of a drag. Her *and* Bluebell. Oh, he'd loved the idea of having them there... but the reality of a baby crying in the morning was something else.

She'd hoped that a big night out would remind him that they could still have a good time together. And here they are the morning after, barely able to look at each other.

'You shouldn't say anything until you've got a lawyer,' he said, but she ignored him. She had Bluebell in her arms and the bag of Bluebell's things dangling from one shoulder, and he didn't even offer to help her carry it.

She took Bluebell upstairs and out into the cold, and somehow she managed to hand her over. Such a small movement, from Leona's arms to the arms of the social worker who was waiting to take her.

Bluebell didn't squall or fuss. She was still watching Leona quite calmly, as if she understood more than Leona did, as if she knew there was nothing else for it.

'We'll take good care of her,' the social worker said.

'You better had.'

It felt like falling off a cliff, or from the top of a multistorey building. Like dying.

Leona leaned forward to touch Bluebell's soft cheek. Her hand was trembling. Bluebell's small one reached out and wrapped itself around her forefinger as she had done so many times before, as she had done just after she had been born.

And then Bluebell let go and Leona turned away because she couldn't bear it – she couldn't look at Bluebell any more. She got into the waiting police car and the door slammed shut, and as they drove away she felt as if her life had stopped and there would never be any point to it again.

*

There's a queue of traffic coming into Kettlebridge – the tail end of rush hour, commuters heading home – but it's quiet heading out of town, the direction Leona has asked the taxi driver to take. Just past the bridge, he turns off the main road and bumps along the single-track road that leads to the lock house.

She could have got this wrong. It's just a hunch. But she has to try… She has to do everything she can to bring Becca back.

Because Leona knows what it is to fear that you will never see your child again. To not care where you are, whether it's a courtroom or a prison cell or the world outside, because nowhere could be as bad as you feel. For time to creep remorselessly on, carrying you away from a loss that you know you will never recover from… And yet you don't want time to pass, you don't want to recover, because that means forgetting, and you want to hold on to every little detail, each remembered smile, what your child's hand felt like in yours, the smell of that skin.

For days, weeks, months, years to go by, as you try to piece a life back together that will always have something missing from it.

No, she won't see Rachel go through all that. Not if she can help it.

At the end of the road she pays the taxi driver and asks him if he might be willing to wait. They are in a turning circle surrounded by trees and banks of hawthorn, beyond which the roof of the lock house is just visible. He looks around, shakes his head, and tells her to call again when she wants collecting.

After he has gone it is very quiet: all she can hear is the steady rush of falling water. She goes through the gate to the bank of the lock and as she approaches the weir the sound of water grows steadily louder and the air seems fresher, as if it has been shaken clean. It is like walking towards the sea.

There is a lone narrowboat moored a little way downstream, but the ice cream kiosk in front of the lock house is closed and there is nobody around. She walks across the lock gates to the small island between the lock and the weir. The view is obscured by trees, by the display showing a map of the course of the Thames from its source to the sea, and by an outbuilding with a sign warning passers-by to be wary of the bees' nest by its side.

It could be a fool's errand: it is very likely that she will find no one here. And then what?

She emerges at one end of the walkway that spans the weir, and sees a lone figure a little way ahead, looking down at the roiling water.

It's a girl. A young girl in jeans and a hooded top. It could be Becca, but she has her hood up so it isn't possible to tell for certain.

Leona sets off towards her. To her right, the river is high and smooth and glassy, pooling at the edge of the weir. To her left, on the low side, it crashes and churns and foams as if it is boiling.

She doesn't call out. The girl might not hear her anyway. She appears to be completely absorbed in the view. But as Leona draws closer the girl turns and Leona sees that it *is* Becca, and she has been crying.

# Chapter Forty-Nine

## Becca

Leona comes towards her as if she's walking across a tightrope. She looks terrified, like everybody's watching her and this is her big chance to prove herself. Eventually she makes it and turns and leans on the walkway barrier so they're both gazing out at the same view of the river downstream, calm and broad as it runs between the meadows towards Kettlebridge.

'I guess you get the prize,' Becca says. 'Congratulations. Are they all out looking, or is it just you?'

'Your dad has just rung the police,' Leona tells her.

'He rang the police? I only went out for a walk. Is that against the law now?'

'No, but it's a good idea to let people know where you are. He's worried about you. Is it OK with you if I call him?'

Becca shrugs. 'If you want.'

Leona gets her phone out. She says, 'People have been trying to ring you. Did you know?'

'I didn't want to talk to anybody. The last few conversations I had didn't go so well.'

Her phone is in her back pocket, switched off. She'd done that as soon as she set out. It had felt good. Really good. Like having the power to turn yourself invisible. Maybe it had been bad, too, but it hadn't felt like it. You couldn't always be on hand the second other people decided they wanted you.

Leona starts talking to Dad, telling him where they are, and the next minute she hands over the phone and says, 'He wants to talk to you.'

And then Becca is speaking to her dad. Which is kind of weird, given that she'd just been thinking about running away and never ever seeing him again. He wants to know if she's OK. She says she is. What's OK anyway? She's not dead and she hasn't started playing with knives. Yet. Although she has definitely been tempted. He tells her to hold on, he's coming to get her, and he's really sorry to have upset her like that, they'd really messed up. Dad never apologises about anything, so that's pretty weird – he's dead stubborn, never backs down if he can help it, and hates admitting when he's in the wrong. He doesn't sound angry either, just relieved. Then he says to give the phone back to Leona.

Leona doesn't say much to him, just listens. Becca stares at the water. Drowning's meant to be nice because your life flashes before you, but what if your life's been awful and grim, or just really boring? Although bits of hers have been all right. Coming here with Mum and Dad when she was little. Paddling in her wellies in the stream in front of the cottage. Playing games with Dad while Mum was at work or coming home on the train. It's just lately that everything has fallen apart. But maybe that's what happens when you grow up.

Leona ends the call and puts her phone away. She says, 'Your mum's been looking for you, too, you know. She went to the Chadstones' house.'

'Really? Guess she must have wanted another fight.'

'I think she wanted to talk to your friend Amelia.'

'Yeah… she's not so much of a friend. I mean, we hung out for a while. But really we just know each other because of our parents. We're kind of into different things.'

'Really? What like?'

'Well, she's into smoking and shoplifting and boys.'

Becca sneaks a look at Leona to see if she's shocked by this. She doesn't appear to be.

Leona says, 'So what are you into?'

'I used to like being at home. But I guess that's ruined now, isn't it?'

'It doesn't have to be. None of what's happened has to be a catastrophe. I know it's all come as a shock, and in retrospect, we could have handled it better, and I'm sorry about that. But if we really want to, we can fix this. All of us.'

'You're going to fix my parents' marriage, are you?'

'I'm afraid I think that's probably broken past repairing,' Leona says gently.

And it's true, and Becca knows it is. She starts crying; she can't help it. She cries hard, and Leona gives her some tissues and then puts a hand on her shoulder and she doesn't move away.

However much you feel like you could cry forever, you never can. By and by Becca stops and then she says, 'I thought it was Mum's fault. She really hurt Dad, you know. She pushed him and he fell on some glass and cut his hand open. He's still got the scar.'

'Yes. I know about that. He told me,' Leona said. 'He said you walked in just after it happened. It must have been a really big shock for you.'

'It was.'

'It might help you to talk to someone about it, you know. Like a counsellor. It can be good to have someone listen to you who isn't involved. Who isn't on anybody's side.'

'I suppose,' Becca says. She hadn't really thought of counselling that way before; it had always just seemed like something her parents wanted her to do so they could feel better about everything. 'Are you in love with Dad?'

'I am,' Leona says.

'I don't get it. He was sleeping with Mrs Chadstone. I don't think he deserved to be hurt like that, but he was pretty awful to Mum. She worked so hard all the time, she was worn out and he didn't even care. He cheated on her, and he made out she'd gone crazy when she was really just sad and angry. How can you be in love with someone who behaves like that?'

'People do worse things,' Leona says.

And then they both stare at the rushing water.

'I did something bad, once,' Leona says. 'I went to prison for it.'

Becca recoils. She gets the feeling Leona is about to tell her what she did, and she's not sure she wants to know. Leona is fiddling with that little pink stone she wears on a chain round her neck. She's taking her time, but she's obviously nervous.

'I got some drugs for a friend, and it turned out they were contaminated and she died,' Leona says. 'I was sentenced to a year in prison for drug supply and Bluebell, my little girl, was fostered. When I came out I was a mess and completely heartbroken, but she was obviously settled and happy, so I decided it would be the right thing to let her foster mother adopt her.'

Drugs! Prison! A lost baby! It all seems a bit unreal – it's the kind of thing the school got people in to warn them about. But it really happened.

It isn't cold, but Becca shivers. She looks at Leona properly for the first time and sees, not the weird tea-towel lady who's suddenly got pregnant by her dad, but a person... someone with her own pain and hopes and fears. Someone who maybe actually is really in love with her dad, because otherwise why would she be here, trying to talk to Becca?

'Is that why you have the bluebell tattoo?' Becca asks.

'It is. Though I don't recommend that you ever get a tattoo, obviously. I'm an example of what *not* to do.'

'Yeah, well.' Becca shrugs, trying to look nonchalant, though actually she's still shocked. 'No offence, but I've never met anyone who's been in prison before.'

'Your mother doesn't know about all that yet. I'm going to have to tell her, and I don't know how she's going to react when I do,'

Leona says. 'It's not easy to tell people about things that you're ashamed of. So, I do understand why your dad told so many lies. He was desperate for you not to find out what he'd been doing. He knew you'd think less of him, and you're very important to him, you know. He once told me you were the only thing in his life that he was really proud of. He really does love you. And your mother does, too. They might not have done a very good job of keeping you out of what's gone wrong between them, but that doesn't mean they don't care. And to be honest, you've given us all a scare tonight. I think we're all going to have to do a bit of soul-searching, and work harder to get it right. I know you must be angry with your dad, but try not to be too hard on him. What happened earlier today was really my fault. I was the one who was pushing to tell you about the baby.'

'Yeah, but if he cares so much about me and what I think, why'd he do what he did?'

Leona sighs. 'Adults aren't always that different to people your age, Becca. I know they ought to be older and wiser. But think of the teenagers you know and then imagine them as grown-ups, with kids of their own and jobs. That's what it's like: they're people you know… just older. Which gives them a whole lot more scope to make mistakes.'

And Becca tries to think about it. Herself, Amelia and her brother, Ollie Pickering, Millie Parker-Jones…

'That's a terrifying prospect,' she says.

Leona smiles as if Becca has just cracked a joke, though she meant it completely seriously. 'So… do you feel like you're ready to come home now?'

'I guess. I have to, don't I? I'm thirteen years old. I can't go anywhere. Not unless I want to end up sleeping on the streets or something. Don't take this the wrong way, but if you're moving in with Dad and you're going to have a baby… babies cry a lot, right? And I'm going to have exams and stuff.'

'Well, the baby's not due just yet. You've got a while to think about it,' Leona says, looking worried again.

'When I'm older I'm going to live in a cave miles away from anywhere, and never talk to anyone,' Becca tells her.

'I think your dad sometimes feels like that, too.'

Then someone calls out: 'BECCA!'

It's Mum, standing at the far end of the walkway, with Henry Chadstone beside her. *Henry?* What's he doing here? Becca pushes past Leona and Mum hurries towards her, and then they're hugging on the walkway and Mum is warm and her cheeks are wet and her hair smells like home, and for some reason it isn't awkward at all.

# Chapter Fifty

## Rachel

### The day of the loss

Becca looked from her father to her mother on the other side of the kitchen table. She seemed relieved that Rachel had agreed to go. Still, her voice faltered as she asked, 'Are you going to get a divorce?'

Mitch considered this for a moment. 'Yes, I think we might.'

Becca said, 'Can I live with you, Daddy?'

'Mitch,' Rachel said, 'please don't. Not like this. We need to talk about all this. Not in front of Becca.'

'Just let us salvage something from what's left of the day, will you? Get what you need and leave us in peace. We can talk tomorrow,' Mitch said.

And so Rachel got to her feet and made her way out of the kitchen and went upstairs to the bedroom. Her bedroom. The room she shared with Mitch. Had shared, until now.

Maybe things would look different in the morning, or in a day or two… he might give her another chance?

But they had seen her as a monster, the way she'd seen her father. What chance was there?

The part of her brain that made lists and did practical things was still almost functioning, but haphazardly, like something broken or squashed that keeps on trying to move. She found a bag and picked up this thing and that thing to put in it. Work clothes. Hairbrush. Underwear. She put in the painting Mitch had done of her years ago and given to her as a present, the study for *Persephone*. 'Heaven help anyone who tries to keep *you* locked up,' he'd said at the time. He had been so much in love with her then…

She picked up the framed photo of her with Becca that sat on the top of the chest of drawers, the one that Mitch had taken the day they first came to see the house, and put it on top of the painting before zipping the bag.

It was like salvaging mementoes from a fire.

Downstairs, the kitchen door was open. Mitch was sitting at the table, resting his bandaged hand on it, and Becca was on her feet and leaning across to light the candles on her thirteenth birthday cake, the one that Rachel had iced that morning.

They looked comfortable together. Peaceful. Best off without her.

She bolted from the house into the cool of the evening, and sat in the car outside and cried.

It didn't change anything. The cottage was right in front of her and her husband and child were both in it and she couldn't go back, and she didn't know where else to go. Everywhere else seemed lifeless and unreal, as if she was at the bottom of an ocean, too far down to ever be found. As if The Deep had claimed her for good.

She had lost her daughter's trust. Would Becca ever want to see her again? It seemed impossible.

There was no one to turn to. She'd have to try and find a cheap hotel for the night. Or sleep in the car. But if she couldn't go home, what did it matter where she was? Or who she was, or what she did next? She was nobody, and nowhere at all.

# Chapter Fifty-One

Mitch turns up at the weir just after she does; the minute she and Becca let go of each other she sees him, waiting patiently on the island between the weir and the lock and watching them.

Becca goes over to him and mumbles an apology, and he holds her and says he's sorry, too. Then Leona heads towards them and says something Rachel doesn't quite hear. Mitch agrees with her, and when Rachel joins them on the island he says, 'I'm going to take Leona back to the house. Would you like to bring Becca? You could drop Henry off on the way.'

Well, yes she would. She would like very much to be with Becca for a little bit longer, and she doesn't mind having Henry along for the ride; and if Leona and Mitch want to have a heart-to-heart, she's very happy to leave them to it.

She sets off across the lock with Becca and Henry, with Mitch and Leona a little way behind. Mitch's car is just behind hers, which is parked haphazardly in the turning circle. She hadn't even remembered to lock it.

Henry offers Becca the passenger seat, and she politely declines and gets in the back. They don't speak on the way. Henry is on his phone, presumably messaging his mother. They are back at the Chadstones' house in no time, and he says to Becca, 'Well, bye. I'll see you around, I guess.'

'Yeah, I guess,' Becca says, and gets out so she can take his seat in the front.

Henry waves before going inside; his face has that unmistakable hangdog look that a boy gets when he's near a girl he likes – the awful vulnerability of the young male who's new to love, who hasn't yet survived heartbreak and has no defences against the prospect of disappointment.

Becca says, 'What was *he* doing with you? Did he just come along for the ride?'

'Oh, he just wanted to help. We were going to look for you in town, but as soon as I'd parked I got a call from your dad saying Leona had found you.'

Rachel turns, pulls out onto the main road and heads for Rose Cottage. It's the kind of evening that feels nostalgic even as you witness it; the hedgerows and houses are bathed in the golden haze of a still summer evening.

*It's over.* Becca is here, beside her, and she's safe. The silence between them is different to the many silences there have been between them in this car before; there is some new quality of understanding in it, as if one or other of them, or maybe both, has let go of something, and is at the beginning of something new.

Rachel feels contentment seeping into her, as warming and gentle as soft sunlight on skin. *This* is who she is – a mother of a daughter, taking care of things, doing what needs to be done. It's someone she thought at one time she had forgotten how to be. But maybe, in spite of everything, it's who she has been all along.

Becca says, 'When we get back, do you think you could stay?'

'I think you should all just get some rest,' Rachel says. 'But anyway, I'll be seeing you really soon.'

Becca sighs again. 'I wish I lived with you.'

And Rachel knows immediately that this is a dangerous wish, for her as well as for Becca. It is what she has yearned for ever since Becca rejected her. But to win Becca back and leave Mitch bereft would be the hollowest of victories. It would hardly be surprising if, now that her father has another child to love, Becca should seek to play off one parent against the other.

It's not as if Mitch and Rachel have merely failed to present a united front, the way that good parents are supposed to do. They have been enemies, and Becca's heart has been what they were fighting for.

'I'll talk about it with your father,' Rachel says. 'We might be able to look again at the arrangements. But there's no rush, Becca. First you need to get home and have something to eat and get a good night's sleep. Everything else will keep.'

They zip along the road that forms the outer boundary of the town and turn onto Rose Lane. Rachel pulls up in front of the little bridge and the front door opens immediately; Mitch must have been looking out for them. He comes out and Becca gets out of the car and mooches towards him, and he puts an arm lightly around her shoulders, a little gesture of affection and regret like someone greeting an injured friend, and both of them wave at Rachel before going back into the house.

Leona is looking on from the bedroom window. Rachel waves at her, too, and Leona raises her hand and holds it still in the air like a stiff little salute, and then waves back.

# Afterword

## Aidan

Two years after the loss

He still minds Mum not coming but he has got used to missing her, which means that he recognises the weird feeling he gets when he remembers she won't ever visit again. There is a hole in everything and it doesn't go away and nothing else fills it up, but other things go on round it and that is why it is sometimes possible to forget. Anyway, it isn't Mum's fault or because she doesn't love him any more. She is carrying on being dead, so has had to stop everything, but he is still going and that is probably how it will be until one day when he is very old, too.

It is bad not being able to touch or smell her but he has plenty of pictures of her that he can go through. Sometimes he has to remind himself that all the pictures are old ones and that they're only in his mind. The pictures don't change, but everything else always keeps changing, usually just when he has got used to it.

Everything is like words, which buzz around like bees and don't stop long enough for you to get a proper look at them, unless you have them safely written down. Written down is like being dead and left behind as a picture in someone's mind, but one that other people can try to see. It is being stopped, but without the rot, like an Egyptian mummy. Or just very slow rot, too slow to see.

Rachel isn't dead yet and probably has quite a long time to go, even though she's a little bit old and has a few white hairs which she turns to brown, but they grow white again. He first knew her when she used to drive Mum in the green car, and she flickered on and off like a light bulb that is nearly going out. Now she glows all the time, like somebody plugged her back in, or maybe she managed to do that herself, which is not something a light bulb can do. He would like to know how she made herself different, but she might not be able to tell him. People often don't know, or don't know how to explain, and sometimes it is best just to let them all just carry on and not ask too many questions, especially when it is about something good like glowing when you used to be nearly going out.

Even when Rachel is just sitting down or walking along, even when she isn't saying anything, she buzzes. She's very busy, always running round – like Mum in that way. Maybe she's worried about stopping if she slows down. She's making a new business and he would like it if that meant her name was on the side of a van or on the top of a shop or on a thing, but she says it isn't like that. It is on her website, though. She has shown him that.

He isn't sure about the Christmas visit. It might not be a good idea. But he goes with her anyway because she's living in the house his mother used to live in, renting it, which means paying money for now but not getting to own it in the future. Becca lives there as well. And he lived in the same house, too, once, when he was a little tiny baby, before he went to the home.

For other people, the place where they live is just *home*, or *his home*, *her home*, *your home*, *their home*, depending on who is talking and who they are talking to. For him, it is *the home*. This is just one of the differences between him and the other people in *the home* and most other people in the world.

But once upon a time, a long, long time ago, he did live at *home*, and this was it. It was *his home*. He can't remember it, but once he has been there he will have lots of pictures in his mind and he will be able to take them out and look at them whenever he likes.

Rachel takes him round the downstairs first. It is brilliant. He spends ages in the kitchen, which is the most interesting room. Rachel is in and out, in and out, taking food to the dining room, and someone comes in and does talking and goes out again. He is told who it is but he can't really take it in, so he pretends to pay attention but doesn't really.

Then Rachel asks if he would like to go to the table and he says he will try.

There are candles on it and he decides to watch them; everything else is too weird, too much. The talk, chat-chat-chat, too fast and then too slow. Everything the others are thinking and feeling and saying is a horrible messy jumble, like tangled wool or the squiggly stuff that brains are made of, the colour of clay. Or like those puzzles in the magazines where you have to follow the path all the way through the maze to the prize and there are dead ends, or sometimes there are several right paths but each path is only right for one pair of things, at the beginning and end of the line.

But the candles are good. He can also watch them in the shiny glass in front of the picture on the wall opposite him, which is called a reflection and is like shadows. The picture behind the glass is of a cold garden with nothing much growing, and the candles look like little lights in the lawn. Next to that picture is a smaller one with no shiny glass, of a tired lady lying on a bed who looks a bit like Rachel. Someone must have taken a long time painting it. Nobody else really notices the pictures or the candles, probably because they are too busy doing all the talking.

There is an awful smell in the room; it turns out to be brussels sprouts. But Rachel has put baked beans and sausage on his plate, and that is OK. The candles carry on being good. They do what they normally do: they burn, and they flicker, and they melt.

He eats a bit even though he isn't really hungry, and the others eat too and keep on saying things. There are four of them, including him. Not too many. He is next to Rachel and opposite Becca, who he recognises though she has changed a lot, which is because she's getting grown up. She's wearing a fluffy jumper and smells of peaches, though not real ones, and she says a few things, not much but a bit more than him.

The fourth person is the one he doesn't know, an old man with white hair called Frank. It would be nice if he was called something like Grandad or Whitebeard, so his name matched what he looked like a bit better, which is how the names work in some of the programmes Aidan likes. But in real life names mostly don't fit like that, unless you're an animal. Frank smells of lemons and leather (not real – it is perfume, but a different one to Becca's) and he keeps looking at Rachel the way a dog or a cat looks at a person when they want something. Rachel doesn't seem to mind this. She keeps on glowing, and buzzing. She's happy, which is catching, like yawns and sneezes.

In between eating their strange dinner they pull noisy crackers and put on hats and read out some jokes, and they give him the cracker toys to look at but they're not particularly good and he doesn't really want them. But nobody is disappointed. They're all smiling a lot as well as everything else, which is a lot to do, more than he could manage.

When he has had as much as he can he asks if can go back to the kitchen, and Rachel says yes. He opens a drawer and looks at the things in it. Rotary whisk, cheese grater, ice cream scoop. The cooker is quiet now. He turns the handle of the rotary whisk for a while, admiring the silver blur it makes. Rachel comes in and makes a pot of coffee, which smells of old plants and burning. It is beyond him how they can drink something like that, but they seem to think it's nice.

The stairs creak. Someone is going up and talking at the same time in a light, high voice. It must be Becca and as Rachel and the old man, Frank, are still downstairs, she must be on her phone.

Other people are usually quiet unless they are saying something to someone, unless they're whistling or humming or singing. Aidan isn't like that himself, and doesn't see why you shouldn't have fun with the up-and-down of words just like other kinds of noises.

The door is open and he can hear what Rachel and Frank are saying and suddenly it starts making sense. Or more sense, anyway. At least now he can make out the words and figure out who is speaking.

Frank says, 'She seems to like him.'

'I know. I thought it would have blown over, especially since Henry's that bit older. But they're still friends. Becca insists that's all it is. In fact, I don't dare ask her about it any more. Last time I mentioned it, she wanted to know if I had a problem with it and I had to insist that I didn't.'

'Do you?'

'Well, it isn't exactly ideal, given the history. But I don't want her thinking it's some kind of *Romeo and Juliet* situation and anyway, as far as I know, they're just friends. It's an unusual friendship… what teenage boy wants to be just friends? But there we are, stranger things have happened, and he does seem to be fond of her. Apparently Amelia teases him about it all the time.'

'Is Becca still in touch with her?'

'Not really. She's been a lot happier since she left St Anne's. I still feel bad about not having realised that it didn't really suit her – I was so busy worrying about paying the fees, it didn't even occur to me that she might be better off at a different school. And she's found Sophie, the counsellor, really helpful.'

Rachel sounds like Coral at the home when she's reading him a story and comes to the last page. It's the way people speak when the up-and-down part of something is evened out, and it's time for the ending.

She carries on talking, but is it definitely Rachel? Maybe not, she's breaking up, going fast and then slow. He finds an interesting straw in the utensils drawer and rolls it fast between his palms so that it looks like something else, its loops all turned into a kind of fuzzy spindle.

You can't really tell what things are like when they're moving, only when they stop. The thing is the same, but it can look completely different, and it can look like something that isn't quite there. Even though it is.

What is around you can trick you, and sometimes you just have to remember and be sure. He is superimposed over where his mother used to stand; he can't see her, he will never see her, but he can almost feel her. It's as close as they can come to touching.

And then he is happy and he forgets all about everybody else until Rachel comes to him and says that it is time for them to go, and would he like to say goodbye to Frank?

*Goodbye.* He manages it, and Rachel looks pleased. Then Rachel says, 'Oh, I nearly forgot,' and puts a Tupperware box of cupcakes into his hands.

'I saw these already,' he says. They were hard to miss, on the worktop next to the tea and coffee things.

'For you,' she tells him. 'If you'd like to take them home.'

He isn't sure. Should he say yes? He takes the lid off and sniffs them. They don't look quite so good as his mother's – not quite so perfectly cake-like. But Coral will probably help him eat them anyway.

He says, 'They're not like Mum's,' and Rachel puts her sad face on so he tries to give her a little hug and she looks startled, which is better, funny even. He sits next to her in her car with the Tupperware on his lap and Becca goes in the back, which is right because she is younger. They drive out to the edge of town and stop at a house he remembers, on the other side of a bridge. There is a big *For Sale* sign in front of it. He knows that this happens sometimes, but he doesn't understand – how can you sell *your home*, a place that belongs to you like your body does?

Rachel says, 'Do you want to see the baby?'

'What baby?'

'Becca's dad's baby,' Rachel says, as if she has explained this to him a thousand times before and he has forgotten, which might be the case.

He says OK. He likes babies a lot – it is easy to know how they're feeling, like with cats and dogs, and they haven't learned how to talk yet. Also, he doesn't get to see them all that often. There aren't any in the home.

They all get out of the car and walk over the bridge, and a man opens the door. 'This is Mitch,' Rachel says. 'Becca's dad.'

But she doesn't need to tell him – he already knows. Mitch looks a bit like Becca but not at all like Rachel. There is something about him – a kind of stubborn crossness – that reminds him of the people at the home that like to sit and watch TV all the time, and don't do the activities. He looks happier than they do, though. He looks quite pleased with himself.

They go into a living room where a woman with long yellow hair is sitting with the baby lying in her arms. She has lovely shiny bangles, all silvery, and blue flowers drawn on the skin by her hand, which is called a tattoo. There is a pink stone on a little chain round her neck, which the baby is fiddling with and which Aidan would quite like to touch, too, though he doesn't really know how to ask, and then the woman detaches the baby's fingers from the jewel which might mean the baby shouldn't do that and he shouldn't either.

Becca sits down and the woman tells her to position her arms just so, then very slowly and carefully transfers the baby into them. The baby doesn't cry; it looks very sleepy. It is quite a big baby, or at least, not a really little one. It has a bit of hair, and when it yawns he sees a flash of tiny teeth.

'Up all night,' the woman says.

'Way to go,' says Becca, which makes no sense at all.

The room is quite interesting, with a few things for him to look at; the best is a basket of eggs by the fireplace, made of cold smooth stone. Rachel tells him they are alabaster. There are pictures of different things and photographs in shining frames, and they're all right too. One of the photographs is of Becca standing on a stage, and another one is of a girl with yellow hair who looks a bit like the woman with yellow hair, cuddling a baby who looks a bit like the baby Becca is cuddling now, though it is almost impossible to know for sure if it is the same. Maybe babies are quite alike, like eggs.

After a bit Rachel says they had better head off and the yellow-haired woman says, 'Wouldn't you like to hold her?'

The look that passes between the two of them makes him think of when you get very dark clouds and then light, bright light, the kind he couldn't quite make out round Mum but knew was there.

'Yes,' says Rachel.

She holds the baby very carefully. Her body is all stiff as if it is hurting her, even though it is still sleeping and can't really do anything. Then she relaxes. The baby stirs and snuffles but doesn't cry. After a bit Rachel gives the baby back to the yellow-haired woman, and the woman looks at Aidan and asks, 'Would you like to hold her?'

He says no as hard as he can. 'No-no-no-no-no.' He is not at all sure about holding something precious that can break, which is what a baby is.

Rachel says, 'I'm not sure that's such a good idea.'

But the woman says, 'I'm sure it'll be fine.'

He sits the way Rachel and Becca had done, and the fat slightly moist-seeming bundle of the baby is put into his arms.

It stretches a bit and sits up – it must be bored of sleeping now. It wants to get moving. Then it opens its eyes and looks at him and smiles, and wraps its little hand round his finger. Like bindweed, which grows by clinging on.

The yellow-haired woman takes the baby back off him and goodbyes are said. How strange it is, all these people who were little tiny babies once. One day they will stop living and people will sing hymns for them. Though perhaps not quite so many people as sang hymns for his mother.

He and Rachel leave Becca there. Rachel hugs Becca but he doesn't – there is only so much cuddling he can do. They go out to the car and then they are on their way back to the home.

Rachel drives quite fast but doesn't break the speed limit. It is odd how you can go really quite fast in a car and it quickly feels normal, even as if it should always be like that and will carry on forever.

She says, 'I hope the day was OK.'

He says it was and remembers not to mention the bad smell of the brussels sprouts, and to say thank you. But he wants to tell her something else, something important. The words start to coalesce in his head, ready to come out. Something about his mother.

He needs to explain that she hadn't really gone anywhere, because they had been in her house and it hadn't felt as if she was missing. There has been a big rearrangement, yes, but she's definitely around somewhere. There are many things he isn't sure about, but he is absolutely certain about this…

But then the words elude him. He is conscious of the speed of the car on the road, pushing on through everything like a rocket soaring into space, but at the same time he is as safe and comfy with Rachel as if Mum was right here with them.

He hasn't lost her. As long as he can feel like this, she hasn't really gone. Realising this, he understands also that he is happy, and it no longer seems to matter that there is so much it is impossible to say.

# A Letter from Ali

Thank you for choosing to read *Lost Daughter*. If you want to keep up to date with my latest releases, just sign up at the following link. I can promise that your email address will never be shared and you can unsubscribe at any time.

*www.bookouture.com/ali-mercer*

There was never really any question about who would have custody of me when my parents broke up. It was 1980, and I was seven years old; after the split I lived with my mum. I visited my dad, who lived abroad, in the summer holidays, and saw him now and then during the year.

Decades later, this novel got started with a question. What if those roles were reversed? What would it be like, as a mother, to be the absent parent – the one who rings up at Christmas, and who, on a day-to-day basis, isn't there, and can't be there?

By this time, the old assumptions of the *Peter and Jane* books – Jane helps Mummy bake, Peter helps Daddy with the car – had long since given way. The days of 'Wait until your father gets home!' had gone. Fatherhood looked different, and motherhood did, too. Just as there were women in the boardroom and daughters who admired the handbags their mums carried for work, there were stay-at-home dads, dads who used baby carriers and changed nappies, dads at the school gate, dads on parental leave. The balance had shifted; in lots of households, including my own, the work of family life was shared out in a different way. But then – what happens if you stop sharing? It was a prospect that scared me – and since storytelling is a way of making sense of your fears, I began to write about it.

Throughout my own children's childhoods, my other half got them up and out of the house most days of the week – which, at times, was a really challenging and exhausting task, given that our son is autistic and has learning difficulties, and went through phases of being very resistant to getting ready for school. Having a child with disabilities shaped our experience of parenting and changed our horizons. It fed into what I was writing, too. I became aware that there had been a time when parents of autistic children were routinely advised to put them in institutional care. That got me thinking: what would it be like to be separated from your child because you had been persuaded that separation was the right thing to do, was indeed the only thing to do – even if you had doubts about it yourself?

In *Lost Daughter*, Rachel attends a group for mothers who live apart from their children, and a noticeboard with photos of the children is displayed during the meetings. That idea came from a parenting course I went on, which was run by the National Autistic Society. It was a really powerful way of having the children there, too, even though actually, they were all at school; it was a way of bringing them into the room with us.

Finally, while I was writing *Lost Daughter*, my dad passed away. I learned what a dislocating experience grief is, and how vividly people can return in your thoughts after they've gone. That final separation is a shock. But even that isn't the end.

Loss is as universal as love, the flipside of the coin, and it has its moments of both darkness and illumination – the light is always love, the only way to get through the dark bits. And so this book is dedicated to my dad, with all my love.

Thank you so much to all my readers – I hope *Lost Daughter* has touched you, made you smile and maybe even made you tear up a little. If you enjoyed reading my book, I would be so grateful if you could write a review. I'd love to know what you thought, and it's really helpful for other readers when they're looking for something new.

Do get in touch – I'm often on Twitter or Instagram (too often!) and you can also contact me through my Facebook page.

All good wishes to you and yours,
Ali Mercer

 AliMercerwriter

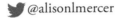 @alisonlmercer

 alimercerwriter

alimercerwriter.com

# Acknowledgements

Thank you to Judith Murdoch, my agent, and Kathryn Taussig and all the team at Bookouture for giving this book its chance.

Thank you to my family, with a special mention for Tom, Izzy and Mr P (without whom, chaos is come again).

Thank you to the good people of Abingdon, the oldest town in England (probably) – and to all my patient readers who asked from time to time how the new book was coming along. Thanks also to my friends, especially Nanu and Luli Segal and Helen Rumbelow, and to everyone I had the good luck to spend time with at the North Cornwall Book Festival in 2015, in particular Patrick Gale, Patricia Duncker and Neel Mukherjee.

And finally, thank you to all those whose work provided useful insights and information as I was reading around the subject matter of this novel, including the website of MATCH, a charity that supports mothers who live apart from their children: *www.matchmothers.org*.

My son's autism and learning difficulties prompted me to read numerous non-fiction books that fed indirectly into the writing of this one, including the following:

- For a first-person perspective on what it is like to be autistic – Temple Grandin's *Thinking in Pictures*; *The Reason I Jump* and *Fall Down 7 Times Get Up 8*, by Naoki Higashida.
- The autobiography of the mother of an autistic son – *Let IT Go*, by the entrepreneur and philanthropist Dame Stephanie Shirley, who came to the UK as a child refugee on the Kindertransport.

- On the history of autism, and society's attitudes to and treatment of autistic people – Steve Silberman's *Neurotribes* and *In a Different Key: The Story of Autism*, by John Donvan and Caren Zucker.
- A big, wide-ranging study of relationships between parents and children, which includes a chapter on autism – Andrew Solomon's *Far from the Tree: Parents, Children and the Search for Identity*.

There are lots more books, both non-fiction and novels, about the kinds of experiences and family situations I've explored in *Lost Daughter* – more than I have space to list here, and I'm sure there are plenty I don't know about. Do get in touch with your thoughts and recommendations. I'd love to hear from you.

Printed in Great Britain
by Amazon